S0-DOP-348

Mom
Christmas 1976

The Flame of the Borgias

The Flame of the Borgias

JEAN BRIGGS

Harper & Row, Publishers

New York, Evanston, San Francisco, London

For information address Harper & Row, Publishers, Inc., 10 East 53rd Street, New York, N.Y. 10022.

FIRST U.S. EDITION

Library of Congress Cataloging in Publication Data

Briggs, Jean.

The flame of the Borgias.

1. Bembo, Pietro, Cardinal, 1470-1547, in fiction, drama, poetry, etc. 2. Borgia, Lucrezia, 1480-1519—Fiction. I. Title.

PZ4.B8535FL3 [PR6052.R4435] 823'.9'14 74-15864

ISBN 0-06-010463-5

CONTENTS

MAJOR CHARACTERS

PIETRO BEMBO
born Venice, 1470 – died Rome, 1547
poet, scholar, Cardinal

HIS FAMILY
BERNARDO, his father: Senator of the Republic of Venice
CARLO, his brother
BARTOLOMMEO, his half-brother: Bernardo's illegitimate son
JACOPO, his uncle: Bernardo's brother and partner
ALVISE, his cousin
GIOVANNI MATTEO, his cousin (known as his nephew): Alvise's son
MARCELLA, his niece: daughter of his sister, Antonia
TORQUATO, his younger son by his mistress, Morosina
CATERINA CORNARO, Queen of Cyprus: his kinswoman

NICOLA BRUNO, of Sicily, his secretary
LICO, his servant
MARCO, his gondolier

HIS FRIENDS
CARDINAL BERNARDO DOVIZII DA BIBBIENA, of Florence: companion of Pope Leo X, formerly Cardinal Giovanni de Medici
RAFFAELLO (RAPHAEL) SANZIO, of Urbino: painter
LUDOVICO ARIOSTO, of Ferrara: poet, in the service of Cardinal Ippolito d'Este
ERCOLE STROZZI, of Ferrara: poet, member of Ferrara's ruling council of Twelve

ALDO MANUZIO, publisher: settled in Venice

THE RULING FAMILIES

THE ESTE OF FERRARA

ERCOLE I, Duke of Ferrara

ALFONSO (later Duke Alfonso I) } his sons
CARDINAL IPPOLITO }

LUCREZIA BORGIA, Alfonso's wife: daughter of Pope Alessandro VI, sister of Cesare Borgia

GIULIO, Duke Ercole's illegitimate son

THE GONZAGA OF MANTUA

FRANCESCO, Marquis of Mantua

ISABELLA, his wife: daughter of Duke Ercole of Ferrara

THE MONTEFELTRO OF URBINO

ELISABETTA, wife of Duke Guidobaldo I: sister of Francesco Gonzaga of Mantua

OTHERS LIVING IN FERRARA

ANGELA BORGIA, Lucrezia's cousin

TITO VESPASIANO STROZZI, father of Ercole Strozzi: leader of Ferrara's ruling council of Twelve

ANTONIO TEBALDEO, Lucrezia's secretary

ALESSANDRO PIO, agent of Cardinal Ippolito: later Prince of Sassuola and husband of Angela Borgia

BARBARA, wife of Ercole Bentivoglio of Bologna: later wife of Ercole Strozzi

BEMBINO, Pietro Bembo's dog

NOTE

This account of the relationship between Pietro Bembo and Lucrezia Borgia in the years 1502–1505 is based on the letters written by Pietro Bembo during this period, and on the few of Lucrezia Borgia's which have survived.

The crystal case containing a strand of Lucrezia Borgia's hair, which is mentioned in the book, is now in the Ambrosiana Library in Milan, together with Lucrezia's letters to Pietro Bembo.

PROLOGUE

Villa Bozza, 1519

The villa of Father Pietro Bembo, Apostolic Secretary to Pope Leo X, lay beside the river Brenta, a few miles outside Padua. In the grounds of his villa Bembo cultivated strawberries, and on a hot June afternoon he was kneeling among the beds, searching for the first of the season's crop. To protect him from the sun he was wearing a peasant's broad-brimmed leather hat, and he carried a basket lined with green leaves for his fruit.

When the basket was full, he carried it to the small wood that was his favourite refuge in the heat of summer. The trees had been planted on rising ground, and from a marble bench set at the edge of the wood he could enjoy a long view of the winding river as it moved sluggishly between rushes and willows towards the lagoon of Venice.

The bench that afternoon was already occupied by the papal treasurer, Cardinal Bernardo Bibbiena. The Cardinal lay full-length, one cushion supporting his head and another the heels of his pale-coloured, gold-tooled boots. He had been watching Bembo as he worked, and now he was looking beyond the fruit garden towards the villa, its steps descending to the river. In the sunlight the water was milky green. Along the opposite bank passed the road to Padua. The air was very still. Only a distant horseman, raising the dry dust of the road, disturbed the afternoon peace.

Bembo came gratefully out of the sun into the shade of the trees. He was a tall, lean man in his middle years, with traces of grey in his short, dark beard. His face was glistening with sweat as he looked down at Bibbiena, but his expression was triumphant. He handed the basket to his friend. 'There you are, Bernardo. Ripe strawberries!'

He lifted Bibbiena's feet off the bench to make room for himself and noticed the boots. He said, laughing, 'If you have to walk anywhere, I suppose you take these off.'

The Cardinal waved a finger at him. 'The Church should never disparage gifts that – '

'Ah, a gift.'

' – gifts that are offered from a full heart.'

'And a full purse?'

'The lady is indeed rich,' conceded Bibbiena. He paused to bite into a strawberry. 'But she is also one of the most devout members of my Roman parish.'

'Devoted, perhaps,' murmured Bembo, 'but hardly devout, surely.'

'My dear Pietro, try one of your own strawberries. The juice might sweeten your imagination.' His bland gaze met Bembo's restless and brilliant eyes, incongruous under the ancient brim of his hat. 'Must you wear that appalling hat?'

Bembo pulled it off. 'I find it useful when I'm working in the sun,' he said mildly. He brushed a streak of soil from his faded woollen robe.

Bibbiena, whose own dress was of yellow silk, shook his head. 'But why work in the sun like a peasant?'

'I enjoy it,' said Bembo. 'Many of us ageing Venetians discover a need for the open fields which we lack on our island.' He smiled at his guest. 'You've no idea, Bernardo, of the pleasure there is in picking one's own fruit and vegetables for the supper table.'

Bibbiena glanced at Bembo's hands, browned and roughened after six weeks in the country. He raised his eyebrows without answering.

Bembo went on. 'I think of all the things I grow here the strawberries give me most satisfaction. It's not merely their flavour that pleases me, but a bowl of them picked for supper makes the whole table smell sweet and fresh. You will notice it tonight, Bernardo.'

Bibbiena doubted this. He did not share Bembo's appreciation of such simple experiences. He ate another strawberry.

'Well, you may not understand a fine pair of boots when you see them,' he said, 'but you know how to cultivate a delicious strawberry.'

'It isn't difficult here. The soil is so fertile.'

Bibbiena looked at Bembo's land with its green fields, its groves of chestnut saplings, its orchard, its vineyard and its rose garden. He noticed Bembo's mistress, Morosina, walking among the roses with a child in her arms.

'The soil is indeed fertile,' he murmured.

Bembo smiled and said nothing. As they watched, a young man darted through the curtain of ivy that trailed from Bembo's pergola, making the child laugh with delight. The young man moved from side to side, sketching swiftly on a pad.

'Raffaello,' said Bembo fondly, 'has a way with my little Lucillo.'

Bibbiena glanced sideways at his friend. This newly revealed paternalism in Bembo both surprised and amused him. His own affairs were by choice of a more transient and less domestic nature, and he could remember a time when Bembo's had been the same. That had been in the earlier years of their friendship, when they had been two of the brightest wits at the court of Urbino. Raffaello Sanzio, who was a native of Urbino, had painted Bembo in those days as a lively gallant, with a pearl gleaming in one ear and a book of sonnets open in his hand.

Raffaello had left the rose-garden and came to join them in the wood. He threw himself on the ground beside the bench, dropping his charcoal and paper. 'I am dismissed,' he announced. 'The baby must sleep.'

Bembo bent down to pick up the pad. 'May I look?'

Raffaello smiled and nodded. Some of the sketches were merely of a finger or a strand of hair, but one in strong, quick lines had caught Lucillo laughing. Bembo laughed himself, and Raffaello seized the sheet from his hand.

'Ah, yes,' he said, pleased. 'I must use that one.' He thrust the sketch at Bibbiena. 'Bernardo, I'll use this head for the child playing with the dolphin.' He slid a hand under Bibbiena's cushions and pulled out a bundle of drawings made in yellow ink on red paper. 'Look, Pietro, let me show you. These are my plans for Bernardo's bathroom in the Vatican.' He tossed the drawings into Bembo's lap. 'They're based on a Roman bath design from a villa just excavated at Tivoli.' He spoke excitedly, moving his hands about. 'You see, Venus with her dolphins – that would be Lucillo there – and a mermaid, and sea-nymphs – '

'With Bernardo splashing about among them?' enquired Bembo. 'In the Vatican?'

'I am not aware of any theological heresy in dolphins,' murmured Bibbiena, looking at him.

Raffaello, on his knees beside Bembo, was still poring over his plans. 'But you can see, Pietro,' he said with a sigh, 'that the room is impossible for murals. It was built for storage. With those alcoves and the roof vaulting, the space is too broken – '

But Bembo, gazing at the plans, observed with amazement that the movement of Raffaello's figures was so perfectly adapted to the space that it seemed as if the perverse angles of Bibbiena's bathroom had been deliberately moulded to the painter's designs.

He was about to remark on this when Raffaello's darting attention was caught by something else. 'Look,' he cried, pointing towards the road, 'look at that rider. Whatever makes a man travel at that speed in this heat?'

Bibbiena, raising his head, saw again the horseman that he had noticed some minutes earlier. 'Perhaps he is an ardent lover,' he suggested.

'Or a surprised one?' said Raffaello, laughing.

Bembo was staring at the man. 'I believe he's coming here.' He made a sudden, nervous gesture. 'Could he be from the Vatican?'

'With a summons from the Pope, demanding your return to Rome?' asked Bibbiena. 'It's not unlikely. You have made so many excuses to previous messengers that the Holy Father may well have lost his temper in the matter. Sooner or later, Pietro, you will have to go back. You've been ill, it's true, but you can't go on suffering from the effects of your fever for ever.'

'I never want to set foot in Rome again,' muttered Bembo. 'The stench of the Tiber under my window – '

Bibbiena waved this aside and spoke to Bembo with severity. 'Pietro, a few years ago your one thought was to gain some sort of preferment that would take you to Rome. Many of us in the Vatican worked hard for you until you were given what you wanted. You came to Rome. You became papal secretary. Now, after seven years in that office, when you are beginning to exercise real influence in Rome, you suddenly tire of it. I can't understand you.'

'I hate the back-biting and place-seeking in Rome.'

'Come now, Pietro, that isn't new. You find it in every court where there are high offices to be filled.'

'Not in Venice,' said Bembo quickly. 'There is none of that in Venice. Every single office, from that of doge to clerk in the Arsenal, is filled by election.'

'Oh, Venice.' Bibbiena looked impatient. 'Venetians always have to live in a different world from the rest of us. And why are you so suddenly concerned with Venice? You dress like a Roman and speak like a Tuscan. You have refused, for as long as I've known you, to live in Venice and you rarely visit it. I remember how you used to write to me about Venice – "I swear by God, Bernardo, that I could never, never settle down to the grasping mercantile life there – " '

'Yes, that's still true,' said Bembo. 'I wouldn't want to live in Venice. But that doesn't mean that I have no respect for her way of government, especially after the political corruption I've seen in Rome.'

Bibbiena took a breath. 'Pietro, would you hold your present powerful office if you'd had to take your chance in a string of your long-winded Venetian elections? It has been no disadvantage to you that I am your friend, and that I have known Pope Leo since our childhood in Florence.' Bembo flushed slightly and Bibbiena added in a more kindly tone. 'Don't misunderstand me. No one could fill your papal office more brilliantly than you do. What angers me is that you refuse to work for the rewards that could be yours.'

'I have all the rewards I need,' said Bembo.

'Or deserve? Look at your position now. You have a shrewd understanding of Vatican diplomacy, and the Pope relies on your judgement in dealing with your slippery countrymen. Your classical scholarship is respected throughout Europe. You have a gift for oratory and you can exert a calculated charm that is invaluable in negotiation.' Bibbiena paused for a moment. 'Pietro, believe me, in a few years, with a little wise lobbying on the part of your friends, a Cardinal's hat could be yours.'

Bembo laughed gently. 'Bernardo, even if what you say is true, I should not want it. I have Morosina and the child now.'

Bibbiena shrugged his shoulders. 'Yes. But you could take a quiet villa in the suburbs – '

'And visit them in secret? No, I will not do that.'

Bibbiena stared at him. 'Do you seriously advance that as a reason for rejecting your ambitions, for abandoning your future?'

Bembo's eyes rested on his green fields and he said patiently, 'Bernardo, I think you make the mistake of supposing that we share the same ambitions. I'm not rejecting mine. I've satisfied them. That's why my attitude to Rome has changed. It's true that ten years ago I was doing all I could to find a place in the Vatican, and you assumed that this was because, like you, I sought influence and position.' Bembo shook his head. 'All I've ever wanted for myself was the opportunity to study and to write. When I was young, our house was wealthy enough to allow me to do this. I studied in Florence and Ferrara and Padua; at an age when most rich young Venetians sail with the galley-fleets to the Levant to learn trade and navigation, I spent two years in Messina, learning Greek.

'But by the time we met in Urbino, Bernardo, my father had lost his fortune. I needed money. All I had to sell was my scholarship, and the only market for that was the Church. When I got to Rome, my benefices enabled me to redeem my father's mortgage on this villa. Now that he's dead, I've been able to enlarge it and make a home here for Morosina, and for my brother and his son. I have a place in which I can live quietly, and sufficient means to be able to go back to my writing as soon as Rome permits me the leisure. Bernardo, haven't I worked hard enough during these seven years to hope for this? My illness, if you like, has made my longing to retire here all the more urgent.'

Bibbiena was silent, frowning. Bembo added, 'You enjoy political manoeuvring and intrigue. It disturbs me.'

'What disturbs me,' said Bibbiena shortly, 'is waste. If a man has gifts, he should use them.'

'Ah,' Bembo answered, 'but you have already admitted that I have a gift for growing strawberries. That talent will be wasted if I go back to Rome.'

Raffaello laughed. He bent forward to scoop up his drawings, which still lay in Bembo's lap. 'Pietro,' he said quietly, 'that horseman did stop here. Cola is coming out to find you. I think that's probably the reason.'

Bembo turned hastily towards the villa. His Sicilian secretary, Nicola Bruno, was hurrying across the terrace.

'What is it, Cola?' Bembo called out as Bruno approached the wood. 'Is it Rome?'

Bruno addressed himself formally to Bibbiena. 'Your eminence will forgive my disturbing your rest.' He looked at Bembo. 'Pietro, Messer Ariosto is here from Ferrara.'

Bembo shouted with relief and pleasure. 'Ludovico Ariosto?' He threw out his arms. 'Cola, bring him out here – '

Bruno interrupted him. 'I think you should come into the house,' he said. 'He is very tired from the ride, and says he has urgent news for you.'

Bembo stared at Bruno, and then he shivered. He rose from the bench and with a murmured apology followed Bruno into the villa.

Ariosto was waiting for him in the cool, quiet room in which he kept his books and manuscripts, his pictures and his treasured Roman bronzes. Cases lined with coloured silk held his carefully arranged collection of medals and gems. Ariosto was leaning against one of these cases, his eyes closed, coughing.

Bembo caught his arm in concern. He saw that Bruno had set out wine for Ariosto, but that it was untouched.

The spasm of coughing passed and Ariosto opened inflamed eyes. 'Pietro, I'm sorry,' he gasped, 'the dust – '

'Ludovico, you're exhausted. Sit down and drink a little wine.'

'Yes, later, perhaps.' Ariosto took another breath and then said carefully, 'Pietro, I have some news which I believe may concern you, but I am not certain of this. If I am wrong, you must forgive me.'

'Is it news from Ferrara?'

'Yes.'

Bembo's expression was wary, but he said lightly, 'Tell me.'

'It is not good news.' Ariosto hesitated. 'The Duchess of Ferrara – ' He felt a slight movement in Bembo's fingers which still rested on his arm. Bembo was staring at him. Ariosto moved his head to avoid Bembo's eyes. 'The duchess is – ' he sighed, 'dying, Pietro.'

He felt Bembo turn away, releasing his arm. After a moment, Bembo asked, 'In childbirth?'

'No. From the fever that sometimes follows.'

'Are you sure? Once before – '

Ariosto looked at him, putting out a hand as if to ward off hope. 'Yes, I know that before now she has been at the point of death, and has recovered. But not this time.' He sighed again. 'Within a day or so, perhaps a few hours, she will be dead.'

Bembo walked to his desk and slowly lowered himself into his chair, laying his hands on the top of the desk. 'Lucrezia,' he said quietly, and then again, 'Lucrezia.'

Ariosto poured wine into a glass and drank it. Bembo turned his head towards him. 'Did she ask you to come?'

Ariosto smiled sadly, 'Is that likely, Pietro?'

Bembo shook his head. 'Yet you said you knew. How?'

'Pietro, I wasn't sure. If you think I guessed because of some indiscretion on your part, that isn't so.' Ariosto stared thoughtfully into his glass. 'We're both poets. In our time we've both flattered great ladies with our meaningless conceits. To most people they sound the same as when we say what is true. But another poet may hear a difference.'

There was a silence in the room until Bembo stirred and leaned across the desk towards Ariosto. 'I am grateful to you for this.'

'No, no. I owe you a great deal. If what I suspected was true, I didn't want you to hear of her death from a stranger.' He paused. 'I thought, too, that these last hours – '

Bembo nodded. Ariosto filled a second glass and placed it in front of Bembo. He lifted it without putting it to his lips. 'Is she in much pain?'

'It is difficult to know, Pietro. She says very little. The child was born over a week ago. It was so weak that it was not expected to live, and it was baptised at once by the bedside. But the child has survived, and it is the duchess who is dying. Much of the time she lies in a delirium, but in her lucid moments she screams and struggles to live. Last night she lost both sight and hearing. They say it was terrible to watch her. This morning she became quieter, barely conscious. Pray God she stays so till the end.'

Bembo set down the wine-glass and rose from his chair. 'Is she alone?'

'The duke sat near her for several hours last night. Even he was moved to pity for her, and wept. He hasn't visited his mistress for five days. If he resents the waiting while his wife dies, he has at least had enough dignity not to show it. Her children wait at her door hour after hour, but she doesn't ask for them. She seems to want no one. The only thing which gives her any comfort is the agnus-dei she holds in her hand.'

'Agnus-dei?' said Bembo, startled.

'Yes. She usually wears it round her neck. It looks like Venetian work – gold and enamel. You would know the kind.'

Bembo nodded. He appeared to Ariosto to be unnaturally disturbed.

'Many pious ladies wear an agnus-dei,' Ariosto explained. 'In these last years the duchess has shown great religious devotion. I've heard that she sometimes has a hair shirt beneath her court dress.'

'A hair shirt!' Bembo groaned softly.

Ariosto swallowed another mouthful of wine and wiped his eyes. 'Pietro, I mustn't stay. I don't want Ippolito to know I've come here. He thought I was riding only as far as Rovigo.'

'Ippolito d'Este is there?' asked Bembo angrily.

'Oh, yes. He kneels in prayer beside the duchess with every display of elegant grief,' said Ariosto, 'and he consoles his sorrowing brother as a good Cardinal should.'

Bembo swore suddenly and violently in the dialect of Venice. 'How is it possible – '

'That he flourishes? Doesn't your Bible warn you that the evil do? After knowing Ippolito all this time, why are you still surprised?'

Bembo was pacing round the room. He stopped in front of a wall decorated with portraits. Hanging beside Raffaello's Urbino portrait of Bembo himself was a small canvas executed in the sombre style of Ferrara. Compared with Raffaello's work it was stiff and flat, yet there was enough skill in the painting to suggest an air of shrewdness and mischief in the sitter. Bembo stood looking at the face of the man who had once been his closest friend.

'Ercole Strozzi?' asked Ariosto. When Bembo nodded, he added, 'It must be ten years since he died.'

Bembo corrected him harshly. 'It is eleven years since Cardinal Ippolito arranged his murder. Of course, no one in Ferrara would admit their Cardinal's guilt.'

'No one in Ferrara would dare,' muttered Ariosto, 'especially someone like me, employed in his household.'

'But you know it's true.'

Ariosto closed his eyes wearily for a moment. When he opened them he said, 'Yes, Pietro, I do know. Ippolito and the Bentivoglio arranged it together. But what use is that? Ippolito can – '

He broke off, hearing the murmur of voices on the terrace outside. Bibbiena appeared at the door.

'My dear Pietro,' he said brightly, 'you must forgive my impertinence in disturbing you. But I understand from Bruno that Messer Ariosto can stay only a short while, and I cannot allow him to leave without expressing my congratulations on his *Orlando Furioso*.' Bibbiena advanced into the room with a hand outstretched towards Ariosto. 'Messer Ariosto, I am sure that Father Bembo will have told you how avidly your poem is being discussed in Rome. Even his holiness the Pope is reading it with pleasure.'

Bembo said with an effort. 'We had not yet spoken of this. I apologise, Ludovico.'

Ariosto was surprised and confused by the Cardinal's praise. He bent quickly to kiss his ring. 'Your eminence is too good. If my work has any value, much is due to Father Bembo here. He read the early drafts and suggested many ideas.'

'I merely,' protested Bembo, 'corrected a few words.'

Bibbiena smiled. 'I wish, Messer Ariosto, that you had some hours of leisure to share with myself and Messer Raffaello Sanzio, who tells me that the Pope has commissioned him to paint scenery for one of your comedies. Bruno, however, has charged us not to delay you. He is anxious for you to eat before you leave and has food ready for you.'

'Oh, no, I thank your eminence – ' Ariosto dismissed the prospect of food.

'I was warned that you would refuse,' Bibbiena said, 'and instructed to say that there is a dish of turnips in wine and vinegar.'

Ariosto smiled apologetically. 'Eminence,' he explained, 'I am indifferent to most food, but I have a passion for turnips and Nicola Bruno knows this.' He shrugged his shoulders. 'The weakness of the flesh, eminence. You understand?'

When Ariosto had eaten, and had set out for Rovigo on a fresh horse from Bembo's stables, Bembo returned to his study and sat down again at his desk. Within a few moments Bibbiena followed him and busied himself studying a case of intaglios. After a silence he said, 'This Roman emerald of yours is rather fine.'

Bembo sighed. 'Bernardo, what is it? You deliberately interrupted when Ludovico was here, and now I'll swear you are watching me.'

Bibbiena glanced at Bembo over his shoulder. 'Yes, as a matter of fact, I am. You must blame Bruno. He was sure from Ariosto's manner that his news was bad, and he was afraid that a shock might cause another bout of your fever. You are certainly pale.'

Bembo clenched a hand. 'I feel tired from working too long in the sun. It was unwise.'

'Ah,' said Bibbiena. He made no attempt to leave, but resumed his study of the emerald. He waited before beginning again. 'As I came in I heard Ariosto mention the name "Ippolito". Were you talking about Cardinal d'Este?'

Bembo let his head rest on the back of his chair. 'Yes. Did you hear what we were saying?'

'No, only the name. Do you know him well, Pietro? I have worked with him occasionally. He's a fine mathematician, and I respect him as an administrator. He's very fashionable now in Rome, with everyone reading Ariosto's praise of him in the *Orlando*. One envies his being the patron of such a writer.'

Bibbiena glanced up to find Bembo's eyes fixed on him with disturbing intensity. 'Ariosto,' said Bembo grimly, 'is a member of Ippolito's household. The money paid to him by Ippolito supports four younger brothers and five sisters as well as himself and his son. That is how you should measure his adulation of Ippolito.' He breathed deeply. 'I presume that the twenty-two wounds that killed Ercole Strozzi were evidence of the mathematical skill to which you referred.'

Bibbiena stared at Bembo. 'Ercole Strozzi? Ercole Strozzi was killed by thieves. I don't understand you.'

'Does a thief waste time striking twenty-two blows when one or two would be enough?' Bembo rose from his desk and walked about the room. 'Do you know what happened to Strozzi, Bernardo? He was pulled from his mule one night at the mouth of an alleyway. He was lame and always had to walk with a crutch. When his body was found it was lying beside him, broken. Hair had been torn out of his scalp. He had been stabbed over and over again, and then left to bleed to death.'

'But why should you believe that Cardinal d'Este played any part in this?' demanded Bibbiena. 'Have you any proof?'

'No. None that you would accept. I can only tell you, Bernardo, that Strozzi was put to death by a man who enjoyed the mutilation of his victim as much as the killing. And Ippolito is such a man.'

Bibbiena protested. 'I can hardly envisage Cardinal d'Este performing such an act – '

'Oh, he doesn't plunge in the knife himself,' said Bembo savagely. 'He likes to watch the spectacles he devises. Strozzi had a quarrel with the Bentivoglio family at the time. Ippolito used them. There was a man called Alessandro Pio, whose mother was a Bentivoglio – '

With a groan, Bembo put a hand across his eyes. He had been speaking again in the Venetian dialect which Bibbiena could follow only with difficulty. He had never before heard Bembo use anything but the pure Italian of Tuscany which he believed should be the common tongue of all Italians. Bembo was not a man of wild judgements, and Bibbiena found himself disquieted by the evident strength of Bembo's feeling.

'If what you say is true,' he said slowly, 'then Ippolito d'Este is a monster.'

'There are times, yes, when he is.'

'Is that what Ariosto came here to talk about?'

'No. That is no news to either of us.'

'Then he told you something that reminded you of Strozzi's death and Ippolito's enmity towards him?'

Bembo was still moving about the room. He said in distress, 'It was something that reminded me of a time when I knew them both in Ferrara.' He paused by the case of intaglios and took out the Roman emerald. It was a pale, cloudy stone cut with the figure of Minerva. 'Did you notice the carving on this, Bernardo?'

It was a clumsy change of subject, and they were both aware of it. Bibbiena nevertheless looked again at the gem in Bembo's hand. 'Yes,' he answered, 'beautiful. And the stone itself is lovely with this misting.'

'Ah, but these old Roman stones from Egypt can't compare with the emeralds coming from Spanish America,' Bembo went on busily. 'You won't agree because you admire nothing that isn't antique Roman, but the new stones are magnificent, deep in colour and flawlessly clear. I remember once seeing – '

He broke off, appalled by the treachery of his mind. He was looking at a necklace of emeralds shaped like a snake, lying against the throat of Lucrezia Borgia.

Bibbiena was watching him, and he added awkwardly, 'It was a necklace of Spanish stones that belonged to the Duchess of Ferrara. Superior to anything Roman.'

'How pre-occupied you are this afternoon with Ferrara,' said Bibbiena. 'I suppose it is not surprising after Ariosto's visit. Shall I replace this?' He removed the emerald from Bembo's hand.

The two men looked at each other for a moment. Then Bembo gave a shaky laugh. 'It is difficult enough to keep one's own counsel without one's memory playing tricks.'

'You are saying – ?'

Bembo sighed. 'I am admitting that Bruno was right. Ariosto did bring bad news.' He fell silent, and Bibbiena waited. 'Ariosto came to tell me that the Duchess of Ferrara is dying.'

Bibbiena was shocked. 'This is indeed bad news, and unexpected. Her death will be a great loss to Ferrara and the duke.'

'A loss to the duke!' cried Bembo. 'Do you know he once said that his greatest ambition was to see his wife and his mistress pregnant at the same time? He will have to go to the trouble now of marrying again. I should say that her death is not so much a loss as an inconvenience.'

'And if this is so,' asked Bibbiena softly, 'what is that to you?'

Bembo glanced at him angrily and turned away without answering. 'Why,' continued Bibbiena, 'did Ariosto undertake that arduous ride to bring you the news? Is he doing the same service for everyone who during the last twenty years passed a few months in Ferrara?'

Bembo stood undecided for a moment. Then with a gesture of resignation he went back to his desk. From the side he pulled out a small concealed drawer, its outline disguised by the pattern of inlaid woods. Inside was a velvet-covered box which he unlocked with a thin key that hung on a chain under his belt. He first removed a thick bundle of letters. Then he lifted out an ornament designed to stand on a shelf or table. A wand of onyx supported two rectangular crystal wafers, held together in a narrow frame of gilded bronze set with seed pearls and small jewels. Two tiny medallions dropped from the lower corners of the frame. Preserved between the crystal wafers was a strand of pale yellow hair.

Bembo offered the ornament to Bibbiena who looked first at the little heraldic medallions. They were alike. One side was white, with the red bull of the house of Borgia; the other dark blue and carrying the white eagle of the dukes of Ferrara. 'Lucrezia Borgia, Duchess of Ferrara,' murmured Bibbiena, translating the device. 'This is her hair?'

Bembo nodded.

'Yes, I remember the colour,' added Bibbiena, 'unusual in a woman of Spanish blood. It's like – ' he hesitated, seeking an apt description.

' – like clear amber,' said Bembo, surprised to find a long-forgotten phrase on his lips. The whole line came into his mind: 'Hair, like clear amber, as by a miracle blown across fresh drifts of snow.' He was back in a small room in Ferrara on a dark winter afternoon; stretched beside him was Lucrezia, her fair skin streaked by the long hair that was the colour of pale yellow amber. And now the hair shirt, he thought in anguish.

He put his head in his hands. 'I should have gone back with Ariosto.'

Bibbiena heard the muffled words and raised his eyebrows. 'What do you mean?'

Bembo raised tormented eyes to the Cardinal. 'Bernardo,' he said desperately, 'I loved Lucrezia. For three years she was a part of every thought that entered my mind. Now she is dying, and in great distress. Hasn't she a right to whatever comfort I can give her?'

'How long is it,' asked Bibbiena, 'since you last saw her?'

'Fourteen years.'

'My dear Pietro – fourteen years! One becomes a different person in fourteen years. Naturally, you are upset by Ariosto's news. But you have no obligation in the matter. One's responsibility is to the present, not the past.'

'Obligations?' Bembo stared through the window, although he was not aware of what he was seeing. 'You and I, Bernardo,' he said, 'we measure life in different ways. You judge it by the sum of all its experiences. To me what counts is the quality of its most intense moments.' Bibbiena was unresponsive and Bembo tried again. 'Life to you is like a corridor so evenly illuminated that you can see every stone in exact proportion to the others. To me it is like a dark room lit only in rare places, but lit with flares of great brilliance.'

He took the crystal ornament in his hands. 'I am nearly fifty. Lucrezia and I were lovers for three years. During those three years the time I actually spent with her was so brief that I count it in hours rather than days or weeks. At one period we were separated for sixteen months – '

Bibbiena interrupted. 'Sixteen months? Within those three years? Pietro – !'

'Oh yes, in one sense Lucrezia takes up only a negligible part of my fifty years. But during those few hours I passed with her, I knew the only perfect moments of my life. She is the brightest light in my dark room. So what is sixteen months? What is fourteen years? What does past or present mean?' He looked up at Bibbiena. 'Shouldn't I be with her now?'

'Haven't you answered that question yourself?' said Bibbiena. 'If you really believe that you ought to be with her, you wouldn't be here now, talking about it.'

Bembo flinched. 'But why? If this is the choice I've made, why?'

'Why?' Bibbiena felt impatient. 'Because you know that for

the sake of an act of self-indulgence you cannot bring embarrassment and hurt to those who do not deserve it.'

'You mean Morosina?'

'Morosina, Ariosto, the Pope, the duchess's children, the duchess herself – '

'Lucrezia? Why Lucrezia?'

'You would ruin her public reputation.'

'Bernardo, do you really think she cares about that now?'

'All that any of us have to leave behind in this world, Pietro, is our public reputation.'

Bembo shook his head passionately. 'No, no. Reputation is only what others choose to think of us. What matters in life is what we have felt. Don't we leave that behind?' Bembo was aware of Bibbiena watching him closely. He read his mind and added wearily, 'Bernardo, I'm not feverish.'

The two men were silent. Bembo picked up the crystal ornament and laid it back in its velvet box. He placed the bundle of letters on top.

Bibbiena frowned. 'You've kept the letters for fourteen years?'

'Some, but others are more recent,' said Bembo. 'The last one was written only a few months ago.'

Bibbiena looked incredulous. 'You went on writing?'

Bembo's fingers lingered briefly on the pile of letters. 'Yes, why not? It was only occasionally, of course, in the last few years.' He locked the box and replaced it in the drawer.

'So you were writing to each other,' said Bibbiena curiously, 'when you were living in Urbino?'

Bembo nodded.

'You and I spent six years together there, yet not once did you give any hint of what had happened.' Bibbiena paused, recalling the past. 'I remember, after supper we would sit with the duke and duchess, some dozen or so of us, and talk or play games or read each other's verses. You used to insist that your sonnets were just metrical exercises, but I sometimes wondered if you were thinking of a woman left in Venice that you still wanted. Yet you amused yourself as light-heartedly as the rest of us, and I decided that I was probably wrong. Not once did it occur to me that if there was a woman it might be Lucrezia of Ferrara.' Bibbiena considered for a moment. 'And yet perhaps I should have suspected it. You dedicated your book to her – '

He walked to the shelf where Bembo kept his own published works, and took down a copy of *The Asolani*. It was the most widely read of Bembo's books, completed shortly before he settled in Urbino. Set in the hill-town of Asolo, which belonged to the Queen of Cyprus, Bembo's kinswoman, it sought to explore different states of love. Bibbiena turned to the dedication and read aloud, ' "to Madonna Lucrezia d'Este Borgia, most illustrious Duchess of Ferrara, from Pietro Bembo".' Bibbiena glanced down the page. 'I really think I can forgive myself for not guessing from this. "Your beauty surpasses that of other ladies – " ' Bibbiena winced. 'It reads like any dedication by any ambitious writer to any patroness.'

'That was the intention,' murmured Bembo.

'Ah, so you were adept at devious diplomacy even then,' said Bibbiena.

Bembo felt a sudden reaction of exhaustion. 'Not by choice,' he muttered.

Bibbiena was still scanning the dedication. 'Ah, I find the ubiquitous Strozzi here,' he exclaimed. He read aloud again, ' "Since I cannot come myself, I hope these lines may speak in my place to you, and to Messer Ercole Strozzi – ".' Bibbiena closed the book. 'He played a part in this?'

'Oh, yes,' said Bembo. 'He had a part in this. In fact, it all began with Ercole Strozzi.'

'In Ferrara?'

'No, in Venice.' Bembo closed his eyes. 'On a Sunday morning in early summer.' The details were coming back to him with amazing clarity. He had been sitting in the cabin of his gondola, its leather curtains drawn apart because he was reading. Bembino, his white dog, had been asleep across his feet.

Suddenly Marco, his gondolier, had given a shout and stopped rowing. Another boatman had cut across their path –

ONE

Venice, 1502

I

Marco was shouting abuse. Bembino woke up and barked. For the third time, Bembo shouted, 'Marco!'

If he heard, Marco took no notice. Other boatmen on the canal were slowing their oars to encourage his most fluent obscenities with cheers and whistles. The dog, panting with excitement, clambered across Bembo to reach Marco's rowing platform and kicked the book from Bembo's lap.

Irritably, Bembo brushed away the white hairs sprinkled on his black gown and bent down to retrieve the book. He knelt on the seat, leaned out of the cabin and struck Marco on the ankle with it.

Marco's heated face glared down at him. He was enjoying himself and resented the interruption.

'Marco, get on. Get on, I tell you!'

Marco roared. 'What, leave this foreign pig? He cut across us – '

'That had nothing to do with it. You picked a quarrel because he was born on the other side of the canal from you. Half Venice was born on the other side of the canal. I refuse,' Bembo snapped, 'to be made the centre of a public brawl every time I set foot in this boat.'

He drew in his head, caught a foot in the trailing sleeve of his gown and fell backwards into the cabin. Bembino leapt on top of him. Marco called out in concern, 'Pierottino!'

'I can't get up,' said Bembo. Then as he pushed Bembino aside, and came to his knees, he saw through the open curtains of the cabin a man standing by the edge of the canal. He was at the top of a flight of steps that led into a narrow alley. From the style of his dress he was not Venetian, and he was looking about him with a kind of exasperated bewilderment, gesturing to a servant who stood behind him. Bembo stared at him. The man turned, and Bembo saw his crutch.

'Strozzi?' he said aloud. He pulled himself to his feet. 'Marco, row over to those steps over there.' He thrust a hand out, pointing.

The foreign pig had slipped away while Marco's attention was diverted. Marco, with a shrug, swung the gondola round and pointed its hatchet prow towards the bank. Strozzi had already begun to limp away from the edge of the water. 'Marco, quickly,' cried Bembo, afraid of losing Strozzi in the warren of Venice's streets.

Marco, pleased to display his skill, manoeuvred the long wooden boat as though it were a black eel from the lagoon. As he brought it alongside the steps, Bembo leapt sure-footed from the rocking deck to the slippery stones. Strozzi had disappeared into the darkness of the alley, but as Bembo ran over the muddy, unpaved earth he saw him emerge into a patch of light at the other end.

'Ercole,' he yelled, 'Ercole!'

Ercole Strozzi heard the voice, paused thoughtfully, and was in the act of pivoting himself round on his crutch when Bembo burst from the alley, black gown flapping loose, Bembino splashing through the puddles at his heels.

'Ercole,' gasped Bembo again. Then he laughed, laid his hands on Strozzi's shoulders, and in the Venetian manner kissed him on both cheeks.

Strozzi regarded him coolly. 'My dear Pietro, you appear like Apollo in a masque, suddenly let down from the roof in a creaking cloud.' He gazed about him. 'Yet I see no cloud. Surely you have not materialised through these walls? It is well known how you islanders of the lagoon cherish the black arts.'

Bembo laughed again. Nothing ever appeared to startle or

disconcert Strozzi. 'My cloud, as you call it, is moored by the steps on the canal.'

Strozzi shuddered. 'You refer, I imagine, to one of those incredible boats of yours that stick out of the water at both ends. However did anyone conceive of such a thing?'

'They say,' said Bembo, 'that a crescent moon once fell from the sky to hide two lovers. That was the first gondola.'

'Are they all,' enquired Strozzi, 'constructed for the same purpose?'

Bembo looked at his friend with pleasure. It seemed to him that when Strozzi was present the air took on a glinting, flashing quality. It was an illusion partly suggested by Strozzi's fondness for metal decoration on his dress. He was wearing then a dark mantle patterned with small, burnished studs which threw out darts of light as he moved. But it was more than that; the effect was also created by the bright eyes, the crisp voice, the quick movements and the sharp wit.

'Ercole,' demanded Bembo, 'what are you doing in this obscure part of Venice?'

'I am not *doing* anything,' said Strozzi. 'I happen to be lost, though not through any want of sense in myself. I appreciate that Venetians consider themselves beyond many of the laws which other Italians observe, but I would have thought that even here the laws of geometry might apply. This, however, is not so.' Strozzi shifted his crutch. 'I left my inn to walk for a few minutes before dining. I moved in four directions to form a square and should, therefore, have returned to the point at which I started. But no. Venice, apparently, does not acknowledge the right angle. So here I stand. Tell me, Pietro, are your streets indirect and confused because such is the state of your minds, or are you a devious people because from birth you never know what it is to cover even the smallest distance by moving in a straight line?'

'Ercole,' said Bembo quickly before Strozzi could begin talking again, 'tell me why you are here?'

Strozzi gestured vaguely. 'I have certain commissions here. We can talk about them later. For the time being, Pietro, just show me how to find my inn and my dinner.'

'But you must dine with us, of course,' said Bembo. 'And you will stay at the Ca' Bembo.'

Strozzi offered courteous protests and Bembo as courteously dismissed them. Strozzi was led back to the canal and with misgiving allowed himself to be lowered into the gondola. He sat perched on Bembo's cushions, looking with disfavour at the city floating around him. His eye was accustomed to the sombre palaces of Ferrara, not to walls brazenly awash with glass, tricked out with mosaic and gilding and coloured stone.

Bembo was watching Strozzi's face. He was aware that, despite Strozzi's jesting, despite even their friendship, Strozzi seriously regarded Venetians as a suspect and alien people, the enemies of his native Ferrara. Twenty years had passed since the last war between the two states, and Venice considered that it had acted with magnanimity in victory by demanding only that a Venetian vice-domino should be appointed to advise on the conduct of affairs in Ferrara. The office still existed, with Venice blandly ignoring the resentment of the Ferrarese. It had once been held by Bembo's father, Bernardo, and it was during this period that Ercole Strozzi and Pietro Bembo, attracted by their common talent as poets, had first become friends.

The gondola approached the wooden-walled bridge of the Rialto. Nearby behind a broad quay, stood the Ca' Bembo. It was an ancient, dignified building with balconies of white marble. Marco turned the boat into the narrow side-stream that served the water-gates of the palace and there, beneath gondola posts painted in the black and gold colours of the Bembo family, Strozzi was restored to land.

Bembo escorted him through a series of apartments to his father's library. There was light everywhere, from open windows, from walls and floors of polished marble. The library itself was hung in the Venetian fashion with gilded leather, shimmering with ripples of light from the sun-flecked water of the canal. Senator Bernardo Bembo was seated at his reading-desk, surrounded by his distinguished collection of manuscripts and printed books. As a young man he had taken doctorates in both philosophy and law at the University of Padua and his books reflected these studies, as well as his life-long interest in the Roman poets. Yet the book he was reading as his son entered the room was a cloth-bound manual of maritime insurance.

He glanced up, peered for a moment at Strozzi and then rose with a cry of surprise and pleasure. Strozzi saw that he was wearing the red silk robe of the Venetian senator. Over his left shoulder was the red stole of cut velvet derived from the toga of the Roman senators, of whom the Venetians believed themselves to be the spiritual successors.

While Bernardo Bembo embraced Strozzi, his son explained where he had found him. 'Ercole,' said the Senator, 'it is an honour to receive you in our house. I am only distressed that you did not choose to come here as soon as you reached Venice. Your father showed us such kindness during our stay in Ferrara that I am grateful to be able to return some small part of his hospitality to his son.'

Strozzi kissed the Senator's hand. 'Sir, you are very good. My visit was arranged in haste, and it would have been too great a discourtesy to have presented myself here without warning.'

'Well, you are here now,' said the Senator, 'rescued by Pietro from the wilderness of Sant'Angelo, or Sant'Anzolo as we Venetians call it.'

'Are we sure that Ercole wished to be rescued?' said a voice behind them. Strozzi turned and saw Carlo, Bembo's brother, smiling at him. Carlo was two years younger than Bembo, like him in feature, but slighter, with the fresh colour and light brown hair that suggested Alpine blood. He shook his brother's arm playfully. 'Did it never occur to you, Pietro, that you discovered Ercole at a most unfortunate moment? He comes to Venice in secret, he arranges an assignation in a quiet part of the city, and then, just as his hand is on the latch and the longed-for moment has arrived, you blunder upon him, tactlessly drag him away and embarrass him with hospitality he cannot refuse.?'

Strozzi's eyes twinkled. 'Carlo, I won't deny that there have been occasions when I should have cursed Pietro's appearance, but this, I assure you, was not one of them.' He drew off one of his gloves. 'Curiously enough, however, my visit does concern a lady.'

He removed the second glove while they waited. 'You spoke of commissions,' said Bembo impatiently.

'Yes,' said Strozzi. He smiled brightly at his audience. 'I am here to buy silks and a cradle for the Duke of Ferrara's new daughter-in-law.'

Carlo stared at him. 'You can't be serious,' He laughed uncertainly.

'Yes, I am.'

'For Lucrezia Borgia?' Bembo spoke the name with distaste.

'Yes.'

'If that's all you've come for,' asked Carlo suspiciously, 'why the need for haste?'

'It's quite simple,' said Strozzi. 'Madonna Lucrezia is pregnant – hence, of course, the cradle – and she had the whim to dress herself and her ladies in new silks. Cardinal Ippolito, always the kindly brother-in-law when it suits him, offered to send her what she wanted when he returned to Rome.' Strozzi smiled crookedly at Carlo. 'I prefer the lady to be in debt to me rather than to Ippolito. So I pointed out to her that the markets of Venice are superior to those of Rome, and that I was free to leave for Venice at once. Here I am.'

'So the object of your visit,' said the Senator, 'was to score off Cardinal Ippolito.'

'It was one of my reasons,' Strozzi answered bluntly. He paused. 'But I also wished to please Madonna Lucrezia. I will serve her in any way that I can.' He saw Bembo frown and added, 'Yes, Pietro, the Borgia.'

'We thought Ippolito was still in Rome,' said Carlo.

'He was until a few days ago. It is rumoured that he tried to seduce Cesare Borgia's mistress, and had to leave in a hurry. Not that the episode has changed him in any way. He brought a new singing-boy back with him – small and dark, the kind he likes best. They say Ippolito is very pleased with his performance.' Strozzi coughed lightly. 'Perhaps he sings as well. I have already enquired of Ippolito when we may hear him.'

Carlo laughed, but Bembo shook his head. 'Ercole, don't goad him too far.'

'I'm lame,' said Strozzi. 'I must have some sport.'

Bernardo Bembo looked serious. 'Ercole, Pietro is right. For the sake of my friendship with your father, allow me to say this to you. You make the mistake of thinking that because Ippolito lacks your quickness of tongue he also lacks intelligence. He has a shrewd, perceptive mind. Because his vanity is ridiculous and his private behaviour amuses you, you under-estimate him. He is clever, he is vicious, and to certain situations he has abnormal reactions that rational men cannot comprehend. It is a very dangerous combination of qualities.'

Strozzi bowed his head politely, but both the Senator and Bembo were aware that he had received the advice as a piece of elderly and unnecessary caution. The Senator prudently dropped the matter. 'Well, shall we dine?' he said.

II

Strozzi dined with the members of the Bembo family at a long table presided over by the Senator's wife, Elena. He had already met in Ferrara Bartolommeo, the Senator's natural son who had been born before his marriage, and Antonia, Bembo's widowed sister, who shared with her three daughters an apartment on the far side of the courtyard. He encountered now for the first time Bernardo's brother and business partner, Jacopo Bembo, who lived on an upper floor of the palace. It being Sunday, there were also present at the table a number of their young bachelor kinsmen.

Venice, Strozzi had often observed, was a city of bachelors, due largely to the barbarous Venetian practice of bequeathing property not to the eldest son but to all surviving sons jointly. To preserve the inheritance it was the custom for only one brother in such a partnership to marry so that his sons might form the joint partnership of the next generation. So it had been arranged between Bernardo and Jacopo Bembo, and it would not be long, Strozzi supposed, before a similar choice would have to be made by Pietro and Carlo.

The other young bachelors sitting along the table were all connected in some way with the trading interests of their house. Leonardo Bembo, introduced to Strozzi as the son of the Venetian consul in Constantinople, acted as an agent in that city for several family concerns. Domenico was leaving shortly for the Barbary coast as the galley-master of a trading convoy. Girolamo was on a brief visit from Bruges, where he handled Levantine merchandise imported by his two brothers in Venice for the markets of northern Europe. Their conversation was on the buying price of cotton in the Syrian ports.

This could only be a household in Venice, thought Strozzi, fuming at the prospect of having to eat in silence because he had nothing to say about cotton. Seated about him were the members of one of the oldest patrician families in the Republic. The nobility of their class was evident in the appointments of their table, their manners, the way in which they were served, yet they talked together like a guild of shop-keepers.

Strozzi had hoped to engage the attention of the only other person present who, like himself, was neither a member of the family nor a Venetian, but Nicola Bruno, the secretary whom Bembo had brought back with him from Sciliy ten years earlier, was joining as volubly in the discussion as if he were native to it.

Only Pietro Bembo himself, who sat beside Strozzi, seemed as bored as he was. He took no part in the conversation but passed the time crumbling up his bread. He heard Strozzi sigh, and turned towards him. 'I thought you would be enjoying all this talk about cloth since you are now the Borgia's haberdasher,' he whispered.

Strozzi smiled. 'Why does she offend you so much?'

'The whole Borgia pack offends me,' said Bembo. 'Was there ever a Pope as corrupt as Alessandro? The son, Cesare, is violent and evil. He killed his own brother, yet the Pope still dotes on him. They use the Papacy simply to aggrandise themselves. Cesare wanted a kingdom, so the papal armies made war without cause on a peaceable state like Urbino. As for the depravity of the daughter – '

'Do you,' murmured Strozzi, 'accept the Roman view that Madonna Lucrezia is daughter, wife and daughter-in-law of the Pope?'

Bembo hesitated. 'I find it difficult to believe that even a Borgia would commit incest with both her father and brother. But, Ercole, the fact that the story is spreading is significant. I can't understand how Ferrara could accept such an alliance. Alfonso was certainly an unwilling bridegroom.'

'True,' Strozzi agreed.

'Can one blame him when one remembers what happened to the Borgia's other husbands? The last one, that little duke of Bisceglie, was almost certainly murdered by Cesare. And Sforza? Sforza was divorced for impotence by a papal court to which Lucrezia swore she was a virgin when she was plainly six months pregnant!'

'The child she was carrying at the papal hearing,' said Strozzi reasonably, 'was probably not Sforza's.'

Bembo's mouth opened. 'Does that make her any the less shameless?' His voice had risen, and the Senator, who liked the conversation at his table to be general, looked at him sharply. Bembo went on in a whisper, 'This is the woman you've chosen as your duchess?'

'There was no choice,' said Strozzi quietly. 'You've just mentioned Urbino. Cesare was about to take Urbino. Ferrara would have been next, but the Pope was prepared to spare Ferrara in return for a hereditary crown for his daughter.'

'If Cesare had invaded your border, Venice would have protected you.'

'With respect, Pietro, we preferred the Borgia marriage.'

'And you let yourself become a runner of errands.'

'Only because it pleases me to do so,' said Strozzi. 'Pietro, I was as much opposed to this wedding as everyone else. But when

I saw Lucrezia, I realised that she wasn't the woman that the stories about her suggest. She wasn't coarse or arrogant or greedy. She had, in fact, a kind of simplicity. She seemed vulnerable and lonely.'

'Well, you won't find her so simple and vulnerable when she starts organising the kind of entertainments she used to like in Rome. Wasn't there one party with the Pope and Cesare where they were amused by fifty naked prostitutes?'

A lull had fallen in the conversation about cotton and Bembo's voice carried across the table. His cousins turned to look at him curiously. Strozzi hid a smile. 'There is supposed to have been,' he said, 'although I've never met anyone who was actually present.'

Bembo stood up as his mother rose from her seat at the end of the meal. 'Ercole, your court at Ferrara has such dignity and restraint. She'll change all that,' he muttered.

Jacopo, preparing to follow his sister-in-law from the table, leaned towards them. 'Change, did you say? Change? There's too much change, Messer Strozzi. They've even pulled down the latrines in the Piazza San Marco. That's the Senate for you.' He glared at Bernardo.

The Senator moved to Jacopo's side. 'You know as well as I do, Jacopo, that they were an offence to anyone walking in the square. The decision to remove them should have been made years ago.' He held out an arm to Jacopo, who ignored him.

'Judge, your help, please,' he said, and turned to place his hands in Carlo's. Carlo raised him gently to his feet and fetched his stick. Jacopo looked into his face. 'Carlo, those latrines have been there since before I was born – '

Carlo led him away from the table. 'Yes, yes,' he said.

'Judge? The old man has fancies?' asked Strozzi.

Bembo smiled. 'No. Carlo was recently elected a judge of the civil appeal court. At thirty, he's the youngest judge Venice has known for years.'

'Ah, then you couldn't do better, my dear Pietro, than to learn a little impartiality from him – especially about – '

'Yes, I know,' said Bembo. 'Lucrezia Borgia.' He shook his head.

III

At five o'clock next morning, Carlo unlocked the warehouses of the Ca' Bembo and gave orders to his workmen for the day. At six, Bartolommeo was in the counting-house on the mezzanine floor, working with his clerks at the account books. By six-thirty, Pietro was up, reading Latin; and by seven, Elena Bembo had approved her cook's purchases from the Rialto market and was sitting at her lace-work. Shortly before eight, the Senator left by gondola for a meeting of the ducal council, and Antonia's music master arrived for her clavichord lesson. At nine o'clock, Jacopo shuffled into the counting-house to peer at the letters from the Bembo agents abroad. At ten, Strozzi appeared in the courtyard and, leaning his crutch against the well-head, pulled on his perfumed gloves, ready to face the day.

Carlo came smiling to the doorway of one of the warehouses, and Strozzi limped towards him, sniffing the air. 'I can smell cinnamon, and cloves – and something else?'

'Cheese,' said Carlo.

Strozzi wrinkled his nose in disgust. 'I can just about bear to think of your selling pearls or ivory or sables, but cheese!'

Carlo laughed. 'We do have some fine goods to please you, Ercole. Look here.' He opened the small wooden box that he was carrying. 'Gold thread from Constantinople for London. We sold a hundred boxes last year. I shall sell two hundred this year if I can get them safely across the Alps.'

'I thought,' said Strozzi, 'that you Venetians never did anything by land if you could do it by water.'

'Oh, we will do anything unnatural if it makes a profit. You see, Ercole, because of our success with the thread last season, other houses have bought for the same market. They will send their boxes by the galley-fleet that sails later in the summer, as we did last year. Ours, therefore, will have to go by the quicker route, overland to Bruges. My cousin, Girolamo, will ship the thread from there to London, and our whole purchase should be sold before the galleys arrive to bring down the price.'

'But the Alpine route will presumably be more expensive.'

'Yes. And there is the risk that the Emperor might close his borders to Venetian trade.'

'Ah,' said Strozzi intrigued. Trade bored him, but the Florentine branch of his family were bankers and he enjoyed balancing financial hazards. He embarked with Carlo on a series of calculations.

'Assuming, then,' he said after a while, 'that the thread reaches London and is sold at your estimated thirty per cent profit – '

'Then our agent in London buys English cloth and pewter with the proceeds. I already have a buyer in Apulia for the pewter. The cloth will be shipped to Syria, and the price I get from that will buy raw cotton – '

'That damned Syrian cotton again,' muttered Strozzi.

' – to sell here in Venice to the Augsberg merchants who will be coming for the winter fair. The overall profit should be between sixty and seventy.'

Strozzi gave Carlo a sly smile of approval. 'Yes, well I recall that I have some cloth-buying of my own to do. Could you leave your cheese unattended?'

Within a few minutes, Bembo had been roused from his books and they were being ferried across the great canal to the warehouse of the Brothers Bartempelli at the sign of the golden calyx. The weekday noise and activity on the water appalled Strozzi. The twin drawbridge at the centre of the Rialto bridge was open to admit a string of round-ships, the sturdy slow-moving sailing vessels that carried heavy freight in and out of Venice. Marco thrust the gondola forward beneath a high prow, and waves smacked their shallow flanks. Strozzi groaned and closed his eyes. From another round-ship, already moored, sacks of coal were crashing on to the quay outside the Ca' Bembo, and Bartolommeo was shouting numbers aloud as they were heaved into wooden sheds.

Strozzi was relieved to enter the quiet warehouse. Here the finest fabrics of the house were laid out for his inspection – cloths of gold and silver, the splendidly-dyed red Venetian velvet, velvets thickly gilded with fruits and leaves.

Strozzi was thoughtful, and then shook his head. 'They are beautiful, yes, but too bold. The duchess is slight, and her colouring is pale.' He turned to glance at pastel silks and painted muslins from Tuscany.

'No,' said Carlo. 'Insipid.'

Strozzi replied with feeling. 'You Venetians can appreciate nothing that is delicate and simple. Your senses are coarsened. Your food is too spiced, your wines too sweet, you blend your perfumes with too much musk. Everything for you must be rich, heavy – ' he pushed the cloth of gold aside, '– everything gilded. Don't you even gild your bread on saints' days?'

Carlo remained good-humoured. 'We also put gold in our glass to turn it red. But can you blame us? We have to exist in the middle of a grey waste of sea and sky.'

Strozzi ignored him and considered the grass-green taffeta that the merchants were unfolding. He nodded. 'Surely this,' said Bembo, pulling out a length of pure white silk, 'would be even more appropriate to your simple, blameless lady?'

Strozzi handled the white silk. Smiling slowly, he said, 'How perceptive and thoughtful, Pietro. I thank you for the suggestion.' Then he reached for a roll of scarlet velvet. 'And what would you say to this for me?' He draped it across his shoulders. 'You will notice that it is red, Cardinal's red.'

The deliberation in his voice caused Bembo to glance at his brother and then look carefully at Strozzi. 'Yes, it is Cardinal's red. What of it?'

Strozzi walked a few steps, trailing the velvet. 'I am hoping,' he said lightly, 'that Madonna Lucrezia will use her influence to win me a Cardinal's hat.'

Carlo shrugged his shoulders helplessly.

'Why not?' asked Strozzi. 'The duke paid five thousand ducats for Ippolito's. I shall have five thousand ducats, and the Pope's daughter to plead for me.'

'So now,' said Bembo flatly. 'we learn the truth behind your concern for the lady and her whims.'

'Why should you think my service to her insincere because at the same time I perform a service for myself?'

Carlo unwound the red velvet from Strozzi's shoulders and restored it to the merchants. 'Are you ready, Ercole? The next warehouse you should visit is by the exchange. We can walk.'

The street door of the Bartempelli warehouse opened on to a narrow lane that led to the oldest part of the city, the little piazza of San Giacomo. The ancient church which gave it its name filled one side, and on the others were the porticoed buildings of the exchange. It was shortly after eleven o'clock and the piazza was filled with groups of men. A few of them were citizens in coloured clothes, but the majority were patricians and, like Bembo and his brother, wore the long black robe which they held to be the privilege of their class. On their heads were plain brimless caps of black felt, and at their throats narrow bands of white linen without pleating or embroidery. They moved from group to group, exchanging their grave Venetian courtesies, but their heads turned like hawks to catch at scraps of passing talk.

'Merchants meet here,' Carlo said to Strozzi, 'twice a day for news of ships and cargoes. Look, there's Uncle Jacopo.' Jacopo was standing on the steps of the church, leaning on his stick, a cape of rabbit fur across his shoulders. He saw Carlo and beckoned to him impatiently.

Carlo nodded back. 'Give me three minutes, Pietro,' he said quickly and slipped away into the crowd.

Bembo, with an obvious reluctance to walk in the piazza, turned aside under the empty portico and sat down on a bench. 'Sit down, Ercole. He will probably be gone much longer than three minutes.' He sighed. 'He doesn't dislike this place, as I do.' He stared at the waiting groups of merchants. 'They are always looking over their shoulders, expecting bad news. It makes them grasping and anxious.'

He folded his arms. 'I suppose it's hardly surprising. At any moment one of them may hear that he's lost twenty or thirty thousand ducats.'

'On one voyage?'

'Oh yes, if it's through shipwreck. My father and Jacopo lost thirty thousand ducats overnight. Their galley was damaged during a storm, got separated from its convoy and was taken by a pirate fleet out of Palermo. They were carrying a quantity of currency in gold – '

'Why not use bills of exchange?'

'They're not accepted outside Christian Europe. The Turks and the Arabs will trade only for gold and silver coin.'

'Oh,' said Strozzi. 'Heathens in two senses of the word.'

Bembo nodded. 'A disaster like that can ruin a fortune and destroy a trading house for ever.'

'But not yours. You still trade.' Strozzi smiled. 'There's all that Syrian cotton.'

'Yes, we trade,' said Bembo wearily,' but under severe limitations. My father had to borrow from the State to repay his creditors, and he also had to support the loss of the galley itself. The Republic owns all the trading galleys and hires them by auction for each voyage, but if one is lost at sea the merchant who hired it is liable to the State for its cost. Ercole, after seventeen years we are still discharging the debt, and a state debtor is not allowed to hire ships. All he can do is buy unwanted space in other merchants' galleys.' Bembo shrugged his shoulders. 'We make moderate profits, and we own a monopoly for the sale of coal in Venice which makes a fair income. It's enough to maintain our household and pay the interest on the loan. But it's not enough to repay the principal which would allow us to hire our own galleys again and rebuild our capital.'

Strozzi shook his head. 'As a banker, Pietro, I would advise you to sell your assets in Venice and buy land.'

'Land?' cried Bembo. 'To a Venetian land is simply a convenient place to change cargoes.' He stood up to see what Carlo was doing. He was still talking to his uncle, who was banging his stick on the ground.

Bembo sat down again. 'My uncle and my brother are having another of their disagreements on the best way of not losing money.' He smiled at Strozzi. 'As you heard yesterday, my Uncle Jacopo dislikes change. He still wants to go on trading the way he did twenty years ago, buying Cretan wine in bulk for London. Carlo prefers to buy what he thinks will be in demand at any given moment, no matter where. As things are, Carlo's is the only practicable method.'

Carlo was now strolling in the piazza, head thrust forward, smiling, eyes alert. Bembo looked at him fondly. 'In a moment, he'll sniff the air and say, "We must buy fish from the Black Sea and amber from Beirut". And he'll be right. He understands these things.'

'But you don't?'

Bembo rubbed a hand across his eyes. 'No, I don't.'

Strozzi said gently, 'You seem – what shall I say – disenchanted.'

Bembo was silent, fumbling with his long sleeve. He spoke suddenly. 'Ercole, I can't work here. I can't. In the last five months, I haven't finished a dozen pages of my book. There's no place here in Venice for writers, no respect for them.'

'Yet Petrarch preferred writing in Venice to any other city.'

'Petrarch,' said Bembo bitterly, 'was not born here. He was not dedicated in his cradle to the belief that before everything else and in every circumstance he must think of the honour of the Comune and San Marco.'

Strozzi laughed at his vehemence. 'Are you?'

'Not in so many words. That's the oath the captains of our trading galleys take before each voyage. But we're all in effect bound by it. If one practises law or banking, this is acceptable to the honour of Venice, but not if one writes. This is not enough, nor is scholarship. Of course, if one chooses to be a scholar in one's leisure, as my father does, this is a desirable accomplishment; as a way of life it is fit only for priests, and you know what we think of them in Venice.' Bembo looked at Strozzi in desperation. 'I can't work here because all the time I'm distracted by the thought of obligations I don't understand how to discharge.'

'Pietro,' said Strozzi, 'if you can't work here, why not spend a few months in Ferrara?'

Bembo was startled. 'Ferrara?'

'I don't mean in the city, but in our villa at Ostellato. We rarely use it, and it's very quiet there on the marshes. You could write there undisturbed.'

Bembo nodded thoughtfully. 'Yes, I think perhaps I could – '

He broke off as Carlo hurried towards him. 'Pietro,' said Carlo, laughing excitedly, 'Rethimo wine is up half a ducat on five hundred litres. I thought it might rise. Thank God we stopped Jacopo purchasing.'

'Carlo, I've already told Pietro that you'd be wiser to buy land,' said Strozzi.

'No,' Carlo's blue eyes glinted. He turned to look at the map of Venetian trade routes painted on the wall under the portico. 'No. Give me ten years and I'll have Bembo galleys sailing again into Alexandria and Cadiz.' His hands made swift movements across the map. 'But only,' he added, 'if I can keep Uncle Jacopo occupied with petitions to the Senate on the restoration of the latrines in the Piazza San Marco.'

He took Strozzi's arm and pulled him to his feet. 'You've been idle for long enough, Ercole. Shall we look now at some silks from China?'

'I had supposed,' answered Strozzi, 'that that was our objective when we left the last warehouse.'

Carlo laughed as they crossed the piazza into the street of goldsmiths. He squeezed Strozzi's elbow. 'More evidence, you see, Ercole, of our degenerate appetite for gold. And do you realise that for the past ten minutes you have been sitting beneath twenty-five millions of ducats in gold?' He pointed to the windows above the porticoes of the exchange. 'Inside there is the largest treasury of gold in Europe.'

'I don't doubt it,' said Strozzi tartly. 'Everything in Venice always is the largest of its kind in Europe, from the violets in your flower market to your brothel for foreign seamen.'

Carlo stopped at a door between two goldsmiths' booths. He glanced at the brothel which stood a few feet away at the end of the Rialto bridge. A naked girl at an upper window beckoned to him.

'Surely,' said Carlo, 'a Cardinal presumptive should have put a knowledge of such things away from him.' He pushed open the door and went in to the warehouse.

IV

Carlo stood beside Strozzi, pointing a finger at him. 'Ercole, I'm trying to understand. Why? Why this extraordinary notion to become a Cardinal?'

Strozzi was resting in Senator Bembo's library, a cushion under his lame foot. He was content with life, and pleased with himself. He had finished with the Venetian cloth houses, and with the warehouses owned by the communities of German, Turkish and Dalmatian merchants. An extravagant number of boxes was waiting to be removed by water to Ferrara.

He looked up at Carlo, who was dressed to preside at the afternoon session of the civil court of appeal. 'You're not examining a recalcitrant witness now, Carlo.'

'Ercole,' persisted Carlo, 'you're not even in minor orders, and you've certainly never shown any inclination towards a life of prayer and humility.'

'One of the benefits of a corrupt church,' said Strozzi airily, 'is that anyone with suitable influence and enough money may aspire to a cardinalcy, not merely the saints on whom the delights of power would be wasted. Carlo, I like a role of authority. I like diplomacy, which I see as the art of manoeuvring people to their disadvantage.'

Senator Bembo appeared puzzled. 'But you already have great power in Ferrara. Your father has led the duke's council for nearly thirty years, and you have shared the office with him for the last ten.'

Strozzi leaned forward. 'Yes, we have control now, under the present duke. But he is an old man, and his son, Alfonso, has no love for either of us. As soon as he can, he'll remove us from power and probably seize the estates we've acquired in office.' He spread out his hands. 'So what else should I do but join the college of Cardinals and warm my empty fingers in the papal treasury?' He was aware of the Senator's shrewd glance. 'You, of course, sir, will not look kindly on such a philosophy of power.'

'Certainly to myself as a Venetian,' said Bernardo Bembo courteously, 'the exercise of government and the exercise of power are not the same thing, as they are elsewhere. We prefer that no man should hold any one office long enough for him to use it to his own advantage. Unlike your father, I have served Venice in many different ways during my life-time.'

Strozzi nodded. The Senator had acted as ambassador to both Lorenzo de Medici and King Henry of England. He had been governor of Bergamo and Padua, and was shortly to hold this office in Verona. He had held many internal posts in Venice itself.

He glanced at Carlo. 'Our system of appointing judges is also designed to prevent corruption in law. Carlo will serve as a judge in the civil court for only eight months. Then, if he is re-elected, he will be transferred to the criminal court for eight months, and so on.'

'Ah,' said Strozzi, 'but the doge is elected for his life-time. This will surely attract a man who craves power. If I were a Venetian I would have to be doge. Yes, think of his pomp: ermine and cloth of gold, silver trumpeters in crimson preceding him, a gilded barge trailing red silk behind it on the water – '

'You dislike gilding,' interrupted Carlo, 'and first you would have to be elected.'

Strozzi waved away the objections. 'Any ambitious man with money and unscrupulous supporters can dictate an election.'

Carlo shook his head. 'Not here. Ercole, do you know how the doge is elected?'

'Oh, you put little black and white balls in urns, or something.'

'That's only at the end,' said Carlo. 'Now, listen. The doge is chosen by the Greater Council, of which every man of patrician birth over twenty-five is a member. There are about two thousand of us at the moment. The process of election is begun by the youngest member of the Council, who chooses thirty others – '

'Yes, well he can choose his own family – '

'Wait a minute, Ercole. The thirty then elect nine of their own number, and their function is to select a further group of forty. The forty then elect twelve of their own number, and this body of twelve chooses twenty-five. From among themselves they elect nine – '

'Oh, not again,' muttered Strozzi.

' – who choose a further number of forty-five. This group reduces itself to eleven, and it is these eleven who choose the forty-one members of the Council who will ballot for the doge. They must reach a majority of twenty-five.'

Strozzi was silent. Then he coughed delicately. 'It does strain belief,' he murmured, 'to think that someone, at some time, must have sat down to work out that improbable arrangement of numbers. What a sinister and inhuman process.'

'It is a very effective process,' snapped Carlo, 'for stopping men like you bribing their way to power. It has given us stability. It has protected us from civil war – '

'Perhaps,' interrupted Strozzi, 'but all the same I think I prefer the warm and velvety corruption of the papal court. I seem to remember that your doge wears chains at his coronation to remind him that he is the slave of the Republic.' He shivered. 'Barbarous.'

Then he wriggled his foot comfortably on its cushion. 'I'm not surprised, Senator, that you can allow only one man to hold office for life. You really wouldn't have time to choose many others.'

The Senator smiled. 'Permanent appointments are sometimes made to one or two of our larger embassies – Constantinople, for example, or Vienna.' A look of regret passed across his face. 'It was always my ambition that Pietro should one day hold such an office.'

Pietro Bembo, who had been standing on the balcony with a book in his hand, turned at the sound of his name.

'Now I fear,' added the Senator, 'that it may never be possible. In Venice, as you will realise, Ercole, high office does not bring high reward. Because here we regard service to the State as a privilege, we receive only a token recompense for office. Our own fortunes have to support us, and only a very rich man can serve Venice abroad with the dignity that she demands.' Bernardo Bembo sighed. 'Once my brother and I controlled such a fortune. Now we do not. Our losses in trade mean that Pietro will be denied the honour of serving Venice in high office.'

Pietro stepped into the room, his fingers marking a page. 'Father,' he said quietly, 'it is not an honour which I particularly seek.'

The Senator frowned. 'It is one which I believe you would be well fitted to discharge.'

Strozzi saw in the look that Bembo gave his father a curious mingling of anger and shame. 'But my election to office does not depend on your good opinion,' he said. 'Three times last year, Father, at your suggestion, I stood as candidate for a post in a minor embassy. I was defeated on each occasion, humiliatingly defeated – ' He snapped the book shut. 'If this room were filled with all the gold in the Rialto exchange, the possibility of my serving in Vienna would be just as remote as it is now.'

'Pietro,' said the Senator patiently, 'all the men of our family who dined here yesterday had come from the weekly meeting of the Greater Council – all, that is, except you. How can you expect votes when you make so little effort to be known by the assembly? As a younger man you spent many years with me outside Venice. Now we are back, but you still insist on speaking Tuscan instead of Venetian, and you make no secret of your liking for the life of the Italian ducal courts. In an ambassador these factors would be an advantage, but you must realise that they make you appear a stranger to your fellow members of the Council. You need to win their trust. These initial defeats are inevitable, but when you begin to show more interest in state concerns you will find that your votes will increase.'

'I resent – ' began Bembo hotly. Carlo shook his head quickly, and started to talk again to Strozzi of his ambitions. A few minutes later a bell rang nearby, and both Carlo and the Senator rose to leave, Carlo for his sitting of the civil court and Bernardo for a meeting of the Senate.

Bembo and Strozzi were left alone. 'All for the Comune and San Marco, eh?' said Strozzi, and Bembo threw down his book.

'When does your father leave for Verona?'

'In September,' said Bembo irritably.

'Then isn't that just the time for you to come to Ostellato? Pietro, why do you hesitate? Ah – ' Strozzi suddenly struck his head. 'What a fool I am! Of course, you won't want to leave Venice in September. That's when Maria Savorgnan will be coming back.'

Bembo said nothing, but looked more distracted than ever.

V

Strozzi was strolling with Carlo beside the doge's palace. Other Italians could take their outdoor exercise in the saddle. Venetians walked in the late afternoon in the Piazza San Marco.

Foreign merchants mingled with them. Apart from the Venetian Jews in their jewelled chains and caps of red felt, Strozzi saw Spaniards, bands of Germans, Greeks with long black hair falling across their shoulders, Turks wearing long brocade robes and white silk turbans, Levantine Jews in turbans of yellow, Hungarians, Dalmatians and Persians.

'Too many heathens and heretics,' grumbled Strozzi as they brushed against him.

There was hardly a Christian priest to be seen. Venice did not welcome priests who were not prepared to put the interests of the

Republic before those of the Church. The only women in the square were courtesans. They walked bare-headed under silken umbrellas carried by their maids, perfumed and wearing dresses extravagantly trimmed with gold lace.

Carlo and Strozzi reached the edge of the water, turned and walked back towards the basilica. Bembo was a few paces ahead of them, moving slowly, from time to time acknowledging a greeting. The Venetians, Strozzi noticed, did not salute an acquaintance, as other Italians did, by removing their caps. Instead, with a singularly graceful movement, they placed the right hand over the heart and inclined their heads. Bembo performed this action in a grave, unhurried manner, without breaking the rhythm of his steps.

As Strozzi watched, one of the courtesans stopped to address Bembo. She had pale, bleached hair and wore diamonds. Bembo bowed low over the hand which she offered him, and they fell into rapid conversation. Strozzi drew Carlo behind one of the pillars of the basilica and stared, engrossed.

'Carlo,' he whispered, 'what's happened between Pietro and the charming widow Savorgnan? A year ago he couldn't speak ten words without mentioning her name – '

Carlo nodded. 'A year ago, Marco was carrying letters between them sometimes twice a day, even when they'd seen each other. And every night he was climbing up to her room on that ridiculous rope ladder they used.'

'Pietro is always regarded by my father,' said Strozzi, 'as a man of scholarly prudence. It was hardly prudent to climb into a bedroom overlooking a public street night after night. He might have known they'd be caught.'

'I suppose there was nothing else they could do,' said Carlo, defending his brother. 'They used to meet in the daytime in Marco's house, until Maria's brothers-in-law became suspicious of her absences. They tried to be careful, Ercole. Pietro used to wait some distance away from the house in the campo San Trovaso between one o'clock and two. When the Savorgnan brothers were in bed and it was safe, Maria used to put a candle in her window, which was at the corner of the house on the first floor. As soon as Bembo was below, she dropped the ladder. They went on like this for five months without being seen. Then one night Paolo Savorgnan got out of his bed and went down into his counting house just in time to see a pair of boots disappearing up past the grilled window. He made such a noise that Bembo escaped before they broke into Maria's room.'

'And then,' added Strozzi, 'when she was turned out of the Savorgnan house, he placed her in a convent until I was able to find lodgings for her in Ferrara. And that wasn't the end. He used to visit her every two or three months and spend several days with her.'

'He hasn't been since August,' said Carlo. 'He went in August, stayed one hour, and came back. She still writes to him, but he won't open her letters. I have to read them and answer them for him.'

'Then what happened in August?'

Carlo shook his head. 'I don't know. But I sometimes suspect that Pietro was discovered on his ladder because Maria had deliberately contrived to betray them, hoping that Pietro would be forced to marry her. If she told him this, or he found it out, I think he would have left her.'

Strozzi blinked. 'For something as trivial as that?'

'Yes,' said Carlo carefully. 'I don't think it would be trivial to Pietro.' He hesitated. 'Candour between lovers is very precious to him. He believed he shared this with Maria. If he discovered suddenly that this was not so, his disillusionment would be very great.'

Strozzi looked at Bembo and the courtesan. 'Does he think she gives him candour?' He grunted. 'At least he doesn't have to use secret ladders to get to her.'

Carlo suddenly laughed. 'Ercole, do you think – ? Ercole, Pietro couldn't afford her. Do you know what they're talking about? Walk past them with me and you'll hear.'

They emerged from the portico of the basilica and strolled

slowly past Bembo and his companion. They were discussing Greek syntax.

Strozzi leaned heavily on his crutch. 'I suppose I shouldn't be surprised,' he said. 'In a city where a former ambassador to the King of England sells coal outside his palace, it is only to be expected that courtesans should speak Greek.'

'She holds a salon,' explained Carlo, 'to which she invites the leading scholars in Venice.'

'I see,' said Strozzi. 'Then if she is not the one, for whom does he now swing about on ladders at midnight?'

'There has been no other lady since Maria. Now, don't ask any more questions, Ercole. There's nothing more to find out. Shall we walk in the other direction?'

Strozzi nodded, and they began to walk the length of the piazza. 'It's nine months since August,' he said. A little while later, he murmured, 'Candour – how interesting. Honesty, directness, candour.' He became then so wrapped in his own thoughts that Carlo looked at him suspiciously.

'What are you planning, Ercole?'

'Planning?' said Strozzi. 'I was merely hoping that Pietro would decide to come to Ostellato.'

'I hope so, too. His work is important to me, and I know that he finds it difficult to write here in Venice. He needs to be away from – '

'From electors and widows, it would seem,' said Strozzi.

They turned, and were facing the squat Byzantine domes of the basilica. From its roof the golden lion of San Marco stirred on a pennant of red silk. The same winged lion peered from the flag-poles; on a field of blue starred with gold it strode against the wall of the clock-tower. The Venetians called their colonisation 'planting the lion', and the beast had now been loosed among the Alps, to the borders of Milan in the west, and eastwards as far as Crete and the Aegean. There were many beside the Ferrarese, thought Strozzi, who wanted to see it tarnished and dismembered.

'From your expression,' said Carlo, 'you would appear to be planning something particularly unpleasant for Pietro's visit.'

'As it happens, I am pondering on the paradox of Venice.' Strozzi glanced at Carlo's black robe. 'You dress yourselves and govern your state with the austere discipline of classical Rome. Yet you surround yourselves with Levantine opulence.'

He gestured towards the basilica. The late afternoon sun was blazing full on its gold mosaic and on the gilded bronze of the four Greek horses above the porch. Among its coloured pillars moved the turbaned Eastern merchants, and as they greeted one another Strozzi suddenly recognised how oriental in style was the Venetian form of salutation. There was something of the East, too, in the way that Venetian women spent the day on the loggias of their palaces or in little gardens built on stilts among the roofs, venturing out in their gondolas only in the evening, their faces veiled with transparent black gauze.

Yet in this same city, Strozzi recalled, a courtesan could be treated in public as an equal by a man of Bembo's birth. He turned his attention again to Bembo. He had concluded his conversation with the lady and was looking round the square for them.

'Have you made up your mind to come to Ostellato?' Strozzi asked as soon as Bembo joined them.

Bembo looked at his brother. 'Carlo,' he said, 'our dear friend, Ercole, appears rather anxious for me to go. Could it be that after his usual fashion he intends to do himself a service, as well as one for me, in sending me to Ostellato?'

'I think, Pietro, that it would be unwise to go unprepared for such a probability.'

'Oh, don't worry,' said Strozzi coolly, 'I'll find some use for you, Pietro.'

TWO

Ostellato, 1502

I

Bembo leaned out of a window in the villa at Ostellato and contentedly surveyed the river winding across the marshes towards the desolate lagoon of Comacchio. It was a day of crystal November sunshine, windless, the water serene under a pale, clear sky.

It was four weeks since Bembo had arrived at Ostellato with his servant Lico, Bembino and a boatload of books. At first he had been tense and restless, but as the days slipped past he had fallen into the placid ways of this isolated place. He rode and hunted across the marshes, fished in the river and interested himself in the work of the gardeners. He had begun to work again on his book. In the calm, undisturbed atmosphere of Ostellato, ideas were forming clearly and precisely in his mind, and he was able to transfer them without effort to paper. He was beginning to feel that lifting of the spirit, that quiet excitement that came to him when his writing was going well.

He was working in a small room in one of the towers of the villa. Its window was fringed by the branches of a tree, and an outside stair led down to the herb-garden. Bembo had chosen the room for its seclusion, and its broad view of the river and the marshes. He sat down at his desk and arranged his notes. As he drew out a fresh sheet of paper, his eye caught a paragraph that he had written many months earlier. 'Love,' he read, in the words of the most cynical of his characters, 'converts us calm, studious, philosophical beings into dangerous night prowlers, leapers over walls . . . ' Bembo, remembering his rope ladder, smiled at this wry self-portrait, and then was amazed to realise that he *was* smiling and that the memory no longer disturbed him.

He settled down to read what he had written on the previous day. Then he reached for the jar in which he kept his quills and discovered that they needed sharpening. This was something that Nicola Bruno always did for him in Venice. He stood up to look for a knife, and saw one on the window-ledge.

As he stood by the window, sharpening his quills, his attention was caught by two things: Bembino sprawled across a bed of herbs, and a barge moving down the river from the direction of Ferrara.

Bembo leaned out of the window. 'Binbo, get off! Binbo.' Bembino peered at him through a fringe of white hair and moved grudgingly on to the path.

Bembo raised his eyes to the river. The barge, as far as he could see, was an ornamental one with a canopy. He sharpened the remaining quills in the jar and laid them on the desk. The black silhouette of the barge was gradually assuming colour and detail as it came closer. It appeared to carry bundles of coloured cloth, but these he saw a few minutes later were the bunched skirts of the women sitting under the canopy. The sound of voices and snatches of music began to reach him through the still air.

There seemed to be little doubt that the barge was coming towards the villa. Bembo watched it with an ill grace, resenting the presence of strangers in what, after four weeks alone there, he was tending to think of as his own villa.

A moment later, he felt ashamed of his attitude, especially when he saw Strozzi helped out of the barge. He wondered if he should greet Strozzi and his guests, or if he should remain discreetly out of sight in his tower. A dozen or so people were now moving across the garden behind Strozzi, untidy swatches of colour on the precise paths. They had a lute and drums, and – Bembo stared – a fool jingling his bells. They swept under Bembo's window and round a corner out of sight, although he could still hear Strozzi's raised voice and a spatter of laughter from time to time.

Then even this died away. Bembo hesitated, still uncertain what to do. At last, reluctantly, he put on his belt and fastened the cuffs of his black gown.

He was still buttoning the neck when the door of his room suddenly opened and a young woman ran in. At the sight of Bembo standing in the middle of the room, she stopped short, gave a faint shriek of alarm and clutched her face in her hands. It was a pale, pleasing face, and under the broad-brimmed hat of black velvet there were coils of fair hair twisted with tiny pearls. Bembo noticed this, startled as he was. He also noticed that the red silk of her dress was too bright for her pale colouring.

'Sir – ' She was out of breath as though she had been running. 'Forgive me. I thought – ' She made an effort to breathe evenly. 'You must forgive me.'

She turned, kicking the red silk skirts behind her, and ran back through the door. Once safely outside, she leaned back into the room to pull the door shut behind her, but as she did so she saw the books stacked about the room and the papers spread on Bembo's desk. From the papers her eyes moved slowly and with growing apprehension to Bembo's face. Bembo, one eyebrow raised in a sense of mild outrage, stared back at her.

'You are not – ?' she began hesitantly, and then stopped. 'Mother of God, I believe you are.'

'You believe that I am what, madonna?' asked Bembo coldly.

His tone made the pale cheeks flush. 'The hermit,' she said timidly. 'Messer Strozzi's hermit.'

'His what?' cried Bembo. He looked furious. 'I suspect,' he said, after a moment, 'that it is quite probable that I am.'

The young woman let go of the latch of the door to which she had been clinging, and walked back into the room. 'It is time,' she said simply, 'that I learned not to be such a fool.'

Bembo was disconcerted by the directness of her manner. 'Madonna?'

'Sir,' she said with an air of apology, 'may I explain? Messer Strozzi told us that he had lent his villa to a hermit who was devoting his life to study. He said that the hermit had given up the world because a woman had once deceived him – ' She glanced at

Bembo's face, and went on hastily, ' – and he wished never to speak to another woman again. From the way he spoke I imagined an old man with a long white beard and a disagreeable smell.' She looked at Bembo's smooth dark hair, his strong nose, and the firm throat rising from his loose white collar, and she laughed softly.

Bembo smiled suddenly, and the dark eyes that until then had regarded her with polite displeasure seemed to grow lighter, more brilliant. 'So you came here,' he said gently, 'to torment an old man, like a second Saint Anthony in the wilderness, with visions of the world he had renounced.' He indicated with his hand the richness of her dress.

She looked down at herself, ashamed. 'Yes, it seems a stupid idea, now – and unkind, which is worse.' She raised her head to him in her quick, direct way. 'It would have been unforgivable if you had really been the old man we imagined.'

'But you see,' said Bembo, warming to her distress, 'I am not.'

'No,' said the young woman miserably, 'and I have interrupted your work. Please forgive me.' She hesitated. 'Messer Strozzi suggested that we play a game. We must all search for the hermit –' She bit her lip as Bembo frowned. 'How could I have been such a fool to believe him? It isn't even a good story. However, he promised a prize to the one who found you first. He said you would have found a place to hide as soon as you heard us coming.'

Bembo, embarrassed by Strozzi's perception, said nothing.

'Then,' she went on, 'Messer Strozzi drew lots to decide which part of the villa each of us was to search.'

'Ah,' said Bembo. 'Did Messer Strozzi draw the lots?'

'Yes.' They looked at each other with understanding. 'He told me that my part lay through the door on the other side of this room, which he said was empty.'

'The only other door in this room leads back to the garden.'

'Could he have made a mistake?'

'In his own house?' said Bembo.

'But why not?' demanded a voice brightly. 'I rarely use this villa, and never this wing.' Strozzi was standing in the doorway, leaning on his crutch. 'Yet despite my mistake, your highness's instinct for scholarship still led her to our hermit.'

Highness! Bembo glared at Strozzi, angry and confused. Then he turned his head to look at Lucrezia Borgia. Her fool and the swarm of ladies were pushing their way into the room behind Strozzi.

'Then where,' Lucrezia was asking, 'is my prize, Messer Ercole?'

Strozzi stretched out a hand towards Bembo. 'Here, madonna. May I present to you Messer Pietro Bembo, Cavalier of the Most Serene Republic of Venice, who begs to be received as your highness's devoted servant.'

Lucrezia's mouth opened with something like alarm. 'You are Messer Pietro Bembo?' She closed her eyes to compose herself, and then took a step towards him, holding out her hand.

Bembo forced himself to brush aside his anger and to offer the courtesies demanded by the occasion. Taking Lucrezia's hand, he said with fluent grace, 'To be accepted as the servant of Madonna Lucrezia would be the greatest of prizes for me, though hardly for her highness. Yet how can I hope that she will grant me such a privilege when I have behaved with such blind stupidity in her presence? Madonna, it is now I who must beseech your forgiveness in that I did not recognise from your beauty that lady whom Ariosto has sung as one to whom all other women are as copper to gold, as the wild poppy to the rose. In my defence, I can only plead that it was this very beauty that dazzled my mind and bereft me of my reason.' Even as the words fell from his lips, it occurred to Bembo that she did have, in fact, a kind of beauty – the fugitive kind that weariness or cold can extinguish. Now, looking up at him, her cheeks slightly flushed, the beauty was beginning to flicker like an uncertain candle-flame.

Bembo bowed low to kiss her fingers and his mother's agnus-dei, which he wore on a long chain round his neck, swung forward from the unfastened neck of his gown.

Lucrezia jumped back and then smiled. Bembo caught the jewel in his left hand. 'I doubt, madonna, if that is the first time that a pious emblem has prevented a kiss.'

'You do not admire piety?'

Bembo thrust the agnus-dei inside his shirt. 'Not if it is obtrusive, madonna,' he said, kissing her hand.

She introduced him then to her ladies, coming last of all to a young girl with black eyes, and black hair hanging loose on her shoulders. 'This is my cousin, Madonna Angela Borgia.'

Bembo bent over a thin hand wearing too many rings, which he suspected were borrowed from Lucrezia. He guessed that she was perhaps fifteen or sixteen. 'It is hardly just,' he said gravely, 'that one family should claim so much beauty.'

Angela Borgia showed her small white teeth in pleasure. 'Why do you make Messer Bembo stay in this lonely place?' She pouted at Strozzi. 'Why can't you bring him to Ferrara?'

'My child,' said Strozzi, 'he knows that he will be welcome in Ferrara whenever he chooses, but he has come from Venice to work and not to waste his time complimenting you.'

'Why shouldn't he compliment me? Am I not the future Duchess of Urbino?' She looked at Bembo and tossed her black hair. 'I am betrothed to the Duke of Urbino's heir,' she said pertly.

'Yes, madonna, I know,' said Bembo. He was a frequent guest of the exiled Duke and Duchess of Urbino in Venice, and also knew how bitterly they resented the betrothal to Cesare Borgia's kinswoman. 'I have always loved Urbino,' he added. 'If you were its duchess, I would have even more cause to do so.'

Lucrezia was standing beside Bembo's window. 'This window will be beautiful when the leaves are out,' she said. 'Will you still be at Ostellato then?'

'I hardly know, madonna. That depends very much on my family in Venice.'

Lucrezia nodded and leaned from the window. 'Whose dog is that? Does it belong to Messer Strozzi or is it yours?'

Bembo looked out of the window and frowned. Bembino was back on the herb bed. 'It is mine, madonna.'

Lucrezia laughed and brought her hands together in a movement that made her bracelets tinkle. 'I was sure of it. It is not the sort of pet dog that Messer Strozzi would have.' She turned to Bembo. 'I should like to see it.'

Bembo opened the door to the stair, and followed her as she stepped out. 'And what sort of dog do you think Messer Strozzi would choose, madonna?' he asked.

Lucrezia considered this as she descended the steps. 'Oh, it would never sit in the dirt, but always on a silk cushion, and it would have long fine fur and a face like a fox.'

'I doubt if such a dog exists.'

From the step below she turned to look up at him, her eyes dancing. 'But that is why he has no dog.'

'Ah,' said Bembo, 'so you knew Bembino was mine because he had the long white hair of a hermit.'

She laughed with delight at the name. 'Bembino,' she repeated. 'Messer Bembo's Bembino.'

They stood in the herb-garden and Bembo called the dog. He came slowly, wagging his tail, his curly white coat dusty and tangled. Lucrezia bent down to stroke him, and then knelt on the path and put her arms round his neck.

Her noisy company were overflowing the garden round them. The fool capered about, barking like a dog. Bembino put out his tongue and licked Lucrezia's cheek. She laid her head on his white fur and closed her eyes.

'Madonna,' shouted the fool, 'only let me be your dog and I will lick more than your cheek!'

Bembo longed to seize the fool and throw him in the river. He felt a fierce distaste for the whole sniggering company. It seemed as though a transparent wall had arisen round him, making them as unreal as cardboard figures. In their midst was Lucrezia, stroking the dog, unaware of them. He wondered what had happened to her if the friendliness of a strange dog meant comfort. As he watched her, she opened her eyes and half-smiled at him – and she was beside him on his side of the transparent wall.

He held out an arm to help her rise to her feet. With the sun falling on her face, Bembo could see faint drawn lines under her eyes and in her cheeks. She seemed suddenly tired.

'You should not stay out here too long, even in this autumn sun,' he said gently.

She looked at him in surprise. 'I think you have not been well,' he added. 'You should take care.'

She gazed at him wonderingly, then turned her head quickly. 'Oh, I am well enough, Messer Bembo,' she said lightly. 'Thank you. But it is time that we should go. We have disturbed you enough.'

'Highness, that was not what I meant.'

Lucrezia turned to him impulsively, and her hand brushed his sleeve. 'Oh no, I understood.'

They walked together towards the boat, both silent. Lucrezia glanced up at the blue and gold clock above Strozzi's stables. 'Do you know,' she said softly, 'that it is only twenty-five minutes since I came to Ostellato. It is such a short time.'

'It is long enough,' said Bembo.

She nodded. 'Yes, it is. Will you come to Ferrara?'

Bembo's brilliant eyes rested on hers. 'I don't know when it will be possible, but I will come.'

She nodded again, and they smiled slowly at each other.

A few minutes later the barge had gone, disturbing the smooth water with its bright reflection. For a long time Bembo could hear the twanging of music, the fool's voice and the shrieks of laughter.

II

Strozzi returned to Ostellato a week later, this time alone.

'What game are we playing today?' asked Bembo coldly.

'You can't expect me to invent diversions for you every week,' said Strozzi.

'I would hardly have called being humiliated and embarrassed a diversion.'

'I had my reasons for it,' said Strozzi. He suddenly leaned forward and put a hand against Bembo's forehead. 'Pietro, have you any fever, any sickness, any pain?'

Bembo snatched Strozzi's hand away. 'Of course not. What are you talking about?'

Strozzi folded his arms complacently. 'So. You have been in the same room with the Borgia, you have spoken to her, you have even touched her, yet you are not diseased, not corrupted. Would you have admitted this to be possible if I had not brought her here, and contrived for you to meet her without prejudice? She, too, would never have consented to see you unless we had played our little game.'

Bembo was startled. 'Not consented to see me?'

'No. You repel her, or rather your name does. The duke, I'm afraid, gave her the impression that you were a hair-splitting pedant. Whenever he talks about his beloved Roman drama he is inclined to say, "Messer Bembo is of the opinion that Plautus meant such-and-such" or "Messer Bembo translates the line so, if I remember him rightly". Madonna Lucrezia prefers to have people who are comfortable rather than brilliant around her.'

'I still don't see,' said Bembo explosively, 'why you had to call me a hermit – giving up the world – not speaking to women.'

'It wasn't entirely inaccurate,' said Strozzi. 'It had a grain of truth. And it was very important in persuading Lucrezia to come. Women cannot resist an opportunity to meet a man who has no time for their sex. Each one of them believes in her heart that she is the one woman who could change his mind.' He smiled at Bembo. 'Did she change yours?'

Bembo frowned and busied himself straightening a line of books.

'Did you really not guess who she was?' Strozzi asked after a moment.

Bembo left his books and sat down. 'No. I suppose I should have done from her jewels and the court fool. But she was so unlike the other ladies of her rank that I've met. There was such a directness in her manner. There was a simplicity about her – ' He glanced at Strozzi. 'Isn't that what you said about her in Venice?'

Strozzi nodded. 'She was so undemanding,' Bembo went on,

trying to express a feeling, 'almost unaware of herself. That's rare in any woman.'

Strozzi knew when to remain silent. He sat waiting, while Bembo lifted and put down the papers on his desk.

'Lucrezia – ?' he began diffidently.

'Yes,' said Strozzi.

'Has she been ill?'

'She had a stillborn child eight weeks ago.'

'Of course,' murmured Bembo. 'You bought a cradle in Venice.'

'This was the first child of the marriage with Alfonso,' said Strozzi, 'but she has a son by young Bisceglie. The duke wouldn't allow her to bring him to Ferrara. I suspect that she grieves for him, and a new child would have comforted her. But it was not to be, such is the devious will of God.' He shrugged his shoulders. 'I've heard her weeping as though she had forgotten what she was weeping for, but had no strength nor will to stop. This is my other excuse for that ridiculous game the other day – to try to amuse her for a few hours.'

Bembo was moved, and he said nothing. Strozzi was silent, too, until he added, 'She never says so, but I doubt if she has known any happiness since she came to Ferrara. Alfonso, as you know, resented being forced into the marriage, and since she arrived he's made no secret of this. During the day he ignores her. It's true that he dutifully spends his nights with her, but then all women are alike to Alfonso.

'His sister, Isabella, has done all she can to alienate the old Ferrarese court from Lucrezia. In fact, Pietro, the only people she could trust during her first year here were the Spaniards she brought with her from Rome. Then a few weeks ago, when she was still too weak to stand, they were sent away from her.'

'How could anyone be so cruel?' said Bembo angrily.

'Oh, people are when they think themselves threatened. When the child was born, everyone thought she was dying. Even Lucrezia did. Then one night, without any warning, Cesare Borgia came riding into Ferrara with no more than a handful of men. He ignored the duke and Alfonso, went straight to her room, turned out all the Ferrarese, and locked the doors behind them. He had brought his own doctors. He stayed with her for three days. On the third day, they could be heard laughing and whispering together in Spanish. When he left, as abruptly as he came, her life was no longer in danger.'

'His doctors were more skilled than yours?'

'I don't think so. But he loves her.'

Bembo found himself moved to wonder by the action of a man whom until now he had considered a monster. Strozzi read his thoughts. 'He's a strange man,' he said. 'I think his visit probably saved her life, but it had unhappy results for her. The little courtiers who'd been turned out by Cesare swore to the duke that Lucrezia and her Spaniards were plotting for Cesare. They'd always been jealous of the Spanish officials in her household, and now every phrase spoken in Spanish became a threat to the safety of Ferrara. I don't think the duke believed this. But he and Lucrezia are always quarrelling about the size of her allowance, and he was delighted to have a reason for sending them all back to Rome and saving money. He even sent away an old nurse who'd looked after her since she was a child.

'The duke wrote to the Pope saying that the Ferrarese were so enchanted by their new duchess that they begged to be allowed to serve her. The Pope wasn't pleased, of course, but he has his reasons for keeping peace with Ferrara at the moment, so he did nothing.'

Bembo thought of Lucrezia kneeling beside his dog. 'At least, she has her cousin with her,' he said.

'Angela Borgia? Yes, as she was the Pope's niece, she couldn't be dismissed with the servants. But she's very young, Pietro, generous at heart but vain and frivolous. She's not the best companion for a lonely woman in Lucrezia's state.'

'And there is no other?'

'No other companion?' Strozzi's eyes glinted unpleasantly. 'Yes, there is someone who devotes part of every day to her, who advises her on her books, her clothes, her household – ' He broke off angrily. 'I refer to the good Ippolito.'

Bembo clenched a hand. 'Cardinal Ippolito?'

'Why not? Your father was right when he called Ippolito shrewd and perceptive. He understood Lucrezia's loneliness. He began to pay visits to the little Bisceglie child in Rome and brought news of him back to Lucrezia. A brilliant move, eh, Pietro? Lucrezia now thinks of him as the only member of the Este who has shown her any kindness.'

'But why should this matter to Ippolito?'

'He hates Alfonso and likes to be contrary. If Alfonso ignores Lucrezia, he will always be at her side. Besides, he likes to be worshipped, and there are few enough of us in Ferrara to do that. Lucrezia was new, and ignorant.'

'Even so, Ercole, how can she be so easily deceived by him – '

'Oh she tends to accept things as they seem until she learns better. After all, she believed my tale about a hermit. So far, Ippolito has been charming to her because nothing has happened to cross him.' Strozzi grunted. 'The sooner it does, the better for all of us. Let her once see him in one of his fits of jealousy – '

Strozzi smiled crookedly and was lost in his own thoughts.

'Ercole,' said Bembo, 'did you have a reason for coming today, other than to gloat?'

'Have I gloated?'

'Not in so many words, no.'

'As a matter of fact,' said Strozzi laughing, 'there is a reason for my visit, and I was forgetting it. Pietro, the winter season begins next month in Ferrara, and my father is giving a ball for Madonna Lucrezia. We should like to begin the entertainment with a masque, and to please the duke I think it should be done in the style of the old Roman comedies. If I provide you with the plot, would you write the dialogue?'

Bembo's response was guarded. 'Why not write it yourself? You know what kind of thing you want.'

Strozzi's hesitation was barely perceptible. 'I can manage a sonnet well enough, but I can't do dialogue. You can. I would be extraordinarily grateful if you would help me out.' He paused.

'I'm sure it will amuse Madonna Lucrezia, too, to hear something produced by the hermit.'

Bembo looked at him wildly, and Strozzi added with a solemn air, 'I promised you when you agreed to stay here that I wouldn't try to persuade you to come to Ferrara. I'm not breaking that promise, Pietro. There will be no need at all for you to leave Ostellato – unless you yourself choose to do so.'

'Yes, I see,' said Bembo bleakly.

'Then will you do it?'

Bembo smiled suddenly. 'Well, you said you would make use of me. If it's for nothing worse than this, I can hardly complain.'

'True,' murmured Strozzi and he stared out of the window.

III

Isabella d'Este, wife of Francesco Gonzaga of Mantua, was spending a week at her father's court in Ferrara. There were two things she wished to take back with her after the visit; one was the bronze cupid by Michelangelo which Tito Vespasiano Strozzi had recently acquired in Florence, and the other was Pietro Bembo.

On the afternoon before her departure she commanded Tito Strozzi to receive her in his gallery so that she could view the bronze cupid.

Isabella was a handsome woman, imperious in manner, a rapacious collector of fine objects. She was also, like her brother Ippolito, immoderately vain, and saw herself as surpassingly beautiful, with the right to possess anything she chose to admire. She considered that, once acquainted with her desire for the bronze cupid, Tito Strozzi should feel privileged to offer it to her as a gift. The fact that she detested both Tito and his son, Ercole, and made no secret of it, would have seemed to her irrelevant.

She advanced into the Strozzi gallery wearing a dress of black velvet boldly patterned with notes of music in gold, and a turban of emerald green silk. Tito and Ercole Strozzi followed her.

She paused before the bronze cupid and her eyes narrowed with the lust of acquisition. 'It is not well set off here,' she announced. 'Now in my own gallery of Mantua it could be appreciated as it deserves.'

Ercole Strozzi moved to her side. 'Then your highness,' he murmured, 'there is only one thing to be done. We must – ' he coughed behind a gloved hand,' – copy in this room the style of your gallery in Mantua.'

Isabella shot him a sharp, irritated glance. 'You are welcome to bring it to Mantua to see it displayed in the way I suggest,' she said.

'How gracious of your highness,' said Tito Strozzi, 'but I could not dream of so inconveniencing you. My son can travel to Mantua and have sketches made.' He bowed to her. 'Since your highness is clearly pleased by this bronze, may I be so bold as to offer her as a gift a drawing of the figure. I should be honoured to commission one.'

Isabella snapped open her fan. 'Thank you, Messer Strozzi. I can retain the image in my mind without the help of a drawing.'

She moved along the gallery, beckoning Ercole to accompany her. After several moments of heavy silence, she said, 'I would have you know, Messer Ercole, that I am not pleased.'

Strozzi's eyes widened. 'With me, madonna? But I am desolate if I have unwittingly offended you.'

'I had expected to meet Messer Pietro Bembo while I was here in Ferrara. He is your guest, is he not? I was informed so, in a letter from Venice written by my sister-in-law, the Duchess of Urbino.'

'Yes, he is our guest, but he is living at our villa of Ostellato.'

'I have been here for six days. I had assumed that you would bring him to court.'

'Madonna, that is just what I dare not do. He came here to work, and asks to be allowed to live like a hermit. I swore to him that in no circumstances would I even ask him to attend court.'

'He did not know when he demanded that promise that I should be here,' Isabella announced. 'He holds me in the greatest affection and would never forgo an opportunity to be with me. I begin to wonder if you have kept from him the news of my visit.'

'If I had, could you blame me?' whispered Strozzi. 'Had Messer Bembo been here, I might not have had this opportunity myself to be with your highness.'

Isabella saw nothing remarkable in this statement. She accepted it with a nod. 'I can, of course, understand Messer Bembo's reluctance to attend the Borgia's court. The only people he would meet there are milliners and pawnbrokers.'

'Pawnbrokers?' murmured Strozzi.

'Do you know why she doesn't wear the Este pearls? She has pawned them. Pawned my mother's pearls!' Isabella snorted with indignation.

'Your dear father, the duke, is somewhat mean with her allowance,' said Strozzi.

'Nonsense. Her extravagance is outrageous. She has sixty pairs of silk slippers alone, fifty dresses – '

'Your highness's intelligence system would baffle even our sly neighbours, the Venetians,' Strozzi interrupted. 'I seem to remember, madonna, that when you saw her wearing the pearls at her wedding, you declared yourself made ill by the sight of your sainted mother's pearls round the neck of the bastard daughter of an upstart Spanish priest. Wouldn't you think a pawnbroker preferable?'

Strozzi's voice was mild and courteous. Isabella was uncertain of him. 'Her birth is only too evident,' she said spitefully, 'in the vulgarity of her behaviour. She wears too many trinkets and smiles too much to please everyone. She performs dances in public – '

'That is the custom among the ladies of Moorish Spain where her father was born.'

'It is not an atmosphere in which Messer Bembo would choose to find himself. He is accustomed to the elegance of my sister-in-law's court in Venice, which is modelled on mine. He can't stay at Ostellato for ever. He is a man of wit and scholarship who needs the conversation of others like him. This he would find in Mantua where I am surrounded by men of taste and learning.'

'You mean, madonna,' said Strozzi, 'that your court at Mantua would form as perfect a setting for Pietro Bembo as for the bronze cupid.'

'Yes,' said Isabella complacently. She turned her head to look again at the little Michelangelo figure. 'It would make a most fitting gift to one who was worthy of it.'

'You embarrass me, madonna. This is a gift to myself from my father. As such I would never, never part with it.'

Isabella swept out of the gallery, down the stairway and into her carriage.

'That cripple of a Strozzi!' she said to her lady-in-waiting as she took her seat.

Ercole Strozzi heard her as he bowed. 'Let us, for God's sake, breathe some fresh air,' he muttered to his father as the carriage moved away.

They walked through the outer and inner courtyards to a garden set against the southern wall of their land. Four little boys of varying ages were splashing each other with water from an ornamental fountain. They were Strozzi's natural sons, Cesare, Filippo, Romano and Lorenzo. Once a month they were collected from the homes of their four mothers and brought to visit their father. Strozzi enjoyed seeing them, but once he had heard them repeat their lessons and consulted his tailor about their needs, he was rapidly bored by their chatter.

He put a hand to his head and groaned. 'The noise they make – '

A spray of water fell on his sleeve. Strozzi glared at his children and they fell silent. The youngest opened his mouth to howl.

Tito Strozzi said quickly, 'Why not go and play in the stables, eh?' He patted the frightened child on the head. 'If you behave quietly, in an hour's time you shall go to see the giraffes.' A visit to the giraffes in the duke's park just outside the city was a favourite treat. The children's faces brightened, but they restrained their shouts of excitement until they had walked sedately out of their father's sight.

Strozzi sighed with relief and eased his lame foot. 'So you kept your bronze cupid,' he said to his father.

'And you kept Pietro Bembo.'

They smiled companionably at each other. 'You would appear,' said Tito, 'to have a strong reason for keeping Pietro in Ferrara.' He spoke with the precise courtesy which he always assumed when enquiring into his son's affairs.

'I want to offer him the peaceful conditions that will help him to write.'

'I see,' said Tito, nodding gravely. 'That is why you took Madonna Lucrezia there with, I believe, drums and a fool – '

'I didn't say it was the only reason.' Strozzi took his father's arm and they walked to a bench in the sun. Tito took the crutch and propped it against a wall, and they sat down together. 'They have both of them, Pietro and Lucrezia, been in low spirits,' Strozzi went on. 'I thought I saw in each of them something that would please the other. It seemed kind to bring them together.'

'One is moved, my son, by your charity,' said Tito Strozzi. 'Might I ask if this charity has any reference, however remote, to Cardinal Ippolito?'

Strozzi clasped his hands behind his head and gazed up at the sky. 'Let us consider Cardinal Ippolito for a moment. I think Ippolito has enjoyed his influence on Lucrezia for long enough. If Lucrezia trusts anyone, she tends to be uncritical of them; if she loves them as well, she will do without question whatever they wish. Isn't this why she lied to the papal court and ruined Sforza? Her father requested it of her, and she loves her father.'

'Agreed,' said Tito. 'And this can be a matter of concern if she trusts someone like Ippolito.'

'But it would be very different if she trusted someone favourable to us – especially if she also fell in love with him.' Strozzi looked at his father. 'It would certainly be useful if her lover were a friend who was in one's debt. He might even persuade her to procure one a Cardinal's hat.'

'With that, as you know, I have no sympathy,' said Tito Strozzi. 'But with your reasons for keeping Pietro here I would have no quarrel. His presence could be a service to Ferrara.'

'I hadn't thought of him as being of service to Ferrara,' Strozzi protested. 'Only to me – and Lucrezia.'

'Then you should have thought of it. As far as Lucrezia is concerned, if it isn't Bembo, it will be someone else. I have no wish to see the court and the duchy disrupted and put to shame by an adventurer. Pietro is an excellent choice. He has no ambition for power, so he won't use her for himself.' He paused and then smiled. 'And he is kind, and Lucrezia needs kindness.' Then he added briskly, 'Though how she will ever enjoy it while he stays at Ostellato is presumably something that you are considering.'

'He is writing his play for our ball. What author can resist an opportunity to see his own work performed? Could he have a better excuse?'

'No, but his pride may be delicate. He has insisted that he will not come to court.'

'Father, if the ball is here, the court will be coming to him. It is a nice distinction that should appeal to a scholarly mind.'

There was a sudden outburst of young voices from the direction of the stables. Strozzi flinched. 'They're loose again.'

Tito stood up and reached for his son's crutch. 'Ercole, they are not a pack of animals. You ought to spend some time with them. Get up.'

'And risk being drowned by that little wretch again?'

'He splashed you with two or three tiny drops of water which have not even marked your sleeve.'

Strozzi, with an ill grace, took his father's arm. As they walked towards the stables, Tito said, 'Have you ever thought of increasing the number?'

Strozzi looked at him, 'You mean you want a legitimate heir?'

'Yes. Why not?'

Strozzi said in mild reproof, 'You know the answer to that. When Barbara Bentivoglio is a widow, then I will marry. But not before.'

'Bentivoglio is not, as I understand it, a sickly man.'

'No, he is not. So you must resign yourself to seeing me in my Cardinal's silks.'

Tito Strozzi shrugged his shoulders. It was not an unfamiliar conversation.

Ercole put a hand on his father's wrist. 'I'll tell you what I will do. When I'm Pope, I'll legitimise all this lot for you – as long as you don't expect me to go to the giraffes with you.'

IV

A dozen out-riders wearing the white and silver livery of Lucrezia d'Este Borgia flanked her litter as it passed under the portico of the Strozzi palace on a mild December evening. Bembo watched it arrive from a window overlooking the street. Then he hurried towards the ballroom to see Lucrezia herself as she climbed the stairs. She was walking between Tito Strozzi and Ercole, smiling and turning her head from one to the other. She wore a white dress, and under the torches that burned on the staircase her hair was the colour of pale amber.

Behind her, hovering like a huge bat of scarlet silk, came Cardinal Ippolito d'Este. He was a large blond man, florid, with pale eyes. His hair was worn at a length that had once provoked a stout rebuke from the Pope, but Ippolito was indifferent to papal displeasure and still arranged it in curling strands across his shoulders. He carried his gloves so that he could display the white hands of which he was excessively vain, and which he treated daily with lemon juice. His expression, as he followed Lucrezia into the ballroom, was both insolent and arrogant.

Lucrezia's chair faced the white and gold proscenium of Strozzi's theatre. As soon as she was seated, Strozzi offered her a small bunch of winter roses arranged round a tiny scroll. Lucrezia drew out the scroll and untied its silk ribbon. It carried a sonnet in Latin comparing Lucrezia's presence in Ferrara to the roses blooming in the frozen ground.

Lucrezia, smiling with pleasure, showed the scroll to Ippolito, who was leaning on the back of her chair. He took the paper as though its surface might irritate the delicate skin of his fingers. He read with deliberate slowness. Then he said in his sweet, precise voice, 'Strozzi, in the fifth line your metre is lame.' He glanced at Strozzi's crippled foot. 'Like your body.'

Strozzi also looked at his foot. When he raised his head he was smiling. 'Your eminence never ceases to provoke my amazement,' he said loudly, attracting attention. 'A week ago I knew you to be ignorant of the principles of Latin verse. Yet within the last few days you have acquired the metrical skill which it has taken a fool like me fifteen years to achieve.'

Ippolito's face became darker in colour and his mouth moved. Tito Strozzi placed himself in front of his son and said quickly, 'Your eminence honours my son by reading his verse with such attention. Madonna Lucrezia must forgive him if his lines are not worthy of his subject, but in a few minutes she will hear language that is impeccable in style. Messer Pietro Bembo has written our masque.'

Lucrezia held the roses to her face. 'I have heard the duke speak of Messer Bembo's scholarship,' she said gravely. 'He is here, Messer Strozzi?'

'He is, madonna. He insists on prompting the lines for his masque, but will beg to be presented to you later.'

Lucrezia laid the roses carefully in her lap. 'Yes,' she said. 'Yes.'

There was noise and music on the staircase outside as the duke arrived with his eldest son, Alfonso. Tito Strozzi, seizing an excuse to separate Ercole from the Cardinal, turned to Lucrezia. 'As the duke is already here, I suggest, if your highness pleases, that my son should retire to prepare for his part in our entertainment.'

Lucrezia nodded. She wanted to sit quietly, nursing her pleasure at the thought of seeing Pietro Bembo again. When Ippolito spoke to her, she ignored him.

Bembo was sitting on a stool at the side of the stage with a bundle of loose papers on his lap. Strozzi saw him for the first time that night when he climbed to the platform from which, as Apollo, he would enter his chariot of gilded cardboard. He leaned over the rail of his platform and whispered Bembo's name.

Bembo glanced up, annoyed at the interruption, and saw

Strozzi's bearded face, incongruously crowned with a sunburst of gilded feathers, suspended above him. He laughed.

'Have more respect,' said Strozzi, waving a finger at him. 'Otherwise, I'll have you trussed up and sent to Isabella.'

'Ssh!' Bembo tried to find his place.

Strozzi folded his gold satin arms on the rail and smiled. He noted with satisfaction that Bembo no longer dressed in Venetian black. He wore pale grey velvet and silk, with a single fine ornament of a baroque pearl set in enamelled gold. His hair was no longer dressed clipped close to his head in the Venetian manner. Absorbed in his script, he looked, thought Strozzi, quite different from the man who had sat beside him under the porticoes of the Rialto exchange.

'Ercole!' Strozzi became aware of Bembo's arm waving towards his chariot. He stepped calmly aboard and was lowered creakily to the ground amid the applause of his guests. Bembo heard him begin the lines which ended the masque. He spoke them well, drawing laughter and more applause.

Despite the heat from the hundreds of wax candles round the stage, Bembo found himself suddenly shivering. Until then he had been waiting happily for the end of the play, when he could enter the ballroom and speak again to Lucrezia. Now that the moment had almost come, he was tormented by anxious thoughts. Suppose they found no means of speaking together? What if she were not the same here with the court as she had been at Ostellato? Suppose she had been bored by the masque and already left? He threw down the script, pushed his way round the back of the stage and ran along the empty corridor to the doors of the ballroom.

At first he could distinguish nothing but rows of faces. Then he saw her in her white dress, leaning forward as she watched Strozzi's antics. He felt a singing sensation of relief that for a moment left him breathless. He stepped farther into the room, edging his way towards her. The stealthy movement caught her attention and she turned to look in his direction. Bembo stood still, gazing at her. Everyone else in the room was absorbed in the action on the stage. She glanced away without giving any sign of recognition, but from the way she gently laid her head against the back of her chair he knew that she had seen him. Joy, like a stream, flowed between them.

Then the masque was over. Sound and movement erupted in the ballroom, thrusting a barrier between them. Strozzi came from the front of the stage still wearing his golden costume but without his plumes. One arm was round the shoulders of an exceptionally handsome young man. They stopped in front of Bembo.

'Highness,' said Strozzi, 'this is Messer Pietro Bembo, who wrote our masque. Do you remember him? He has lived in Ferrara before.' He spoke carefully as if to a child. 'Pietro, you know Don Giulio d'Este.'

Giulio was the duke's natural son. During her life-time the duchess had brought him up as one of her own children, and he still lived at his father's court. As Bembo bowed, Giulio grasped his hand eagerly and gazed at him with the most beautiful eyes Bembo had ever seen in a man. 'Yes, yes, Messer Bembo,' he said. 'I enjoyed your play. I can never understand a lot of words said together, but it was very pretty to watch.'

His smile and his ingenuousness were disarming, and Bembo found himself smiling back as he expressed his thanks.

Strozzi led them towards the dais where Lucrezia was sitting with the duke, her husband and Ippolito. It was evident that Alfonso and his brother were pointedly ignoring each other, and that the duke was in an ill humour with both of them.

'Giulio, you should join your brothers now,' said Strozzi.

Giulio shook his head. 'No, I don't want to sit with them. They're all quarrelling again.'

'Oh, how sad,' murmured Strozzi solicitously. 'What happened?'

'Ippolito had one of his wild days,' said Giulio. 'He set some of his men on Alfonso's grooms and one of them was killed. Then he wouldn't tell my father which of his servants had done the killing. My father was furious. He said he paid out five thousand ducats to make Ippolito a Cardinal and not one pennysworth of Christian obedience had he seen in return for his money. He called Ippolito a monster, and Ippolito said that if he was a monster, so was Alfonso. He told him some of the things Alfonso likes to do when he spends all day in a brothel – ' Giulio broke off, suddenly remembering Bembo's presence.

'Don't worry, Giulio,' said Strozzi. 'Messer Bembo is a Venetian, and Venetians are never embarrassed by anything that makes a profit.'

'Oh,' said Giulio, 'well, he likes two or three women, Ercole, to tie him to a bed so that he can't move – '

'Not now, Giulio,' said Strozzi gently.

Giulio nodded obediently. 'So now my father is angry with Alfonso, too. He told him that he was not an intolerant man, but he was repelled by grossness of conduct.' Giulio looked bewildered. 'He made Alfonso stay with him all day and come to the ball with him. Alfonso wasn't pleased. He wanted to finish painting a set of majolica plates.'

'Alfonso has a workshop in the castle,' Strozzi murmured to Bembo. They all looked at Alfonso. He sat with his arms stiffly folded across his chest, a stocky young man with a crisp brown beard.

'So you are the only one in favour,' said Strozzi to Giulio.

'No, he's cross with me, too. He says I've been spending too much time with Angela Borgia. I'm not allowed to visit Madonna Lucrezia's apartments more than twice a week to see her because she is betrothed. It isn't fair, Ercole. Ippolito is there every day.'

'Then it must have been Ippolito,' said Strozzi ruthlessly, 'who told the duke that you were enjoying the company of Madonna Angela. He's jealous, Giulo. But be patient. Things will change. And no one has forbidden you to meet here in this house. If you wait in the little room behind the stage, I will send her to you.'

Giulio's dark, lustrous eyes shone. 'But go quietly, Giulio, quietly,' said Strozzi.

Bembo watched Giulio slip away out of sight. 'You seem to be very much in his confidence, Ercole,' he said with mild disapproval.

'I am very fond of him,' said Strozzi. 'He knows this and he likes to talk to me. His wits, as you will have gathered, are not of the sharpest, but he soaks up everything he hears like a sponge, even when he doesn't understand its significance. He is very useful to me, so I think it prudent to do him a favour whenever I can.'

He took Bembo's arm and continued towards the dais. 'Now it is time to do a favour for you.'

Bembo drew back his arm. 'I mean,' said Strozzi soothingly, 'that the duke is waiting for you.'

Duke Ercole was listening to something that Lucrezia was saying. Bembo was sure that she had seen them approaching – it would have been difficult to ignore them with Strozzi in his gold robes – but she kept her eyes intently on the duke. Bembo sensed that she felt, as he did, a kind of shyness, now that they were to be face to face again.

The duke peered at them through his spectacles. He was a small, spare man with a face that in repose appeared wary and withdrawn. His coolness of manner in public had earned him the name of 'the Diamond' among his people, few of them ever having witnessed the passions to which he could be roused by the behaviour of his sons. The style of his dress was old-fashioned, because he believed it wasteful to spend money on new garments when the old ones were still wearable.

He recognised Bembo, and rose from his chair. 'So, Ercole, you have brought our Pietro Bembo back to us at last,' he said. He clasped Bembo in his arms and embraced him warmly. 'How long is it since I've seen you?'

'Five years, highness,' said Bembo, 'when my father left.'

'Ah, your father.' The duke chuckled. 'I did not enjoy his zealous, incorruptible pursuit of Venetian interests, but I admired him dearly for his integrity and his scholarship. And they tell me you have become an even greater scholar than him – in Greek, as well as in Latin.'

Bembo, remembering Lucrezia's horror of scholarship, said diffidently, 'I am inclined to think, highness, that one can only appreciate Latin fully if one knows Greek.'

The duke nodded. 'Then you will come and read Greek to me one day, and talk to me about the drama of the Greeks.'

Ippolito, choosing to be contrary whenever an opportunity arose, said, 'I see no value in reading Greek. I have never heard of anyone in the Vatican needing it to improve his Latin.'

'Yes, but with respect, eminence,' Bembo answered courteously, 'much of the Latin written in the Vatican is not classical in style, but debased. Besides, Greek has a richer vocabulary than other tongues.' He let his eyes rest for a moment on Lucrezia's bright hair and her white dress. 'In what other language can one find a single, perfect word to describe Madonna Lucrezia as she appears tonight?'

He turned to Lucrezia. 'Madonna, the Greeks created the most precious statues in their temples of gold and ivory. The mingling of pure gold and shining ivory they called – in my poor translation – chryselephantine.' His eyes dwelt again, more slowly, on her hair and her dress. 'Until this night, the beauty of its sound alone has enchanted me. Now I understand, for the first time, how much more beautiful is the image it describes.'

Lucrezia, who had been listening for much of the evening with indifference to the flattery of Strozzi's guests, now looked away and dropped some of her roses.

The duke was smiling at the facility of Bembo's compliment. Strozzi leaned towards him. 'Your highness is surely not deceived into thinking these fine words were spoken in praise of Madonna Lucrezia,' he said. 'Messer Bembo is merely applauding his own taste, since it was he who insisted that I buy this white silk in Venice. You cannot deny, Messer Pietro, that it was you who convinced me that this was the true colour for my lady.'

Bembo felt himself flushing. Lucrezia laughed and said, 'How could this be possible since he had never seen me?'

Strozzi regarded her solemnly. 'Messer Bembo had heard much about you, and he is one who can discern unerringly what is true and what is false in hearsay.'

'So Messer Bembo assisted you during your expedition to Venice, Strozzi,' said Ippolito nastily. He glanced quickly at his father who had turned his head away to listen to Tito Strozzi. 'What commission did you pay him for selling you the silk?'

The insult was so clumsy and pointless that Bembo was almost amused, and had nothing to say. Strozzi, however, put his mouth to Ippolito's ear with an appearance of friendship that startled Ippolito as much as Bembo.

'One shares your distaste for Venetian cupidity,' murmured Strozzi, 'but you must allow Messer Bembo to escort you sometime through the warehouses of Venice.'

Ippolito looked at Strozzi suspiciously. 'I have no need to go to Venice to buy silks.'

'Not for silks, no, eminence. Your own are exquisite. I was thinking rather of perfumes.' Strozzi assured himself that his father and the duke were still occupied together. 'There is one they make from Arabic oils – '

Ippolito was interested. Strozzi sank his voice to a whisper, ' – that is said to make one irresistible to men.'

Only Bembo and Angela Borgia overheard what he said. Bembo was horrified, but Angela Borgia laughed aloud.

Ippolito pulled himself away from Strozzi, his clenched hand raised. The duke glanced round and saw him.

'Ippolito,' he said in a low voice, 'get out of my sight! I will not endure another of your acts of temper.'

Ippolito opened his mouth angrily, but the duke waved him away. 'Do not dare to speak in front of your host and his guests. I have had enough.'

Strozzi stood with head bowed as the Cardinal made his savage departure. The duke, upset by the incident, left shortly afterwards, taking Alfonso with him. As he stepped off the dais, Alfonso nodded curtly to his wife and to Tito Strozzi, but his face was as expressionless as it had been throughout the evening.

In the upheaval of the duke's leave-takings, Strozzi drew Angela Borgia aside and whispered to her. For a brief instant, Bembo was standing alone beside Lucrezia.

She glanced up at him. 'Messer Bembo, I fear you must be greatly offended by the Cardinal's words. Not for anything would I have you feel displeased tonight.'

Bembo shook his head gently. 'Highness, how could I be? I am only sorry that his speaking as he did has caused you uneasiness.'

Lucrezia took a quick breath. 'Nothing really matters, does it, except that you are here? You have come.'

'As I promised,' said Bembo. He bent down to retrieve one of the roses that she had dropped earlier.

'At least this time we recognised each other,' she said as he raised his head.

Bembo thrust the rose into the posy. 'I think we did the first time.'

Tito Strozzi and his guests were closing round them again. Bembo bowed to her in the Venetian manner with his hand over his heart, and moved away from her side. Music for the dancing was beginning, and he stood in a corner where he could look at Lucrezia while appearing to watch the dancers.

She was receiving a number of Tito's guests. After a while, although appearing to listen to what was said to her, she was searching the room with her eyes. Then she found him, looked at him for a moment with an expression of delight, and glanced quickly down at her roses. Bembo had drunk no wine that evening, but he felt himself growing light-headed with excitement. They had hardly spoken a dozen sentences together, but he had no doubt of what she would become to him, although he would not have been able to explain why he was so sure, even to himself.

His thoughts were broken by Strozzi, who came to lean against the wall beside him. Bembo glanced at the gilded crutch he was using. 'It's a pity your tongue doesn't need that instead of your foot.'

Strozzi looked bewildered. 'My dear Pietro – ?'

'You know very well what I'm talking about. That insane remark to Ippolito.'

'Oh, the perfume,' said Strozzi. 'I thought you meant the white silk.'

'Do not imagine that I shall ever forget that,' said Bembo with feeling. 'But at least it wasn't dangerous. What you said to Ippolito was. That is precisely the sort of thing my father warned you about.'

'Ippolito insulted you,' said Strozzi, 'and you are my guest. What else could I do?'

Bembo groaned. Strozzi raised his eyebrows. 'You lack a proper respect for your host. I have just limped all the way across the floor to tell you something that should please you, and I find myself treated in this surly fashion.' He laid a hand on Bembo's arm and added quietly, 'Pietro, look. Look at Madonna Lucrezia.'

Lucrezia was rising from her chair. Tito Strozzi clapped his hands together and announced that at his request – he smiled briefly at his son standing beside Bembo – the duchess had consented to perform one of the ancient dances of Catalan.

She danced alone, to the beat of a tambourine. The rhythm was slow and languorous with a flavour of Moorish Spain. Her head swayed and the candlelight gleamed on the chain of emeralds coiled round her throat in the form of a snake. Bembo's breath was caught by the delicacy of her movements with their subtly alien quality.

'You should like this. You Venetians are half Turks.' Strozzi's voice in his ear made Bembo start.

'Turks are not Moors.'

'All heathens,' said Strozzi.

Lucrezia was close enough for him to see the ruby eyes glittering in the gold and emerald head of the snake. The room was hot and he longed to lay his fingers on the cool stones. But the dance was ending, and Lucrezia was sinking to the ground in the floating white silk dress. Bembo thought of snow – of the light, white flakes falling on the slopes round his beloved Asolo.

The snowflakes were still spinning in his brain when, towards dawn, he followed the servant who was lighting the way to his room. The guests had gone. Strozzi and his father were still drinking in the ballroom among the dying candles. Lico was asleep on a stool, his head against the wall. Bembo woke him gently and sent him away.

He sat down at the table where Lico had left his writing things. The snowflakes in his mind were forming into words. Picking up a quill, he wrote 'whiteness' and stared at it. His scholar's mind translated it into the Latin 'candor' and then played at turning it back again – candour, clarity, simplicity. Lucrezia danced before him in the white, snowflake dress. He gripped the pen again in his cold fingers. 'I renew my sense of that strange whiteness of her mind'. He sighed, and the pen straggled across the page. He laid his head on the table and slept.

V

The first heavy snow of the winter fell in Ferrara towards the end of January, blocking the roads out of the city. Bembo, who had set out for Ostellato in the early afternoon, was forced to turn back.

Since the Strozzi ball, he had ridden into Ferrara several times on the excuse of reading Greek with the duke. When he left the palace he would walk the short distance to the castle, where Alfonso and Lucrezia had their apartments, and would wander up and down beside the moat, observing every movement behind her window. He was in that early state of love when merely to gaze at the rooms where Lucrezia lived gave him pleasure. Now, with the city enclosed in snow, he felt a child-like satisfaction in knowing that they were both beleaguered within the same walls.

The snow was still falling in the evening as Bembo idly watched Strozzi dress for court. The costume was magnificent, even for Strozzi: bronze satin glittering with jet and furred with black sables. Bembo spoke of it.

'Tonight is a great occasion – The Torch Ball,' said Strozzi impatiently, as if Bembo should have remembered.

Having been reminded, Bembo did remember. The Torch Ball, held in the middle of the winter, was an ancient custom in Ferrara. It was given in the castle by the first lady of the ruling house. It took its name from the dance performed at midnight, when the ladies were given lighted torches and searched for their partners in the darkness. Bembo had been present in the past, when Alfonso's mother had presided. Tonight it would be Lucrezia.

'As you have to stay in Ferrara, why not come with me?' asked Strozzi.

Bembo, still in his riding dress, watched the snowflakes drifting past the window and shook his head. As Tito Strozzi had suspected, pride still prevented him from attending Lucrezia's court after the fierceness of his earlier refusals. He muttered something about not having a suitable costume.

Strozzi was holding a small looking-glass. 'Alfonso is in Hungary,' he said.

Bembo realised that Strozzi was watching him through the glass. He moved his seat. 'Is he?'

'He has gone to study the Hungarian method of founding cannon,' Strozzi added, 'so he will be away some time.' He selected a pair of gloves. 'Will you change your mind and come?'

Bembo shook his head bleakly. From a window he watched Strozzi and his torchbearers ride towards the palace. When they had gone the street was dark and deserted. On the opposite side of the road, through the snow, Bembo could see the Casa Romei. It had once been a great private house, but was now owned by a sisterhood of nuns, and Lucrezia retreated there from time to time to live quietly among them. He now knew that she had gone there after her child had died, and that she had still been there when he was travelling along the Po with his boatload of books towards Ostellato. That had been only three months ago, yet now he could hardly conceive of a life that took no account of Lucrezia's existence.

He went restlessly to bed. The clocks were striking half past eleven when he pulled off his twisted sheets, shouted for Lico, and started dressing again in desperate haste. He reached the castle a few minutes before midnight and came breathlessly into the hall as the candles were being extinguished.

Lucrezia was standing alone in the centre of the darkened room. To the sound of pipes a single lighted torch was carried in, and placed in her hand. She was wearing a dress of pale gold, and as she raised the flame above her head it shimmered across the folds of her skirt, and cast spinning flecks of gold on the floor as she moved. She walked slowly round the room, illuminating first one face, then another. She was smiling, teasing with her hesitation, then standing on tiptoe to search the remotest corners with the swaying flame. Bembo suddenly knew that she would find him, despite his obscure place beside the doorway.

Lucrezia paused, turned and swung the torch in a half-circle. As its light passed across the entrance to the hall, she recognised him. She stood quite still, and then with quick steps, almost running, came towards him. The people standing between them parted as though melted by the flame. Lucrezia stopped before him, her eyes shining in the light, and spoke the formal words of the dance. 'Will you, sir, accept this torch from me?'

Bembo took the torch from her hand and bent towards her. 'Your highness does too much honour to a stranger.'

'You forget, Messer Bembo,' she whispered, 'that I, too, am a stranger here.'

Bembo took her hand. 'Then let us form a league together and make strangers of everyone else.'

He moved beside her, stepping into the tiny points of light reflected from her dress. 'You gild my path as well as my sight, madonna,' he said as he led her into the pattern of the dance.

The brilliance of the torch blinded them to everything beyond the circle of light in which they moved. 'It is like living in a special world of our own,' murmured Lucrezia. 'There is no room for anyone else in our world, no one else exists.'

But even as she spoke other torches were appearing, and other ladies were seeking their partners. The room was growing brighter; figures and shapes were forming. Lucrezia sighed. 'Our enchanted world is dissolving already.'

'No, madonna,' said Bembo. 'Once one has discovered an enchanted world, it exists for ever.'

Lucrezia's eyes fled to the torch. She said breathlessly, 'I think a flame is one of the most beautiful things in the world.'

'That is why we use it to describe whatever we think is most precious in life – truth, the spirit, love.'

Lucrezia's hand stirred in his. She turned her head towards the windows of the hall. 'Oh, look,' she cried. 'It's snowing again. I should like to see it.'

She let go his hand and led him through the dancers across the hall, along a painted corridor and out on to a square terrace that overlooked the moat and the street. The orange trees that grew in tubs set on the paved floor were shrouded in straw that was glistening with snow. It was falling thickly in big, light flakes. Lucrezia ran to the battlemented wall and looked down. Bembo, following her, saw far below them the black water of the moat stark against the white ground.

'It is so quiet,' she whispered, 'that I can almost hear our flame burning.'

'I think,' said Bembo, after a moment, 'that it is going out.'

Like a child Lucrezia held out her hands to the flame as though to hold it. 'No, I don't want it to die.'

'No. I think this is better.' He raised the torch and threw it over the wall of the terrace. They watched it fall and touch the water. Bembo turned to Lucrezia, who was gazing sadly after it.

'Do you remember *The Song of Songs*, madonna? "No waters can quench – " ' He stopped, hearing a sound behind him. He twisted round, and saw Ippolito d'Este stepping through the doorway from the painted corridor. On his heels came Strozzi, limping with amazing speed, and behind him Angela Borgia, a cloak folded over one arm.

Lucrezia and Bembo stood facing them, the snow lying on their hair.

Strozzi pushed his way past Ippolito, talking rapidly. 'A thousand, thousand pardons, your highness. In the darkness I tripped over this wretched foot of mine. Madonna Angela, who was bringing your cloak, came to my rescue, but I fear her kindness to me meant that you were left shivering and unattended.' He took the cloak and laid it across her shoulders.

Alone with Bembo, Lucrezia had been unaware of the cold. Now she was shaking. 'If you take a chill, madonna,' said Strozzi, 'I shall hold Messer Bembo entirely to blame. If he had not praised the roof-gardens of Venice with such arrogance, I should never have insisted on his seeing this one here.'

Ippolito was staring at them, his round pale eyes observing every change of expression on their faces.

Strozzi went on chattering. 'To be fair, of course, one must imagine this garden as it is in spring, filled with the scent of white blossom, or in summer when the golden fruit appears. White and gold! Are these not the colours, Messer Bembo, which you thought so fitting to her highness – ?'

'Strozzi!' Ippolito broke in rudely. 'Let Messer Bembo speak, unless he has nothing to say.'

'What can I say,' said Bembo, 'other than to admit, Messer Strozzi, that on this one occasion you shame me by being right? Yet how could I guess that behind these battlements was hidden a garden as pleasing as this?'

'So the hidden surprises of our castle interest you?' said Ippolito with a thin smile. 'There are others, Messer Bembo. I should enjoy showing them to you.'

'Your eminence is very good,' said Bembo carefully. 'I should be honoured if some day – '

'Why not now?' asked Ippolito. With a sudden movement he fastened his hand on Bembo's arm and drew him towards the doorway.

Bembo, caught by surprise, turned his head awkwardly to look at Lucrezia. 'Madonna, forgive me – '

'There is no need for you to take leave of her,' said Ippolito. 'She shall come with us. There are places here that even she has not seen although she has lived in this castle for over a year. It would seem that the time has now arrived when she should.'

'The duchess cannot leave her guests,' said Strozzi.

'She left them just now for Messer Bembo's sake,' snapped Ippolito. 'For his sake she can leave them a little longer.'

Strozzi's mood changed suddenly. His face took on a look of pleasurable anticipation. He rubbed his hands together. 'Yes, yes, why not? We'll all come. Dancing becomes tedious. A diversion would be very welcome, I thank your eminence. Now where are we going first?'

Ippolito, disappointed by the collapse of Strozzi's opposition, said moodily, 'To the courtyard.'

Strozzi nodded and laid Lucrezia's trembling fingers on his arm. She was too frightened to speak, and walked stiffly beside him as they followed Ippolito and Bembo into the castle.

They descended not by a staircase but by a huge spiral ramp which lay behind secret doors in the ancient council chamber. 'This is another hidden feature of the castle for Messer Bembo to remember,' said Ippolito. 'Duke Borso built it so that he could ride straight from the hunt to his council without dismounting. It also gave him the advantage of surprise.' He laughed, his pleasure in the expedition revived by Lucrezia's distress.

No one answered him, and they walked on in silence. The ramp ended under the portico that surrounded the courtyard, close to a low, mean door. Ippolito led Bembo towards it.

'Ippolito, where are you going?' cried a voice behind them. Giulio, who had been following Angela since she left the hall, came thundering down the ramp and put an arm round her shoulders. 'That's the entrance to the dungeons.'

Ippolito glared at his brother. 'You were not asked to come.'

Giulio placed his arm more closely round Angela and whistled softly.

Ippolito swung away angrily and shouted for the turnkey. The man appeared, lifted a torch from an iron wall bracket and unlocked the door. He stepped inside, and Bembo was waved to follow him. He found himself at the top of a flight of steep, uneven steps. The ceiling was so low that in climbing down he had to crouch to pass beneath it.

He heard Lucrezia cry out, 'It's too dark. I can't see.' He turned back to reach her, but Ippolito blocked the way and forced him to go on. Then, gratefully, he heard Giulio sing out, 'Don't be afraid, madonna. I'm here behind you. It isn't far to the bottom.'

At the foot of the steps, Ippolito pushed past Bembo and strode off through a tangle of low, dark passages. He stopped finally in a large, square stone chamber, bare and low-roofed. The only light and air came from a single thin slit in one wall. Ippolito ordered the turnkey to raise his torch so that they could all see the prison, and then he turned to Lucrezia. 'This is indeed a night of torches for you, my sister, though this one is not so pretty as the one you gave Messer Bembo.'

The harsh light threw dark pockets of shadow under their eyes and cheekbones. The cell was bitterly cold, yet the air was thick. To Bembo it had the stench of despair. 'Do you know where you are?' asked Ippolito. He seized the torch and held it close to Bembo's face so that he could watch him.

Bembo tried to breathe. 'No, eminence.'

'We are standing, Messer Bembo, immediately under the terrace with the little garden that pleased you so much.'

Bembo looked back at him. 'It is difficult to believe,' he said, 'that two such different places should rest on the same foundations. They hardly belong to the same world.'

Ippolito gave his unpleasant laugh. 'Ah, but for some people they did. There have been those who amused themselves in the sunlight among the orange trees and then came down into the darkness to die. You see, Messer Bembo, this part of the prison is used for members of my own family who betray their house. My grandfather kept his son, Ugo, in this very chamber.'

Angela cried out. 'Why was he such a monster?'

Ippolito smiled at her. 'Before I answer that, let me show you something else. Let me show you the cell of the Duchess Paragina.'

He led them back through the labyrinth of tunnels to a place that was far worse than the one they had just left. It was a narrow sliver of a cell, less than five feet wide. At one end was an iron-bound door which barely reached Bembo's chest, and in the thickness of the outer wall a slit even smaller than that of Ugo's prison. The other end of the cell disappeared in darkness, despite the spill of torchlight from the open doorway.

Lucrezia stumbled towards the darkness, away from Ippolito. Bembo followed as closely as he dared.

'You asked what happened to Ugo,' said Ippolito. 'My grandfather, as you may know, took as his second wife Paragina Malatesta of Rimini. She was seventeen when she came here as a bride. Ugo foolishly fell in love with her. One day my grandfather glanced into a mirror – it still hangs in the room where you were dancing tonight, Messer Bembo – and he saw a look pass between them that betrayed the secret. They were brought down here. Next day, Ugo's head was struck off in front of Paragina. She was left in this cell. It was bare, as it is now, and she was allowed no light.'

Ippolito turned in Lucrezia's direction. 'I wonder, my dear sister, if you can imagine what this cell is like without light? Let me show you.'

Lucrezia began to cry out in protest, but Ippolito was already calling to the turnkey to close and lock the door. It was dragged into place, cutting them off from the light of the torch. Bembo would not have believed that any darkness could be so complete. Not even the faintest glimmer of Lucrezia's gold dress was visible. They heard the key turning in the lock, and an iron mace being clamped into position.

Bembo heard Lucrezia's gasping breath and sensed the panic rising in her. He reached out and sought for her hand in the darkness. 'Close your eyes and hold my hand tightly,' he whispered. 'It will be easier.'

'Did you say something, Messer Bembo?' asked Ippolito.

Bembo stood quite still. Then he said, 'Yes. I thought I could hear water.'

'Yes, you can. It is the moat against the outer wall. The floor of this cell is earth, and when the water in the moat rises it is flooded.' Ippolito's voice was growing more excited. 'The prisoner has to lie or sit in the water. They kept Paragina here for a long time before they took her out to die. Nobody really knows how she died.' He gave a high chuckle.

Lucrezia shuddered and grasped desperately at Bembo's hand. For a moment he could think of nothing but her fingers locked in his.

At the other end of the cell there was a loud yawning noise, and then Strozzi's voice. 'Is this all we've come down here for? Everyone knows that old tale.'

Ippolito was angry. 'Not everyone. I doubt if Messer Bembo had heard of it, or even our duchess.'

'Then, in that case,' said Strozzi, 'wouldn't it be wiser not to mention it? Your grandfather was mad, and at times you remind me of him.'

'Do you call my grandfather mad,' cried Ippolito, 'because he avenged the honour of his house?'

'The honour of his house!' Strozzi repeated the phrase with contempt. 'Your grandfather hated Ugo. There was never any proof that Paragina betrayed him.'

'It was enough,' declared Ippolito in a shrill voice, 'that she betrayed him in her heart – ' He stopped abruptly, hearing another sound in the cell. Angela Borgia was giggling. The noise rose to a delighted shriek.

There was a small rattle as though a button or trinket had fallen to the ground. 'Giulio!' murmured Angela.

'Some of us, at least,' observed Strozzi, 'appear to appreciate your little treat, Ippolito.'

Ippolito uttered a low cry. His silks rustled in a hasty movement and he struck on the door, swearing at the turnkey for the length of time he took to unfasten the locks. When it was at last open, the flickering light showed Angela clutching at her dress and Giulio groping on the floor.

Ippolito looked at them with a mixture of disgust and spite, then without speaking turned and stooped under the low doorway. Strozzi put out a hand to stop the others following. 'Let him go alone. Giulio, fetch a lantern.'

Giulio looked up from his knees. 'I must find what was dropped first.'

Angela laid a hand lightly on his shoulder. 'Get up, Giulio. There was nothing.'

'But I heard it – '

'I knocked my bracelet against the wall to make it sound as if I'd dropped something,' said Angela impatiently.

'Yes, that was very well done, my child,' said Strozzi. 'I trust that my response was suitable?'

'Yes, that was very well done, too,' said Angela pertly.

Lucrezia's cold fingers still clung to Bembo's hand. 'Ercole,' Bembo called urgently, 'let's leave this place.'

'Please,' whispered Lucrezia, 'please.'

Strozzi nodded. 'Get the lantern, Giulio. I'll explain what happened later.'

Giulio fetched a lantern from the passage outside the cell, and guided them himself to the stairs. Bembo climbed them backwards a step ahead of Lucrezia, so that she need not let go his hand. She was still badly shaken, almost afraid to move. Bembo encouraged her gently. 'Be careful, madonna, this tread is uneven. Now bend your head a little!' She did as he told her, hardly taking her eyes from his face.

They stood at last in the courtyard, breathing in the sharp, sweet air. Lucrezia shivered and gasped with relief. Reluctantly, Bembo took his hand away from hers. Above them were the windows of the hall, the torch dance still in progress.

Lucrezia stared in amazement at the windows, then shook her head and sought the private way to her own apartments. When Bembo entered them beside Strozzi, she was standing with her hands to her face, tears on her cheeks.

'There is no need to distress yourself, madonna,' said Strozzi. 'You will never have to visit those cells again.'

'How can you be sure?' sobbed Lucrezia. 'Ippolito wants to shut me down there like the Duchess Paragina.'

'Ippolito has no power to do anything of the kind,' said Strozzi brusquely. 'He wanted to frighten you, as he obviously has. He enjoys seeing people frightened. You must understand that about him.'

Lucrezia sank into a chair, twisting her hands together. 'He has never been anything but kind to me before. Why has he changed?'

'He hasn't changed,' answered Strozzi. 'You've had a chance tonight to see him as he is. Until now, it has suited his purpose to be thought kind by his brother's wife.'

'But why should he be different tonight?'

Strozzi sighed. 'You gave the torch to Messer Bembo. Ippolito took it for granted that you would choose him.'

'The torch? Just that?'

'Ah, but it wasn't just the torch, was it?' said Strozzi softly, and he looked from Lucrezia to Bembo. 'And then, after that, you invited him to walk alone with you on the terrace.'

'To look at the snow,' cried Lucrezia helplessly. 'Oh, what shall I do?'

'There is no need for you to do anything,' said Bembo. 'I shall leave Ferrara in the morning, and the Cardinal will think that he has frightened me with his talk of Ugo and honour. I shall stay away, and that will satisfy him.'

The tears sprang again into Lucrezia's eyes. 'No,' she said.

Bembo knelt beside her chair. 'If I stay now, he will go on persecuting us, and you when I am not with you, until we become afraid not only of seeing him, but each other. If I am not here, he will not try to hurt you.'

'No,' said Strozzi tartly, 'he will be looking for other victims.'

'Why should anyone worry about Ippolito?' demanded Angela, tossing her hair. 'It's easy to deal with Ippolito.' She was still pleased with herself and she spoke with the foolish confidence of the very young. She put her arm boldly round Giulio's waist and rubbed her cheek against his sleeve. 'Isn't it, Giulio?'

'Angela – ' said Bembo, concerned for her, and for the harm she could cause Lucrezia, 'Angela, you must be careful – '

Angela laughed.

'Messer Bembo is right,' said Strozzi unexpectedly. 'You had your game with Ippolito tonight, and that must be enough.' He turned to Lucrezia who was staring dispiritedly at the hands in her lap. 'You must remember, highness, that Ippolito won't be here for ever. Sooner or later, he will create trouble for himself, and go back to Rome. It's only a matter of waiting for the right time for Messer Bembo to return.'

Lucrezia raised her head and gazed at Bembo. Crying had drowned her pretty looks, and the gold dress was too bright for her pallid skin. Bembo felt an infinite tenderness and longing for her. She leaned towards him and whispered so that no one else in the room could hear. 'Do you think it will ever come, the right time?'

'Of course. Why else should I be staying at Ostellato this winter?'

She laughed and cried at the same time. 'You are not going back to Venice?'

Bembo shook his head, moved almost to tears himself by her need for him. 'Then he has not destroyed it – our special world?'

'How could he?' said Bembo. 'He is one of the strangers we made league against.' Candles were burning on Lucrezia's desk; he reached for one of them and held it between them. 'Whenever I see a flame, I shall think of our torch, and how it protected us from the rest of the world. You must do the same.' He set the candle down and traced with his finger the circle of light which it threw on the black velvet cover of the desk.

Lucrezia stared at the circle of light. 'When you threw the torch into the moat, you began to say something.'

'They were not my words, but King Solomon's. He said that no waters could quench love, and no rivers could drown it.'

'And is it true?'

'That is what he wrote,' said Bembo, 'and his wisdom is proverbial.' He bent his head to kiss her fingers.

THREE

Ferrara, 1503

I

Through February and March, Bembo worked on his book alone at Ostellato. When the rain and wind raced across the desolate, swollen marshes, Strozzi offered him refuge in Ferrara, but he refused to return to the city while Ippolito was still living there.

Lucrezia, during these weeks, did all she could to avoid meeting Ippolito. She spent days at a time among the sisters of the Casa Romei, where a suite of four rooms was always kept ready for her; she rode in the country round Ferrara from early morning until evening; she ate in her room, with only her dwarf and two or three ladies for company.

Strozzi, whenever his duties allowed him the time, went between them, talking to Lucrezia of Ostellato and to Bembo of the castle at Ferrara.

One morning early in April, he arrived in Lucrezia's apartments in a mood of elation. He clapped his hands to command attention and then announced, 'Your highness, ladies, I have news that will amaze you!'

He kept them waiting while he drew off his gloves. 'Cardinal Ippolito has left Ferrara for Rome. In haste. And I can tell you why.'

Angela Borgia ran across the room. 'Then tell us why.'

Strozzi smiled at her, and then at the rest of his audience. 'I warn you, ladies, to prepare yourselves.' He paused. 'Ippolito has fathered a daughter.'

Angela shrieked. 'It's not possible. Not that old – '

'Ssh!' Strozzi put a finger to his lips. 'I assure you it is true. Ippolito always prefers a nice, dark-eyed singing-boy, but if one is not to hand he will make shift with – ' Strozzi coughed, ' – second best.'

He glanced at Lucrezia. 'The duke, your highness, is furious and Ippolito had to get out of his reach. He won't dare to return for several weeks.'

Lucrezia bowed her head and invited Strozzi to sit beside her. 'Have you noticed,' he said when he was settled, 'how sweet and warm the air has become since Ippolito departed.' He fanned himself with a sheet of folded and sealed paper which by sleight of hand had appeared in his fingers.

'I had mistakenly supposed it to be the spring,' said Lucrezia, smiling. She paused, and then added, 'The countryside will be much pleasanter now, in this weather.'

'Indeed, indeed,' Strozzi agreed. He continued to fan himself.

'Especially on the marshes,' said Lucrezia timidly, 'near your own villa.'

'At Ostellato? Yes. The winter can be very hard there, madonna. Do you know, by an extraordinary coincidence, I wrote to Messer Bembo this morning to assure him, that isolated though he has been in these last few weeks, he has not been forgotten in Ferrara.' He tapped the paper. 'This is the very letter.'

'Oh,' said Lucrezia, clasping her hands together and staring at it.

Strozzi lowered his voice. 'I took the liberty, madonna, of mentioning how often we speak of him here. You would have no objection to my sending it?'

Lucrezia blushed faintly and shook her head. 'But Messer Strozzi,' she said, 'you have not addressed your letter.'

Strozzi regarded the blank outer covers of the letter as though in surprise. 'Your highness is right. I left in such haste – ' He glanced towards Lucrezia's desk, set out with quills, wax and ink.

Lucrezia nodded. 'Please use them.' She followed him to the desk, watching as he selected a quill and dipped it into her silver ink-pot. With the pen poised over the paper, Strozzi turned to Lucrezia as though struck by a sudden thought. 'Your highness, why not write it for me? Wouldn't that be fitting? This is your room and your pen. Messer Bembo will then have proof that what I say is true.'

Lucrezia's fingers flew to her throat and twisted themselves in her necklace. 'Shall I?'

'If you would like Messer Bembo to address himself again to your highness,' said Strozzi gently, 'you must give him some indication that this would not be displeasing to you.'

'Oh, yes,' said Lucrezia. She sat down at the desk and took the pen that Strozzi offered her. Then very slowly and with great care she wrote across the white paper 'Messer Pietro Bembo'.

As Strozzi sanded the wet ink for her, she asked, 'Does he know yet about the Cardinal?'

'No,' murmured Strozzi, 'but I promise you that he will before long.'

He rode himself to Ostellato next day, arriving in a drizzle of spring rain. Strozzi hated getting wet, and when Bembo came to meet him he said shortly, 'I have a letter for you.'

'From Venice?'

'No.' Strozzi threw his wet cloak on the floor and shook the rain from his cap. 'As a matter of fact, it comes from me.'

'Dear God,' said Bembo. He took the letter, broke the seal and read it hastily. Then he looked at Strozzi in bewilderment. 'I don't understand. For one thing, I've never minded the isolation here. And why give me this when you're here yourself – '

'Pietro,' interrupted Strozzi, 'where is your scholar's sharp eye for detail? Look at the superscription.'

Bembo turned over the letter. 'It isn't even written by you. Someone else – ' He hesitated. 'Ah, someone else,' he repeated slowly. 'You were with her yesterday and spoke of this letter?' Strozzi nodded. 'And she wrote my name?'

'Yes,' said Strozzi. He paused. 'Ippolito, by the way, has left Ferrara.'

'Ah.' Bembo glanced at the letter. 'I see.'

He was aware that Strozzi was manipulating them. But he smiled to himself recalling things of which Strozzi knew nothing –

the look that had passed between them at the Strozzi ball, their hands linked together in the prison cell, the words they had whispered together.

He turned to look out of a window. 'Will you reply to it?' Strozzi called to him.

Bembo laughed. 'Can one reply to the superscription on a letter?'

Strozzi limped to his side. 'One can reply to a gesture that says "I remember".'

Bembo nodded. A spatter of rain beat against the window. 'Damned rain, it's getting worse,' muttered Strozzi. Bembo said nothing. He was thinking that if the drops of rain on the glass had been falling among the mountains they would have been frozen into dancing flakes of white snow. On the river a fisherman was rowing out to catch eels. Black eels, green snakes, a necklace of emeralds gliding across Lucrezia's throat. Was there anything, he wondered, that couldn't remind him of her?

The snake persisted in his mind. He sent to Lucrezia a set of Latin verses, 'On her highness's Necklace' contrived in the artificial manner of court poetry, 'I sing of a snake from the waters of Tagus, transmuted in gold . . . '

The lines pleased Lucrezia, but much more to her was the sight of his writing on the paper, and the paper itself which had come from his hands. His fingers had touched it, and now it touched hers.

II

Strozzi showed a copy of the poem to his father. Tito was a poet of no small distinction himself, and he approved Bembo's verses both for their discretion and their impeccable classical style. 'So Ippolito left only three days ago,' he said, 'yet Pietro and Lucrezia have each been assured, with a delicacy which I applaud both in you and them, that the other's interest still lives.'

'Yes, after ten weeks,' said Strozzi. 'Would you have waited ten weeks, not knowing whether it might have been twenty?'

Tito shrugged his shoulders. 'A violent, precipitate affair would not have served your purpose. The fact is that they have waited. And you must make sure that there are no more episodes like the one at the Torch Ball. You must continue to exercise the same care and discretion that you have just shown.'

'What happened at the Torch Ball was hardly my fault,' protested Strozzi mildly. 'I didn't know Pietro was there until I saw Ippolito follow him on to the terrace. At least, it opened Lucrezia's eyes to Ippolito.'

'But it also roused Ippolito's antagonism against Pietro, and that was not wise. What you must do now, Ercole, is to find a way of bringing Pietro back to Ferrara so that it is not obvious that he has been waiting for Ippolito to leave. Neither Lucrezia nor Pietro must make the first move in this, a fact that must be observed by the whole court. And Alfonso. In our concern about Ippolito, we must not forget Alfonso.'

Strozzi grunted. 'Alfonso. Since he came back from Hungary he has been too occupied even to visit Lucrezia. Instead of his daily excursions to the brothels, he spends both day and night with a certain Laura. He leaves her at times to attend to the training of his gunners, but for precious little else.' He looked at his father. 'In the circumstances, I don't think it should be difficult to arrange matters.'

III

A few days later, Ercole Strozzi sought an audience with the duke in order to present him with a small gift.

He found the duke sitting alone, except for his lutanist. It was evening, but there was no fire in the room and it was lit by only a meagre number of candles.

'What's this, Ercole,' said the duke, peering at him, 'a gift? Eh?'

Strozzi smiled and laid before him a small piece of carved ivory. The duke gave a long sigh of pleasure and bent down to study the workmanship. In his later years he had become frugal in most things, but two things he loved and on these he lavished money with an extravagance that shocked his daughter, Isabella – the theatre he had built inside his palace, and his collection of ivories.

'Your highness is pleased with it?' asked Strozzi.

The duke's eyes were shining. 'It's exquisite, exquisite. But why are you parting with such a piece?'

'A single piece is lost,' said Strozzi. 'It needs to be part of a fine collection such as your highness possesses.'

The duke clasped Strozzi in his arms, and then unlocked the marquetry cabinet which housed his ivories. He took out each piece in turn, fondled it lovingly and set it on a table. When the collection was complete, he arranged and re-arranged it until he was satisfied that the new piece was displayed to the best advantage.

Strozzi endured this ritual as patiently as he could. Then he murmured, 'How Messer Bembo would have delighted in the sight of such pieces.'

'Messer Bembo understands ivories?' enquired the duke.

'It was he,' declared Strozzi untruthfully, 'who showed me in Venice where to find the piece that you honoured me by accepting tonight.'

'Then why didn't you bring him with you?' said the duke testily.

Strozzi looked away, as if avoiding the need to answer. The duke sighed. 'Ercole, to tell the truth, I am very disappointed that Messer Bembo never visits me now. We were reading Aristophanes together, and then in the middle of a scene he stopped coming. I hope,' he added wistfully, 'that it was because the roads were bad.'

'The roads were not bad,' said Strozzi with a curt shake of his head. 'Nor does he stay at Ostellato through any choice of his own, but because he feels that he is forced to – ' He broke off with an exclamation of annoyance, as though he had spoken without thinking.

'Why does he feel that he is forced to stay at Ostellato?' demanded the duke.

Strozzi fidgeted with a ring. 'Your highness must forgive me if I do not answer your question,' he said in a soft, unhappy voice. 'I beg you not to insist – '

'I do insist.'

'No,' cried Strozzi. 'To speak would be an act of disloyalty against a member of your illustrious house – '

'Ercole, I command you.'

Strozzi bowed his head helplessly. 'If you command, highness, what can I do?' He took a deep breath. 'My lord, Messer Bembo remains at Ostellato because of an attack made against him by – forgive me – Cardinal Ippolito.'

'Ippolito!' The duke half rose from his chair.

'You spoke a moment ago, my lord, of Messer Bembo's visits to read Greek with you. One afternoon last winter he found, after he had left you, that the road back to Ostellato was blocked with snow. As he had to remain that night in Ferrara, I persuaded him to attend a ball at the castle. Cardinal Ippolito was also present. During the course of the evening, he forced Messer Bembo to accompany him to the dungeons, where he insisted on locking him into a cell in complete darkness as though he were a prisoner condemned to death. This, he made quite clear, was intended as a warning to Messer Bembo.'

'Ippolito did that?' The duke stood up and walked round his table. The lutanist went on quietly playing in his corner. 'Why?' shouted the duke.

'I would not presume to guess at the Cardinal's reasons,' murmured Strozzi. 'However, the only reason we could have in Ferrara for imprisoning a Venetian in our dungeons would be for spying. Perhaps he suspected that Messer Bembo was abusing his private visits to you to spy for the Republic.' Strozzi looked bewildered. 'What other possible reason could he have?'

The duke shook his head and a tear formed in the corner of his eye. 'I am distressed beyond words, Ercole, that our good Messer Bembo should have been made to suffer this infamous treatment.'

He sniffed. 'Ippolito knows my respect and affection for him.'

'Oh, indeed he does,' said Strossi meaningly.

The duke's distress increased. 'But Messer Bembo should have come to me – '

'My lord, how could he? He had no means of knowing whether you shared your son's suspicions. Rather than be unjustly dismissed from your presence, he preferred to withdraw to Ostellato.'

'Yes, yes, I see,' mumbled the duke. 'Ercole, he must come back at once.'

Strozzi smiled. 'I know that he will rejoice in the opportunity.' He paused. 'Might I suggest, however, that since many people must have heard what happened that night Messer Bembo should in fairness be received publicly at court, not merely by your highness in private.'

'Just, very just,' agreed the duke. 'I rarely hold court myself now, but Alfonso can receive him.'

'Don Alfonso is seldom in residence at the castle. He has his duties – ' Strozzi coughed, ' – in the field.'

'Then what's his wife for? Let her do it.'

'Madonna Lucrezia?' Strozzi sounded dubious. 'If you say so, my lord – '

'I do say so. She is to welcome him at my court. You will help me see to it.'

Strozzi bowed.

When he left, the duke was again sitting alone at his table, one hand resting on his new piece of ivory, the other beating time to the music of the lute.

IV

Lucrezia chose to wait for Bembo on the terrace overlooking the castle moat. When Bembo caught his first glimpse of her since the night of the Torch Ball, she was sitting under a silk awning feeding her parrot in its cage of gold wire. She wore a green dress sewn with pearls and silver thread, and her hair was loose on her shoulders, one strand above each ear drawn back and tied together with a ribbon. Her orange trees were already in blossom.

Her ladies sat around her, or leaned against the battlements gazing into the street. In the warmest corner of the terrace, Giulio was asleep, his head on Angela's shoulder. Strozzi was beside Lucrezia, listening to a man in sober blue silk who was reading aloud to them.

As Bembo stepped on to the terrace, he smelt the scent of the orange flowers. The man in blue silk turned his head and Bembo saw that it was Ludovico Ariosto.

Ariosto's dark, melancholy face was changed by a smile. Lucrezia stood up, her hand outstretched.

Bembo touched her fingers, and Lucrezia's cheeks glowed. The breeze blew a strand of hair across her mouth. 'Highness,' said Bembo, 'I thought as I came out here that I was breathing the scent of the orange flowers. I see now that it is the hair loosed from your ribbon that casts this perfume about us.'

Ariosto laughed with delight and held out his arms to Bembo. 'You see, madonna, our Messer Pietro's tongue is as quick as I promised you.' He embraced Bembo. 'I am glad to see you here in Ferrara again.'

Lucrezia thanked Bembo for his compliment. 'I have also to thank you, sir,' she added, 'for your poem to me. When I read it, I remembered that you had once mentioned to me the lines that Messer Ariosto wrote for my wedding. The duke has commanded me to make you welcome at court, and I hoped that it would please you if I invited Messer Ariosto to read to us.'

Bembo detected Strozzi's schooling in this. He glanced towards him, but Strozzi was engaged in annoying the parrot by running his finger across the wires of its cage. He knew that Strozzi had visited the duke, but not what had passed between them.

'Madonna,' he said, 'you could have done nothing to make this occasion more agreeable to me. I thank you. I believe,' he added seriously, 'that Messer Ariosto's writing will one day bring the greatest honour not only to Ferrara, but to Italy.'

Ariosto was moved to awkwardness by Bembo's words and

the sincerity with which they were spoken. He said wryly, 'What a pity, Messer Pietro, that you are not my master instead of Cardinal Ippolito. He sees me as one whose fluency with words makes him a useful messenger.' He shrugged his shoulders.

'I interrupted you when I arrived,' said Bembo. He turned to Lucrezia, 'May I beg your highness to ask Messer Ariosto to continue?'

Lucrezia nodded, sat down again and waved Strozzi to be silent. Ariosto fixed his large, expressive eyes on Bembo. 'These poems,' he said, tapping his manuscript, 'tell the wretched story of what love has done to me. They are so heavy with tragedy that most people assume them to be comic inventions.'

He began to read. After a while, Lucrezia's glance stole by degrees across the terrace towards Bembo. When she raised her eyes to his face, she found him watching her. They both looked quickly away.

Angela Borgia made a sudden, petulant movement that woke Giulio. 'Why do all these poems have to be written in Latin?'

Ariosto, arrested in the middle of a line, stared at her. Strozzi answered. 'They are love poems. One cannot write about such noble sentiments in the same language that one uses for ordering fish.'

'The Romans did,' said Angela sulkily.

'The Romans did not regard love, as we do, as an enlightenment. They saw it as an affliction.'

'Then, surely,' said Bembo, disagreeing with Strozzi, 'that is all the more reason for not writing of love in their tongue. Love comes freely from the heart; shouldn't we speak of it, even in poetry, in the words which are native to our thoughts?'

'But, Messer Bembo,' said Lucrezia gently, 'your poem to me was written in Latin, not Italian.'

'Madonna, that was the poem of a servant to his lady,' answered Bembo smiling. 'A servant must circumscribe the thoughts of his heart.'

'I don't want poems written to me that I can't understand,' said Angela.

'Madonna,' said Strozzi tartly, 'poems are not composed for the women to whom they may be addressed. They are intended for other poets who can appreciate the wit and facility of their style.'

Ariosto turned to Bembo. 'Messer Pietro, you would have us write our love poetry in Italian. But what is Italian? A Roman can't understand a Venetian, nor a Florentine a Sicilian – '

'True,' said Bembo. 'We must all learn to write in the least corrupted form of the language, which is Tuscan, the dialect of Dante and Petrarch.'

'But it is still a dialect,' said Strozzi. 'You cannot write in a language which has no established grammatical structure, as Latin has.'

'But of course it has a structure,' cried Bembo. 'All that needs to be done is to study it and define it – '

Angela gave a scream of boredom. 'Can't we play a game?'

Giulio sat up. 'Hide-and-Seek?' he said amiably.

Several of Lucrezia's ladies clapped their hands together. 'The ladies hide,' cried Angela. She glanced at Lucrezia for her permission.

Lucrezia looked helplessly at her guests and sighed. 'Yes.'

Giulio leapt to his feet, shouting 'Forfeits!' Angela and the other ladies were already scampering away into the castle, laughing and shrieking. Lucrezia rose and followed more slowly.

'I hardly think,' murmured Strozzi, 'that this is how Isabella's discussions on poetry are organised in Mantua. Shall we join in, Ludovico?' He turned to Bembo. 'Pietro?'

Bembo shook his head. He was disconcerted by the sudden change in the nature of the occasion and irritated by the descent into childishness. When the other men had gone, he lingered for a moment among the orange trees, and then wandered through the windows that opened on to the terrace from Lucrezia's apartments.

As always in a strange room, Bembo was drawn towards the books. Lucrezia's numbered only a score or so, and were contained on a single shelf. Each volume was bound in purple velvet with silver mounts and clasps of gold. Most of them, Bembo observed bleakly, were devotional works printed in Spanish and included the letters of Saint Catherine of Siena. There was a beautiful Petrarch manuscript and an edition of Dante, though not the one which he himself had prepared for Aldo Manuzio's press in Venice. He found a collection of Spanish songs and proverbs, many of them copied out by Lucrezia herself, and it was this book that he was reading when he was disturbed by a movement behind him.

He turned and saw Lucrezia standing inside the window, with the sun blazing on her hair and catching the silver threads of her dress. She was smiling, holding out her hands to him. 'Messer Bembo, I give in,' she said. 'You have found me and I must pay the forfeit.'

Bembo laid aside the book and walked towards her. She took his head in her hands and drawing it down touched her lips to his hair. Then she looked into his face. 'How are you, Messer Pietro?'

Bembo, trembling, took her hands, turned them over and kissed the palms. 'I am well, madonna.'

'It was not so silly after all, was it, to play this game?' asked Lucrezia. 'It has given us a few moments alone together.'

Bembo smiled. 'I should have remembered that if it were not for a silly game we might never have met.'

Lucrezia eyes were shining as she gazed at him. 'Now that you are here, I feel as if you had never been away from me.' She laughed. 'What happened to all those long, miserable days and hours?'

'They melted like the snow falling on our torch-flame.'

'And now it is summer and there are no more flames.'

'No more flames, madonna? But they follow you everywhere. Look into the moat and you will see a thousand flames where the sun strikes the water. Your hair in this light is alive with fire – ' He snatched up her book and moved the clasp to catch the light. 'Isn't this burning?'

Amused, she laughed again. 'Yes, they are everywhere.'

'Did you doubt it?' said Bembo gently.

Lucrezia looked at him with her level, candid gaze. 'I don't think so. But it was a long time.'

'Yes,' said Bembo. 'For some, perhaps.'

'For the strangers. Not us,' said Lucrezia breathlessly.

'Not us,' said Bembo.

Three of Lucrezia's ladies, shepherded by Strozzi, came chattering into the room.

Lucrezia and Bembo drew apart and became intent on the book he was carrying. 'Do you read Spanish, Messer Bembo?' Bembo nodded. 'Do you know the lines that begin "*Yo pienso si me muriese*"?'

Bembo translated the words. ' "I think if I should die"? No, madonna.'

'May I show you?' Lucrezia sat down to turn the pages. Bembo read the poem over her shoulder. It was filled with bizarre conceits of love and death, and he was puzzled at the choice until suddenly, in the last line, he saw the word 'flame'. He smiled. 'Ah, yes.'

'You see, you were right,' whispered Lucrezia. 'They are everywhere.'

Strozzi was trying to hear what they were saying. 'Madonna,' he said, 'I have no Spanish, nor have your ladies here. Would you be gracious enough to ask Messer Bembo to translate for us?'

'I should, of course, be pleased to do so,' said Bembo, 'but perhaps your highness will agree that this is not the time to read a poem of this kind.' He turned his head towards the adjoining rooms and passages where the game was still noisily in progress. 'Perhaps,' he went on, seizing his opportunity, 'I might copy the poem and when I have studied it send a translation to you.'

He added hastily before Strozzi could interfere, 'It is not difficult, madonna, to translate the thought of these lines, but to transfer them from the poetic style of one language to that of another demands care.'

'Messer Bembo,' said Lucrezia, 'I should be most grateful for such a kindness. We shall then be able to enjoy your translation at leisure.' She stood up, handing him the book. 'I hope you will be able to write to me soon,' she said softly.

'That was my hope, too,' he murmured.

They had no further chance to be alone again that afternoon. Ariosto was anxious to spend as much time as he could with Bembo. He was leaving shortly to join Ippolito in Rome and feared that it might be some time before they would meet again.

'The Cardinal then plans a long stay in Rome?' asked Bembo carefully.

'For perhaps six or seven months, yes,' said Ariosto.

Bembo tried to hide his pleasure. He snatched a glance at Lucrezia. Six or seven months, and the duke's blessing. What lay beyond they could think about later.

V

Bembo was writing to Lucrezia from Ostellato.

His desk stood by the open window. The leaves that brushed against the frame were bright green in the sunlight, like flickering pointed green flames consuming the stonework. Bembo smiled at this recurring image in his thoughts. At their first meeting, Lucrezia had stood by this same window and had asked him if he would still be at Ostellato when the leaves were out. He had not been aware then that he was already committed to her and had answered, he recalled, that it depended on matters in Venice. With a sense of guilt, he realised how very little matters in Venice now concerned him, yet even as he reproached himself for his indifference his thoughts were returning to Lucrezia. He gazed at the tranquil marshes that had so delighted him when he first arrived at Ostellato, and wished for the hot, sour streets of Ferrara.

He had turned Lucrezia's Spanish verses into a tolerable Tuscan lyric. Yet he was not happy with it, as he explained to her in his letter, because the thoughts conceived by a poet in one language sound alien in another. He offered her, as a kind of apology, a little Spanish song which he himself had written. As it was only a simple piece, he begged her not to let it out of her own hands because he would be ashamed for anyone else to read such unpolished lines. 'This favour I implore of your highness,' he went on, 'and then I will know that it is safe for me to send you other things from time to time.' He put down his pen, wondering if she would understand what he was telling her. Strozzi was coming to fetch the letter, but even with Strozzi acting as bearer, Bembo was wary of speaking openly. He hoped wryly that he had not disparaged without cause his flawless little Spanish song.

He took up his pen again. 'I have nothing else to tell you, except that this solitary life of mine – this hermit-like state – that I once enjoyed so much, now no longer pleases me as it used to do. Is this the sign of something, or the beginning of an illness? I would like your highness to search in her books to discover whether her thoughts on this conform with mine.'

From the window, Bembo saw Strozzi's boat approaching the villa. 'I commend myself to your thoughts – ' He hesitated. A hundred times, a thousand times? It was true, but he had used the phrases so many times before without meaning them. So had others. He glanced again at the shining leaves. 'I commend myself to your thoughts as many times as there are leaves in this little garden which, as I sit beside the open window writing to you, I can see beneath me.'

He added the words that ended all his letters to those who were dear to him. 'Keep well'.

VI

Bembo's letter lay in Lucrezia's pocket as she took her place beside the duke for one of the private family meals which he imposed weekly on his sons and daughter-in-law. On this occasion only Lucrezia and Alfonso were present. Giulio was in disgrace for wild behaviour with a band of what the duke considered to be unseemly companions.

Lucrezia usually attended these gatherings in a mood of sullen resentment because the duke still refused to increase her allowance. On this June afternoon, however, she surprised her father-in-law by the sweetness of her temper. He concluded that Alfonso must have resumed the attentions he paid her when they were first married, and that there might soon be the prospect of another heir. He was not, therefore, pleased when Alfonso announced that he wished to spend the next three months away from Ferrara, inspecting the defences of the Adriatic coast.

The duke petulantly demanded his reasons. Alfonso found it difficult to explain to others what in his own mind was eminently clear and sensible. He shifted his chair reluctantly to face his father.

'Within a year, perhaps in six months, I shall be able to build cannon in Ferrara that will have a greater range than anything else in Italy, and in the greater part of Europe.' Alfonso's slow voice deprived the statement of any arrogance. 'By a careful disposition along the banks of the Po, we could halt any fleet that Venice sent against us.'

Alfonso looked at his father and saw that this argument had produced the expected change in the duke's attitude. He was now eager for information. 'Do you know the range of their ships' cannon?'

'I could probably guess at it,' said Alfonso, 'but I need to be certain what they are building in their Arsenal now.'

The duke smiled on his son. 'So you think we might defeat Venice?'

'I didn't say that,' said Alfonso patiently. 'I think we shall be able to prevent their fleet threatening Ferrara, so they will no longer be able to take their influence for granted.' Having taken the trouble to explain his thoughts, Alfonso was prepared to continue. 'I don't, of course, believe as you do that Venetian influence is harmful to us.'

The duke glared at him. 'Have you forgotten the humiliations of the last war with Venice?'

'That was twenty years ago,' said Alfonso. 'They've treated us fairly since then. My lord, we are a small, vulnerable state. If we shake off the Venetians, we shall have to accept the influence of someone else.'

'Yes,' said the duke. 'I am considering an alliance with the French.'

'Foreigners!' muttered Alfonso. 'There are too many already in Italy. The Venetians are at least Italians like us.' He pulled away his chair.

'We need the help of foreigners if we are ever to destroy Venice,' shouted the duke.

Alfonso decided to try again. 'Here in the north we need a strong Venice, not a helpless one.' He paused. 'Think, my new cannon mounted in their war-galleys. With that speed and range we could be invincible against the Turks – '

'The Turks?' The duke struck the table. 'They're no concern of ours.'

'But why not? If we could re-take Constantinople and share a trade percentage with the Venetians – '

The argument raged on. Lucrezia could feel Bembo's letter hidden under her silk skirt, and she became lost in her own thoughts. She remembered well the garden and the window of which he wrote, and his 'hermit-like' state. For him, as for her, it would seem that every moment passed together could be recalled with brilliant clarity. It was as though a new life, like a fresh shoot, was beginning to grow between them, hidden and enfolded by the outer leaves of their two separate lives.

The duke startled her by striking the table again. 'I am still duke here, Alfonso,' he was shouting, 'and while I am, the guiding principle of our policy will be the destruction of Venice.'

Alfonso turned his back on his father.

The duke, with no apparent sense of incongruity, turned to Lucrezia and enquired if Messer Bembo had been pleased with his reception at her court. 'He was kind enough,' said Lucrezia a trifle breathlessly, 'to translate a Spanish poem for me, so I think perhaps that he was.'

'Good, good. I am very glad,' said the duke. 'I hope he will return soon.'

'I hope so, too,' said Lucrezia meekly. She looked at Alfonso.

With a fork dipped into his wine, he was working out a design on the linen cloth for a new set of majolica plates.

VII

Lucrezia's secretary wrote to enquire of Messer Pietro Bembo if he would graciously consider assisting the duchess in inventing a Latin device for a new medal which she was having designed.

On the afternoon before he rode into Ferrara, Bembo was running along the edge of the river, throwing sticks for Bembino. He was elated at the prospect of seeing Lucrezia again, and in a burst of energy flung the stick too hard, wrenching his neck.

He awoke during the night, unable to move his head without severe pain. By morning he was unable even to lift himself in bed without Lico's help. He could have wept with fury and disappointment. 'And what will the duchess think, waiting for me?' he cried out to Lico.

Lico, he gasped, must go at once to Ferrara with a letter that he must place in the hands of the duchess herself. When Lico demurred at leaving him alone in such a state and suggested sending one of Strozzi's house-servants, Bembo groaned. 'No, it must be you, Lico. Someone I trust.'

Lico fetched cushions to support him, laid a board across his lap and stood beside him, holding the ink-horn. Bembo described as briefly as he could what had happened, adding recklessly, 'However, the pain seems to be a little easier, so I will be able to see you soon, certainly within two days. And if I am not better, I will still see you within two days, otherwise the injury to my neck will spread to my heart, and that would be much more serious. I must see you . . .'

He wondered if she could have any idea how much he wanted her. It was close in the room, and he was sweating with the effort of writing. He thought desperately of her cool hands touching his face, her lips on his hair. With any other woman not of her rank he would have seized her in his arms and explored her mouth with his – 'Here it is very hot,' he wrote, scoring the paper. 'I myself have never known it worse than this, because all my body seems to burn and to be on fire. I wonder if you feel it in the same way. I should think not; ladies are supposed, by nature, to feel the heat less than we do'.

When the letter was sealed, Bembo was suddenly alarmed at what he had written and called Lico back. But Lico had already gone.

Lico returned later in the day with oils and salves bought in Ferrara to rub into Bembo's neck. After two days of Lico's care, the stiffness and pain were reduced, though not greatly. Nevertheless, despite Lico's objections, Bembo declared himself well enough to ride to Ferrara.

He suffered the journey in silence, sitting rigid in the saddle, his teeth clenched. At the Strozzi palace, Tito in concern offered him a stick which he refused, but he found himself unable to climb the marble staircase to Lucrezia's apartments without help. He clung first to the walls of the staircase and then to the arm of one of the guards, while Strozzi at the top leaned on his crutch laughing.

Shaken and irritable, he stepped carefully behind Strozzi into Lucrezia's presence, and was upset to find her rooms crowded with visitors and petitioners. Lucrezia herself was sitting in a high-backed chair, embroidering linen with gold thread and listening first to one, then another. The dwarf sat at her feet threading her needles.

She saw Bembo and pricked her finger, but several minutes had to pass before she was able to speak to him. When at last he stood in front of her, the linen with its speck of blood was screwed up in her hands. 'You have been able to come, Messer Bembo,' she said formally. 'I hope you are well again.' She saw then how pale he was. 'But you are not well!' She jumped up, spilling thread and needles from her lap. 'You are still in pain. You mustn't stand.'

She asked her secretary to fetch a chair. 'I want a chair, too. I want a chair, too,' chanted the dwarf, jingling his bells as he imitated Bembo's awkward steps.

Strozzi began to laugh again and tossed the dwarf a coin.

'A chair is unnecessary,' said Bembo curtly to Lucrezia. 'I am quite capable of standing in your highness's presence.'

He saw that his manner had distressed her, but for that moment he could feel nothing but his annoyance with Strozzi and the dwarf.

Lucrezia had seated herself again and her secretary was laying before her the designs for her medal. She glanced up at Bembo and then raised a hand to shield her eyes. 'Messer Bembo,' she said, 'you are standing against the light. When I look up it hurts my eyes. It would be more comfortable for me if you would sit while we consider these drawings.'

Bembo was suddenly ashamed. 'You must forgive me,' he whispered. Lucrezia's eyes shone again and she asked the dwarf to pass her a fan. 'It is very hot here,' she said.

Bembo stared at her. He could not answer her because a servant was arranging cushions on a chair behind him. He lowered himself into it, flinching. Lucrezia saw, and bit her lip. Then she added, 'I was grateful for your letter.'

'It was written with some difficulty,' said Bembo. 'I trust your highness was able to understand it.'

Lucrezia moved her fan. 'Yes. I understood.'

'And you received my earlier letter, too – with the translation?'

'Yes, I thank you. And for the little Spanish song.' She looked at him over the black and white feathers. 'I have not shown it to anyone else.'

The dwarf was watching them, walking round Bembo and peering under his chair. 'What is it?' snapped Bembo.

'I have always heard,' said the dwarf, 'that Venetians are born with fish tails. Where, sir, do you keep yours?'

There was a murmur of laughter at this sally. Bembo closed his eyes and heard Lucrezia gently dismiss the dwarf. 'Messer Bembo,' she said, and he looked at her, 'I have heard much worse of Venetians: that their tails are forked and their feet cloven. If it is true then we have much in common. I am a Borgia and they say that we also belong to the devil's brood.'

She spoke lightly, but Bembo was aware that something was disturbing her. 'Madonna, what are you thinking?' he asked gently.

She hesitated. 'There are many stories told about the Borgia, about me. Many are not true. Some are.' Her eyes searched his, as though warning him that she would neither deny nor excuse anything that he might have heard about her.

'Yes. I think I know most of them,' said Bembo. He respected her own candour too much to protest for courtesy's sake that he had never believed them. 'But I shall have enough stories of my own to remember about you. Why should I concern myself with any others?'

Lucrezia sat quite still. The fingers on her fan were shaking slightly, and she squeezed her eyes as though trying to suppress tears. Then she called to Angela and spoke to her behind her fan.

Angela left them and came back carrying a small gilded chest which she laid in Lucrezia's lap. Lucrezia opened the lid and took out an ornament made of two thin oblong pieces of crystal set face to face in a rim of gilded bronze. It was decorated with seed pearls and small gems and mounted on a column of onyx. Between the little slabs of crystal were pressed two locks of hair, one crisp and flecked with grey, the other smoother and more silky.

'This is my brother's hair,' said Lucrezia, pointing to the smoother strand, 'and the other piece my father's.' She held out the ornament to Bembo. He sensed that she was trying in some way to share her family, those she loved, with him. He studied it slowly and with attention to please her. From the lower corners of the crystals hung two tiny medallions, each bearing on one side the red Borgia bull and on the other the white eagle of the Este.

'My father gave me this before I left Rome.' Lucrezia spoke softly, and Bembo imagined that it had been a long time since she had dared to mention him in Ferrara. 'I am hoping that I may be allowed to meet him in September. I miss him. However he may seem to princes and ambassadors, he was always kind to me. Cesare, too, always tried to protect me.'

Bembo thought of Cesare riding through the night to be with her when she was ill in Ferrara, and nodded. He recalled, too, that Cesare was believed to have killed the young Duke of Bisceglie of whom it was said she was very fond. He sighed, and realised that some of her ladies were regarding them with curious looks. He moved the ornament in his hands and said loudly, 'This crystal, madonna, is flawless.'

Lucrezia gasped and fluttered her fan. 'Is that one of your Greek words, Messer Bembo?'

Bembo smiled. 'Crystal? Yes, it means "ice".' He went on talking. 'When the Greeks first discovered veins of crystal beneath the snow of the Alps, they believed it to be water frozen too hard ever to melt again.'

The thought pleased Lucrezia and took her mind from her father and Cesare. 'You like snow,' she said unexpectedly. 'You often write about it.'

'Do I?' he said, surprised.

'Yes. I know, because Messer Strozzi gave me a book of your sonnets last winter.'

'Did he?' said Bembo. 'I see. Most poets, madonna, tend to use certain images over and over again, sometimes without knowing it.' He paused. 'Once when I was a very young man I was staying at Asolo and I saw the snow on the mountains. It is always beautiful there, but that winter, with the snow thick and white on the peaks and the stillness of winter lying everywhere, I thought it was the most beautiful thing I had ever seen. Since then, whenever I've encountered something I thought beautiful, I suppose I've been reminded of my snow-peaks.'

Lucrezia was listening with her head on her hand, absorbed in hearing him talk about himself. He wanted to tell her then that it was only when he saw her dancing in her white dress that he understood the true nature of his image, and that he would never use it again to describe anything but her. He tried, stiffly, to lean towards her.

But Strozzi was suddenly there, dangling between them a piece of the gold thread that Lucrezia had dropped. 'Madonna,' he said, 'if you are ever in need of gold thread of the finest quality from Constantinople, let me advise you to apply to Messer Bembo's brother, Carlo, in Venice. I'm sure, as Cardinal Ippolito would be anxious to point out, he'll make a good price for you.'

Bembo let his head fall back on his cushions. Were they never to be able to speak alone for more than a few seconds, never to be able to share a thought undisturbed?

Lucrezia was bending over him. 'Is the pain worse, Messer Bembo?'

'Madonna, no,' said Bembo, 'no.'

'Then tell me – ?'

Bembo raised his head and looked at her helplessly. Around the room people watched Lucrezia idly as they waited to speak to her; Strozzi was only a few yards away; Lucrezia's secretary was hovering to collect the drawings of the medal. 'It is not possible, madonna.'

The crystal ornament still lay in his hands. He held it out to her and as she leaned forward to take it, he muttered, 'I wish my heart were made of crystal. Then you could read what was in it, and know what I want to say to you. But it is not.'

'Oh, Messer Pietro – ' Lucrezia turned her head away and laid the ornament back in its chest.

Bembo snatched up the drawings and stared at them. The first one showed the obverse of the medal: Lucrezia in profile, with the strands of hair tied at the back of her head with a ribbon. He looked at the second sheet to see what device she had chosen for the reverse. 'A flame,' he murmured.

'Yes,' said Lucrezia. 'You once explained to me, Messer Bembo, that a flame often symbolises that aspect of life which is most precious to us.'

Bembo went on studying the design. 'So everyone who receives your medal, madonna, will see in your flame the thing which to him is the breath of life.'

'Yes, oh yes,' said Lucrezia.

Bembo beckoned to her secretary. 'In the space for the legend, write "Est anima".'

Strozzi, who had limped up to look over Bembo's shoulder, said, 'Anima – the breath of life. With the flame. Yes, that's good, Pietro. I like that: anima.'

Bembo addressed himself to Lucrezia, deliberately assuming the lofty manner of the scholar giving instruction. 'It is a useful word in Latin, capable of fine variation. Cicero, for example, uses it for the soul, with particular felicity when that term is an endearment.' His glance lingered for a moment on the drawing of Lucrezia's profile before he returned it to her secretary.

'Cicero,' said Lucrezia.

Bembo dragged himself painfully to his feet. 'Exactly so, madonna.' He wondered if she understood. If only hearts, he thought bitterly, were made of crystal.

That night in the Strozzi palace, he was haunted by the phrase. Still in discomfort, with nerves overwrought, he slept fitfully. Between waking and uneasy dreaming, he was tormented by curious memories – torches blazing after dark in the squares of Venice, crystal glass being drawn from the fires of Murano, an astrologer gazing into a ball of crystal to warn him as a child that he would never find happiness in Venice, a human heart laid bare in the dissecting room of the University of Padua. He woke with a cry, to find Lico shaking him.

He spent the next day scribbling words on paper, reluctant to eat or rest. By evening he was exhausted, but calmer, with a new sonnet completed. Its first line 'Had I a flawless crystal for a heart' was in time to become the most famous line he wrote.

The poem, carefully couched, spoke of the hidden injury in his heart and begged at least for mercy, although this was not, in fact, a powerful enough medicine for the wound. He made a copy and addressed it to Lucrezia. Then, before he sealed the paper, he wrote inside the cover with a trembling hand, 'Gazing into my crystal, about which we spoke yesterday when I offered my respects to your highness, I read these verses. It would be dearer to me than the most precious treasure to learn from your highness what she reads in hers.'

The jerky strokes of the pen, more than the words themselves, suggested the urgency of the plea he was making. He sealed the letter hastily, and asked for a servant to carry to Lucrezia some lines expressing his thanks to her for her courtesy to him on the previous day.

He went back to Ostellato to wait and hope for a reply from Lucrezia. Several days passed, and he grew more and more anxious as he watched the road for a messenger. He decided that if she didn't answer him he would go back to Venice. Yet she would answer; he was sure of it, just as he was sure that from their first meeting they had shared a discovery of their need for each other. But he wanted her now to tell him that it was so.

He walked up and down the paths of Strozzi's garden, he walked across the marshes and along the river-bank. On mid-summer day he came back to the villa to find her servant waiting for him.

His hands were shaking as he tore open the seal. She had written in Italian, although some of the words she had spelt as if they were Spanish. The letter was short, yet its laboured style suggested the effort and caution that had gone into its composition. 'My own Messer Pietro, with regard to the desire which you have to know what likeness there is between your crystal and ours, for so one may rightly think of it and call it, I do not know what else I might say or find except an extreme conformity, perhaps never before equalled at any other time.'

Bembo leaned against his window with the letter in his hand, staring at the river. After the strain of the past few days, he felt as though the smooth, shining water were flowing through his own body. He experienced a moment of perfect happiness. He folded the letter and thrust it inside his shirt. Lucrezia had not spoken of 'your crystal and mine' but of 'your crystal and ours'; his heart she did not presume to claim, but her own was already given to him. The simplicity of her declaration amazed and humbled him.

At the bottom of her letter she had added, 'From now on, my

name shall be FF'. He wrote that night to FF, enclosing the sheet in covers addressed to the Duchess Lucrezia. 'Now is my crystal more precious to me than all the pearls in the Indian sea because you have made it the equal and the companion of your own. God knows nothing on earth could be more dear to me than the certainty of this. You yourself will one day know this if you do not know it now . . . '

VIII

A few days later, Bembo rented a small house in Ferrara and by the end of June was living in it. It was a quiet house, discreetly hidden in its own orchard. From there he could go as often as he dared to the castle. When he was unable to see Lucrezia for two or three days, he wrote his unsigned letters to FF and sent them to Angela Borgia.

'Why FF?' Bembo had whispered to her one day when they were supposed to be studying a volume of Catullus. Lucrezia had drawn two wavering triangles in the margin with her finger.

Bembo had shaken his head. It was some time before he had finally understood. 'Flames? Why two?' he had asked, and been surprised when Lucrezia blushed. 'Two joined together, like the crystals,' she had said. To hide their smiles, Bembo had hastily begun to read aloud.

When the heat grew oppressive in July, Lucrezia moved from her apartments in the castle to the villa of Belvedere. Belvedere was an island of wooded parkland in the Po just outside Ferrara, and the villa itself overlooked rose gardens laid out round a bronze fountain. To protect it from the river, the island was circled by a wall which was broken at intervals by little crenellated loggias.

One afternoon, when most of Lucrezia's household was asleep, Bembo sat in one of the loggias talking to her secretary, Antonio Tebaldeo. Tebaldeo was an aspiring scholar himself, and he had never before met a scholar of Bembo's distinction who also displayed the wit and manners of a courtier. He grasped every opportunity he could to share Bembo's company, and on that afternoon was earnestly discussing the structure of Bembo's sonnets.

Bembo was listening with only half an ear. Below him, on the strip of shore between the wall and the edge of the river, Lucrezia was walking, idly picking up pebbles and sticks. Angela was trailing listlessly behind her.

Lucrezia glanced up, for the fourth or fifth time, at the loggia. 'Antonio,' said Bembo suddenly, 'I think we could discuss this more usefully if we had the text. I believe her highness has a copy inside the villa. I've seen it somewhere.'

Tebaldeo agreed with him, and set off happily towards the villa. As soon as he had disappeared among the trees, Bembo left the loggia and climbed the steps down to the beach.

Lucrezia, when she saw him coming, wrote something with a stick in the wet sand near the water. Bembo quickened his steps, but when he was almost close enough to see the letters she rubbed them out with her foot.

'Why did you do that?' asked Bembo.

'I want you to guess what I wrote.'

'How can I?' said Bembo laughing. 'Tell me.'

'You must try. It was one word – ' She gasped as a breeze from the river blew her hair across her mouth.

Bembo put out a hand to lift it away. Then he drew it back. His hand, his mouth, his whole body ached to feel the touch of her hair. If once he felt it, how could he stop himself from folding her in his arms –

Lucrezia was watching him gravely, waiting without speaking. Bembo looked at the long strands of hair falling now against her bare neck and shoulders. 'Amber on snow,' he said abstractedly.

'You can't have amber in the Alps,' said Lucrezia, smiling at him.

'I can have anything I want. In my imagination.'

Lucrezia turned round so that the wind blew her hair back from her face. As she turned she stumbled slightly, and sighed. Bembo caught her arm to steady her. 'Madonna, what is it?'

'I don't know. My head aches – '

Bembo looked at her anxiously. 'Is it fever?'

They stared at each other, appalled by the realisation that illness could mean separation.

'No, no,' cried Lucrezia. 'It must be the heat.'

Angela had seen her stumble and was hurrying towards them. Bembo noticed, too, that Tebaldeo had returned and was peering through the canopy of leaves that hung over the front of the loggia.

'I would like,' Bembo said urgently to Lucrezia, 'something of yours to keep – '

She had no time to answer him before Angela reached them.

Next day the signs of fever were obvious in Lucrezia. The duke insisted that she must be sent away from the unhealthy air of Ferrara to one of his distant country estates. Lucrezia sobbed and protested, but the duke was about to engage himself in a quarrel with the Pope and was determined to give him no grounds to complain that his daughter was being neglected.

Before she left, however, Lucrezia sent to Bembo's house in Ferrara a long strand of amber-yellow hair, and with it the crystal case that had once contained the locks of her father and her brother.

IX

One evening, towards the end of July, Bembo was strolling with Strozzi in the gardens at Ostellato.

When he had first heard of Lucrezia's fever, Bembo had been almost as distraught as Lucrezia. They had grown used to seeing each other several times a week. Now they were suddenly separated, without any chance to say goodbye and with no means of knowing when they might meet again. 'The fever is not dangerous, and she will be well in two or three weeks,' Strozzi had said patiently. 'Why not go into the country yourself until she comes back to Ferrara? We'll both go to Ostellato.' Bembo had finally agreed, and when they were ready to leave had written a note to FF, 'I am writing to you, light of my life, not because I need to tell you how much grief this parting has caused me, but to beg you to take care of yourself and your health so that my own will not be in danger . . . I must go now. I kiss your hand'.

As though Strozzi were reading his thoughts, Bembo heard him speak Lucrezia's name. He looked at him, startled.

'I was saying,' Strozzi repeated, 'that I believe Madonna Lucrezia plans to go to Rome in September.'

'Ah yes,' said Bembo. 'To see her father.'

Strozzi limped a few steps without speaking, Then he said, 'When I was in Venice, Pietro, I spoke to you about my hope of acquiring a Cardinal's hat.' He smiled. 'It occasioned, I recall, some amazement in Carlo and yourself.'

'Yes, I remember,' said Bembo shortly. He had suddenly realised what Strozzi might be going to ask of him.

'This visit to the Pope.' Strozzi went on, 'would give Lucrezia an opportunity to persuade him to consider my request.'

He glanced sideways at Bembo. Bembo was staring at his boots. 'Pietro,' said Strozzi delicately, 'I would be eternally in your gratitude if you would beg Lucrezia to speak for me.'

It was repugnant to Bembo to ask favours of anyone, least of all Lucrezia. But he owed Strozzi more than he could ever repay, as Strozzi had intended he should. He made an effort to disguise his reluctance and with his gaze fixed on the marshes said, 'When she is well, Ercole, I will ask her.'

'My dear Pietro,' murmured Strozzi. Then he added brightly, 'I was sure you would. I am asking you now, Pietro, because I shall be leaving in a few days for Florence. As you agreed to speak to Lucrezia, I can arrange while I'm there for our banking house to have five thousand Florentine gold ducats ready for transfer to the papal treasury.'

'You seem to take my success for granted,' Bembo said unhappily.

'Pietro, if I asked her, or my father asked her, she would try to help us. If you ask, she will turn the Vatican upside down to please you. Of course, I take your success for granted.'

Bembo's face expressed his anger. Strozzi merely laughed. 'You know me well enough to know that I intended to use you.'

Bembo smiled, despite himself. 'But, Ercole, I still can't understand why you want this.'

'My Cardinal's hat? Why not? You Venetians have a ridiculously foolish abhorrence for anything to do with the Papacy. I explained my reasons to you in Venice – '

'Yes, I know,' said Bembo. 'You want to assure your future. But couldn't you do that just as well by marrying an heiress with a city or two in her dowry?'

To Bembo's surprise, Strozzi fell silent. Then he said in a mild voice, 'Do you know, Pietro, that you may not believe this. I have a disinclination to marry purely for expediency.'

Bembo became thoughtful. 'Ercole,' he said slowly, 'when a man makes a remark like that, it usually implies that he has – ' he hesitated, ' – committed his affections.'

'Yes.' Strozzi sighed. 'You're right. There is a lady.'

'Here in Ferrara?'

'Yes.' Strozzi shifted his crutch. 'Does it surprise you that I can be discreet if it suits me? Believe me, it has been necessary.' He faced Bembo in the fading evening light. 'It is a very odd business,' he said amiably. 'May I talk about it?'

Bembo took his arm and they sat down together on a bench. After a moment, Strozzi began to speak. 'The lady, Pietro, is the wife of Ercole Bentivoglio of Bologna. The man is brutish and depraved. Barbara finally ran away from him when she learned that he had sold her to his bishop for a thousand ducats. Isabella hid her in Mantua until she was able to arrange a refuge here in Ferrara in the convent of San Rocco. Barbara is suing the papal courts for consent to live apart from her husband and for the return of her dowry. The dowry, of course, is the chief reason why the Bentivoglio want her back. The duke, as well as Isabella and the Duchess of Urbino, are all supporting her petition, but it could take a very long time to settle it. In the meantime, she remains her husband's property, and dare not move outside the sanctuary of the convent.'

'But the Bentivoglio surely couldn't abduct her from Ferrara,' said Bembo.

'Unfortunately, Ippolito has taken their side in the matter. His household officers have instructions to take her if they can and deliver her to the Bentivoglio. He is also obstructing her petition in Rome.'

'How long have you known her?' asked Bembo gently.

'Eighteen months,' said Strozzi. 'As soon as she arrived at San Rocco, the duke sent me to her as his agent to offer what help she needed.' He smiled. 'I am still observing his instructions.'

'Yet you still want to go to Rome?' Bembo was bewildered, able only to imagine his own feelings had Lucrezia been in Barbara Bentivoglio's position.

'Barbara is very dear to me,' answered Strozzi. 'She is the only woman I would choose to make my wife. But I'm not a troubadour lover like you. I doubt if I would have stayed all these weeks at Ostellato, as you did, not even sure that you would see Lucrezia again. Even if Barbara eventually wins her claims in the courts, she will still be Bentivoglio's wife. Even if she were willing to become my mistress, I don't know that I would want that. So what, Pietro, is the point of sacrificing an opportunity for power, which is also something I desire strongly?'

They were both silent. Then Strozzi laughed and struck Bembo's shoulder. 'How extraordinary it is that at dusk we can talk freely about things that we would never dream of mentioning in clear daylight. Shall we go in?'

They walked slowly back to the villa. Lico was waiting on the steps to tell Bembo that a letter had arrived from the duchess and was lying on his desk. He laughed, gripped Strozzi's arm and leapt up the stairs to his room. The letter, from the duchess and not FF, informed him sedately that Lucrezia had almost recovered from her fever and would return to Ferrara at the beginning of August. Bembo snatched up a pen and replied in courtier's fashion. 'I have just received this minute your highness's sweetest letter, full of the honey that is gathered from the flower of her words and no others . . . ' It was a pretty conceit, and only Lucrezia would understand that it was not as trivial as it seemed.

He arranged to return to Ferrara on the last day of July. The day before was so hot that Bembo found it impossible to work. He walked idly by the river, and then sat down on the bank to watch a man fishing in mid-stream from a shallow boat. The man was using a conical net on a long flexible pole. Every time he lifted the net dripping from the water, the smooth reflection of the boat was shivered into fragments, like a piece of dark glass that would miraculously be made whole again within a few seconds.

Bembo's eyes grew heavy as he watched the net dipping in and out of the water. Water and glass were confused in his mind as he drifted into sleep. Some time later he thought he was standing before a furnace in Murano. The sweat ran down his cheeks. He opened his eyes and found himself lying in the sun at Ostellato.

He stumbled to his feet, his head aching, his eyes tormented by the dancing light on the water. At supper he had lost all appetite for food, but his thirst was unquenchable. Next morning the pain in his eyes and his temples was so violent that he felt hardly able to stand. But when he tried to grasp at solid objects for support, they wavered and shrank from his touch.

He insisted on leaving Ostellato, struggling to hide his weakness from Lico. During the journey he was seized by a fit of shivering so severe that he had to stop his horse and grip the saddle helplessly until it passed. By the time he reached his house in Ferrara, he was delirious and his servants had to carry him to his bed.

X

On the day that Bembo fell ill with malaria, plague broke out in Rome. Cardinal Ippolito set out on one of his unexpected journeys to Ferrara. Within a week of his arrival, he had given the duke cause to regret it. While leading a hunting party, Ippolito had amused himself by riding through farms and villages slaughtering livestock and chickens.

As they sat at supper that night, the duke enquired bitterly of every dish that was set before them whether it owed anything to the Cardinal's apprentice butchery. Ippolito, pleasantly tired by his day's exercise, ignored him.

It was one of the duke's private family meals and Lucrezia was present. 'I have two sons,' he complained to her, 'nobly born and liberally educated. One wants to work in a foundry, the other in a shambles.'

Lucrezia hardly heard what he said. She felt helpless and lonely and frightened. Ten days earlier, she had returned to Ferrara, excited at seeing Bembo again; but during those ten days he had neither visited her nor written to her. Strozzi was unable to help her because he was in Florence, and she dared not send a messenger to Bembo's house to ask where he was. At times she was in despair, thinking he had gone back to Venice, no longer wanting her. At others, she would refuse to believe this, tormenting herself then with the fear that he was dead, and wishing that she could die, too.

Her food, scarcely touched, was removed. She looked so white and listless that even the duke noticed and forgot Ippolito's sins for a moment to ask if she still had the fever.

'Fever?' said Ippolito. 'She hasn't any fever. She's pining for Alfonso. Isn't that the cause of those red eyes, madonna?'

Lucrezia's white face flushed. 'Be quiet, Ippolito,' snapped the duke. He had recently learned of Alfonso's new mistress, Laura, and had no wish to have her discussed in front of his daughter-in-law. 'Why can't you leave your brother alone?'

'My brother?' said Ippolito. 'Why should you take my remark as an attack on Alfonso? I was merely trying to find out who was the cause of my sister's tears. Because she has been crying. Haven't you, madonna?'

The duke struck Ippolito on the wrist and turned his head to hear what a servant was trying to say to him. 'Yes, let him come, let him come.' He addressed himself to Lucrezia. 'Messer Strozzi is back from Florence. He has a message that he says is important – for both of us.'

'Us, my lord?'

'You and me.'

Strozzi came limping swiftly into the room and bowed. 'Your highness is gracious to see me. The message I bring for you and Madonna Lucrezia is from Messer Bembo – ' Lucrezia gasped, and Strozzi glancing round suddenly recognised Ippolito sitting in the duke's feeble candlelight.

It was not often that anyone saw Strozzi taken aback. He had not known that Ippolito had left Rome.

He recovered his brightness quickly. 'Your highness must forgive me. I had not been informed that you were entertaining his eminence. My message can, of course, wait until the morning.' He began to withdraw.

'Ercole, wait,' said the duke. 'Never mind Ippolito. What have you come to say?'

Strozzi glanced uneasily at Lucrezia. It was unlikely that she would be able to hear about Bembo's illness without betraying her feelings. In front of the duke, who hardly noticed what she did and said, this would not have been dangerous. With Ippolito present, it was a different matter. 'Madonna – ' he murmured, trying to warn her.

'Yes, she's listening,' said the duke. 'Go on.'

'Well, my lord, I returned from Florence a few hours ago, and sent a servant to Messer Bembo's house with some books he had asked me to buy. The man came back with the news that Messer Bembo was ill – '

Lucrezia gave a cry. 'Your highness is too tender-hearted,' said Strozzi, looking at her.

'My father and I have since been to visit him. He is beginning to recover, but he was delirious for several days and so unable to send word of his illness to you, my lord, or her highness. His one thought was that you should not think his absence was due to negligence.'

As Strozzi had feared, Lucrezia's distress was obvious. Since there was no way of hiding it, he drew attention to it. 'Madonna,' he said, 'I beg you not to alarm yourself in this way. Messer Bembo has malaria, not plague. None of your ladies will be in any danger.'

Lucrezia put her hand gratefully on Strozzi's. 'I understand,' she said. 'Thank you.'

Strozzi smiled and nodded slightly. Then he took a step nearer the duke and whispered, 'Your highness knows that Messer Bembo is much attached to one of the ladies of Madonna Lucrezia?'

The duke shook his head. 'Ah,' said Strozzi. 'Then you can understand now why she was so alarmed by Messer Bembo's illness. Had it been plague – ' He shrugged his shoulders.

The duke's eyes twinkled. 'Which one is it?'

Strozzi put a finger to his lips. 'Messer Bembo is discreet, and so is her highness.'

The duke chuckled. 'Then we must get him well for the poor lady's sake. I shall send my own physician. And he must be visited. I am not well enough to go myself, but Ippolito shall go on my behalf.' He called out to his son, 'Ippolito, you will visit Messer Bembo tomorrow with my good wishes for his recovery.'

Ippolito stared at his father. 'You expect me to visit the Venetian?'

'After your conduct towards him last winter, it is the least you can do,' said the duke. 'You can take the opportunity to apologise for the insulting and degrading treatment that you offered him.'

'What treatment?'

'Have you forgotten,' shouted the duke, 'that you accused him of spying on me and threatened him with our dungeons?'

Ippolito looked at Strozzi, who was studying the ceiling. 'I had forgotten,' he answered with suspicious mildness, 'but now that you have reminded me, I shall not forget again. You may be sure of that.'

'You'll go tomorrow,' persisted the duke. 'It's a priest's duty to comfort the sick.'

'I'll go with pleasure if he gets any worse,' said Ippolito. He smiled spitefully at Lucrezia. 'I should enjoy hearing his last confession. Until then someone else can go.' He rose from his seat, turned his back insolently on his father, who had opened his mouth to speak, and walked from the room.

The duke struck the table in fury. 'My lord,' said Strozzi quickly, 'I think his eminence is right. Someone else should visit Messer Bembo on your behalf. It would not perhaps encourage his recovery to find Cardinal Ippolito at his bedside.' Strozzi moved to include Lucrezia in their conversation. 'I wonder if Madonna Lucrezia might be willing to convey your greetings? Next time she drives in the city, she might perhaps stop for a few moments at Messer Bembo's house.' He made a performance of winking at the duke. 'She could take one or two of her ladies – '

The duke was pleased at the prospect of a harmless conspiracy. He tapped a cheek with his finger. 'One lady at least, eh?' he whispered. 'Much better for him than Ippolito.'

He leaned towards Lucrezia. 'My dear daughter – '

XI

Lucrezia travelled to Bembo's house escorted by her out-riders, six of her ladies, her secretary and Ercole Strozzi. She wore white silk, with a pendant of crystals set in enamelled gold. She could not explain her love in words as Bembo could, but she had other ways of showing it.

She was silent during most of the journey, contained in her own excitement. She spoke only once to Strozzi, who was riding beside her. 'I wish, she said, 'that you hadn't had to pretend that Messer Pietro and one of my ladies – ' She stopped, embarrassed, and fidgeted with her pendant.

'Madonna,' said Strozzi in surprise, 'what more useful rumour could I have started? I wish it had occurred to me before.'

They rode through the orchard to Bembo's house, and Lucrezia's carriage stopped in the wide flagged passage that ran through the house from the entrance to the garden beyond. Lico was waiting at the foot of a shallow spiral stair to help her alight. The stair led them directly into a salon which stretched across the front of the house. On a long table Lico had arranged wine and sweet cakes.

Lucrezia swallowed a token sip of wine while Strozzi went to prepare Bembo for the visit. In the short time that Bembo had rented the house, Lico had imposed on it that air of quiet, decorous behaviour that characterised the great households of Venice, and Strozzi found himself treading with care. Bembo's sick-room, he observed, was fresh and cool, its walls hung with spotless herb-scented linen.

He returned to Lucrezia to suggest that as few people as possible should visit Messer Bembo's bedside to avoid exhausting the sick man. Perhaps her highness and her cousin – ?

Lucrezia agreed to do whatever Messer Strozzi considered wise. She rose and allowed Lico to conduct her through a door which led to the private rooms at the back of the house. They entered a small vestibule which Lucrezia saw was also used by Bembo as a study, for books and papers were piled on a table under the window.

Lico opened another door, leading into an adjoining room, and invited Lucrezia to enter. As she stepped over the threshold, Strozzi caught Angela Borgia by the arm and drew her back. 'Madonna,' he said, 'I must urge you to look at the view from this window.' He pulled the door shut behind Lucrezia.

Bembo lay with his head on a low pillow, watching the door. He was thinner, Lucrezia saw with distress, the flesh under his eyes dark and sunken.

When he realised that Lucrezia had come alone into the room, he struggled to sit up. He was weaker than he thought, and the effort of raising himself left him helpless. He clutched at the bed-hangings.

Lucrezia was quickly at his side. She slipped her arms under his and lowered him carefully back to his pillow. 'No, you must lie still,' she said. As she began to draw her hands away, he laid his on her shoulders and held her there. 'Lucrezia,' he said. It was the first time he had ever spoken her name to her. She laid her head for the moment on the pillow beside his.

When she sat up there were tears in Bembo's eyes. His face and neck were damp with sweat. She recognised that he was suffering from the weakness and languor that followed the most violent attacks of the fever. Linen and fresh water stood near his bed.

Lucrezia moistened a pad of linen and bathed his face. Then she loosened the cord at the neck of his shirt, and as her fingers brushed against his throat he trembled and sighed, 'Your fingers are cooler than the water.' He caught her hand and raised it to his lips.

He was wearing the agnus-dei that she had seen at their first meeting. She eased the gold chain carefully as she bathed his neck. Bembo closed his eyes and murmured, 'White dress – '

When he opened his eyes again to look at her, he said, 'I thought I should die because I didn't know how to find you. Now I think I shall die of joy because you are here.'

Lucrezia knelt on the floor so that he could see and speak to her more easily. 'I, too,' she said, 'because I am near you.'

They watched each other tenderly. 'A pair of crystals,' Bembo whispered.

Lucrezia nodded. 'And yet I was afraid that I might never see you again.'

'My love, why?'

'This must be what you call a paradox,' she said shyly. It was a word he often used and he smiled, recognising it. 'Why?' he asked again, gently.

'Because,' said Lucrezia simply, 'I cannot believe what I know is true. I do not understand why you should love me. So I am always saying to myself, "Some day he will look at me and see the plain truth of what I really am. And he will realise that I am nothing, and he will go away. But I shan't be able to blame him, because he is so much".'

Bembo reached out for her hand. 'Goose,' he said shakily, 'my dear white goose.' He tried to frown at her. 'You must take me for a fool. I saw the truth the first time I met you. I loved you because – ' he sought for words, ' – you were unaware of yourself. You are now. That's why you are so ungenerous to yourself.' He swallowed painfully, what little voice he had almost exhausted. There was so much more he wanted to say to her to explain so strange a reason for loving. But he shook his head, laughing at his own weakness.

Strozzi was tapping delicately on the door. Lucrezia bent over Bembo and kissed his hair, the chain that rested against his throat, the hand that held hers. She had not understood the words he had said to her, but she knew his meaning. She called Strozzi.

'I think, madonna,' he said, as he ushered Angela into the room, 'that your highness has spent as much time here as the duke would reasonably expect.' He looked thoughtfully at Bembo. 'In a day or so, I hope it will be possible to move him to Ostellato.'

Bembo shook his head on the pillow. 'No,' he said hoarsely, 'no, I shall stay here.'

'The air here is bad for fever.'

'No,' gasped Bembo, looking at Lucrezia.

Strozzi also turned to look at Lucrezia. 'I am surprised, madonna, that you, too, remain here in the city. This is plague weather. And now that Cardinal Ippolito has arrived from Rome, who knows what to expect? I wonder that you haven't considered going to Medelana.'

'Medelana?' repeated Lucrezia, bewildered by Strozzi's remarks. 'I don't know Medelana.'

'Oh, you should, madonna,' said Strossi. 'Although it is rarely used, it is one of the most agreeable of the duke's villas. Very isolated. It is admittedly small, so that one can take only a limited household, but is that a disadvantage?' He gave his attention to the view from the window. 'It is, as it happens, only twenty minutes' ride from Ostellato.'

Bembo and Lucrezia looked at each other.

'May I remind you, madonna,' added Strozzi after a moment, 'that Don Alfonso will soon be returning to Ferrara. I'm sure he would be relieved to find you safely removed from the danger of infection.'

They were clasping hands like two happy children. 'Madonna, will you go?' Bembo asked her. Lucrezia nodded, too overjoyed for words.

'I shall be strong enough to ride in a few days,' Bembo said.

'Oh, but you must take care.'

Bembo glanced at Strozzi, who was listening intently. 'Of my crystal?' he murmured.

Lucrezia smiled at him. 'Of course, because it is mine,' she whispered.

Strozzi had caught the mention of crystal, and as he rode back to the castle he wondered what they could have been talking about. Surely Bembo hadn't given her a crystal ball to read the future. Venetians, even scholars like Bembo, had a heathenish faith in the power of such practices. It was one of the many ways by which they contemptuously gave offence to the Church. It afforded Strozzi a certain sardonic amusement to reflect that it was on one of these heretical Venetians that he had reposed his chief hopes for acquiring a Cardinal's hat – hopes which, he trusted, might soon begin to be realised in the seclusion of Medelana.

Bembo, left alone, fell into an exhausted and contented sleep, and lay undisturbed until morning. When he awoke he felt stronger. His mind was clearer, his skin cool and dry. While Lico washed him, changed the linen and administered his draughts, Bembo relived exquisitely every moment of Lucrezia's visit. He begged Lico to fetch him pens and paper. Lico, observing his patient's improvement, agreed that he might write a few lines.

Bembo, uncertain of the safety of writing to FF, addressed himself to the duchess. He sat for a long time, pen in hand, searching for words that would tell Lucrezia what her visit had meant to him without being indiscreet. Finally, he confessed to her, 'For a long time I have had this pen in my hand, wanting to thank you for your great kindness in condescending to come yesterday to my house, even to my bedside, to comfort me and spend some little time with me. But I can find no way to begin – I think, perhaps, because my debt to you is infinite and words, which are finite, cannot describe it. Your visit has taken from me all the weakness of the fever from which I was suffering . . . I cherish in my soul the memory of my debt to you.'

He laid down his pen. Then he snatched it up again and added, with a simplicity worthy of Lucrezia herself, 'I hope to be able to get up tomorrow'.

FOUR

Medelana, 1503

I

Lucrezia was waiting for Bembo at Medelana, and he rode to her between fields of ripe wheat, each blade like a yellow flame lighting his path.

The duke had made no objection to Lucrezia's sudden wish to leave Ferrara. He had merely requested that she should be accompanied by a member of his family, and had been content to accept her suggestion of Giulio.

When Bembo arrived he was met by Angela Borgia. She led him away from the house and across the park. 'Where are we going?' Bembo asked.

'Where you want to go,' said Angela. She stopped at a wicket set in the wall of an old garden. Half-smiling, she motioned him to enter. Bembo saw white birds on the grass, and on the archways of clipped yews that sheltered the paths. At the far end of the garden was a pergola hidden from the windows of the villa by the trees outside the wall. Angela nodded towards it, and handed Bembo a key.

'Lock the gate behind me,' she said, and left him alone.

Bembo turned the key in the lock and began to run along the path towards the pergola. Lucrezia, sitting beneath it, heard his footsteps and started up. They met in each other's arms under the dark canopy of leaves. Bembo bent his head and kissed her long and gently on the mouth.

They drew apart and gazed at each other in complete happiness. Bembo was still pale from his illness, and Lucrezia put her hands to his face anxiously.

'Pietro, are you well yet?'

Bembo nodded and smiled faintly. 'Of course.' He kissed her again, more fiercely, with her head cradled against his arm. They clung to each other with the hunger of many months of waiting. When Bembo raised his head to look at her again, her face was alight with its candle-like beauty.

He laughed and swung her off her feet. 'Now all the bells of Venice are ringing in my head,' he cried.

'The bells of Venice?' Lucrezia gasped for breath as he set her down.

He let her go for a moment and cupped his palms together. 'Yes. They are not like other bells because they float between sea and sky. When they ring it is like a clap of joy leaping across the water to the whole world.' He brought his palms together, and the birds flew up.

'Like snow upside-down,' said Lucrezia delightedly, watching them.

They sat under the pergola, heads touching, fingers laced together. 'One day I shall come to Venice,' she murmured after a while, 'and I shall require a kiss for every one of your bells that I hear.'

'Sweetheart,' asked Bembo softly, 'have you any idea how many bells there are in Venice? They are as thick as the leaves on these trees.' He put his lips to her hair. 'I shall have every one of them ring every quarter of every hour. And every night – ' he turned her face gently towards his, ' – shall be Easter night, when the bells ring without ceasing – '

During the next few days, Bembo rode every afternoon to Medelana. They sought as often as they could to meet in the garden, but if it were not wise they were content to be patient. Apart from her visit to the Pope in September, Lucrezia planned to stay in the country until the middle of November. They had three months to pass in the seclusion of Medelana. Bembo thought occasionally of the desperate, avid nature of his meetings with Maria Savorgnan and was amazed that love could have a core of tranquillity.

'It must be,' he said to Lucrezia, 'because of your extreme conformity.' The quaint, prim little phrase that she had used in her letter to him always amused him, although he could never think of a better one. '*Our* extreme conformity,' said Lucrezia.

On days when Lucrezia had no other company, Bembo remained to sup at Medelana. After supper, her household played cards. Lucrezia would allow no money to be staked, so they played for little marzipan cakes made specially for the purpose by Lucrezia's pastrycook. Lucrezia would watch the game for a few minutes, then go out on to the balcony where Bembo would be waiting for her. There they would stand talking in the moonlight, their fingers touching under the balustrade.

One night the moon was hidden by clouds. Bembo stood looking up at the dark sky. 'I don't often wish I were back in Venice,' he said, 'but tonight I do.'

'Why?' asked Lucrezia.

'Because on a night like this, I should take you out on to the lagoon in a gondola. All gondolas are alike, and on the water under a black sky there is no more safe and private meeting-place. The only light you would see would be the little flame of the lantern swinging at our prow. Well,' he laughed softly, 'you might see other little lanterns bobbing here and there.'

'And there we should hear your bells?'

Bembo glanced at the thickening clouds and drew Lucrezia behind a shutter. 'Oh, you can hear them anywhere if you try.' He lifted his head and listened to the perfect silence of the garden beneath them.

'Deafening,' he said, reaching for her.

II

On another warm August night, Pope Alessandro and his son, Cesare Borgia, supped at a villa outside Rome. Next day they were both ill. A week later the Pope was dead.

Ippolito brought the news to Ferrara. The duke, when he heard it, shouted with joy and embraced his son as though Ippolito himself had administered the poison which was assumed to be the cause of Alessandro's death.

'And Cesare?' he asked, pulling off his spectacles to wipe his eyes.

'The Roman mob would have killed him if he hadn't escaped in time to the Castel Sant'Angelo. He won't get out alive unless he's clever, and he's still too ill to move.'

The duke rubbed his hands together. 'So the Borgia are finished, eh? Finished. No more threats on our borders from Cesare – '

'And Lucrezia can be divorced,' said Ippolito. 'She's no use to us any more.'

For once father and son were in accord. The duke nodded delightedly. 'We'll make a French marriage for Alfonso, and with the French we can contain Venice.'

'There will, of course, be problems about a divorce,' said Ippolito. 'We can't use either of the usual excuses, consanguinity or non-consummation.'

'Then we can sue to have the annulment of Lucrezia's first marriage rescinded on the grounds that it was awarded on false evidence, as everyone knows it was,' said the duke. 'Then the marriage to Alfonso will be nullified.'

'Yes, but so will her second marriage to Bisceglie. Then the child of the union would be illegitimate and unable to inherit his father's property. He's a kinsman of the King of Spain, and we can't afford a dispute with Spain.'

'Well,' said the duke impatiently, 'there'll be a way.' He pointed a finger at Ippolito. 'I'll tell you, Ippolito, when you get back to Rome you are to lobby for Cardinal della Rovere as the next Pope.'

'A soldier – ' said Ippolito with approval.

'And a Genoese, who hates the Venetians. If he thinks we can bring in the French here in place of them, he'll find a means to the divorce.'

Ippolito drew on his gloves. 'It would help, wouldn't it, if we could find some error in Lucrezia? An error of treachery. Complicity with Cesare, or a lover perhaps.'

The duke peered at his son. 'Ippolito, I want no false evidence.'

Ippolito's eyes widened. 'False evidence? No, nor do I,' he said, picking up his riding-cloak.

'Where are you going?'

'To Medelana, of course.'

The duke waved this aside. 'There's no reason for that. I'll send a messenger later, Ippolito. You stay here with me.'

'Lucrezia surely has a right to courtesy,' declared Ippolito. He did not add that he was excited by the opportunity to pounce unexpectedly on Medelana at night.

The duke grunted. 'Well, well, I suppose so,' he admitted. 'If you must go, you can convey my command that there shall be no public expression of grief in Ferrara for the Pope's death. No one, not even the household at Medelana, is to wear mourning.'

Even Ippolito was startled by this. 'I am not behaving spitefully for the sake of it,' snapped the duke. 'The Pope's daughter, of course, may do as she likes, but I want it understood in Italy that we repudiate completely the Borgia connection.'

Ippolito shrugged his shoulders. As he reached the door, he paused. 'What happened, by the way, to your Venetian? I see his house is closed.'

'If you refer,' said the duke, 'to Messer Bembo, kindly use his name in my presence. He is recovering at Ostellato.'

'Yes,' murmured Ippolito, 'of course.'

He rode hard to Medelana, outdistancing his escort. Only his captain, Alessandro Pio, kept pace with him. Pio had worked for many years in Ippolito's service, and he recognised the signs of elation which often preceded a mood of violence. He heard Ippolito laughing to himself, and once he called out, 'Did you know, Alessandro, that we have an old law in Ferrara that condemns adulterous wives to the stake?'

'A very old law that is never observed,' said Pio pleasantly. 'It would be hard on us bachelors if it were, eh, my lord?'

Ippolito appeared not to hear him. 'If the husband agrees to take back the wife, then her life is spared. But why should Alfonso do that?'

They arrived at Medelana before dawn. Ippolito refused to wait for the servants to dress and announce him, but hurried ahead to Lucrezia's door and pushed it open.

Lucrezia awoke with a scream. She was alone. One of her ladies was within sight in an adjoining room. Ippolito stared at his brother's wife. Pio, who had reached his side, saw thwarted rage beginning to work in his face. He thrust himself in front of Ippolito. 'Your highness's forgiveness, but the Cardinal has very urgent news for you. May I beg you to receive us as soon as possible?'

He drew Ippolito away from the door. 'Eminence,' he said, 'you must prepare yourself to comfort the distress of the ladies here. They will need you.' Ippolito turned to him, and Pio saw his savagery giving way to a relish for the scene to come.

When Lucrezia appeared, pale and frightened, Ippolito had recovered sufficiently to receive her with a grave air of composure, He broke the news of Alessandro's death with every mark of sympathy and concern for her. She refused at first to believe it, then lay sobbing uncontrollably in Angela's arms. For the benefit of Lucrezia's ladies, Ippolito played the kindly brother and attempted to comfort her himself, but when he put out his hands to touch her she screamed.

Ippolito left her and summoned her household to hear the duke's decree against mourning. Giulio's mouth fell open. 'That's not right, and it's cruel,' he cried.

Ippolito chose not to explain the duke's reason. 'It's cruel,' said Giulio again.

'Eminence,' said Tebaldeo, 'few of us here feel regret for the Pope's death, but for Madonna Lucrezia's sake we would think it only fitting to wear mourning.'

Ippolito ignored him. 'Giulio, those who disobey the duke's orders will be punished. I myself have business in Rome now, but I shall leave one of my officers here to see that his wishes are carried out.' He glanced at Alessandro Pio. 'He will also oversee the management of the household.'

'Madonna Lucrezia is under my protection,' protested Giulio. 'I don't want your man here.'

'He nevertheless stays. You have no idea, Giulio, of what may need to be done in a house of bereavement.'

'That's not why you want him here – ' Giulio shouted.

'Go away, Giulio,' interrupted Ippolito shrilly. He snapped his fingers for Tebaldeo. 'I want to see Madonna Angela Borgia.'

Angela Borgia sent word that she was walking on the terrace. If the Cardinal wished to speak to her, he must go to her there.

Ippolito went out on to the terrace. Angela was waiting for him, wearing a black dress.

'Are you not aware, madonna,' he said pleasantly, 'that the duke has forbidden mourning?'

'I often wear black,' said Angela. She put her hands on her hips. 'Am I expected to strip myself naked to show my obedience?'

Ippolito's gaze flickered over her body, lean and quick like a boy's. He looked into her black eyes. 'Besides,' she added, 'you forget I am not one of your Ferrarese.'

'No, you are not. What *are* you now? Yesterday you were the niece of the Pope, the most powerful man in the world. You were the future Duchess of Urbino. You know, of course, that the Duke of Urbino will repudiate the betrothal now that your uncle is dead? He won't let his heir marry the niece of a discredited priest. Because that is now what you are. Nothing.'

Angela, without answering, tried to push her way past Ippolito. He caught her in his arms. 'Don't run away, my sweet. I'm only trying to make you understand that you will have to learn to be grateful now for anything that is offered to you.' He gripped her more tightly. 'But I'll be kind to you. All you have to do is tell me what happens in this house – '

Angela called out in fright, 'Giulio, Giulio!'

Ippolito took his hands away from her and pushed her against the wall of the villa. 'Giulio,' he said angrily, 'why does it always have to be Giulio with you?'

His face, with its round, pale eyes, was thrust close to hers. Angela blurted out stupidly, 'He has beautiful eyes.'

Ippolito laughed. 'Is that all?' He stroked her arm. 'You need more than eyes.' He pressed himself against her. 'Let me show you – '

Alessandro Pio had heard Angela's cry for Giulio and came out on to the terrace. When he saw Ippolito he stopped. Ippolito glanced at him over his shoulder and Angela was able to pull herself free. She ran along the terrace out of Ippolito's reach. Then she turned to face him. 'I would rather,' she shouted, 'have Giulio's little finger than your whole body!'

Ippolito, as he mounted his horse to leave Medelana, was brooding and silent. Giulio was waiting to wish him a safe journey. He looked up at his brother with the dark, beautiful eyes that Angela admired. With sudden savagery, Ippolito raised his riding whip to strike Giulio's face. Giulio jerked back his head, caught the blow on his shoulder and stumbled back against Alessandro Pio.

III

Bembo learned of the Pope's death from a hasty note sent by Angela Borgia. The event as such was of little interest to him, but he was concerned for Lucrezia and the grief she would be suffering. For discretion's sake he allowed two anxious days to pass, and then, dressing himself in the robe of a Venetian patrician, he rode to Medelana on the excuse of presenting his formal condolences.

Tebaldeo tried to dissuade him from seeing Lucrezia. It would be a waste of Messer Bembo's time, he explained. Her highness had shut herself up without light and food, she had hardly spoken since the Cardinal's visit and she would listen to none of those who tried to console her.

Bembo, feeling cold despite the heat, begged Tebaldeo to admit him. Tebaldeo sighed, led him to Lucrezia's apartments and left him alone in the doorway.

Bembo was unprepared for the extreme form of Spanish

mourning which he found before him. In place of the familiar room with its balcony, he was in a dark cell. The walls and furniture were draped in black velvet. Black hangings covered the windows, blocking out the air and the daylight. The only illumination came from candles burning before a make-shift altar.

Bembo took a step forward, unable to see clearly. Then as his eyes became accustomed to the darkness, he realised that he had almost stumbled over Lucrezia. She lay on the floor, her head towards the altar, her fingers clutching the black coverings on the floor. She was sobbing.

Bembo was appalled by her grief. He wanted to lift her in his arms and carry her into the air and light. He bent over her, but a rustle of cloth made him glance up and he saw Angela Borgia beside him, making a warning movement with her hand. He became aware then that a man, who must have followed him to Lucrezia's apartments, was waiting in the doorway behind him.

Bembo stood watching Lucrezia helplessly, suffering anguish himself at having to see her suffer alone, and be unable to comfort her. She still lay with her face hidden from him. He struggled to think of a few words of conventional condolence, but his brain and his tongue seemed paralysed. He laid his hand on his heart, bowed and turned miserably away from her.

In the doorway, the man inclined his head courteously and stood aside for Bembo to pass. Bembo thought he recognised one of Ippolito's men.

He hurried out of the villa, avoiding people. In a quiet corner behind the stables, he laid his head against the bricks and let the tears come into his own eyes. She didn't even know that he had been beside her. He loved her with his life, and he was having to accept the truth that whenever she had most need of him he would not be able to help her.

He looked round quickly, hearing a step on the path. Tebaldeo had sought him out to bid him goodbye.

'Are you unwell, Messer Bembo?' asked Tebaldeo, seeing his face. 'A recurrence of your fever, perhaps – '

'No, no.' Bembo laughed awkwardly, and brushed a hand across his forehead. 'I find the heat somewhat trying.'

'Ah, yes.' Tebaldeo noted Bembo's heavy black robe and the band of white linen fastened tightly round his throat. He lowered his voice. 'How did you find her highness?'

Bembo said with an effort, 'Oh, you were right. She appeared to be in some distress and so I withdrew without offering my consolations. Perhaps you would be good enough to do so for me when a suitable moment arrives.' He hesitated. 'Messer Tebaldeo, you will not forget?'

'No, of course not, Messer Bembo.'

They walked to the entrance to the stables. 'I thought,' said Bembo diffidently, 'that I saw one of Cardinal Ippolito's men inside the villa.'

Tebaldeo frowned. 'Yes, that would have been Messer Alessandro Pio. He has been left here to – to look after matters.'

'For how long?' asked Bembo sharply.

Tebaldeo shook his head. 'I don't know. I suppose while her highness is in mourning. Six weeks.'

'Six weeks,' said Bembo, closing his eyes.

'Are you sure you're well enough to ride?' said Tebaldeo.

Bembo nodded, grasped his hand, and set out for Ostellato. He rode slowly and listlessly, and when he arrived found Strozzi waiting for him.

Strozzi's mood was hard and angry. 'You've come from Medelana?'

Bembo sighed. 'Yes.'

'Did you know one of Ippolito's men was there?'

'Yes, I saw him. Does it matter? I didn't even speak to Lucrezia. Ercole, her grief is terrible.'

'So is mine,' said Strozzi grimly.

Bembo suddenly understood what the Pope's death had done to Strozzi's ambitions for a place in Rome. He went up to him. 'Ercole, I'm sorry,' he said, hardly knowing what to say. 'Does this have to mean the end of your hopes? Perhaps under another Pope – '

'There is unlikely to be another Pope with Alessandro's measure of greed and complacency,' interrupted Strozzi. 'It is even less likely that he will have a daughter whom I shall be in a position to use – a daughter, incidentally, whose stupid exhibition of grief must be stopped.'

'Ercole!' cried Bembo. Strozzi shot him a glance, unmoved, and for the first time Bembo recognised the ruthlessness that made Strozzi hated in some parts of Ferrara.

'You won't know, of course,' he said to Bembo, 'that there is talk in Ferrara of divorcing Lucrezia.'

Bembo stared at him and his eyes became brilliant with excitement. He saw Lucrezia sewing with her gold thread on the balcony of the Ca' Bembo, or living with him among the mountains at Asolo.

'I don't want this divorce,' said Strozzi. 'My future will have to lie now in Ferrara, not Rome, and when Alfonso is duke my only hope of influence is through his wife. A Frenchwoman will not be as malleable as Lucrezia.' He looked at Bembo and, reading his thoughts, added more gently, 'I wouldn't oppose a divorce if it weren't against Lucrezia's interests, too – and yours.'

'How can it be against our interests?' murmured Bembo, his mind dazed.

'Pietro, think: if Lucrezia is divorced, she will be returned with her dowry to her family, which now means Cesare. Do you know what has been happening in Rome? They stripped the Pope's body and dragged it naked over the floors of the Vatican before they stuffed it into a coffin too small for it. They haven't taken Cesare yet, but they're slaughtering his men in the streets and burning their houses. That's how the Borgia are hated. Do you want to send Lucrezia back to that?

'Of course, Cesare might escape and his army might hold the Romagna and Urbino for him. Then he'll want allies, and he'll buy them with Lucrezia and her dowry. God knows what sort of man she might find herself married to. Pietro, once she ceases to be a Duchess of Ferrara, she will be exposed to all kinds of danger. And you will not be able to protect her. Can you understand, the divorce must be dropped.' Strozzi's voice had again become abrupt. 'You can help, Pietro, by persuading her not to display her grief so publicly.'

'Why,' cried Bembo, 'is it so shameful for Lucrezia to show grief for her father?'

'It is not shameful, but ill-advised. Ippolito, for one, is trying to make sure it is misunderstood.'

Bembo shook his head. 'Misunderstood? No.'

'Oh, yes, Pietro. You and I, we know that her sorrow is real, but very few people can understand how anyone, even a daughter, could care for that disgusting old man. Ippolito is suggesting instead that she is prostrate with fright at Medelana because neither the Pope nor Cesare can save her any longer from the consequences of her guilty behaviour. People are beginning to remember the old stories of her depravity in Rome, and she's even been accused of conniving in the death of young Bisceglie.'

'No one would believe that,' said Bembo.

'You would have believed it a year ago.'

Bembo looked down at his hands. 'Yes, yes, I would,' he agreed miserably after a moment.

'Pietro, members of the court, the council, and foreign ambassadors will all go to Medelana to offer condolences. If they find Lucrezia in the state described by Ippolito, they will be inclined to accept what he says and regard her as unfit to be Alfonso's wife. If, on the other hand, they are met by a woman who, though bereaved, is calm, confident of her position, concerned with affairs in Ferrara rather than in Rome, then Ippolito will be discredited and it will be difficult for him to gain support for the divorce. To force such a woman into a contrived repudiation would create a scandal among foreign courts, and no ruler would marry a daughter or sister into such a family.'

'Yes,' said Bembo slowly, 'yes, I suppose so. But what can I do about it? I daren't see her again, I certainly can't speak to her.'

'No, but you can write to her. I'll get a letter to her through Giulio. Write to her, and try to make her understand, Pietro, but be very careful.'

Bembo climbed the stairs to his room and leaned against the window. He knew that what Strozzi said had to be true, yet he was remembering how for one exultant moment he had believed in the possibility of a life shared with Lucrezia. It had been a brief moment only, yet in its passing he felt an intolerable sense of loss. He stared at the strip of luminous sky above the rim of the marshes. Beyond lay the lagoon. He felt adrift on a waste no less desolate and formless. The days at Medelana were over before they had barely begun. Now he had to live through six weeks before he could hope to see Lucrezia again, six weeks that had to be endured without knowing what might happen when they were over.

It was past midnight when he began to write. 'Yesterday I came to your highness – partly to express to you the great sorrow I feel at your loss, and partly to offer you what comfort I could for I had heard that you were distressed beyond measure. But I was able to do neither the one, nor the other. As soon as I saw you lying in the darkness in your black dress, weeping and inconsolable, I was so overwhelmed that I stood there for some time without being able to say anything. Seeing you like that, I was so confused that I was more in need of comfort than able to give it, and as you saw, or might have seen, I left dumb and stammering . . .

'Remembering as you do my loyalty and devotion to you, you will understand how great is my pain for yours . . . As to consolation, I know nothing to say to you: you have suffered so much already that you have learned how to bear suffering bravely. Besides which, you must not let anyone think you mourn less for your father's death than for the state of your fortunes.' Bembo stared at what he had written. Lucrezia read and re-read every word of his letters. He hoped it was enough.

When the letter was finished, he inscribed it to 'Her Illustrious Highness, the Duchess of Ferrara, at Medelana'. Then he took off his agate ring carved with the chevron and three roses of his family, and impressed it into the hot wax of the seal.

IV

Alfonso broke his journey along the northern coasts of Italy to visit Medelana and offer his wife his dutiful, if belated, sympathy.

He then rode on to pay his respects to his father in Ferrara. He found him with Ippolito and Tito Strozzi, apparently involved in a discussion on some matter of policy. What surprised Alfonso was the affability which Ippolito was displaying towards the duke.

'Shouldn't you be in Rome?' Alfonso asked him coldly.

'Brother, I shall be,' said Ippolito, 'just as soon as we have settled the business at issue.' He spoke with a gaiety that grated on Alfonso's nerves.

Alfonso turned to his father. 'I have just come from Medelana –'

'Ah,' cried Ippolito, 'the very business itself. You need not have wasted your time. You will soon be rid of Lucrezia.'

Alfonso folded his arms and looked at Ippolito. 'Rid of Lucrezia?' he enquired slowly.

'A divorce,' said Tito Strozzi. 'His eminence has been working on possible grounds, as well as amassing information on suitable royal brides from France.'

Alfonso breathed heavily. 'Without consulting me?'

'You were not here,' said the duke testily. 'I didn't know where you were, and the matter has a certain urgency. We learned this morning that the King of France secretly undertakes to support us if we apply to the new Pope for a dissolution of your marriage.'

'I never wanted the Borgia marriage – ' Alfonso began.

'True,' nodded the duke, 'but at the time it was a necessity. You shall be released from it as soon as possible.'

'I never wanted the Borgia marriage,' repeated Alfonso loudly, 'but Madonna Lucrezia is now my wife and I will not divorce her.'

Tito Strozzi quietly raised an eyebrow and waited for the storm to break.

'Why?' roared the duke.

'Because he's against a French alliance,' cried Ippolito, 'and he's against it because we want it.'

Alfonso, unmoved by his brother's outburst, said, 'I've always been opposed to inviting more foreign influence into Italy. But that isn't my only reason.'

'Your highness is perhaps prudently thinking of the dowry,' murmured Tito. 'France is not likely to offer us a dowry as large as the Borgia one, which – ' he glanced at the duke, ' – we shall have to relinquish, of course, in the event of a divorce.'

Alfonso grunted in agreement. He had other reasons, too, which he did not propose to mention. He had married twice for the sake of Ferrara, and he was determined that if he ever took a third bride it was going to be his mistress, Laura. His first wife, Anna Sforza, had humiliated him by preferring to sleep with a Negress, and he didn't want to risk another Anna. As things stood, he was content enough with Lucrezia. She was compliant, and had shown herself capable of child-bearing. She behaved to him with deference in public, and never interfered in matters of state as his sister, Isabella, did in Mantua. She was also indifferent to the existence of his mistress and the nights he spent with her.

The duke was biting his lip and muttering, 'What you say about the dowry, Tito, is right, yes, yes.'

Ippolito shouted, 'Are a few hundred ducats more important than ridding Ferrara of the Borgia?'

'Not a few hundred, but several thousand,' interrupted Tito.

Ippolito glared at him. 'Do you want a wife,' he went on, addressing his brother, 'who acknowledges her guilt in conspiring against us by shutting herself up in the darkness – ?'

Alfonso shouted back, 'What guilt? What darkness? What are you talking about, Ippolito? Do you forget I've just come back from Medelana? I was there for two hours. No one was shut up in any darkness. Madonna Lucrezia wore mourning and no company were present, as is fitting. But she was dining in public with her household. We spoke of my journey. Well, Ippolito?'

'You are easily deceived,' sneered Ippolito.

'Not when you have a hand in things,' said Alfonso, crossing the room after his brother. 'The woman is harmless. What do you want?'

Ippolito retreated a step. 'They say her father made a pact with the devil,' he spat out. 'When he died his body turned black and swollen, and that's proof of it. And you think his daughter is harmless?'

'Oh God,' said Alfonso in disgust. 'Stop lying, Ippolito.'

Before Ippolito could speak again, Tito Strozzi said blandly, 'I must confess that I begin to see much wisdom in Don Alfonso's attitude. It would appear from what he says – and we have no choice but to believe him – that the accounts of Madonna Lucrezia's disturbing behaviour are not based in fact.' He bowed his head to Alfonso. 'We must be grateful to him for his timely arrival, which may well have saved us from an act that would gravely discredit Ferrara. Certainly Madonna Lucrezia's position is no longer of any political value to us, but this is not without its advantages. No one can exert pressure on us through her – '

'Be quiet,' said the duke to Ippolito, who was trying to interrupt.

'Thank you, my lord. I was about to add that if we still wish to arrange a French marriage, there is always Don Giulio.'

Long after Ippolito had galloped away to the hunt, and Alfonso had hurried to see his mistress before resuming his broken journey, Tito Strozzi and the duke went on talking.

Within a week, all talk of a divorce had been dropped in Ferrara. Before a second week was out, the duke, who had never felt any personal animosity towards Lucrezia, was corresponding courteously with Medelana, although he was never able to bring himself to express any regrets for Pope Alessandro's death.

By the beginning of Lucrezia's fourth week of mourning, her future as the next ruling duchess was acknowledged throughout Ferrara. Bembo at Ostellato heard the news with a relief that was not unmixed with despair.

V

Senator Bembo had meanwhile arrived in Venice at the end of his term of office as Governor of Verona. He was disappointed that

Pietro had not returned from Ferrara to greet him, and wrote to him suggesting that it was now time to resume his affairs in Venice.

Bembo, dragging out the time at Ostellato, delayed answering day after day. A second letter, more commanding in tone, arrived. The Senator had secured Bembo's nomination for the post of ambassador to France. The elections would fall in November, and he was required in Venice as soon as possible to prepare for them.

Forced into activity, Bembo sent a cry of help to Carlo. He would never, never, he wrote, stand for office. He must stay in Ferrara. He had been ill, and Carlo must remind their father of this. He would come home to Venice soon, but he couldn't promise when it would be. Carlo was disturbed by the unusual style of his brother's letter, but to his father he merely urged the imprudence of persuading Pietro to travel before he was strong again.

Thanks to Carlo, the end of September was reached without further demands from the Ca' Bembo. Then it was at last October, and Lucrezia's period of mourning was over. The nobility of Ferrara flocked to Medelana to welcome the duchess back to public life and to ensure her good will in the future.

Twenty minutes' ride away, Bembo waited nervously at Ostellato, making himself face the thought that until then he had pushed to the back of his mind. Lucrezia had had to endure a great deal alone in the past few weeks. It was not unlikely that she might be changed by it. What if she had travelled too far ever to return to their garden with its canopied walks and the white birds?

Then a note came, written in Tebaldeo's hand. The duchess had a pair of crystals that she would like to have re-set. She would welcome Messer Bembo's advice on jewellers in Venice.

VI

Bembo locked the garden door behind him. Lucrezia was waiting, walking up and down on the paths. The first cool wind of autumn was in the air, stirring the leaves at her feet and blowing her black gauze veil above her head.

She turned and held out her hands. 'Pietro!' At the expression in her eyes, Bembo laughed and wondered why he had been afraid.

'What is it?' she said, as his arms went round her.

Bembo kissed her mouth, her face and her hair. 'Oh, there were times,' he whispered, 'when I thought you might never be waiting for me in this garden again.'

Lucrezia lifted her head. 'And I used to think you might have gone back to Venice.'

Bembo smiled. 'Our trouble is that we don't understand – ' he kissed her again, ' – our own extreme conformity.'

'We are just not used to it yet,' said Lucrezia, laughing back. 'Yet here we are – '

'And you are safe, I thank God.'

Lucrezia sighed and laid her head against him. 'Yes, safe. You see, I realised what you were telling me to do in your letter.'

'Oh Lucrezia, it wasn't what I wanted to tell you.'

'No, no, I understood that. This is difficult for us, but anything else could be much worse. Yet it ought to be so simple. Ferrara no longer has any use for me, and I should be glad to leave Ferrara. What harm could we do, being together? But it isn't so simple to the rest of the world – '

' – to the strangers, no,' said Bembo.

With their arms linked, they began to walk towards the pergola. 'I should have been born in Venice,' said Lucrezia.

Bembo touched her black veil. 'You look like a Venetian in this. And many of our women are fair, like you. But you are not,' he added sadly, 'a Venetian. If you were you would belong to me as you ought.'

'In your gondola with its little lamp?'

'In my gondola, in my bed – ' Bembo stopped. 'Lucrezia, I shouldn't – '

Lucrezia stood still and faced Bembo. 'Why not? Pietro. If I look so much like a Venetian, can't you pretend that I am one?'

Bembo, mouth parted, stared at her. 'Lucrezia?'

Lucrezia grasped his wrists and said simply, 'Pietro, I love you. Surely, you can understand. I'm answering your question.'

Bembo continued to stare at her, but his eyes were growing brilliant. When he said nothing, she said, 'I mean the question that you asked me in a letter once – '

'When the weather was hot at Ostellato.' Bembo had suddenly found his voice. 'Yes. Yes, I know the one.' He bent his head and kissed her hand. 'My dear love.'

After a while, he said, 'But the risk – '

'Yes, there is a risk,' said Lucrezia, 'but it could never be less than it is here.'

'Where is Alessandro Pio?'

'I dismissed him,' said Lucrezia briskly, 'and sent him to Rome after his master.'

Bembo smiled at the new strength in her manner, but then he shook his head. 'Even so, it would be dangerous.'

'Pietro,' said Lucrezia, 'when we came here in August, we thought the days here would never end. We had so much time that we could afford to be careful. Then suddenly my father died, and I realised how uncertain life really is. Overnight everything can change. We could be together today, and tomorrow you could find I had been taken away from you. The risk can't be compared with our loss if that should happen.'

Bembo touched her face gently. 'I think you really must be a Venetian. That is a good Venetian argument. If I had only myself to think of in this, I would say that you are right, I would agree. But, my darling, are you sure?'

Lucrezia nodded. 'Yes, I am.' She put her arm round his neck. 'Pietro, please.'

Bembo laughed softly. 'Dear goose, my love, I don't need persuading.'

He left her then and rode back to Ostellato with her promise to send for him as soon as she could make it possible. He wrote next morning to FF, longing to share his excitement with her. 'There could be nothing more precious to me than the words I heard you say yesterday'. He added, teasing her, 'In duty to conformity, I think perhaps you might have said them to me earlier . . . I could write of so many things that I didn't know how to tell you yesterday, but if you are not able to understand me from the way I behave, or to read the truth in my eyes and face, then how can I expect to explain myself to you on paper. I really think the flames in which FF has encircled me must be the strongest and clearest ever felt in the heart of anyone who loved . . . '

The letter was a long one, as were most of his letters to FF, and it suddenly occurred to Bembo that if Lucrezia had kept them all they must make a dangerously thick bundle. 'I beg you to burn all my letters,' he advised her. 'Keep this one as a token, if you must. Perhaps in several years' time you might happen to read it again.'

He added the date, the fifth of October, 1503, and addressed the cover to Angela Borgia. Lico carried it to Medelana, and returned with an invitation from Madonna Angela to sup at the villa next day.

VII

Lucrezia led the way in to supper with her hand resting on Giulio's arm. As Bembo followed with her other guests, Angela Borgia brushed against him.

'Are you a patient man?' she whispered.

'I would say so, yes. Why do you ask?'

Angela ignored his question. Waving her fan in front of her face, she said, 'If you are, find an excuse to leave after supper and wait near the stables.'

Before Bembo could answer, she darted away, her black eyes laughing at him over the edge of the fan.

At the table, Bembo found himself seated at some distance from Lucrezia. Apart from his formal greeting to her on arrival, they had not spoken to each other. As they ate, they avoided exchanging glances and if their eyes met by chance looked away hastily. To Bembo, hardly able to swallow his food, the procession of dishes seemed interminable, and he noticed that Lucrezia played with the chains round her neck more often than she touched her fork.

Lucrezia rose at last. The company was a large one and she had arranged music for dancing. Shortly after the dancing had begun, Bembo made his way to Lucrezia's chair and begged her permission to leave because he was expecting urgent letters from Venice. Lucrezia, clutching at her chains again, nodded and trusted that the news from Venice would be pleasing to him.

Bembo left the villa and wandered quietly round the stables, avoiding the grooms. He felt apprehensive and a little foolish. After a few moments, Angela, muffled in a hooded cloak, came skimming through the shadows to meet him. Without offering him any greeting or explanation, she instructed him to put up the hood of his own cloak and follow her without speaking.

She led him by a devious route to one of the servants' entrances to the villa. As she pushed open the door, she turned her face to his. 'Kiss me,' she said.

Bembo stammered. 'Madonna – '

Angela sighed impatiently. 'Then pretend to kiss me.' She leaned towards him and Bembo obediently placed his cheek next to hers. 'I don't think anyone has been watching us,' she told him crossly, 'but if they have, and they recognise us under these hoods, they will think you are coming to me, not my cousin.'

Inside the door on a stone ledge a candle had been left burning. Angela picked it up and climbed the narrow stairway ahead of them. On a small landing, where a second stair met their own, she stopped. 'Down there are my cousin's rooms.' They climbed another flight. 'These are mine.'

They crossed a small servant's room and entered Angela's bedroom. She lit the candles which stood by the bed. It was spread with Lucrezia's gold-lace linen.

'This is where you will need your patience,' Angela announced. 'My cousin will come as soon as she can, but she must watch the dancing first. Will you mind staying here alone?'

'No, of course not.' Bembo regarded her gently. 'Madonna, how can we thank you?'

Angela tossed her hair. 'Lucrezia is going to give me a gold dress, like hers.' She glanced at the bed and then laughed. 'I wish Ippolito could know about this. His face would turn purple, like the colour of raspberries in milk.'

She was barely seventeen. Bembo was not sure whether she was being flippant or serious, and the uncertainty disturbed him.

When she had gone, he sat by her window. It overlooked a small courtyard with a brick well, and was lit by the fires burning in the kitchens. After a while, he felt in the pocket of his cloak for one of the books which he always carried. He opened it to read, but his excitement and uneasiness made it impossible for him to concentrate on the printed words. After several fruitless attempts, he laid aside the book and walked up and down the room, or stared into the courtyard.

He was roused at last by the whisper of women's voices. Then the door opened, and Lucrezia stood on the threshold, her hair hanging loose on her shoulders. They were both so shaken by relief and joy that they could only cling to each other breathlessly, without speaking.

Then Bembo held Lucrezia away from him. 'What if someone finds your room empty?'

'Angela has said she feels unwell. It is natural that I should sit with her. If anyone comes up the stairs, she will hear.'

They lay together naked between Lucrezia's gold-laced sheets. Once or twice during those first hours which they shared as lovers, Bembo was fleetingly aware of the rattle of well-chains in the courtyard below. Years afterwards, a similar sound could flood his mind with memories of that night.

Angela roused them before the first servants were stirring. A little later, when she came to fetch Bembo, she found them sitting side by side on the bed, fastening the laces of Bembo's sleeves. Their fingers were barely moving. When their eyes met, they smiled slowly at each other and the laces were lost as they put their faces together to kiss.

Angela threw Bembo's cloak across the bed. 'It's late,' she said impatiently.

They kissed for the last time a dozen times as they crossed the room. Lucrezia followed Bembo to the head of the stairs, and their fingers touched for as long as it was possible as he descended. Then he raised his hood and walked beside Angela into the dark night.

They fetched his horse and led it over the grass to muffle the sound of its hooves. Angela let him out of a small gate in a part of the grounds that he had never seen before. As he mounted his horse outside, she said, 'Don't ride straight for Ostellato. Take the road for Ferrara and turn back across the fields. Someone could be watching.'

Bembo bent down. 'Madonna Angela, you are my guardian angel. I wouldn't dare to disobey you.'

VIII

Two nights later, Bembo returned to Medelana. He arrived in the dark and let himself through the gate that Angela had shown him. He tethered his horse, crossed the grounds and climbed the stair to Angela's room. Angela met him outside her door. She smiled her sly smile and wished him good-night.

Lucrezia was waiting for him, sitting by the window overlooking the well. The firelight and the candlelight glowed on her face. Bembo experienced the wonder of a love that was constantly renewing itself. He took her hands. 'I've loved you since that first day at Ostellato and yet, looking at you now, I feel as though I've been struck with love for the first time. Is that a special paradox for a hermit?'

'Not a hermit,' said Lucrezia.

An hour or so before dawn, Bembo was woken from a brief sleep by the sound of Angela moving about in the adjoining room. Lucrezia was curled beside him, sleeping with her head against his shoulder. As he touched her hair, she stirred, opened her eyes and put an arm across him. Bembo settled himself to hold her more comfortably. 'I thought,' he whispered, 'that we could never be as happy again as we were last August.' He held her more tightly. 'Yet now – '

After a moment he added, 'I like your word.'

'Word?' said Lucrezia drowsily.

'Conformity,' He sighed. 'Oh, my love.'

'You used to laugh at it.'

Bembo smiled and bent over her again. 'Did I?'

Later that morning at Ostellato, Bembo was roused by the rattle of his bed curtains along their rod. He opened his eyes and saw Strozzi looking down at him.

'So there you are,' said Strozzi unnecessarily. 'I want to talk to you.'

From the brilliance of the light striking his eyes, Bembo realised that it must be noon. He turned over on his face. 'Ercole, later?' he suggested. He closed his eyes again.

'Pietro,' said Strozzi sharply, 'you have to go back to Venice.'

Bembo smiled into his pillow. 'Not Venice,' he murmured, 'not now.'

Strozzi shook him. 'Listen to me, Pietro. Alfonso is coming to Ostellato.'

Bembo sat up with a cry and grabbed Strozzi's arm. 'Lucrezia?'

Strozzi looked at him coldly. As the sleep cleared from his brain, Bembo realised that he had betrayed himself as Strozzi probably intended that he should.

'Lucrezia? Why are you enquiring about Lucrezia?' demanded

Strozzi. 'Isn't she still at Medelana? Surely you would know that better than I do. You were at Medelana until the early hours of this morning. Lico tells me you were playing cards with Giulio and his friends. I had always understood that you disliked cards, but if you weren't playing cards what else could have kept you there?'

Bembo got out of bed and put on his robe. He faced Strozzi. 'Very well, Ercole,' he said. 'I admit that I was not playing cards with Giulio last night.' He spread out his hands. 'Do you want me to say anything else?'

Strozzi sat down on the edge of the bed. 'Christ,' he said. 'Christ!' His breathing was uneven. 'I knew it was true, and yet I couldn't believe it. I couldn't believe either of you could be so stupid.' He struck the floor with his crutch. 'What the hell were you trying to do? Put a son on the throne of Ferrara? Alfonso won't enjoy that bit of Venetian influence.'

Bembo's anger flared as high as Strozzi's. 'Isn't this what you wanted? Isn't this why you brought me to Ferrara?'

'Not for this, no!' shouted Strozzi.

They were both suddenly aware of the ugliness of the quarrel, and made an effort at control.

'It is true,' said Strozzi, labouring for words, 'that I wanted you to meet – '

'For your advantage,' Bembo interrupted.

'For the advantage of yourself and Lucrezia as well. You were both lonely and dispirited. I saw qualities in both of you that could be matched. It was to be expected that if you did respond to each other's company, there would grow up between you – ' he waved a hand in the air, ' – a certain something. Enough to give a little vivacity to your meetings.'

It surprised Bembo that with so much perception Strozzi should lack a little more. 'Ercole,' he said, 'I can't dole out a specified measure of affection like cheese.'

'But you have no choice,' Strozzi argued. 'You know the manners of courts. You understand as well as anyone how to exploit the courtier's code of devotion, and you know its limitations. You've engaged in the exercise often enough with Isabella of Mantua and the ladies of Urbino.'

'And you thought this was the same?' asked Bembo bitterly.

'You had no right,' snapped Strozzi, growing angry again, 'to regard it as anything different.' He sat on the bed, pale with shock, disturbed and confused beneath his anger. Bembo, looking at him, felt his own guilt in this. He bent down to pick up Strozzi's crutch, which had fallen on the floor.

'Ercole,' he said, 'we acted discreetly.'

Strozzi grunted. Bembo made an effort to explain. 'Ercole,' he said again, 'there occur very occasionally in life moments when circumstances seem to conspire to make the impossible possible. To refuse them, even for a careful man, is like insulting fate – '

'Pietro,' said Strozzi wearily, 'have you any notion of the danger in which you've placed us all?'

'Well, it's done now,' said Bembo. 'When will Alfonso be here?'

'In three or four days.'

'Three or four days,' cried Bembo. 'I thought you meant he would be here in an hour or so. Ercole, these tricks of yours.'

'It was no trick. I came to tell you about his visit and suggest that you went to Venice while he was here. It seemed a sensible opportunity to do as your father asks.'

'Why is he coming?'

'I'm surprised that you ask.'

'Ercole,' said Bembo severely, 'that's enough. There hasn't been time for anyone to reach him from Medelana and for him to arrange to be coming here.'

Strozzi shrugged his shoulders. 'If you must know, he's coming for the hunting. Or so he says. The duke gave this estate to my father. I suspect that Alfonso is warning us that he means to repossess it. Why he's chosen this particular time, I don't know. It's possible that he's been listening to Ippolito about you, but I doubt it. Thanks to the duke, the court in Ferrara thinks you are pursuing one of Lucrezia's ladies. Even so, it's better that Alfonso shouldn't find you here. Out of sight, out of mind.'

Bembo with some reluctance nodded.

Strozzi pulled himself up on his crutch. 'So you will leave today?'

'Why should I leave today? You say he won't be here for three or four days. That probably means five or six.'

'There's hardly much point in your going if you're seen walking out of one door as Alfonso marches in at another.'

Bembo took a breath. 'Tomorrow then. I must go to Medelana today.'

'Pietro!' Strozzi banged the floor again with his crutch.

'I will not go,' said Bembo, gritting his teeth, 'until I have spoken to Lucrezia.'

IX

Lucrezia came running along the gravelled paths of the walled garden. Bembo caught her gratefully in his arms. 'Thank goodness you've come.'

'I daren't stay long. Pietro, what is it?'

'Did you know Don Alfonso was coming to Ostellato?'

'Yes, I heard this morning.'

'Oh, my love, if anything should happen to you because of me–'

Lucrezia shook her head. 'Pietro, why should it? His orders were drafted over a week ago, before –'

'Yes. Before.' Bembo sighed with relief. 'I thought they must have been. Lucrezia, I think I should go back to Venice for a few days while your husband is at Ostellato, but I shan't go unless you feel safe.'

'Venice? Oh.' Lucrezia held him tightly.

'Sweetheart, it's the last thing I want to do.' He kissed her tenderly. 'But Ercole thinks it would be wise, and I can see the sense of it, too. I don't know how well we could hide what has happened. Our brains as well as out hearts have probably turned to crystal now – or mine has.' He confessed to her how easily Strozzi had been able to trap him that morning.

Lucrezia was silent. Then she said, 'Pietro, you will come back?'

'My darling, I told you, I shall be gone only a few days.'

'Yes, but when you are there, it may not be so easy to leave again. Your father wants you to stand for election. Supposing you can't refuse him. You may be chosen, and then you will have to go away to France.'

She was on the verge of tears, Bembo took her face in his hands. 'You mustn't imagine that Venice thinks as highly of me as you do,' he said. 'Lucrezia, believe me, I have no intention of allowing my fellow-countrymen the satisfaction of expressing their opinion of me in public, nor of deciding what I should do in the future.' He paused, then added, 'If you don't want me to go, if you feel afraid, Lucrezia, I shall stay. This is what I came here to ask you.'

Lucrezia threw her arms round him. 'You came to ask me? Oh, Pietro. Of course I don't want you to go, but only because I never want you to go anywhere away from me. There's nothing for me to be afraid about. So you must go to Venice. It's right that you should see your family.'

She slipped her fingers inside the opening of his shirt and found his agnus-dei. She drew it out and kissed the small gold and enamelled lamb.

Bembo smiled. 'My mother wore that before I was born,' he explained. 'Venetian women believe that an agnus-dei is a protection in childbirth. She gave it to me when I was a child, as soon as I was old enough to wear it.'

Lucrezia, pleased by this, kissed it again and replaced it carefully inside his shirt. Her hand rested against him, touching his flesh. Then she took her hand away and smoothed his shirt.

A clock chimed, reminding them both of the passing of time. Bembo kissed the palms of her hand. 'I must go.'

By the gate, Bembo took her fiercely in his arms. 'When I tell you in my letters that I kiss your hand, you will know that that is only the beginning of my thoughts,' he whispered.

He wrote to her next morning when it was still dark, before he left Ostellato. 'I am leaving, my sweetest life, and yet I am not leaving, nor will I ever leave you. I live in you. All this night, in sleeping and in long hours of waiting, I have been with you, as I hope to be every other night of my life . . . I kiss with my heart the hand that I shall soon kiss with my lips.'

X

Strozzi, his humour restored, rose early to watch Bembo ride out of the torchlit courtyard at Ostellato on the first part of his journey to the Villa Bozza. Lico and Bembino went with him.

Shortly after dawn they passed the great board that proclaimed, in black Roman lettering on a ground of gold, the frontier of the Republic of Venice. Before seven o'clock they reached Padua. Here they left the horses and took the barge that plied daily between Padua and Venice along the river Brenta.

The travelled through the flat green fields of the Veneto under a vast sky that drenched the landscape with clear, brilliant light. Bembo smelt the familiar smell of sluggish water and felt the movement, known since childhood, of a barge on a slow-moving meandering stream. He was home, and for the greater part of the journey he slept.

Lico woke him as they negotiated the shallow bend half a mile from the Villa Bozza. It was eleven o'clock. Bembo watched his father's fine trees come into sight, and then the house itself, a long low building of pale red brick set at right angles to the river. Carlo was standing at the top of the steps cut into the bank, and as Bembo began to wave he saw Bartolommeo and Nicola Bruno come running out of the villa.

Bembo jumped from the barge and threw himself into Carlo's arms. They swung each other round like two boys, laughing and shouting. Bembino raced up and down the bank, barking. Then Bembo embraced Bartolommeo and grasped Bruno's hands.

Inside the villa, his mother was waiting, and with her his sister and her three small daughters. Bembo kissed them all fondly on each cheek and then looked round for his father, surprised not to see him.

Carlo read his mind and said quickly, 'Our father is in Venice.

He'll be here later.' His glance warned his brother not to question him further.

When they were together in the room which they shared in the villa, Carlo explained, 'I thought it would be wiser to tell you when we were alone. Our father has gone to Venice to confirm your nomination for the election in November.'

Bembo, who was washing, lifted a face dripping with water, 'No, Carlo, no!' he said, appalled. 'Why didn't he wait until he saw me? I've come here to tell him that I can't stand. I won't. I'm not staying, Carlo. I'm going back to Ferrara.'

'I see,' said Carlo. He waited and then asked, 'Why?'

Bembo plunged his face back into the water again and mumbled that Ariosto had suggested he write a grammar of the Tuscan language.

'Then if you still can't work in Venice, wouldn't it be better to go to Florence?'

Bembo hid behind a towel. 'I need to work in a place that's quiet, like Ostellato.'

'But,' said Carlo, 'you spend a lot of time away from Ostellato.'

The two brothers looked at each other. Bembo sat down on the bed and held out a foot to Carlo. Carlo pulled off his boot. 'Pietro, is it a woman?' he said gently. He grasped the second boot.

Bembo frowned, fiddled with the laces of his shirt and tried to sound indifferent. 'Why do you ask that?'

Carlo sat on the bed beside him. 'For the last ten years, Pietro, you've spent the summer here at the Villa Bozza. Whatever you've been doing, you've left it in July to come here. The two summers before that you missed only because you were in Sicily. It wasn't scholarship that kept you away this July, so it must have been the only other thing that you care about – women.

Bembo was indignant. 'I'm not a womaniser.'

'No, of course not, not my fastidious Pietro. Womanisers can take women lightly, but not you. You know, Pietro, there are times in your life when you close yourself up in your own beautiful thoughts and almost disappear from common sight. And this lasts until you discover that what you thought you saw in the lady doesn't really exist.' Carlo laughed and put an arm round his brother. 'This last year of yours in Ferrara has all the signs of another attack.'

'It has nothing of the kind, Carlo,' said Bembo curtly. 'I've been working – '

'Oh? Then it isn't true that you are secretly attached to one of the ladies at the court?'

Bembo stared at him. 'Where did you hear that?'

'Oh, I know a lot more about you,' said Carlo. 'I know that you've rented a house in Ferrara, and I know that – ' he glanced sharply at Bembo, ' – the Borgia herself visited you there when you were ill.' His eyes were bright with amusement at the amazement on his brother's face.

'Pietro, whenever I want news of you, all I have to do is pay my respects to the Duchess of Urbino. She shares confidences with her sister-in-law in Mantua, and Isabella maintains a vast correspondence with the ladies of the court in Ferrara. They have a common dislike of the Borgia which makes their pens fly. And since Elisabetta of Urbino misses you here in Venice, and Isabella is curious as to why you stay so long in Ferrara, they write about you, too.'

'Oh, God,' said Bembo.

'The feeling among the ladies would seem to be that your infatuation will pass,' added Carlo. He handed Bembo a clean shirt.

'And you share that view?' enquired Bembo.

'Well, I can't,' said Carlo. 'You see, I never subscribed to this tale of a mysterious court lady.' He smiled. 'Why should such an innocent affair have to be secret? It has too strong a flavour to me of one of Ercole Strozzi's evasions.' Carlo looked up at the ceiling. 'I think the lady is the Borgia herself.'

Bembo emerged, scarlet-faced and shaken, from the folds of his shirt. 'Why?' he said faintly.

'You never write about her in your letters.'

'Well, Carlo – '

'Pietro, you write about the Strozzi, about Ariosto, Don Giulio,

Ippolito, even her cousin – people you must have met at the duchess's court – but not a word about the duchess herself.'

'There must be a dozen other people I know well in Ferrara that I haven't mentioned,' protested Bembo.

'Ah, but these people, whoever they are, have always been unknown to us. When you first met the duchess your letters were full of her.'

'Only because I wanted you to understand how different she was from what we had always supposed,' said Bembo.

Carlo smiled. 'Pietro,' he asked gently, 'is she so very different?'

Bembo sat and looked at his brother. His face changed and softened as he saw no further need for pretence. He smiled back at Carlo. 'Yes, she is.' He threw himself back on the bed, arms linked behind his head. 'For the first time in my life I feel complete.'

Carlo stood over him. 'Two years ago it was Maria Savorgnan. In two years' time it will be someone else.'

'No,' said Bembo.

Carlo peered at him closely. 'Even so,' he said after a moment, 'is it wise to go back to Ferrara? It will have to end sometime. Isn't it better now while it is still undiscovered?' As Bembo shook his head, still smiling, Carlo added with a touch of desperation, 'Have you any idea of the risks you may be running? You won't be dealing this time with the brothers-in-law of Maria Savorgnan.'

'No, I do know that,' said Bembo quietly.

'Pietro,' pleaded Carlo, 'if you don't want to come back to Venice, you could go to Urbino with the duke and Elisabetta. Cesare Borgia's men have relinquished Urbino, and the court will be back there in a few weeks.'

Bembo sat up and embraced his brother gratefully. 'Carlo, I know you say this for my sake, but I must go back. I know Lucrezia and I can't be lovers for ever. Apart from the danger of our circumstances, life itself is uncertain. This time next year, one of us or both of us may be dead. I daren't waste a moment of what we share. We have been blessed with each other, and it would seem a kind of sin to me to relinquish what we have before we need.'

'But isn't the danger need enough?'

Bembo shook his head. 'Not yet.'

Carlo sighed and walked about the room. 'Pietro, I haven't been asking these questions out of idle curiosity. There's something else I have to tell you about our father's journey to Venice today, something you should be prepared for.'

Carlo's manner made Bembo uneasy. 'Oh?'

'Yes. He won't be coming back alone. He's bringing with him two guests: a Veronese, Count Gambara, and the count's daughter.' He paused. 'The count's marriageable daughter, Pietro.'

They looked at each other. 'Yes?' said Bembo.

'It is hoped on both sides,' Carlo went on, speaking with care, 'that having met Madonna Veronica, you might be encouraged to offer her marriage.'

Bembo's temper rose. 'You thought it would be dangerous for me to go back to Ferrara? What about staying here?'

'I did suggest Urbino,' Carlo reminded him. He added reasonably, 'This is only a suggestion to be explored. After all, one of us has to marry. Our father and Uncle Jacopo decided that, as in their generation, it was more fitting for the ambassador.'

'What ambassador?' cried Bembo. 'Why wasn't I included in these talks?'

'Well, you did give everyone to understand that you were living in an isolated stretch of country, absorbed in your writing. You couldn't be expected to find much opportunity to look for a wife yourself.'

'Why should it suddenly become so urgent to find me a wife?'

'We need the dowry,' said Carlo bluntly. 'What little capital we had left was exhausted by the ceremonial which our father was obliged to keep as governor of Verona. We need capital now, so if there is to be a marriage at all this would be a sensible time.'

'Why do we need capital?'

Carlo sighed. 'Pietro, you know you're not interested in talk about trade. If you must know, I think we ought to start transferring all our Levantine interests to the west, to Bruges and

London and perhaps Gothenburg. For that we should need to strengthen our Alpine route so that we can avoid hiring shipping space until our debt to the Republic is settled.'

Bembo grasped a point. 'You mean we'll do no more trading in the east, not even spices?'

'No. We shall lose the spice trade anyway when the cheap Portuguese sea routes to India improve.'

Bembo tried to be interested. 'Can they improve? They lose two ships out of every three on that route.'

'They used to. Not now. But we ought to expand our markets in the west while everyone else in Venice is still saying what you just said.'

Bembo groaned. 'So to keep your gold thread streaming across the Alps, you want me to marry Veronica Gambara.'

Carlo laughed. '*I* don't want you to marry anyone, unless it would give you happiness.' He hesitated. 'I think our parents feel that if you were married it might help you to settle.'

'Yes, to settle in Venice, eh?' Bembo said bitterly. 'Carlo, I find this interference in my life intolerable. Wouldn't you in my place?'

Carlo shrugged his shoulders. 'Oh, I don't think so,' He smiled apologetically. 'I think I would only regard it as the apportioning of my share of family responsibility.'

'Well, I can't,' said Bembo unhappily. 'And, Carlo, I can't marry. The count had better take his daughter back to Venice because I intend to ignore her.'

But Bembo, with his natural courtesy and his gentleness towards women, did nothing of the kind. When he met her in the gardens of the villa, he walked with her. When she expressed a wish to go on the river, he escorted her. She had been instructed to try to please him with her knowledge of Latin authors and, after she had made her careful little observations, he responded by reading aloud to her from the poets she preferred. Veronica Gambara was not aware that Bembo would have behaved with the same consideration to any woman who was a guest in his father's house, nor that his graceful compliments were a commonplace in the court life to which he was accustomed. She was seventeen and fresh from her convent schooling. When she caught him one evening staring at her with a brooding, abstracted look, she believed that he was sharing her state of enchantment. Bembo was, in fact, at that moment a long way from the Villa Bozza. He was in a room at Medelana with a window that overlooked the kitchen well.

The Senator spent his time in the company of Count Gambara. When Bembo begged for an opportunity to speak to him alone, Bernardo blandly refused, urging him not to waste time when he might be amusing the young countess. The time to talk, he said with nods and glances at the count, would come later.

XI

The days of the visit came at last to an end, and the Senator accompanied his guests on their journey back to Venice.

He returned in the evening with his kinsman, Alvise Bembo, who was spending the night at the villa. Bembo greeted him half-heartedly, seeing yet another delay to his departure, but was suddenly excited to discover that Alvise was on his way to Bologna. He drew him aside and asked if he intended to travel through Ferrara.

'I do indeed,' said Alvise. 'Is there something I could do for you in Ferrara?'

Bembo said gratefully, 'Alvise, I would be in your debt if you would carry a letter for me.'

Alvise nodded, pleased to be able to serve his cousin. Alvise, like Jacopo Bembo, spent his time in trading, but he had little enthusiasm for it. He traded because his grandfather and his father, his brothers and uncles expected him to do so, and because he had no particular talent for anything else. Yet he had a yearning to experience a wider world than that of the Venetian markets and counting-houses. He had spent some time in Bruges, it was true, but that was in the enclosed merchant quarter of the Venetians. In his cousin Pietro he recognised a kindred spirit, one who had the gifts and the will he lacked to ignore the habits of Venice. With his Tuscan speech, the foreign touches in his dress, his talk of anything but trade, Bembo had a distinction and an air that Alvise greatly admired and would have liked to emulate.

Bembo was explaining. 'The letter will be addressed to Medelana, but if you would be kind enough, Alvise, to leave it at the Strozzi palace with Messer Ercole, he will send it on to Medelana for me. Do you know the cathedral in Ferrara? If you take the road that begins by the north wall, you will pass the Strozzi palace on your left.'

'Yes, I understand,' said Alvise. 'Your letter should be in Ferrara by tomorrow afternoon.' He was agreeably surprised by the sudden brilliance of Bembo's smile and the warmth of his thanks.

That night, when Carlo was asleep, Bembo wrote to Lucrezia, 'It is eight days since I left FF, and it seems as if I've been away for eight years, although I swear that not for one hour of this time have I stopped thinking of her. I remember so often, and so easily, what she has said to me on the balcony under the moon, and near the little window that I always see with such delight. I shall never be content until she realises how strong a fire her dear worth has kindled in me. The flame of true love is strong, but strongest when it burns equally in two spirits. Such is the gospel of conformity'.

Bembo stared at the paper, dismayed by the inadequacy of his words. Even in writing to FF, his pen was crippled. He used a plain seal, and in the early morning handed the letter to Alvise.

He watched Alvise riding along the road to Padua which he hoped to be travelling in a day or so himself. He thought about his letter lying that evening in Lucrezia's hands at Medelana. Then he turned away and entered the villa.

Senator Bembo was waiting for him in his study. 'Ah, Pietro,' he said as his son appeared in the doorway, 'I thought you might come. At last we can find time to discuss our affairs. Sit down.'

Bembo murmured vaguely and sat down on a stool in front of

his father. The Senator regarded him with affection. 'Pietro, I have a message for you which I thought you would prefer to hear privately.' He smiled as Bembo glanced at him in surprise. 'It comes from Count Gambara. He will be remaining in Venice for the next ten days. He asks me to offer you his daughter's good wishes and to tell you that she will be happy to receive you there.'

Bembo stared miserably at the floor without answering. Such an invitation, conveyed through the heads of the two families, indicated an agreement that Bembo was free to offer marriage to Madonna Veronica and that her consent would be given.

Desperation made Bembo speak more abruptly than he had intended. 'Father, I shall be returning to Ferrara tomorrow.'

The Senator was momentarily startled by the apparent irrelevance of the remark. Then he observed calmly, 'You have affairs to settle there, of course.'

Bembo shook his head. 'No. I'm going back there to live.' There was a long silence in the room, and then Bembo said urgently, 'Father, I can't marry now.'

He looked up and saw on his father's face not the anger he had expected, but surprise and something like relief. The Senator considered briefly. 'Pietro,' he said in a mild voice, 'I have no wish to arrange a marriage, or even to persuade you to contemplate one, if it's against your inclinations. I will admit that I would have welcomed it. I developed a high regard for the count and his daughter during our stay in Verona, and we had assumed as a family that you might welcome our guidance in selecting a bride. Your bearing with the lady when she was here led me to believe that you approved of our choice. However, I can understand that we were perhaps precipitate, especially in view of the fact that you may well not be fully restored after your illness. The matter can be delayed or dropped, as you please. There is no need on this account for you to leave Venice, and so lose the opportunity to stand for election. That, after all, is at the moment the most important issue.'

Bembo was moved by the forbearance of his father's attitude. It made all the more difficult what he had to say. 'Sir, even if there had been no suggestion of a marriage, my decision would have been the same. I am going back to Ferrara.' He took a quick breath. 'I have no wish to hold office for the State, and I do not intend to submit myself for election. This is what I came home to tell you, and tried to tell you earlier.'

The Senator stared at his son, shocked and incredulous. Then he rose from his chair and said sharply, 'Pietro, you have been allowed to indulge your taste for scholarship for a number of years, and it has given me much pride to see you attain the degree of eminence which is now yours. But it is time now for you to consider your responsibilities to the Republic, and to your family.'

Bembo stood up to face him. 'I am aware that a Venetian is expected to owe loyalty first to the Republic, then to his family and lastly to himself. But I am before anything else myself, Pietro Bembo. It is in the nature of my work as a poet that I must be so. To you, this is selfishness. But the gift to create demands this quality of selfishness if it is to be used.'

The Senator's distress was making Bembo more and more distraught. He was convinced of the justice of what he was saying, yet he could not escape a sense of guilt and ingratitude. Had he not been desperate to return to Lucrezia, he doubted if he would have had the courage to go on. 'Father, there is nothing else to be said.'

Anxious to avoid argument that might give more fruitless pain to both of them Bembo turned his back on his father and made his way towards the door.

'Pietro!' The Senator called out after him. He could not remember an occasion when one of his sons had opposed him with such feeling. More disturbed than angry, he called out again. He hurried across the room and pulled open the door that Bembo had closed between them. In his haste, his foot caught in the hem of his robe and threw him forward. He fell, striking his head on the marble pavement.

He lay unconscious, blood trickling from a wound above his temple. Bembo with tears running from his eyes, helped to carry him to bed. Carlo set out for Venice to fetch a Jewish physician from the ghetto.

For two days, Bernardo remained unconscious. Bembo crouched in his room, watching. When Carlo urged him to rest, he refused. 'How can I? This is my fault.'

On the third day, the Senator stirred. He ate a little food, meticulously prepared by the Jew, and then slept. The physician nodded, stroked the curls of his beard with gold-ringed fingers and announced that there was no longer any danger to his patient's life. 'But,' he warned them, 'you must not expect that he will ever again be as strong as you have known him. There could be a weakness somewhere. For this we must wait.'

Bembo, laughing with relief and exhaustion, rocked his mother in his arms. Then he buried his unshaven face in a pillow and slept. The Senator's condition improved steadily, and a few days later the physician packed his instruments and his drugs, and returned to Venice.

'And now you will be leaving, too?' Carlo asked Bembo. When Bembo hesitated, Carlo added, 'Aren't you expected in Ferrara?'

'Oh yes, yes I am,' said Bembo unhappily. He had promised Lucrezia that he would not be away for more than a few days. It was nearly three weeks. 'But how can I leave?'

'Why shouldn't you? He is much better.'

'But I shall have to stay,' cried Bembo. 'This was all my fault. My selfishness caused it.'

'A loose slipper and a hard paving caused it,' said Carlo. 'Or do you mean that you regret what you said, that you no longer believe it.'

'Of course I believe it,' said Bembo. 'But it wasn't the real reason I wanted to leave.'

'No, I know, but that doesn't make the reason you gave any less true, does it?'

Bembo sighed. 'No. I can never work in Venice.'

'Then what difference does this accident make to the course you know you should follow?' asked Carlo ruthlessly.

'Oh, Carlo, I don't know,' said Bembo wearily.

Later in the day the Senator invited Bembo to sit with him. When he entered the room he found Carlo already there, holding an open book in his hand. The Senator embraced Bembo fondly and they spoke for a few minutes about Bernardo's health. Then he said, 'Carlo and I have been talking about the time we spent in Florence when you were both children.'

'Oh?' Bembo glanced at Carlo, but Carlo had his back to them and was looking out of the window.

'We were recalling,' the Senator went on, 'how highly Lorenzo de Medici spoke of your gifts, young though you were then. I have always treasured his praise of you, and Carlo has been pointing out to me how illogical it would be if I did not rejoice in your determination to employ and perfect those gifts.' He stretched out his hand for the book which Carlo had left on the bed. 'If I needed to be persuaded further, I could hardly ignore this. Perhaps you recognise it?'

Bembo leaned forward and saw that the book was the first printed edition of Pindar's Odes, which he himself had prepared for the presses of Aldo Manuzio during the winter at Ostellato. Bernardo held the page open at Manuzio's preface. 'He describes you, Pietro, so: "*decus eruditorum aetatis nostrae, e magnae spes altera Roma*" – the ornament of learning in our time, and the great hope of the new Rome.'

Bembo, not unaware of the worth of his own scholarship, was nevertheless overwhelmed by his father's acknowledgement of it. He began to mumble, and then fell silent. He knelt down to kiss the Senator's hand, and the Senator's touch rested lightly on his head in blessing. 'Now go back to Ferrara, Pietro, if that is what you want.'

Bembo stood outside his father's door, recovering himself, feeling his excitement mounting. He would go next day to Venice to settle various small matters with Aldo Manuzio, and then he would be on his way again to his dear Medelana.

While he set Lico to prepare for their departure, he wrote eagerly to Lucrezia, 'My father, because of a fall, has been in great danger of his life, and I could not leave him until this moment. Tomorrow I shall be in Venice, and will stay there for two days. Then I shall return again to see my dear half, without whom not only am I not whole, but nothing at all – I lose myself in the single thought that in two hearts lives the same wish . . . '

Lico left next morning to arrange Bembo's rooms at Ostellato and to see the letter delivered at Medelana. Two days later when Bembo followed from Venice, Carlo travelled with him as far as the mainland. The autumn air was cool and Bembo was wrapped in a cloak of characteristically Ferrarese design. It fell in deep straight folds of brown velvet to his calves and its hem was banded with pale brown fur some fifteen inches deep. The arm-slits were furred as lavishly.

'Bizarre and arrogant,' said Carlo, in his neat patrician dress. 'Is this the way you flaunt yourself in Ferrara?'

'Rarely,' said Bembo. 'When I wish to appear bizarre and arrogant in Ferrara, I dress as a Venetian.'

When Bembo had hired a horse to take him to Padua, they lingered for a moment by the water. 'Come back sometime,' said Carlo. He embraced Bembo. 'Be happy, Pietro, but take care.'

'And you,' said Bembo, 'take care.' He clung for a moment to his brother. 'I'm grateful, Carlo.'

Carlo sat in the boat for some time watching him ride away before he let Marco row him back to Venice.

XII

Bembo arrived at the Strozzi palace in the late afternoon. He intended to stay only long enough to offer his respects to Tito Strozzi before going on to Ostellato.

'That I am afraid,' said Tito Strozzi, when Bembo had explained this, 'will not be possible.'

'Why not?' Bembo asked, startled.

Tito urged him to sit down and share the wine he was sipping. 'I have been waiting here to talk to you about it, Pietro. Please sit down. Lico is here.'

'He should be at Ostellato – '

'Yes, I know,' said Tito. 'But, unfortunately, Alfonso is still at Ostellato. When Lico arrived there, he was told by the master of the household that Alfonso's court had eaten the countryside bare and that there was no food to spare for two more mouths.'

Shaken and speechless, Bembo sat down. 'It's true, of course,' Tito went on, 'that they've stripped the estate, but two more mouths could hardly make any difference. This is merely a way of telling you that you will not be welcome there. For what reason I'm not sure.'

'Do you think he's listened to Ippolito?' said Bembo desperately. He thought of the stories that had even reached Carlo in Venice and groaned.

'Now, Pietro,' said Tito Strozzi, patting Bembo's arm, 'this was an attempt to rebuff you with a certain degree of politeness. I doubt if Alfonso would have troubled with courtesies if he even suspected –' Tito hesitated, ' – the truth. It may be that he has heard Ippolito's tales and wants to explode them. On the other hand, he could distrust you as a companion of Ercole's. Perhaps he is not alone, and makes any excuse to keep strangers away. Had you thought of that?'

'Whatever the reason,' cried Bembo, 'it means the same. I can't go to Ostellato.' He swallowed some wine. 'Then I shall ride straight to Medelana.'

'No, you will not,' said Tito with severity. 'It's unlikely, but it is just possible that that curious message was part of a trap to see if you did go straight to Medelana as soon as you knew that Ostellato was closed to you.'

Bembo, near to despair, said, 'Lucrezia will be waiting.'

'Well, for the moment, you can write her a formal little note to acquaint her, as is proper, of your return. Then we will see what can be done.'

When the note reached Lucrezia, she was sitting on her balcony watching the road, as if by willing it she could make Bembo appear. She was unhappy and distracted, having no clearer idea than Tito Strozzi as to why Alfonso was still at Ostellato. Apart from several presents of game, she had received neither visits nor messages from him. That, Angela Borgia had insisted, was because he was not at Ostellato for the hunting at all. 'The game is to deceive you into thinking he is,' she said scornfully to Lucrezia. 'Messer Bembo found it quiet and isolated there. So does Alfonso. And with you close by at Medelana, it makes his stay look innocent.'

Lucrezia was not so sure as Angela. Perhaps because she had something to hide, she felt as though she were being watched.

The arrival of Bembo's note, formally inscribed and delivered openly to her by Tebaldeo, frightened her. She opened it as hastily as she dare with Tebaldeo standing over her. It was written from Ferrara. Bembo apologised for not seeking her permission to return there instead of to Ostellato, but explained that the court of the lord Don Alfonso had stripped the land of food and he was therefore prevented from resuming his stay there. 'I remember,' he went on, 'that I promised you during the summer to spend the winter in Ferrara, and there I shall remain especially as, with the danger of sickness in the city almost passed, you yourself will soon be returning there. I must add that Messer Ercole is threatening to make me stay against my will if I should talk of leaving'.

The letter would have implied to anyone else that Strozzi was determined to prevent Bembo returning to Venice. Lucrezia realised that Bembo was warning her not to expect him at Medelana.

They waited, Bembo in Ferrara and Lucrezia at Medelana, for Alfonso to leave Ostellato. The autumn days slipped away. Bembo tried to work. He sat one afternoon, struggling to fashion the arguments advanced by one of the characters in his book in defence of love. He found after a while that he was not setting down the reasoned observations he had intended, but was describing his own memories – 'There are some who in the act of loving deny each other nothing. What one wishes, in that same moment and with equal pleasure the other does, and together they discover every possible delight . . . ' Bembo pushed the paper aside. When Strozzi arrived unexpectedly to visit him, he was staring miserably out of the window.

Strozzi was wearing a pair of carnation satin sleeves and his beard was perfumed. 'Pietro,' he said pleasantly, 'I am on my way to an afternoon's – ' he coughed, ' – recreation. Why not come with me?' He struck a hand on Bembo's drooping shoulder. 'I can't claim that Ferrara offers the varieties of your establishment by the Rialto Bridge, but we have a sufficient choice of delights.'

'I don't know why you suggest such a thing to me,' muttered Bembo.

'I suggest it,' said Strozzi crisply, 'because it is time you were shaken out of this pining humour of yours.'

'You think catching the pox would improve it?' snapped Bembo. 'Go away, Ercole.'

'Very well,' said Strozzi. 'I'll go, and take my news with me.' He limped towards the door.

'What news?' Bembo bounded across the room after him. 'Ercole, I'm sorry. Come back. What news?'

Strozzi leaned on his crutch in the doorway. 'Do you know Count Alberto Pio of Carpi?'

Bembo was disappointed. 'I haven't met him,' he said listlessly, 'although we've corresponded on points of scholarship. He's the patron of my printer, Manuzio, in Venice.'

'Yes. And he's anxious to meet you while you are in Ferrara. He invites you to Carpi.'

Bembo shook his head. 'Oh, no, Ercole. I can't leave here now.'

'I see,' said Strozzi. He walked through the doorway and reached the head of Bembo's curving stairway. 'A pity,' he called out. 'Madonna Lucrezia will be staying with him the week after next.'

'Ercole, you old fox,' shouted Bembo. He caught up with him half-way down the stairs, and the force of his embrace almost knocked Strozzi off his balance. 'It is my father you should thank,' gasped Strozzi, 'for dropping thoughts into Count Alberto's mind. And now, Pietro, do you think you could let me go? Leave me a little strength for the afternoon.'

Bembo arrived in Alberto Pio's seigniory of Carpi two days before Lucrezia was expected to reach the town after a leisurely journey by barge eastwards along the waterways of Ferrara and Modena.

But before the two days had passed, a messenger brought word that plague had broken out at Medelana and that the duchess was immured within its bounds. Lucrezia, it appeared, had actually been standing on the steps of Medelana, ready to leave, when one of her seamstresses collapsed a few yards away from her. Her physician had diagnosed plague. Within four days, thirty-four members of Lucrezia's household were ill.

Bembo returned from Carpi as soon as courtesy allowed. He prowled the streets of Ferrara, going several times a day to pray in the church of Corpus Domini which enjoyed Lucrezia's especial support. He told his beads for the first time in years.

At Medelana, Lucrezia's physician had the windows barred to keep out the infected air and declared that no one must leave the house itself. Lucrezia could be perverse and wilful at times. If she was to die she wanted to spend her last hours in the walled garden. The weather was as mild and clear as it had been during the previous November when she first saw Bembo. Every day she sat alone under the pergola, making herself work with her gold thread.

The seamstress died, and five more of Lucrezia's servants. The number of those with plague rose to fifty-four.

'Lucrezia?' gasped Bembo to Tito Strozzi.

'Not Lucrezia.'

The mild November air grew colder. In the early winter dusk, with the mists rising from the river, the sombre streets of Ferrara were chilled and bleak. Bembo shivered and rejoiced. This was not the climate in which plague thrived. By the beginning of December, four more people died at Medelana, but for several days there had been no new cases of sickness.

Ten days before Christmas it was announced that the duchess would be returning to Ferrara. As soon as he heard the news from Strozzi, Bembo leapt up, ready to ride to Medelana. 'Pietro, wait,' said Strozzi. 'Alfonso is at Medelana, waiting to escort Lucrezia back to the castle. Whether he does so as a solicitous husband or a gaoler, I don't know.'

Bembo stood bare-headed in the street to watch her enter the castle. He caught only a brief glimpse of her lying in her litter, with Alfonso riding on one side of her and Giulio on the other. The anguish of being kept apart from her overwhelmed him until he remembered that only a few days before his one prayer had been that she should stay alive. He went, perhaps more out of superstition than piety, to Corpus Domini to light a candle in repentance and gratitude.

He attended the first court reception held after Lucrezia's return. Alfonso appeared beside her. He remained only a short time, but even after he had left, the word 'gaoler' lingered in Bembo's mind. Lucrezia was hedged about, even in his absence, by the members of his household, by the duke's watchful councillors, by ladies who had served the former duchess and who still regarded Lucrezia with cold resentment. It had been the same, he supposed, a year ago, but he had not been conscious of it then.

He dared not approach Lucrezia, not even to join in the playful, courtly talk that had once been their way of communicating. Since his visit to Venice, he was obsessed by the fear that Isabella's letter-writers might be observing him. Even when Lucrezia moved about the hall, receiving greetings, he felt constrained to speak only a few, unsmiling words to her.

Lucrezia, understanding the need for caution yet still hurt by it, nodded and walked on without knowing how to answer him. She showed no interest that night in dancing. She stayed, as Bembo did, because they were in the same room together. Bembo could recall a time when this in itself had been happiness enough. Now it caused them both as much distress as pleasure.

He lay awake that night, wondering what they were going to do. He could see no escape from the hopelessness of their position.

Late in the afternoon of the next day he was walking in his garden, to and fro under the dripping evergreens, still in the same nervous, helpless state, when Lico suddenly appeared to fetch him. Lico had rarely seemed to Bembo to look so agitated.

Bembo hurried into the house. Leaning against the door from the street, breathless and frightened, was Lucrezia. She was wearing a plain cloak, and had just lifted from her face a thick veil of the kind worn by widows in Ferrara.

'I was so afraid you wouldn't be here,' she said, half-sobbing with relief. She almost fell against him.

'Lucrezia.' He put his arms round her. 'Are you alone?'

'Yes.' She was shaking with reactions. Bembo asked her no more questions, but guided her up the curving stair to the living quarters of the house. Half-way up, she laid her head on his arm. 'I used to imagine you holding me like this when I was afraid of the plague at Medelana,' she said.

'I'm here now, my pet.'

He sat her in front of his wood fire. Lico brought a mug of hot, spiced wine.

Bembo placed the mug in Lucrezia's cold fingers, covering her hands with his. She took a sip, shuddered and tried to put the mug down. Bembo, kneeling beside her, shook his head. She swallowed again and found the drink not unpleasant. Then warmer, no longer shivering, she leaned her head against the back of the chair and smiled. Bembo unfastened the neck of her cloak.

'Lucrezia, who knows that you've come here?'

'Only Angela.' She grasped his hand. 'Pietro, I had to be with you. I had to talk to you. When you couldn't come back to Medelana, and then we couldn't meet at Carpi, I was longing for the time when we could be together again in Ferrara. But last night I could see that it was going to be almost impossible to be alone with you. And you were so cold – '

'I wasn't cold, love, but I daren't behave in any other way.' He sighed. 'Perhaps I was wrong. It may be just as unwise to seem to ignore you as to be too close to you.'

'I knew you were being careful, yet it still made me feel unhappy. I wondered if we would ever be able to speak to each other again. Then I thought of coming here.'

'You must tell me how you did it.'

'Yes.' Lucrezia nodded obediently. 'This morning I went to my rooms in the Casa Romei. I often spend a day there when I'm tired of the court. I said I wanted to rest and I knew no one would disturb me. Then Angela asked some of the younger nuns to help her slip away while she had the chance. One of them found this cloak and another made the thick veil. They sent the gardener for a public litter and then smuggled me out through the kitchens, thinking, of course, that I was Angela. I got out of the litter at the end of the road and ran the rest of the way here.'

Bembo put his head against hers and laughed gently. 'My dear goose,' he said. 'Have you ever been out alone in the city before?'

She shook her head. 'Not in any city. But I had to do it, didn't I? I was so desperate to see you.' She looked searchingly into his eyes. 'Are you angry with me?'

Bembo kissed her tenderly on the mouth. 'How could I be angry, my brave love?'

He left her side for a moment to glance out of the window, 'Do you think anyone recognised you, or followed you?'

'I didn't notice anyone,' she said. Bembo nodded. He could see no one skulking among the trees in the orchard, or on the road beyond.

'We'll make sure,' he said. 'Sit here by the fire and let me talk to Lico. Lico and I will take you back when it is time.'

He descended the stair to Lico's domain on the ground floor. They talked intently for several minutes, then Bembo returned to Lucrezia. As he reached the head of the stair, he saw Lucrezia still sitting in his chair before the fire. He stood watching her, affected by the simple fitness of her being there at his hearth.

Lucrezia turned to look at him and spoke his thoughts. 'I am feeling what it is like to live in your house. It seems as though I've always known it.'

Bembo held out his hand to her, and she rose and took it.

Later they made love in his bed, the shutters closing out the winter afternoon. Once Bembo raised himself on his arm and looked down at her as she lay on his pillow, her hair spread across her white skin. He remembered how a strand of it had blown across her cheek on the beach by the river. 'Here's my miracle again,' he said, 'amber flowing across snow. Don't tell me again it's impossible.' He smoothed the hair that lay across her breasts.

Lucrezia smiled and held out her arms to him. He lay down again beside her.

In the early evening, they dressed by the light of the flames burning in the fire-place near Bembo's bed. In the outer room, Lico had set out a simple meal, the only one they ever ate alone together. As they ate they hardly took their eyes off each other, still bemused by their complete and perfect satisfaction.

They talked of when they should next meet, both understanding that she must not come again to his house. Now that she was happy and tranquil, he told her of his conversation with Carlo and the letters which passed between Ferrara and Mantua. 'I think it would be unwise if I came to your apartments to see you, even to read to you and your ladies,' Bembo said. 'We must wait until we know more about Alfonso's attitude. I will come, with everyone else, to your balls and your music at court. If I appear cold – ' he leaned across the table to kiss her, ' – you will know that I am not.'

He searched for comfort. 'We will write. And soon it will be spring, and you can go to Belvedere, and we will wait patiently for the summer again at Medelana.'

'Yes. Medelana,' said Lucrezia.

When it was time for her to go, he fetched her cloak and wrapped it round her. They walked slowly down the stair together. In the passage below, Lico was waiting with two horses.

'You will ride behind Lico on one horse,' Bembo explained to her, 'and I shall ride on the other. When we reach the Casa Romei I shall ride straight on. Lico will see you safely back into the house. You must not look at me or talk to me. Do you understand.'

Lucrezia nodded. 'Then we must say good-bye now?'

'Yes, my love.' He held her closely in his arms. 'I think I took this house in the hope that some day I might have you alone with me under my own roof.'

'For one afternoon?'

'One or a hundred. It doesn't really make any difference to the feeling of having shared the house with you.' He bent his head to kiss her for the last time.

They rode at a leisurely pace through the city to avoid attracting attention, Lico in front, Bembo some distance behind. Lico carried a stout wooden stave under his cloak and Bembo wore a sword, with a long knife in his belt. When they were close to the Casa Romei, Bembo rode ahead and Lico turned into the narrow alley that led to the nuns' kitchen quarters.

Bembo turned his horse and rode slowly back past the Casa Romei. A window opened above him. Angela Borgia looked down at him with a smile, and slammed it shut.

With a feeling of relief, Bembo returned home.

XIII

Lucrezia was stitching a little brocade coat for her son, Rodrigo, who since Pope Alessandro's death had been living with his father's aunt in Spain. Five silver-gilt buttons that had once belonged to the young Duke of Bisceglie lay beside her, ready for use. Angela Borgia was tipping out the contents of several jewel boxes to find the sixth.

In front of her, Lucrezia's milliner and her seamstresses were spreading out caps and sleeves and dresses to help her decide as she worked what she should wear that night. The milliner offered her a veil of green gauze. Lucrezia held it against her face and glanced in her mirror. The silver frame of the mirror was set with green enamelled leaves on which tiny pearls rested like drops of dew. Lucrezia smiled at her image encircled by the green gauze and the green leaves, and thought of Bembo's window at Ostellato with the leaves that he had once described to her in a letter. She nodded to the milliner.

'The emeralds,' she said to Angela, and Angela brought her the snake necklace. Since her visit to Bembo's house, Christmas had been celebrated, and they had not seen each other. Tonight, however, the duke was giving his Christmas concert of music in the palace and Bembo was expected to attend. Under the duke's benevolent protection she hoped Bembo might feel less wary of speaking to her than in her own court.

She thought for a moment that it was in her own imagination that she heard his name being spoken. Then she was aware of Tebaldeo beside her.

'Messer Bembo,' said Tebaldeo again.

'A letter?' asked Lucrezia, smiling.

'No, madonna,' said Tebaldeo, frowning at her. 'He is here. He begs to speak to you.'

Lucrezia nodded and stared at the door in alarm. After what they had decided together, he would not have come in this way unless the reason were urgent. As soon as she saw him, her misgivings were confirmed. His face was unusually pale and his movements clumsy with haste.

He looked at her across the litter of silks and trinkets. 'Your highness must forgive my coming at this hour,' he said unevenly. 'I must go to Venice, and I could not leave without offering my duty to you.'

Lucrezia's face had become almost as pale as his. 'You must go to Venice?'

Bembo nodded. 'I have had a letter from my family.'

Lucrezia ordered her servants to leave them. She waved Tebaldeo away after them. Angela crept into another room. As soon as they were alone, she caught hold of Bembo. 'My love, what is it?'

'Lucrezia,' said Bembo distractedly, 'Carlo is ill. I think he may be dying. A letter has just come from my brother, Bartolommeo.'

Lucrezia gave a cry of distress and put her arms more closely round him. Bembo laid his head on hers. 'I must go back at once.'

Lucrezia said quickly, 'Oh, not at once.'

'Love, I must. The letter was written five days ago.'

'Pietro, stay just for tonight. I can't bear it if you leave suddenly like this.' She began to cry, aware that she was being unreasonable, yet unable to help herself. 'I'm so afraid.'

Bembo was surprised. 'Dear heart, why? I shall not be away for long. I promised to spend the winter here, and I will. If Carlo is better, I shall be back in three or four days. If not – ' He stopped, his voice breaking as he faced the possibility of Carlo's death. 'Oh, God, if he's dead – '

He gripped the back of Lucrezia's chair, his head bowed. 'If he's dead,' he said again, 'then there will be nothing at all, Lucrezia, to keep me in Venice.' He raised his head and looked towards her collection of books. 'Lucrezia, let me have your Bible.'

Lucrezia hesitated. 'Why?'

Bembo sighed impatiently. 'Lucrezia, let me have it.'

Reluctantly, she fetched it. He closed his eyes, turned the leaves and allowed the book to fall open at random. Then he opened his eyes and read the leaf in front of him. 'No,' he muttered, and then groaned. 'No!'

Lucrezia tried to close the Bible. He grasped her wrist and tapped the page. 'Listen: *Obdormivit cum patribus suis at sepelierunt eum in civitate David* – He fell asleep with his fathers and they buried him in the city of David.' He turned away. 'He's dead. I know Carlo's dead.'

The grief in his face wrung Lucrezia's heart. 'Pietro, you can't possibly know that.'

'It's written here,' said Bembo, striking the Bible.

Lucrezia faced him. 'No, it isn't. That's superstition. The Church says that what you have just done is abusing God's word. So no comfort can ever come from it.'

'The Church – ' said Bembo contemptuously.

Lucrezia was angry with him for hurting himself. They glared at each other. Then Lucrezia held out a hand. 'Oh, my love, we mustn't quarrel.'

Bembo seized her hand. 'No, not when I need you, when I

need your prayers and your strength.' He kissed her fiercely. 'My dear love.'

'You must go now?'

'Yes, I must. Can't you trust me, goose, to come back? Do you think it's easy for me to leave you.'

Lucrezia gritted her teeth. 'I'm afraid of Venice.'

'Venice? Venice is only a collection of bricks and stones and timber. It won't swallow me alive.' He rocked her gently in his arms. 'Don't worry. I promise you that whatever happens I shall come back.' Moved by her fear, he drew out his agnus-dei on its chain. 'Will you allow me to swear on this? I cherish it because you've kissed it – ' He smiled and wiped away a tear from her nose, ' – so it has nothing to do with your Church. I swear, Lucrezia.'

'Oh, there is no need,' cried Lucrezia. 'But let me kiss it again. Forgive me. I wanted you to stay and I was selfish. Will you forgive me?'

'My soul,' said Bembo, 'there is no need.'

Within less than an hour, he had left Ferrara. A short distance outside the city gate, on the road to Padua, a messenger wearing Lucrezia's colours overtook him and handed him a sealed letter. It had been scribbled in haste, in Lucrezia's confused Spanish-Italian spelling. 'I pray for your brother and for you. FF begs you again to forgive her. Come back to your FF.'

Bembo placed the letter inside his tunic. 'Tell her highness,' he said to the messenger, 'that her command shall be obeyed, not only because it is her wish, but mine also.'

He dismissed the man, and turned his horse towards the north.

FIVE

Venice, 1504

I

Bembo reached Venice by the public ferry from Fusina. The city was crowded for the winter fair and he had difficulty in hiring a gondola to take him from the ferry-stage to the Ca' Bembo. When he eventually found one, the boatman, glancing at his Ferrarese cloak, assumed that he was another foreign merchant and demanded twice the legal fare. Bembo, his nerves raw with anxiety and the delay, burst into low Venetian and loudly recited the penalties that could be imposed for the offence by the magistrates.

He was rowed in sullen silence to the Ca' Bembo. He sat huddled in the cabin, shaken by the violence of his own anger and the time it had wasted. He felt the familiar damp winter air settle on his shoulders. Lanterns by the water and the chinks of light showing through shuttered windows were haloed in mist. Bembo shivered.

They turned into the darkness of the Rio San Salvador. A pallid torch burned by the water-gate of the Ca' Bembo. Marco was sitting on the steps beneath it, his head sunk on his chest, his hands hanging loosely between his knees. At the sound of the boat, he raised his head slowly. Bembo stood up and Marco recognised his movement. 'Pietro?' he called, his voice bewildered.

Bembo called back through the thin, wispy fog and leapt from the boat. Marco caught hold of him and steadied him. 'Pietro,' he whispered, 'why weren't you here?'

Bembo was shaking. 'Carlo – ?'

'He's dead. Our dear boy's dead.'

Bembo wanted to scream. He clung to Marco.

'Dead and buried,' said Marco.

Bembo gasped in horror. He remembered the words he had read in Lucrezia's Bible. 'Buried? Not buried.'

'Yes, this morning. He died the night before last.' Marco's voice was accusing. 'You should have been here with him. He loved you. Why didn't you come back?'

Shaking his head, unable to answer, Bembo turned towards the stairs, grasping at the wall for support.

He reached the first narrow landing and found the great reception doors standing open. Usually at this time of year, the rooms beyond were closed, and the family lived in the smaller rooms on the floor above, where open fires, low ceilings and wooden panelling kept them warmer. But death demanded its own splendour. Bembo stepped into a cavern of cold and darkness, rousing echoes. Other sounds answered, other footsteps and the tap of a stick. From one of the open doorways came a frail, bobbing light.

His father appeared, leaning on a cane. Beside him was Bartolommeo, holding a candlestick. Bembo hurried towards his father, arms outstretched to give comfort. But as Bernardo embraced him, his own grief overwhelmed him. He laid his head on his father's shoulder and wept.

The Senator waited for a time and then roused him gently. 'Pietro, we must all try to bear this bravely for one another's sake.' Other lights came swimming into the room as the rest of the family came to greet Bembo. 'I wish you could have been here this morning. It would have consoled you, as it consoled us all, to have seen the manner in which the Senate chose to lay your brother to rest.'

Bembo looked up. 'The Senate?'

Bernardo nodded. 'Carlo was given a state funeral by the Republic. Never in the greatest moments of our house was one of its members paid greater honour.'

On the Senator's haggard face, there was a faint smile of pride. Bembo sickened, covered his eyes.

In the church of San Salvador, the stone slab which closed the entrance to the Bembo tomb had not yet been replaced. Bembo crouched on the paved floor beside it. Bartolommeo knelt close to him, trying to comfort him as their father had done.

'The whole college of ministers was there,' he whispered, 'the chiefs of justice and the high admiral.' Bartolommeo was barred by his illegitimacy from holding an office of state and he had an uncritical admiration of those who did. 'The doge himself led the procession.'

'Our father should have done that, and you, Bartolommeo,' said Bembo fiercely. He glanced round. The interior of the church was swathed in the black velvet trappings of a state funeral. Tears rushed into his eyes. 'Why couldn't we have buried him under the trees of the Villa Bozza?'

Bartolommeo's literal mind was shocked. 'Pietro, that isn't consecrated ground.' He was puzzled by his brother's attitude. 'I can't remember the Senate giving such a funeral to a man as young as Carlo,' he explained. 'I don't think you should be angry about it. I suppose they were trying to honour him for what he would have done for Venice had he lived. Did you know that he had been elected to serve with the college of ministers during its next session?'

Bembo shook his head. It was the custom in Venice to elect young men of exceptional promise to minor ministerial posts in order to train them in the Venetian practice of government. Bembo was amazed and ashamed that he should not have been aware of Carlo's growing public reputation. He recalled, with bitterness towards himself, how in their last conversations together it had been his affairs, rarely Carlo's, that they had discussed.

He stared into the tomb, and then rose to his feet. Bartolommeo, with a feeling of relief, followed him. 'How long was he ill?' asked Bembo.

'About three weeks.'

'Three weeks!' cried Bembo.

Bartolommeo put a finger to his lips and hastily led his brother to the back of the church. Bembo was indifferent to their surroundings. 'Why didn't you write to me earlier?' he demanded.

'Pietro, ssh! For the first ten days or so the illness didn't seem serious. It was very like the sort of chill you always catch in the winter. Later, when he was feverish, he wouldn't let me write to you.'

'Wouldn't let you write? Not to me?'

'He kept saying,' Bartolommeo whispered patiently, 'that you were concerned with important matters in Ferrara, and he wouldn't have you taken away from them for his sake.'

It was typical of Bartolommeo that he never questioned what those matters were. He always accepted without resentment the fact that his two younger half-brothers involved themselves in activities which he could not hope to understand.

Bembo leaned against the wall behind him, and turned his face towards it. 'Carlo,' he murmured, 'Oh, Carlo.' After a moment he pulled himself up and said, frowning. 'He never suffered from malaria before. It seems strange.'

'Oh, it wasn't the malaria fever,' said Bartolommeo quickly. 'I don't know what it was.'

Bembo looked at him intently. 'You said you thought at first that he had a chill. How did he get that?'

'We think he caught it because he got wet one night on the lagoon. Alvise asked us to go fishing by flares. We were in the marshes beyond Mazzorbo when fog came down suddenly. Alvise's boatman missed the channel and we went aground.'

'Where the marsh-water is foul?'

Bartolommeo nodded. 'Carlo got out to help push the boat clear. The boat shifted suddenly – you know how it is, Pietro – and Carlo fell forward into the water.'

'Did he swallow much?'

Bartolommeo was surprised by the question. He tried to remember. 'I don't know. I suppose he did. I think he was coughing. His clothes were soaked and, you see, he had to sit in them while we felt our way back through the fog to Venice. It took us over three hours. He was put to bed with hot bricks and hot wine, but it must have been too late. The chill had already got into his bones. If only the fog had cleared – '

Bembo shook his head slowly. 'No, Bartolommeo. I don't think it was the wet clothes or the cold that killed him. It was the sour water he swallowed. I've heard other stories like this.' He closed his eyes for a moment. 'Carlo was already dying when you pulled him back into the boat.'

Bartolommeo brushed the back of his hand across his eyes. 'Yet he laughed and made jokes about the smell on his clothes all the way back in the fog. And, Pietro, for the next week he seemed well enough, except that he kept shivering and his throat ached. Then suddenly he had a terrible, violent fever. He was crying out with thirst all the time, and his body seemed to waste away as we watched him. After two or three days his skin turned a yellowish colour and he began to have fits of delirium. That's when I broke my promise to him and wrote to you. The day before he died the delirium passed and he lay quite still, without speaking, as though he were already dead.'

Bembo walked away to perform the act which had brought him to the church. In front of one of the altars, he took a candle and lit it for Carlo's soul. He knelt beside others mourning like himself. They seemed to take comfort from the gesture of caring for their loved ones even beyond death. Bembo felt nothing of this, but he was conscious of a need to express some sort of bond between Carlo and himself. Rising, he glanced briefly at the Christ hanging above the altar and turned his back on it.

By the door of the church he found his cousin, Alvise, waiting for him. 'I heard that you were back,' he said. 'I came to find you.' He breathed heavily. 'I feel that I'm to blame for it. If I hadn't suggested fishing by night – ' He broke off, overcome.

Bembo embraced him. 'Alvise, this is nonsense,' he said gently.

Bartolommeo, who had joined them, nodded. 'If the time for death has come, Alvise, it has come. If one possible cause is evaded, another will take its place.'

There were times when Bembo envied the simple, uncomplicated faith of believers like Bartolommeo. There were times when, as now, he was irritated by it. If Carlo had not swallowed poisoned water, he would still have been alive. However, to spare Alvise distress, he said nothing. He looked at the rows of devotional candles fluttering in the winter draughts, and begged Bartolommeo and Alvise to leave him alone in the church.

II

In the first days of January the Venice winter fair, which lasted from mid-December to mid-February, was at its peak. The western galley fleets from Barbary and the northern Mediterranean, which had left in the spring, both arrived home in the second week of December. Later in the month the fleets from Constantinople and Alexandria returned from their autumn cruises with Levantine and far eastern merchandise. The unarmed sailing ships, which carried the cheaper freight twice a year from Greece and Syria, were also unloading. Warehouses were filled with cotton, spices, furs, carpets, silks, damasks, wool, sugar, musk, dyes, preserved fruits, salt, gold, pearls, wine and gems. Inns, canals and markets overflowed with foreign merchants and seamen back from their voyages.

Two days after Carlo's burial, Senator Bembo stepped from the quiet apartments of the Ca' Bembo into the crowded streets, obstinately intent on attending a meeting of the doge's council of ministers. Elena, his wife, had begged him not to venture out. While he had been occupied with the ceremonies for Carlo's funeral, the Senator had been an example of courage and dignity to his family, supporting and strengthening them in their grief. Yet once this was over, he seemed to shrink before them into a frail and brittle old man. The abrupt change terrified Elena. Until his fall in the autumn he had carried himself, at seventy, with the bearing of a much younger man. Even after the fall, which had caused a stiffness in one leg, his energy had in no way been impaired.

Now, as he emerged from his house, he had to lean heavily on Pietro's arm. He refused to take his gondola to the doge's palace, preferring to walk through the city to greet acquaintances. They moved very slowly into the Mercerie, the street which linked the Rialto with the Piazza San Marco. Carlo always spoke of it as the most splendid street in Europe. He had never travelled outside Italy, but he had been willing to take the word of those who had. It was the only street in Venice that was paved, and was wide enough for seven or eight people to walk abreast. No horses were allowed along its twisting length, so the traveller could wander at will from side to side, looking at worked ivory, coral and crystal, books and maps, singing-birds in wicker cages. Above all, however, it was the street of the mercers, who gave it its name. From their first floor windows were displayed lengths of velvet and cloths of gold or silver.

Beneath these swaying banners of glowing and shimmering fabric, Bembo forced a way for his father. There were thick knots of people outside the shop-booths and his ill-humour was mounting. Their progress grew slower and slower as the Senator stopped to receive the condolences of friends and kinsmen. Bembo, too, they acknowledged, but distantly and without interest, as if they hardly recognised him. Bembo felt his old resentment against Venice beginning to stir. When a perfumer, who was sprinkling Arabic scent on the brick paving outside his booth, jostled against him and spilt several drops on his gown, Bembo spoke out in anger. The Senator looked at him sadly and with reproach.

In silence, Bembo escorted his father across the Piazza San Marco to the palace. Then he pushed his way back to the Ca' Bembo, determined to get away from Venice as soon as he could. For the first time he began to consider the possibility of living permanently outside the Republic.

His mother was waiting for him when he reached the house, anxious to know if the Senator had been over-tired by the walk. 'He got to the end of it in a better temper than I did,' said Bembo irritably. He lifted his sleeve, which reeked of musk.

Elena smiled, and asked him to sit beside her. 'Do you plan to go back to Ferrara?'

Bembo looked away, wondering if the thought showed in his face. 'Yes, I hope so,' he said.

They were both silent. Then Elena spoke again, 'Pietro, I should like to ask you to do something for me.'

Bembo turned to her. 'Of course, if I can.'

Elena hesitated. 'You can see how your father has been affected by Carlo's death. He needs your help. We all do. Will you stay here with us until he is stronger?'

Bembo hesitated only for an instant. 'I'll stay as long as you need me.'

Elena caught his hand gratefully. 'We must hope it won't be more than a few days before he begins to recover.'

Bembo pretended to be deceived. 'I don't see why not,' he said and made an effort to smile at her.

When she had gone, he sat lost in thought for some time. Then he called Lico and instructed him to return to Ferrara to collect his clothes and some of his other belongings. 'We may have to stay in Venice for several weeks,' he said. 'And, Lico, before you go, there will be a letter to take.'

Although Lico was to be the bearer, Bembo wrote formally, not sure if Lico would be able to hand the letter to Lucrezia herself. ' . . . my presentiments, highness, were well-founded. Messer Carlo, my beloved brother, who was always a support and comfort to me, is dead and has taken with him a great part of my heart. I arrived here to find him not only dead, but already buried, so the verse of the Bible which I read when I parted from you was in every way a true omen of the future. I have sent for the things which I left in Ferrara, and I shall be staying here, at least during this time of total bereavement, so as not to leave my elderly father, who is certainly in need of consolation in his grief. Of my return I will say nothing, because I do not know what to say about it. I kiss your hand . . . with all my heart I beg you to think of me . . . '

Lucrezia wept when she read the letter, both for Carlo's death and Bembo's grief for him. She wept for herself, too, since her own premonition had proved as true as Bembo's. But of this she said nothing in the answer which Lico carried back to Venice. She spoke only of her tears for his loss.

The note reached Bembo as he was wearily preparing to ride to Asolo. The Senator's cousin, the Queen of Cyprus, had sent word from her castle at Asolo that she wished to express personally her condolences to her bereaved kinsfolk. Since her rank precluded her from making the journey to Venice, courtesy demanded that one of the Senator's family should travel to Asolo. Bembo gratefully seized the lines from Lucrezia. He abandoned what he was doing to scribble back, 'Your tears have been a very sweet comfort to me in my grief, if anything sweet can be mine in these days. I hold myself in great debt to you . . . '

He gave the letter to Bartolommeo, explaining carefully that he was to take it to Alvise and ask him to deliver it in Ferrara the next time he had business in Bologna.

With his usual lack of curiosity, Bartolommeo took the letter and propped it up on his desk in the counting-house. Then he tapped the ledger that lay open in front of him. 'Pietro, you won't leave, will you, till we've decided what to do about the pewter?'

'Pewter?' said Bembo.

'The English pewter that Carlo bought. Unless we sell it soon, before the end of the fair, we shan't get a good price.'

'Well, I don't know anything about that, do I?' said Bembo pleasantly.

III

Bembo rode across the flat plain of Treviso in a fine drizzle of mist that enclosed him like a cocoon. He passed the night at Treviso with a branch of his mother's family. Next morning the mist still lay on the ground, but thinly, and as he left the city the first foothills of the Alps began to take distant shape. When he had passed through Montebelluno, five peaks rose clearly before him, the further one tipped by the remains of the Roman fort that stood above Asolo. Beyond, hidden in cloud, lay the mountains.

Bembo had always loved Asolo, and he liked the untroubled, leisured life at the small court of the Queen of Cyprus. The queen was an elderly Venetian lady of the patrician house of Cornaro. As a young woman she had been married to the King of Cyprus to further the political interests of the Republic, and her life there had been bitter and turbulent. More than one of Bembo's kinsmen had died a violent death in her service. Venice had finally decided to annex her kingdom, giving her in exchange the seigniory of Asolo, where she settled into a placid exile.

A mile or so before the town, the road to Asolo left the fields and orchards of the plain to ascend steeply and abruptly. Clusters of larches, cypresses and pines appeared. Along the approach to the gate, the ground dropped sheer away into the mist.

As he rode into the twisting, arcaded street, Bembo felt none of the pleasure which he usually experienced at this moment, but only a sense of desolation. It was largely because of the melancholy reason for his visit, yet it had another source. Asolo's winter snow was now associated in his mind with Lucrezia, and to find himself alone in the town made all the more vivid his separation from her.

He pressed on past the lion of Venice carved on the stone fountain in the piazza and up into the courtyard of the castle. He was lodged that night in a room in the watch-tower, with a window that overlooked the courtyard. Overnight the white mist thickened, and by morning he was unable to see the buildings on the other side.

He rose unhurriedly, and left his room at an hour that would have been late for the Ca' Bembo, but was still too early for the court at Asolo. He left the castle, walked through the piazza and took the rough path to the Roman fort. After a few minutes of brisk climbing, he was alone in a white, empty world. He met no one and heard no sound. The path was treacherous from rivulets that had trickled across it and then become frozen. He reached the top, warm with exertion, and leaned against one of the ancient walls to catch his breath. Below him the town was like a drowning Atlantis, submerged in mist, with only the watch-tower of the castle, the campanile in the piazza and the dark tips of the cypresses lifted above it.

The cold was beginning to affect Bembo on his lonely perch when suddenly the mist began to move. He turned his head to look back at the wall of cloud that lay in front of the mountains. Before his eyes, it was drifting away from the higher slopes. Within minutes the whole crescent range of peaks was uncovered, soaring against a sky of brilliant blue, the snow glistening in the sun.

Bembo felt excitement quickening. This glorious sight of the snow, white and remote against the sky-line, was the sight he had cherished in his memory since he had last glimpsed it many winters before. It was in terms of this image that he so often thought of Lucrezia.

He longed for her to be with him to share the moment. Without her, even the most intense pleasure lost its edge, lacking something that was not lacking before he knew her. He looked towards the town. The mist was rolling down the hill, and the floating towers and trees were gradually resuming contact with the earth. He watched the uncovering of the fountain in the piazza, and saw the water in its bowl glint like a tiny sliver of pewter.

Pewter! Bembo recalled with a shock Bartolommeo, Venice and the winter fair. Then, just as the mist had suddenly been blown from the mountains, a veil was twitched from his mind. He saw for the first time what Carlo's death meant in relation to his own future.

He sank down on the damp grass, shaken by the fact that he should have grasped as soon as he had arrived back in Venice – the trading concerns of the Ca' Bembo were now his responsibility.

When he had left for Ostellato eighteen months before, matters were being handled jointly by his father, Jacopo and Carlo. Bernardo had largely dictated the policy of the house, using to advantage his special knowledge of the Senate's deliberations on merchant shipping. Jacopo had organised the day-to-day business of the partnership, appointing and corresponding with agents abroad, hiring seamen, buying and selling on the markets. Carlo had supervised the warehouses, and dealt with legal and banking matters. In the past year, however, Carlo had steadily undertaken more and more of the work of Bernardo and Jacopo. While he was recovering from his fall, the Senator had delegated nearly every decision to Carlo. With Jacopo's memory failing rapidly, Carlo had, in fact, virtually controlled the affairs of the Ca' Bembo in the months before his death.

Bartolommeo remained, but Bartolommeo, by reason of his illegitimacy, was debarred by Venetian law from transacting business for the patrician merchant family to which he belonged. Bembo laid his head in his hands. 'No,' he said uselessly to himself, 'No!' He wondered if this had been in his mother's mind when she had asked him to stay. 'Your father needs your help,' she had said. 'We all need it.' It had never occurred to him that she might mean in the counting-house and in the markets.

He climbed down towards the town, turning his head every few steps to glance at the snow peaks. He had a sense of separating himself not only from the mountains but from Lucrezia.

It was shortly before noon when he arrived back at the castle, still too early to wait on Queen Caterina. He walked about in the garden in front of her apartments. The path surrounding it ran between tall junipers on one side and taller laurels on the other. In winter it was gloomy, but in summer cool and pleasant. Bembo remembered that it was eight years ago, in summer, that he had walked along this same path, thinking about the book he was planning to write on aspects of human and divine love. He had noticed a number of the queen's ladies and her officers passing the heat of the afternoon in the shade of a clump of trees that grew at one end of the garden against the mountain. As he listened to them talking, the idea came to him to cast his book in the form of conversations after the manner of Plato. The speakers should be just such a group of young men and women, and they should sit, as he saw them sitting then, among the wild summer flowers of Asolo, beside a tiny marble canal filled with water trickling from the rock. He decided that he would call the book after them, the people who lived in Asolo – the Asolani.

Now the garden was deserted and silent. Bembo wandered unhappily along the wall that rose from the steep hill-side on which the castle and its garden were poised. The wall was screened with laurels, broken by two openings framed in marble, with seats of marble set in the thickness of the wall, like the windows of a great hall. He paused beside one of them, looking down at the plain beneath him stretching to the horizon. On the rim of the horizon lay Venice.

In quick anger Bembo swore that whatever happened, whatever he would have to sacrifice for Venice, he would finish his book for Lucrezia. It should be dedicated, publicly, to her. That at least they would share. Before the world, now and in the years after they were dead, their names should lie together on the printed page. It seemed to him now that it had always been her book, even from its inception in this garden, long before he knew her. He was often amazed, rereading the earlier pages, to discover that he had expressed thoughts about love which only through his conformity with Lucrezia he had truly comprehended. It was as though his imagination existed on a different plane of time.

The clock on the watch-tower struck the hour of noon. Bembo turned towards the castle. He raised his eyes to the mountains; the cloud was already forming again.

IV

Bembo returned to Venice and shut himself up in the counting-house to study Bartolommeo's ledgers. The Venetian system of venture accounting was necessarily complicated. Bembo pored over records and bank deposits, merchandise accounts, shipping accounts, agents' accounts, merchandise accounts received from agents, buyers' accounts and accounts to be paid. With Bartolommeo's help he finally grasped the principle of these. Then he turned his attention to the pewter and the rest of the stock standing in the warehouse, expecting to find in Carlo's papers some indication of what he intended to do with it.

Bartolommeo shook his head. Carlo, he explained, could carry complex schemes and calculations in his head without needing to commit them to paper, and since he was in the habit of making rapid changes of plan to meet changing situations he rarely troubled to discuss his decisions.

Bembo's head reeled. He sought Jacopo's help. His uncle was sitting before a blazing fire with his feet stretched out on a stool. 'Don't come to me about that pewter,' he said testily. 'Worthless stuff. You should never have bought it. Now take yourself away, Pietro.'

Bembo went to his father. The Senator listened to him with a vague air, then said courteously, 'I am willing to leave any action to your judgement, Pietro.'

In the end it was Alvise who found him a buyer. 'Carlo would probably have got a better price,' he told Bembo, 'but this gives you a fair profit and it gets it off your hands.'

Gratefully, Bembo turned his attention to the rest of his tasks. For a scholar, used to working alone for long periods at a single problem, the fragmented demands of the counting-house, the markets and the warehouses were mentally bewildering and exhausting, and the more tired Bembo became the more elusive was the simplest calculation. Bartolommeo continued to help him, and they were joined by Nicola Bruno. Bruno had a better memory and a shrewder mind than Bartolommeo's but he had never worked in the counting-house before and he despised the routine. Ultimately, everything depended on Bembo.

He was amazed that his family took it wholly for granted that he should assume Carlo's place. After a time, however, he realised that in their eyes he was not in fact taking Carlo's place, but merely undertaking the work that was his by right and duty. He worked hard, hoping that by doing so he was bringing himself nearer to his return to Ferrara, but the harder he worked the more his parents were convinced that he had found satisfaction in his proper state.

The Senator acted on this conviction, roused for the first time from apathy since Carlo's burial. One evening when supper was almost finished, he turned to Bembo with a cheerful expression. 'Pietro, I have some news for you.'

Bembo glanced up warily from his plate. 'Sir?'

The Senator smiled round the table. 'I have been able to secure your nomination for two coming elections. One is for a post with an embassy to the King of France, the other for an embassy to Germany and Spain.'

Bembo half rose to his feet in anger. Bartolommeo pulled him back by his gown.

'You are surprised, Pietro?' asked the Senator kindly.

Bembo sank back into his seat, shaking slightly. 'By the suddenness of it, yes, sir,' he muttered.

'But why wait longer?' enquired the Senator. 'You are admirably fitted for either office. I rather favour the French post myself, but the other would do very well.'

Bembo retired from the table as soon as he dared and took refuge in the empty counting-house. He struck one of the ledgers, furious at his father's bland disregard for all that had passed between them in October. Had no one listened to what he said, or believed that he meant it? Did they think he was so shallow as to have forgotten it himself? Now, because of his father's fragile health, it was impossible to argue with him. He paced up and down the narrow floor, missing Carlo's help. If he lost the election, he would have to submit to a public humiliation which he dreaded. If he won, he might be tied to a post abroad for months to come. There was no question of a refusal. To decline an office to which one had been elected incurred imprisonment or a fine that was quite beyond the resources of the Ca' Bembo.

This, thought Bembo, sitting exhausted in the darkness, is what Lucrezia foresaw. He had laughed at her and told her that Venice was nothing but bricks, stone and timber. He had promised to return to her in a few days. Six weeks had passed, and there was still no end to their separation in sight. How could anyone not born a Venetian understand his delay? His need to explain himself to her was desperate, yet for the moment he had no means of writing freely to her. Since the visit at the beginning of January, Alvise had made no further journeys to Bologna, and Bembo had had to send his last two letters by the public courier, which meant that they could contain little more than polite greetings. He asked himself again how anyone but a Venetian could be expected to understand.

V

But Lucrezia knew more about the manner of life in Venice than Bembo realised. In his absence she had taken care to cultivate the company of the Venetian vice-domino's ladies, and when the vice-domino's niece gave birth to a son in Venice, Lucrezia indicated that she would be pleased to act as his godmother by proxy.

From the talk of the Venetian ladies, she learned not only how to make the paste used in their famous method of bleaching hair in the sunlight, but also the pattern of the merchant year in Venice. She now knew that until the middle of February the trading houses were very busy, but that when the first round-ships sailed again for Syria the winter fair drew to its end, and the pressure of buying and selling became less fierce.

She waited, therefore, until the last week in February and, when there was still no news of Bembo returning, she expressed a wish to visit her new godchild in Venice.

Lucrezia's punctiliousness in fulfilling her obligations towards the Church was well established. She was known to be devout, never appearing in public without carrying a rosary – although it was noted by the observant that her rosaries were always set with the gems to match her dresses. Alfonso, alive to the advantages of piety in a consort, agreed to the proposed visit. The duke, quietly plotting the destruction of Venice, still prudently paid lip-service to his protectors and welcomed his daughter-in-law's journey to aid the deception. Delighted with her success, Lucrezia consulted her calendar and decided that she would be free to leave Ferrara towards the end of March or shortly before Whitsun.

The news that Lucrezia intended to travel to Venice in the third week of March first reached Bembo in a letter from Strozzi, who slipped it in between paragraphs of inconsequential gossip about the court. With the letter in his hand, Bembo wandered towards the Rialto exchange in a bemused state of wonder. The simple daring of Lucrezia's actions always amazed and enchanted him. She had come to his house in Ferrara, and now she was coming to Venice.

He walked round the piazza of San Giacomo and out again without taking in a word of the information he had come to find. He moved idly towards the canal between stalls of fruit and on into the fish market. An elderly senator, with a musk melon under one arm, was sniffing at a box of mullet. He was a man to Bembo's knowledge worth at least two million ducats a year, yet he did his own shopping because he distrusted his cook to bargain as closely as he did. Such parsimony was not uncommon among the merchant princes of Venice and Bembo usually treated it with contempt. On this occasion, however, he startled the old man by greeting him good-humouredly and congratulating him on his fine melon.

As they parted, the noon-day bells began to ring out over the city. It was the custom in Venice at this hour to say aloud an Ave-Maria. The fishmongers and porters in the market tore off their caps and uttered their prayers at such speed that their knees hardly touched the ground. Bembo, who often ignored the bell, chose for once to observe it. He knelt down, heedless of the scales and green slime on the floor of the market, and spoke the words of the prayer with gentleness. Then he rose, resumed his cap and walked between the pillars of the fish market to the edge of the quay.

A pale winter sun was lighting the canal, and Bembo found himself looking at his city with new eyes, discovering a pleasure in the sight that he wanted Lucrezia to share. He smiled at the palaces, soaring out of their own shifting reflections, the bobbing water flickering light back across the fretted stone. There were no smooth surfaces, no solid masses to calm the mind. Instead there was a sharpness of outline, a brightness of colour, a glitter, a restlessness of movement that communicated energy and excitement. Bembo saw a bristling rim of gilded posts springing from the water, windows like spiked crystal wands, a skyline of thin, high chimneys with washing fluttering on poles. He thought of Lucrezia clapping her hands with delight, and then falling silent as she heard the air shimmer with the sound of bells.

He was roused from his dream by the sound of his own name. He glanced down. Alvise was riding on the canal in a small fishing craft. His twelve-year old son, Giovanni Matteo, was leaning on the single oar.

'Uncle,' cried Giovanni Matteo, 'you have fish-scales on your gown.'

'Be quiet,' said Alvise. 'Pietro, where are you going?'

Bembo looked at the smear across the knees of his gown and laughed. 'Home, I think, for fresh clothes.'

'Get in, then, Pietro. We'll take you.'

Bembo climbed down from the quay into the boat. He embraced Alvise and Giovanni Matteo at their opposite ends of the shallow craft, holding it balanced as he moved. Then he sat down beside Alvise.

'I see you've hired a new boatman,' he said, smiling at Giovanni Matteo.

Alvise looked harassed. 'He's in disgrace. He's staying with me today.' He waited until his son had manoeuvred the boat in the direction of the Rialto bridge and then added darkly, 'He's been to the Arsenal again.'

Since his return from Ferrara, Bembo had been a frequent visitor at the house of Alvise, and he understood the significance of the remark. Giovanni Matteo had played truant again. 'Oh,' said Bembo, trying to sound suitably distressed.

Giovanni Matteo had a passion for the sea and ships that was remarkable even in a boy brought up in Venice, and the shipbuilding yards of the Arsenal were both his second home and his idea of paradise. Children were not welcome inside the Arsenal compound, but Giovanni Matteo had ways of getting in and out of the two miles of fortified walls. He had become such a familiar sight in the timber-yards, the hemp-sheds, the sail-makers' stores, the gun foundries and the dry docks that no one troubled any more to chase him out. But yesterday, it appeared, Giovanni Matteo had gone too far.

'He was sent,' Alvise was whispering in a tone of bewildered exasperation, 'to take a parcel of fruit to his mother's aunt, who has been ill. After four hours, I went to fetch him back. His aunt hadn't seen him!'

It was the time of year when the Barbary fleet was being refitted for its spring voyage. Giovanni Matteo had intended to take a quick look at the basin. But the sight of the galleys lying in ranks on the water, their prows thick with fresh gilding, had been too much for him. He had stood and gazed at them. Then, when no one had appeared to be watching, he had rowed out to the nearest and climbed aboard. He had been found some time later in the galley-master's cabin by a carpenter.

'And then he tried to speak to the carpenter as though he *were* a galley-master,' said Alvise distractedly. 'They're proud men, you know, Pietro, those craftsmen in the Arsenal. It doesn't do for a child – or anyone else – to be rude to them.'

'I wasn't being rude,' said Giovanni Matteo. 'I was only pretending. He didn't understand.'

Alvise ignored him. 'If Cousin Domenico hadn't by a lucky chance been inspecting the work on his fleet and taken charge of the boy, I don't know what might have happened. Domenico brought him back, in no good humour, I can tell you.' He waved a finger at his son. 'You wasted Cousin Domenico's time, you gave your mother a lot of unnecessary worry and you embarrassed me.'

Beneath the concern and the embarrassment, Bembo detected a touch of pride in Alvise's manner. So did Giovanni Matteo. His eyes slid towards Bembo with a glint in them that reminded Bembo of Carlo at a similar age. Bembo smiled indulgently.

There had been a growing bond between them since Bembo had realised that, despite his preoccupation with ships, Giovanni Matteo had the makings of a scholar.

One day he had heard the boy working with the Latin tutor Alvise had hired. Bembo had rounded passionately on his cousin. 'Alvise, that man's a heretic. You can't let him teach your son.'

'Pietro, I assure you,' Alvise had said nervously, 'that he's an orthodox believer – '

'I don't mean that. He doesn't teach Ciceronian Latin. Dismiss him.'

Alvise had pointed out the difficulty of finding even bad Latin tutors in Venice. Bembo, after a pause, had then announced that he himself would undertake Giovanni Matteo's classical education. The boy, overawed by Bembo's manner and reputation as a scholar, had at first been terrified of him. But the wealth of legends and anecdotes with which Bembo illuminated every text they studied soon won Giovanni Matteo's adoration. In return he shared his most exciting thoughts about ships with his uncle. Bembo was inclined to think that he was learning more about rigging and tonnage than his pupil about Caesar's Gallic Wars.

Giovanni Matteo rowed under the wooden bridge. 'Will you let me watch Cousin Domenico sail for the Barbary coast?' he asked his father.

'You're not going on your own,' said Alvise, 'and I doubt if I shall have time to stand about.'

Giovanni Matteo looked at Bembo. 'Uncle Pietro – '

'Yes, Gian Matteo?'

'If you took me, it would give you a chance to teach me Latin naval terminology.'

Bembo and Alvise glanced at each other helplessly. 'Now that's enough,' said Alvise. 'Just wait. The Barbary fleet doesn't sail for another month.'

'I know,' said Giovanni Matteo. 'But I like to have something special to think about.'

Bembo felt Strozzi's letter in his pocket. 'Yes, I understand,' he said gently. 'So do I, Gian Matteo.'

VI

In the first week of March, at only a few hours' notice, Francesco Gonzaga, Marquis of Mantua, arrived in Ferrara. The possessive devotion of his wife, Isabella, and her prying interference in his political affairs drove him from time to time to seek peace elsewhere.

He had never met his brother-in-law's new wife, but he had heard a great deal about her from Isabella and his sister, Elisabetta of Urbino. They no longer held to their earlier conviction that being a Borgia she must be depraved, but they were agreed that she was vulgar and spiritless.

Francesco was, therefore, unprepared for the kind of woman who appeared at Alfonso's side to greet him. He found her gentle and without affectation, and after an hour's conversation with her he was enchanted. In the days that followed he spent as much time in her company as he could. His constant attention to her, half-serious, half-playful, startled the court and even attracted Alfonso's notice. Francesco was aware of this and amused by it. His position was privileged, since he had grown up among the duke's sons, and Ferrara also relied on his brilliant generalship to organise its defences.

He postponed his departure for Mantua. The letters flew from the pens of the ladies of Ferrara to Isabella. She wrote, commanding his return. He delayed it a second time.

'But your excellency must go back,' cried Lucrezia. 'Your wife requests it. Besides, I must prepare for my journey to Venice.'

'Why must you go to Venice?' asked Francesco.

'To – to visit my godson,' stammered Lucrezia.

'Well, if that is the only reason, I shall join you there.'

'Your excellency doesn't mean that,' said Lucrezia, twisting her necklace nervously round her fingers.

'Oh, yes, I do.'

Strozzi assured her that Francesco was indeed quite capable of following her to Venice if the mood seized him. 'He's impulsive,' he said, 'and he also enjoys upsetting an apple-cart or two.'

'What am I to do?' Lucrezia sobbed. 'What date is it?'

'The fifteenth – '

A string of pearls broke in Lucrezia's hands and she threw them across the floor. 'If he doesn't leave soon, it'll be too late for me to go. It's almost too late now.' She drew a gasping breath. 'I'll go anyway – '

'Leaving him here? No, madonna, that would be such an unthinkable discourtesy that everyone would ask questions.'

'Oh, why doesn't he go?'

Strozzi forebore to remark that one of the reasons that Francesco lingered in Ferrara was her own unresponsiveness to him. It puzzled him. Women usually found his exuberant admiration irresistible, especially women who were as neglected by their husbands as Lucrezia was.

'Is she a prude?' he enquired of Strozzi. They had been friends since boyhood, and were drinking together in Francesco's rooms in the castle.

'I think not,' said Strozzi.

Francesco reached for another bottle and considered. 'Then there's only one other possibility,' he announced indistinctly. 'She already has a lover.'

'What here? With your wife's harpies watching everything she does?'

Francesco frowned, and then laughed. 'Ah, no, not here. Not possible.' He struck the table with a roar. 'No, of course, not here. Is this why there's such a fuss about going to Venice?'

'Excellency?' Strozzi raised one eyebrow.

Francesco nodded good-humouredly. 'So that's it. And you know about it.'

Strozzi shrugged his shoulders. He filled Francesco's wine-cup. 'Nevertheless, I don't think Madonna Lucrezia will be going to Venice. Your excellency's long stay has prevented it.'

'Venice is a long way away,' said Francesco.

'Perhaps the time has come to discourage such long journeys,' murmured Strozzi.

Francesco leaned across the table. He looked and sounded sober. 'Ercole, when you are arranging shorter journeys, do what you can for me. You know I will not be ungrateful.' He pulled a large diamond ring off his finger and thrust it on to Strozzi's.

'You know that I have always been your servant,' said Strozzi.

The marquis departed at last for Mantua, but too late for Lucrezia to make her stay in Venice before the Easter ceremonies began at court. As soon as he had gone, she disappeared into her own apartments, sent for paper and pens, and dismissed all her attendants except Angela Borgia. Within minutes, Strozzi was begging to be received.

When Strozzi was admitted, Lucrezia was already writing. She glanced up with the pen in her hand. 'Messer Ercole,' she said courteously, 'unless what you have come to say is urgent, would you allow me a few minutes – ?'

'Madonna, it is urgent – that is to say, it is urgent if the letter you are now writing is destined for Venice.'

Lucrezia put down her pen. 'Yes, of course, it is.'

Strozzi sighed. 'I must ask your highness to forgive this impertinence.' He snatched the letter from Lucrezia's table, carried it to the fire-place and threw it on the flames.

Lucrezia jumped up. 'Ercole, how dare you!'

'I dare, madonna,' said Strozzi brusquely, 'for your safety.' He pointed towards the public rooms beyond Lucrezia's doors. 'Out there are a hundred pairs of eyes watching on Isabella's behalf for the first sign that you are writing secretly to Francesco Gonzaga. Some of your pages and your servants have been bribed to tell them whenever you put pen to paper, where your letters go and who carries them.'

'But I'm not writing to Francesco Gonzaga,' cried Lucrezia, stamping her foot.

'No, but is it wise to let them discover a letter to Bembo? Believe me, you must be very careful in the next few weeks.'

Lucrezia gave a cry of despair. 'But there are things I must tell him. I must explain – ' She broke off and held out her hands to Strozzi. 'Messer Ercole, write for me.'

Strozzi hesitated, and became evasive. 'Madonna, I am known to be a close companion of the marquis. I am the first person they would suspect of being a go-between. I have little doubt that some of my own servants have also been bribed.'

Lucrezia fell silent. Then she looked straight at Strozzi. 'If you can't help me, I shall have to find some other way.'

In Venice, Bembo was unaware of the effects of Francesco Gonzaga's visit. As the days slipped away, and no further word reached him about Lucrezia's journey, his elation turned to uneasiness and then to alarm.

Thus preoccupied, he found himself facing the first of the elections for which he had been nominated. His opponent won. The Senator was not disheartened. 'As you know, Pietro,' he said, 'I should have preferred to see you in the French post, but the electors evidently judge you more fitted for the emperor's court, and they may very well be right.'

Ten days later, Bembo was again defeated, by one hundred and thirty-eight votes to forty-three.

Bembo strode out of the doge's palace, making no attempt to disguise his anger. He had not wanted to win, and, in fact, had not expected to do so, but he had assumed that he would lose in an honourable way by some fifteen or twenty votes. Instead he had been almost totally rejected in favour of a man whose talents were negligible and whose family was considerably less distinguished than his own.

Alvise tried to keep pace with Bembo as they crossed the courtyard. 'Your absence from Venice did, of course, weigh against you,' he said, trying to calm him. In his agitation he added without thinking, 'And Carlo was very much respected.'

Bembo saw no connection between the two remarks. 'What do you mean? What has Carlo to do with it? Surely his reputation should be an advantage to me.'

Alvise wiped sweat from his face. 'Pietro, I thought you understood. It's being said that you stayed away from Venice for a year because you were jealous of Carlo.'

Bembo stood still and stared at Alvise. 'What did you say?'

Alvise stumbled on. 'When you didn't come back for Carlo's burial, there was talk that you couldn't even bear to witness the tributes paid to him when he was dead.'

Bembo felt as if he had been struck across the heart. 'People believe this?'

'Some do, I'm afraid.'

At that moment, Bembo hated Venice. He was not unaccustomed to being neglected by his countrymen, but now they had inflicted on him a hurt that he believed he would never forgive. He resolved that as soon as his father was stronger, he would leave Venice and that he would never return.

Meanwhile he felt unable to breathe the air of the city. He went back to the Ca' Bembo to see if any letters had arrived for him from Ferrara. There was nothing. Not waiting to meet his father, he had Marco row him to Murano, to the villa of his friend, Andrea Navagero, who was a poet like himself.

Bembo often stayed with Navagero when he was weary of the lack of green trees and open walks in the centre of Venice. Navagero owned a villa on a tiny spit of land which he had covered with an orchard. The house stood by the water, beside a small quay. The air was warm that evening and they supped under trees thick with blossom, watching the distant towers of Venice darken against a luminous sky. His surroundings and Navagero's amusement at his disgrace eased Bembo's bitterness. But not his anxiety about Lucrezia.

Unable to sleep that night, he sat by a window staring out at the water, consumed by the wretchedness of uncertainty. He wondered if Lucrezia were ill, or whether the mere suggestion of travelling to Venice had placed her under some constraint. Strozzi's silence, too, disturbed him. In either case, it would be dangerous to write to her. He had made himself promise a hundred times in the last few days that he wouldn't write to her until he knew she was safe and well. And a hundred times he had asked himself how she could understand his desperate need of news if he didn't tell her so. Yet, even if he dared, there was no one at present that he could trust to get a letter to his FF. If he wrote openly to the duchess, the letter might be read anywhere between Venice and Lucrezia's apartments; and how, he asked himself hopelessly, could he disguise in a courtier's trivial compliments his cry for help.

Then, suddenly, he remembered Strozzi's fiction of his attachment to one of Lucrezia's ladies. The solution to the problem was so simple that he wondered why he had never thought of it before. He would write to the Duchess Lucrezia and entreat her help with the unresponsive FF.

He lit candles, set out paper and dipped a quill in his ink. He was in despair, he confessed to the duchess, because for so long he had had no news of his beloved FF. Could her highness, for pity's sake, not persuade FF to send him a couple of lines in her own hand so that he would know she was well and remembered him? A grey dawn was rising when Bembo sealed the letter and called Lico to carry it into Venice.

Two days later, when Bembo was watching glass being blown in the factory which Navagero owned on Murano, Marco arrived on the island looking for him. The majordomo of the Duchess of Ferrara, he explained breathlessly, shouting above the roaring of the furnace, was in Venice and asking to meet Messer Pietro Bembo.

Impatient with excitement, Bembo returned to Venice with Marco. It was only after the gondola had been gliding for half an hour across the lagoon and they were entering the canals of the city that Bembo realised that the majordomo's arrival was too early for it to be a result of his letter. Lucrezia must, on her own initiative, have despatched him from Ferrara.

He entered the Ca' Bembo as his family was about to walk into supper. The Senator nodded to him as he appeared in the doorway and bowed to his parents. 'Ah, Pietro,' he said pleasantly, 'you are joining us.' He made no reference to Bembo's hasty retreat to Murano or his unexpected return. With the composure that he had acquired during his years as an ambassador, he merely took his son's arm and added, 'Will you carve?'

VII

It was only his long training in the courtly ideals of nonchalance and discretion that prevented Bembo from embracing the majordomo like a brother. He received him instead with dignity, standing in his black robes in one of the lofty apartments of the Ca' Bembo under a carved and gilded ceiling.

He invited him to drink wine and then politely asked the reason for the majordomo's request to see him. The majordomo sipped his wine and explained that he had come to Venice to prepare for a visit by the Duchess of Ferrara, who wished to see her godson.

'Ah, yes, I had heard something of this,' said Bembo carelessly, 'but I thought the visit had been planned for some time earlier this month.'

The majordomo nodded. 'That was so, Messer Bembo. You are quite right. But her highness had to change her arrangements because of an unexpected stay in Ferrara by the Marquis of Mantua.' He broke off. 'That reminds me, Messer Bembo, that her highness particularly charged me to beg your indulgence because she has not replied to certain letters of yours which were written several weeks ago. Believe me, Messer Bembo, the marquis made such demands on her time that she was forced to neglect everything else.'

'But she is well?'

'Oh, in excellent health, I thank you. I think I may say that she looks more beautiful than ever, despite the exhausting attentions of the marquis. Or, perhaps, I should say – ' he winked, ' – because of them.'

Bembo turned away, and the majordomo recalled having heard that Venetians were austere in some of their attitudes. Being republicans they were, of course, unused to the manners of courts. He moved on. 'You will still be wondering, sir, what her highness's visit has to do with my intrusion here today. Let me tell you. Some years ago, Madonna Isabella visited your city and your father, the Magnifico Bernardo Bembo, showed her the Bellini portraits in this house.'

'Yes, I remember,' said Bembo, his heart beginning to beat more quickly.

'Don Alfonso is considering commissioning Messer Bellini to paint in Ferrara, and her highness wonders if the magnifico would allow her to see the works of which Madonna Isabella has spoken so highly. She hopes that you might be entreated to use your good offices in presenting her request to your father.'

Bembo contrived to retain his gravity of bearing. 'I shall be pleased to be of service to her highness. I am sure that my father will be honoured to receive her here.'

Bembo and Lucrezia's majordomo bowed to each other. Then Bembo escorted him to the Senator's library and explained to his father the nature of the majordomo's mission. It was the Senator's turn to bow. 'It has always been a matter of regret to me,' he said, 'that my term of office in Ferrara ended before her highness's marriage. I am therefore delighted to be offered this privilege of meeting her, and am deeply appreciative of the honour she does my house. I beg you to inform her of my abiding wish to be of service to Don Alfonso and herself.'

As the majordomo left in another flurry of bows, the Senator noted thoughtfully the animation in his son's face. He decided to wait a little longer before telling him that the next diplomatic posts would go for election some time in June.

The majordomo, meanwhile, was addressing himself to more wine while Bembo wrote a note of courtesy to the duchess, confirming the majordomo's visit. He used his words with care; letters carried by one of Lucrezia's officers would not be intercepted, but Bembo suspected that the majordomo himself would slip a hot knife under the seal to see if anything had been said about his own behaviour. 'It was not necessary,' Bembo wrote, 'for your highness to excuse herself for not having written more often to me, since, as long as you remember that I am your servant, this is and always will be enough for me. From your majordomo I have learnt that you had planned to come here during Lent, but were prevented, and that you are now considering a visit at Whitsun. My despair at the one will be the less if the other in due time takes place. I would not plead with your highness to make this journey, since it is not my place to make such a plea. Nevertheless, if you do decide to come, I believe you will be pleasantly entertained here. Much more important, your servant will have a glimpse of you. I hear from those who came from Ferrara that you are more beautiful than ever. I would pray the sky that every day it bestow on you greater beauty, but I consider that it cannot add more to the beauty that you already possess.'

In Ferrara, on the same day, Lucrezia was reading Bembo's earlier letter from Murano. Its distress moved and troubled her. She had sent her majordomo to Venice to reassure him, but she didn't yet know if the majordomo had found Bembo or, if he had, whether his message had conveyed all that she wanted Bembo to understand. She snatched up a pen. If Bembo thought it safe to write about the unknown lady-in-waiting, then she must do the same. She wondered, like Bembo, why they had never thought of this device before. 'Messer Pietro,' she wrote, 'with distinct pleasure I received and read your letter. I thank you most warmly, although on the other hand I am grieved to know that your letter leaves you in such distress at the present moment, and that you feel such anxiety to receive a line or two from the hand of FF. For many good reasons she has not been able to satisfy your request. But being eager to please you and do all you wish, she has persuaded me to write these words in the hope that they may bring some consolation and quiet to your mind. So I pray you in this respect to excuse her, and to accept her good will, which I swear to you is always submissive to your desires and your service.'

She signed the letter boldly 'Lucrezia Estensi de Borgia. From Ferrara, the twenty-eighth day of March'. When it was finished and Tebaldeo was sealing it, she gave a small sigh of satisfaction. If a dozen of Isabella's spies contrived to read it, there was nothing of which they could accuse her – except match-making.

The month of April opened with blue and sparkling weather. It was spring in Venice and Ferrara, and the hearts of Bembo and

Lucrezia were light. Each of them carried about a letter written by the other on the same day. Bembo walked about the Ca' Bembo with a brisk step, already seeing Lucrezia in every room. Lucrezia dwelt on the day when she would enter the house in which Bembo had passed most of his life. Neither of them had reached the point of wondering how they might contrive to meet each other alone. It was enough for the moment to know that in six or seven weeks they would be together under the same roof.

VIII

In a boat not far from the gateway to the Arsenal, Bembo and Giovanni Matteo were watching the triremes of the Barbary fleet manoeuvre the narrow channels of the lagoon before assembling in convoy and raising sail.

Giovanni Matteo gazed hungrily at the long, sleek, shallow hulls designed to carry valuable cargoes swiftly through pirated seas. Each of the galleys was built to the same specification, so that in emergencies damaged fittings on one ship could be replaced by those from another, and seamen trained on one deck were at home on all the others in the fleet. The galleys differed only in the degree of splendour which their captains introduced into their furnishings. Tapestries, vessels of silver, silks and carpets were carried even when the triremes were converted for war so that the capture of a Venetian fighting ship ranked as the richest of possible prizes.

The first galley to leave the Arsenal was accompanied by trumpets, and it was the galley of Domenico Bembo, the fleet-master. Pietro could see his kinsman distantly, strutting on the deck in cloth of gold and ermine. All galley-captains, in Pietro's opinion, were alike in their flashy style of dress and arrogant, loud-spoken manner. Since their office, like other state offices, was elective, he could only assume that this was the type of man Venetians liked to send into foreign ports carrying their flag. His own taste was too fastidious to approve either their clothes or their behaviour.

Giovanni Matteo, on the other hand, worshipped them and longed to imitate them. He waved and shouted as the painted oars flashed past him. The sun shone on the gilded prows, shaped like swords, and on the breastplates of the armed men aboard. Giovanni Matteo fired imaginary cannon at the cannon of the galleys while Bembo clutched at his belt. He bowed to the red and gold pennants of the Republic.

'Come along, Gian Matteo,' said Bembo at last. 'It's Wednesday, and I have a meeting to attend.'

Giovanni Matteo sat down and grasped his oar. He rowed for some time without talking, hardly taking his eyes off the fleet. Then he said, 'I don't think I want to be a merchant.'

'Oh?'

'There are too many risks that you can't do anything about,' explained Giovanni Matteo. 'Your father lost a spice-galley, didn't he?'

'Yes, it was damaged by a storm and then taken by pirates. But such events are not common, Gian Matteo.' Bembo was amused at discovering a fellow non-conformist in his family, but he felt obliged to voice the general attitude. 'You must remember that your father and grandfather are merchants. Most Venetians of our kind are merchants in some degree or other.'

'You weren't.'

'Well, no,' said Bembo, 'but I am now.'

'For good?'

Outmanoeuvred against himself, Bembo hesitated.

'I'm never going to be a merchant,' announced Giovanni Matteo. 'I want to be a galley-captain.'

'Galley-captains are usually traders as well,' Bembo reminded him. 'Cousin Domenico will be buying oil and silk on this voyage.'

'I don't want a cargo-galley,' cried Giovanni Matteo indignantly. 'I want to lead a war fleet against the Turks.'

Bembo took a breath. 'Is there no risk in that?' he enquired.

'No,' said Giovanni Matteo, 'not if you understand your own ships, and know the speed and armament of the enemies'. He paused. 'Well, there are risks, I suppose, but they're the kind that happen round you.'

'I see,' said Bembo. 'And having defeated the Turks in a single encounter, what happens then?'

Giovanni Matteo looked at him. 'Haven't we any other enemies?'

Bembo laughed. 'Of course. Aren't we Venetians? The new Pope is a Genoese and he is collecting allies to fight against us – the emperor, the French, Spain, Ferrara – ' He broke off, realising that when the war did come, Venice and Ferrara would be cut off from each other. There would be no messages, no letters at all.

'But they will have to be fought on land,' Giovanni Matteo was complaining, 'not at sea.'

'What?' said Bembo distractedly, 'Oh, well you will have to be content with founding new colonies on Turkish soil.'

'Could you teach me Turkish?'

'No. But Uncle Jacopo might. He used to speak it fluently.'

'Did he fight the Turks?'

'No, but he often traded in their lands when he was a young man. He went to Constantinople and Cairo, too. He saw the Pyramids. Merchants often see more of the world than admirals.'

Giovanni Matteo, who had been struggling with the startling thought of Uncle Jacopo as a young man, glanced at Bembo shrewdly. 'Is that the translation of a Latin saying?'

'No,' said Bembo, 'I do have some ideas of my own.'

Giovanni Matteo laughed so immoderately at this that he suspected that he was being placated. He realised that they were returning home by a devious route. 'Why are we coming this way?' he demanded.

'I thought,' said Giovanni Matteo with innocence, 'that you would enjoy riding past the ship-building yards.'

'Oh, not more ships,' groaned Bembo.

They were entering a quarter of the city largely occupied by the private ship-builders who constructed the sturdy sailing vessels intended for cheap bulk merchandise. Giovanni Matteo stopped beside one of the yards where carpenters were working on the deep, curving ribs of a hull. These ships were so different in line from the long, light galleys that they were commonly called round-ships, a term applied with some bitterness by those who had suffered their slow, rolling motion.

'There are none of your warships to see here, Admiral,' said Bembo.

'But I should use these as my supply ships.'

'They would be too slow. Your men would starve.'

'They were too slow when they were single-masted,' said Giovanni Matteo excitedly, 'but these are three-masters. With the new rigging, they can manoeuvre almost as fast as the galleys with their oars. With a spritsail and the lateen mizzen – '

He paused, aware of his passenger's growing impatience. He changed tack. 'Uncle, what is the Latin for lateen mizzen?'

Bembo was not deceived by the attempt to divert him. 'I have no idea,' he said crisply, 'whether the Romans had either a lateen mizzen or a word for it. Change places with me. I'll row.'

'I'm not tired.'

'Perhaps not. But I have other things to do today. If I row, we may get back in time for me to do them.'

They changed places. 'Are you going to the Greek Academy this afternoon?' asked Giovanni Matteo.

'Yes,' said Bembo.

Giovanni Matteo slapped the water crossly with his fingers. 'I'd rather speak Turkish than Greek.'

'So I gathered.' Bembo ignored the boy for some minutes. Then he said, 'Do you know how the galleys get their name?' Giovanni Matteo shook his head. Bembo rowed another half-dozen strokes. 'It's from the Greek word for a swordfish.'

Giovanni Matteo took his hand out of the water. 'A swordfish?' His eyes shone. 'That's very good.'

Bembo nodded gravely. 'Do you think so?' He murmured to no one in particular, 'The Greeks were excellent navigators.'

Giovanni Matteo hugged himself. 'Tell me some more Greek words,' he said.

Bembo smiled at him, thinking of someone else who liked to understand Greek words.

He delivered Giovanni Matteo into Alvise's hands, shared a mid-day meal with his cousin and then walked to the printing-house of Aldo Manuzio near the church of Sant'Agostino.

Of the two hundred printing-houses that made Venice the publishing centre of Europe, the Aldine Press of Manuzio was the most distinguished and influential. Manuzio was not only a publisher and printer, but also a classical scholar who had come to believe, as Bembo had, that no one could truly understand the world of antiquity unless he knew as much of Greek as of Latin. Latin texts were being widely printed, but none in Greek, and Manuzio conceived the ambition of putting into print every classical Greek text known to have survived.

Encouraged by his patron, Count Alberto Pio of Carpi, Manuzio had set up his printing-house in Venice. He had chosen Venice because it supported one of the few Greek colonies in Italy, established after the fall of Constantinople to the Turks. The Venetian Senate, too, was sufficiently interested in Greek studies to create a chair of Greek in the University of Padua. It was also the home of Messer Pietro Bembo, who had spent two years studying Greek in Sicily and had returned to Venice with the text of the only Greek grammar known to be in existence.

Bembo had co-operated willingly with Manuzio in his work. Between them they had assembled a number of Greek exiles to assist in the collection and editing of manuscripts. When the first few texts had been published, Manuzio founded his Academy of Greek Studies. The enthusiasts met every Wednesday afternoon to discuss Greek scientific and philisophical thought, using Greek as their only language.

Bembo had always valued his Wednesday afternoons at the Academy, but never more so than in the weeks that followed Carlo's death. Here, among scholars who respected him, he regained something of the confidence that was drained away from him in the counting-house. He was not entirely unsuccessful in his dealings in the exchange, but he lacked Carlo's vast knowledge of the markets from London to the Black Sea. He lacked even more the temperament to back a risk based on calculated timing. He bought and sold small quantities of safe merchandise for certain but moderate profits. Though he judged this the wisest course, he nevertheless suffered the frustration of the perfectionist who is doing something at which he knows he can never excel.

He made his usual witty and informed comments at the meeting, and when the rest of the members had dispersed settled down to proof-read a group of Tuscan sonnets. He had long since persuaded Manuzio that the printing of classical texts was not enough; the Aldine Press must also undertake the dissemination of Italian works in pure Tuscan.

He was making a small grammar correction when Aldo Manuzio came into the room. He looked over Bembo's shoulder. 'When are we going to print this Tuscan grammar of yours?'

Bembo raised his head. 'How do you think I can find time to do that? I want to do it, Aldo, but at the moment it's difficult enough to get a few pages of *The Asolani* written each week.' He stood up and looked out of the window to rest his eyes. After a bright morning, the sky had clouded and it was beginning to rain. Worshippers leaving the church were wrapping woollen cloaks round their shoulders to keep off the fine drops. Manuzio's arm in its woollen sleeve reached across Bembo to fasten the window. As the rain began to fall more heavily, a boy wearing a woollen cape darted into a doorway for shelter. Bembo was suddenly aware, as he had never been before, of wool all around him . . . He stood considering this fact.

'What are you thinking about?' asked Manuzio. 'Your book?'

Bembo turned round, laughing guiltily. 'I was thinking about buying wool.'

Manuzio grunted. 'Ledgers, warehouses, buying wool – you shouldn't be wasting your time on such things.'

'I don't do it from choice,' Bembo pointed out. 'Only because there's no one else.'

'There's no one else to finish your book.'

Bembo sighed. 'No, that's true. Aldo, I promise you I'll have it done by the end of the summer.' He paused. 'It's just that this last part doesn't come easily – '

Bembo leaned his head on his hand. 'I don't know why. What I started out to do was to refute the Church's premise that human and divine love are an antithesis, destructive of each other. Why do priests talk about sacred and profane love? It seems to me to be a blasphemy in itself to call the blessing of love between a man and woman profane. I believe, like Plato, that the two kinds of love are akin, one illuminating the other – provided, of course, that the human love is not false.

'So, in the first part of my book, Aldo, I discuss the embittering ends of human love that *is* falsified or distorted in some way – by self-deception, perhaps, or selfishness. I then contrast this with the tranquillity and delight of true human love.' Bembo faltered slightly and Manuzio smiled to himself. 'In the last section I have to show that it is from this state of love, and only from this, that springs our understanding of, and our longing for, divine love. Which is, of course,' added Bembo bleakly, 'the highest experience of all.'

Manuzio scratched his thick white hair and laughed. 'And that is what you find difficult to write? Shall I tell you why? You're thirty years too young to care about it.' He laughed again at Bembo's look of confusion. 'Since we can't wait all that time for the book, you'll have to rely on rhetoric and the sour grapes of old men like me.' He laid a hand on Bembo's shoulder. 'But you won't get even that on paper if you keep filling your head with the price of wool.'

Bembo smiled. 'In Venice, Aldo, thoughts on commerce take precedence. Haven't you learned that yet?'

'I see,' said Manuzio. 'Well, in that case, let me show you these.' He placed three books in front of Bembo. 'Isabella of Mantua ordered a similar set, but refuses to pay my price of six ducats.'

'Yes, of course she does,' said Bembo. 'She wants you to enjoy the privilege of giving them to her.' He handled the books lovingly, taking pleasure in the feel of the decorated leather binding. They were uniform editions of Horace, Juvenal and Persius, produced in the pocket size which Manuzio had devised to replace the large tomes of the earlier printers. Bembo opened the Horace. One could recognise anywhere a volume published by the Aldine Press with its fine white paper, the beautiful style of its woodcuts and engravings, the clean line of the print elegantly spaced between broad margins.

'These are well worth six ducats,' said Bembo. 'Isabella can be as mean as her father. Is this set for someone else?'

'For Count Alberto Pio.'

'Ah, yes, for your patron,' said Bembo. Then he glanced sharply at Manuzio. 'Aldo, they're going to Carpi, in Ferrara?'

'Yes.'

'Aldo,' asked Bembo eagerly, 'how are you sending the books?'

'My father-in-law is taking them,' said Manuzio. He had a father-in-law younger than himself who was a junior partner in the printing-house. 'Why?'

'Would he take a parcel of books for me to the city of Ferrara, to the castle, to a Madonna Angela Borgia? And give her a letter?'

Manuzio looked hard at Bembo. 'Yes, if it's important to you.'

Bembo seized Manuzio's hand gratefully. 'Yes, it is. I daren't send the letter with anyone I don't know. He mustn't let anyone but Madonna Angela take it, or even let anyone else know he's carrying it.'

'I understand,' said Manuzio. 'Where is this letter?'

'I haven't written it yet. I'll do it now.'

Manuzio nodded. He fetched paper, ink, quills, sand and wax. Observing the brilliance in Bembo's eyes, he went away without saying any more.

Bembo took out Lucrezia's letter, excited by this unexpected opportunity to write to her. He read her words again, although he knew them by heart. 'I am grieved that you feel such anxiety to receive a line or two from the hand of FF. For many good reasons she has not been able to satisfy your request . . . ' He felt almost ashamed now of the anguish he had felt earlier when he had had no news of her. 'I understand every excuse which you made to me in the name of FF, and all those reasons, which you say are many, for her not writing as she wished to do. But,' he explained, 'not for anything can I make myself stop longing for her letters now that I can no longer see and talk to her. Nothing, of course, could ever take from me the memory of her, which moves in my heart every day, every night, every hour, in every place and in every circumstance. But this memory which burns inside me cries out at times for some little relief. For this you must forgive me, and FF in her pity help me. You can imagine what delight her letters will always be to me . . . '

It was Holy Wednesday, and Bembo added, 'I have no wish to bore you on this holy day with a long sermon, so I will end, commending myself without end to your kindness and her pity.'

When Manuzio came to collect the letter, Bembo was again staring out of the window. He turned and gazed thoughtfully at Manuzio. 'Aldo, you wouldn't have any idea, would you – '

'Of what?'

' – of the speed of a three-masted round-ship?'

'Pietro, for God's sake,' said Manuzio.

It was dark when Bembo left the printing-house. He walked home along quays and across squares lit, as public places were in Venice, by torches. The gold flames reflected in the black water of the canals reminded him of the colours of his house. On the bridge by the Ca' Bembo, he paused to watch a gondola pass beneath, its curtains closed, on the way to the lagoon. A few yards away the bells of San Salvador were ringing for Holy Wednesday. Bells, torchlight, curtained gondolas – everything about him seemed to recall moments spent with Lucrezia. He smiled to himself. And now a scheme was growing in his mind that he hoped in time would mean an end to their separation.

IX

In the week that followed Easter, Bembo passed much of his time away from the Ca' Bembo. He visited the guild of weavers and dyers, and talked earnestly with other merchants under the porticoes of the exchange. With Giovanni Matteo in tow, he asked questions in a number of ship-yards, and he spent a whole day in the vast building near the Rialto bridge which housed the warehouses and living quarters of the German merchants resident in Venice.

Then he asked if he might speak to his father and Jacopo together.

'I've been wondering,' he began nervously, 'if we might consider the possibility of buying raw wool from England.'

The two brothers stared at him. Then the Senator said, 'Raw wool? You are not talking about the lengths of English woollen cloth which the galleys import?'

'No, raw wool, that could be woven and dyed here in Venice.'

The Senator said patiently, 'We are not a wool city, like Florence. I don't suppose we weave more than two hundred pieces a year.'

'Yes, I know. That's why there would be room to expand the market, especially as our dyes are more stable than the Florentine ones. No other dyers in Europe can make a red dye that won't fade.'

'The House of Bembo,' interrupted Jacopo testily, 'transports merchandise. It doesn't sell. The profit lies in shipping the stuff.'

'It did once, yes, but not now,' said Bembo. 'Uncle, do you know the cost today of hiring galley space? It's almost doubled since I went to Ferrara eighteen months ago. So has insurance. For a house like ours, having to work on small margins, these outlays are crippling. Now raw wool would be of no interest to pirates, so we could import it in round-ships as bulk intead of luxury freight. The shipping rates would be low and so would the insurance.'

'Round-ships!' muttered Jacopo contemptuously. 'Your wool would have rotted before it reached port.'

'Not if we used one of the new three-masted vessels,' Bembo persisted. 'They have enough sail area to give them the required speed.'

The Senator smiled. 'I see the Latin studies with Gian Matteo are progressing,' he murmured to his son. He turned to Jacopo. 'Pietro is right about the improvement in the round-ships. In time we may have to use them to replace our galleys.'

Jacopo stared at the Senator. 'Replace our galleys? You're talking nonsense, Bernardo. You're getting old.'

'Jacopo,' said the Senator, 'Venice may not be able to afford her galleys much longer. They run at a loss. On the Levantine routes we used to carry a yearly average of three and a half million pounds of spices. Last year we shipped one million only.'

'Because the Portuguese began regular spice shipments by sea from India?' asked Bembo.

The Senator nodded. 'As for the Western fleets, Jacopo, the Senate has to subsidise their hire. The English and the Flemish are building their own trading fleets. That's why we would be unwise to ship any more Cretan wine to London. The English can do it more cheaply themselves.'

Jacopo grunted. 'It won't last. It can't do. Whatever we do, we must maintain our galley fleets. They're the symbol of our maritime power.'

'No,' said the Senator wearily, 'the Republic is not in a position to do this. Look at the government stock which we hold. It was worth a hundred ducats at par; now it fetches five and a half. This speaks for itself. We can't send galleys abroad for prestige alone. To survive will be difficult enough.' He laid a kindly hand on his brother's shoulder. 'Things have changed, Jacopo. We've fought too many Turkish wars without help from the rest of Italy. And just as our treasuries are depleted, we lose our monopoly in trade. To recover, we have to wrest the spice trade back from the Portuguese. And we can only do that by persuading the Senate to remove the monopoly in transporting spices from the galleys. If the round-ships carry spices, we can undercut the Portuguese rates. That's in the long term. In the short term, we have to consider schemes like Pietro's.'

Jacopo sat mumbling to himself, striking the floor with his stick.

Bembo, encouraged by his father's attitude, said, 'Carlo talked to me last autumn about the growth in the Portuguese eastern spice cargoes. He thought we should turn quickly to the west for our profits, to Bruges and London.'

'Ah.' The Senator smiled. Opinions once held by Carlo were now very precious to him. 'So he might well have approved of this idea of yours.'

'Father,' said Bembo earnestly, 'the German merchants are interested in buying woollen cloth dyed in Venice, and they would buy directly from us. That would eliminate the cost of agents and their commissions. If eventually we were to trade in wool alone, we should need only one agent in London.'

'We've always had a network of agents all over the Mediterranean,' grumbled Jacopo.

'What I am trying to do is simplify our operations,' cried Bembo. 'Carlo could think of a dozen projects at once. I have to handle one at a time.'

The simplicity of the operation was, in fact, the whole core of Bembo's scheme. Once established, the process of buying and selling would follow an annual routine which could be left largely to Bartolommeo. He himself would be free to spend most of his time outside Venice.

Jacopo stood up, glared at his nephew and stumped away without speaking to him. The Senator also rose from his chair. 'There is a lot to be said for this proposal,' he said, 'and I'm sure your uncle will come to realise this. We must discuss it with Bartolommeo. But not now, if you will forgive me, Pietro. I am a little tired. May I have your arm?'

They walked companionably across the room, each cheered by the conversation that had taken place. The Senator was delighted that at last Pietro was beginning to accept his family responsibilities. Bembo, for his part, rejoiced in the fact that for the first time since Carlo's death his father was arguing with something of his old authority and perception. While the Senator was trying to decide how long he need wait before re-opening the question of his son's marriage, Bembo was wondering if he would be able to leave Venice before the winter.

The next day Bembo left for the Villa Bozza to make up the accounts for the sales of produce from the estates. While he was there he made a round of visits to the cottages of his father's peasants. Feeling cheerful and at ease, he spent rather longer than usual listening to their complaints and problems. As the day was hot, he even consented to drink a beaker of goat's milk with them.

X

Ippolito d'Este had returned to Ferrara.

He was giving a ball to the duke and nobility of Ferrara to celebrate the completion of the frescoes commissioned for the banqueting hall of his palace. Each of the four walls depicted the Cardinal engaged in activities appropriate to the seasons of the year. In winter he was the scholar, discoursing on mathematics to the learned doctors of the university; in spring the soldier, arrayed in the snow-white armour which he had designed for himself; in summer the musician, playing to ladies in a flowering garden; in autumn the huntsman.

'Even God,' muttered Ercole Strozzi to his father, 'was content with three images.'

He limped about the room until he could place himself, as he liked to do on these occasions, within earshot of the ducal family. Ippolito, dressed in purple silk brocade, ignored him. Strozzi addressed himself to Alfonso. 'Your highness is known to have an appreciation of murals. Might I beg the privilege of hearing your judgement on these?'

Alfonso's gaze lighted on Strozzi and then on his brother. He found the company of both of them uncongenial, but he answered in his usual considered and expressionless manner. 'The design is very fine and well executed, but I prefer the mural style of the Venetians which has more movement and richer colour.'

Ippolito turned round to glare at his brother, his face mottling with temper. 'We all know, brother, that you have a curious liking for anything Venetian.' He shot a spiteful glance at Lucrezia, who still declined to speak to him unless forced to do so. 'As, of course, has your wife.'

Alfonso said nothing. He had no time to waste bickering with Ippolito. His mistress was waiting for him. But his silence goaded instead of pacifying Ippolito. 'This visit planned for Venice occurs at a particularly unfortunate time,' he added, raising his voice. Both Lucrezia and the duke, who were sitting together eating supper with golden forks, heard him and turned their heads.

'A visit to a godchild?' murmured Strozzi.

'But is this really my sister's reason for going?' Ippolito looked at his father and then Alfonso. 'She is not always open in her ways.'

Lucrezia stared nervously at Ippolito. 'Eminence?' she whispered.

Ippolito smiled at her distress. 'Isn't it true, madonna, that you have been engaged in a secret correspondence?'

Lucrezia's fork clattered against her plate, and her face turned pale.

Strozzi laughed quickly. 'But what woman doesn't – with her dressmaker, her jeweller – ?'

Alfonso was frowning. 'What do you mean, Ippolito?'

'I was referring,' said Ippolito pleasantly, 'to the fact that Madonna Lucrezia has recently petitioned the King of Spain to release her brother, Cesare, from the Spanish prison in which he is now confined – confined, may I add, with the consent of the Pope and his allies, of whom Ferrara is one.'

Lucrezia gasped, overwhelmed for a moment with relief at hearing Cesare's name spoken instead of Bembo's. Then from the silence around her she began to realise the gravity of the charge that Ippolito was making against her publicly.

She turned desperately to the duke. 'My lord, it is true that I have written to Spain. I meant no disloyalty to you. Surely anyone whose brother was imprisoned as mine is would have done the same.'

The duke grunted. The candlelight glinted on his spectacles and she was unable to see his eyes.

Ippolito leaned over her. 'The King, we know, has not acceded to your request.'

Lucrezia said miserably, 'No.' She was wondering where and how Ippolito had intercepted her letters, and how many others his agents had read.

'And your highness expects us to believe,' Ippolito was saying, 'that your journey to Venice is to see a godchild?'

Lucrezia looked up in bewilderment at him. 'I don't understand.'

'No? Our new Pope Giulio is your brother's enemy. He also hates the Most Serene Republic of Venice.' Ippolito pronounced the title with a sneer. 'In what more likely place could you solicit help for Cesare Borgia?'

Lucrezia half rose from her chair. 'But this isn't true,' she cried.

'You have written secretly to Spain,' said Ippolito with a shrug of his shoulders. 'How can we be sure that you haven't written secretly to Venice?'

Lucrezia was shaking as she sank back into her chair. She struggled to push away her terror. 'I wrote to Spain for Cesare's sake,' she said slowly, 'but not to Venice, not for Cesare.'

'That I believe,' said the duke unexpectedly. He looked without pleasure at Ippolito. He himself had known about Lucrezia's letters to Spain. He also knew that she had pawned some of her jewels to raise money for Cesare. It suited him not to interfere. Cesare owned lands on the borders of Ferrara and were he released to occupy them, neither Venice nor the Papacy would be able to claim them as an extension of their own territories. Duke Ercole could see advantages in having an impoverished buffer state on his frontier, but he was in no position to admit this either to his Venetian protectors or his papal overlord. Ippolito's interference had brought the matter into the open, and it had to be dealt with in the open.

'There must be no more letters to Spain, madonna,' he said to Lucrezia, 'and I must forbid you to offer any further help to your brother. As far as your visit to the Republic of Venice is concerned, if you wish to dispel the suspicions which the Cardinal has voiced, your course is simple. You must cancel it. For your own sake, and for sake of Ferrara's standing with the Pope, I would advise it.'

He saw Lucrezia's stricken face. He patted her hand. 'You can go later, eh?'

XI

Bembo's birthday fell on the tenth of May. He spent his thirty-fourth in bed with fever. He had been ill for nearly three weeks, the intensity of the sickness varying from day to day. At times, though tired and listless, he was able to dress and walk slowly as far as the Rialto. At others he lay drenched in sweat, his throat parched, too weak to stand or swallow food.

The fever was not malaria, and its cause puzzled Bembo's physicians. Bartolommeo, returning one day from the Villa Bozza, said that two of the children on the estate were ill with a fever that seemed very similar to Bembo's. It was a month since Bembo had been to the villa; the children had been well then, because he remembered sharing a pitcher of milk with them. Later, Bruno recalled that during his boyhood in Sicily he had seen a goatherd affected by the same kind of recurrent weakness.

Ercole Strozzi, who disliked sick-rooms, stood near Bembo's bed, looking down at the great canal and twisting Gonzaga's diamond ring on his finger. He was in a sullen mood, having come unwillingly to Venice at his father's insistence.

'Lucrezia is in a pitiful state,' Tito had said, when Strozzi complained about undertaking the journey. 'I can't risk her doing something foolish that will damage us all. She wants you to explain to Pietro why she can't go to Venice. We have banking affairs to resolve in Venice, and I see no reason why you shouldn't go now instead of later. If we can offer them some tolerably certain hope of meeting each other in the future, then they may both be saved from precipitate acts.'

'What tolerably certain hope?' Strozzi had asked, frowning.

Tito had been writing to Bembo as he spoke. 'Alfonso will

probably be going to England in October, and Ippolito will be in Rome. I shall offer our villa at Codigoro to Lucrezia for the plague months.'

'October, oh,' Strozzi had said with relief. That was another five months away. He doubted if even Bembo could be so stubborn over that period of time. And Gonzaga would be back in Ferrara long before that.

Strozzi stopped playing with his ring and sighed as the rain ran down the window. A steady drizzle had been falling without stopping for five days. Below him, Strozzi saw the gondoliers with dripping sacks across their shoulders pushing their mournful black boats through the choppy leaden water under a leaden sky. The white marble palaces, decorated with green serpentine and apricot-coloured porphyry, had faded into slabs of dismal grey stone, and the gilding, the mosaics, the painted gondola posts looked like bedraggled, tawdy carnival finery.

Bembo was calling to him. Strozzi turned reluctantly. 'Ercole, wait another day, or perhaps two. Then I can come back with you.'

'Pietro, I can't wait.' It wasn't true, but all Strozzi wanted was to get away from Venice, from the rain, from Bembo's disappointment. 'Anyway, look at you. You won't be fit to ride for two or three weeks.' That at least was a fact.

Bembo moved his head on the pillow. 'Ercole, I'm well enough. Just tired today. Surely you could stay another couple of days?'

Strozzi sat down on Bembo's bed. 'Pietro, supposing I could, what then? You would ride back with me on the excuse of keeping me company. In a day or so, you would have to leave again. Would the excuse deceive Ippolito, or anyone else at court who suspected the truth? Would you dare to speak to Lucrezia?'

'We could see each other, we could be in the same room together. After six months that would be some consolation.' Bembo smiled.

'And then you have to wait another five months before you meet at Codigoro.' Strozzi pointed to his father's letter that lay beside Bembo's bed.

'Yes, perhaps.'

'Pietro, listen to me. When you and Lucrezia met at Ostellato, the time was opportune for you to – ' he hesitated, ' – to divert each other. Times pass. Wouldn't it be better now for both of you to accept this?'

'You mean we're no longer of any use to you now that the Cardinal's hat is lost?' Despite his weakness, Bembo chuckled.

'Well, you're right. That's quite true,' said Strozzi. He laughed himself, but there was a note in his voice that suggested to Bembo that his response had not been entirely flippant. 'My father, of course, doesn't agree with me,' Strozzi added. 'He still thinks you a desirably benevolent influence on her highness that must be encouraged. And so he has thought of Codigoro. Do you know Codigoro? It's even more remote than Ostellato.'

'Then there will be less risk of plague,' said Bembo. 'Your father is thoughtful.'

'Sly,' muttered Strozzi. 'Pietro, if you go on now, you can only bring yourself more and more unhappiness. I don't see how the uncertainty and the danger can ever grow less.' Bembo noticed that Strozzi had stopped touching the new ring he was wearing and he seemed for once wholly sincere. 'There comes a time in all liaisons when everything conspires against them, as it does for you now – there was Alfonso's visit to Ostellato, then the plague at Medelana, now your responsibilities here in Venice and the politics of Ferrara. This is the time when a wise man recognises the warnings of fate and stops.'

'Or ignores them and hangs on,' said Bembo, smiling again.

Strozzi threw out his hands. His moment of feeling had passed and he went back to the window. 'Will you at least take Lucrezia a letter from me, even if it isn't a note of farewell?' Bembo asked.

Strozzi smiled despite himself. 'Are you strong enough to sit up and write?

'I have to be,' said Bembo. 'In these lean days a good courier can't be wasted.' He paused. 'Ercole, ask her to write to me if she can.'

'Yes, I will ask her,' said Strozzi, 'but you must try to understand how difficult it is for her. Since the business of the Spanish letters, she's nervous of writing anything at all. If she picks up a pen, she knows that half the court still suspect her of conspiring with Cesare.' He didn't add that the other half would assume that she was sending a secret note to Francesco Gonzaga. 'She thinks everyone is watching her, and of course some of them are.'

'Ippolito's people being among them,' said Bembo bitterly. 'I wonder how much Ippolito really knows.'

'Pietro, since he saw you and Lucrezia standing together in the snow, he has known that there is something to know. But of how much there is to be known, he has only suspicions. If he had more, he would not have been silent about it. As it is, he makes his clever guesses aloud and then he watches. He never was a man for the *coup de grâce.*' Strozzi's eyes narrowed in thought as he spoke on one of his favourite themes. 'He's like a cat with a dying bird. It diverts him to see a victim in misery. If he can't play with physical pain, he'll use fear. And when Lucrezia is frightened, she betrays herself. He hopes that Lucrezia will be frightened little by little into telling him all he wants to hear.'

The sweat poured down Bembo's cheeks. 'If only I had the power to take her away from him,' he gasped.

'The most you can do,' said Strozzi brutally, 'is to stay away from Ferrara so that Ippolito isn't always being reminded of your existence. He hates Lucrezia, but the only way he can harm her is through you.'

The letter which Strozzi carried away with him was brief, for Bembo found the effort of writing more difficult than he had thought. 'I was hoping,' he scrawled, 'to be coming now with Messer Ercole to offer my duty to your highness. I have been harassed for so long with troubles that I don't need to tell you how much it would have comforted me. But a strange illness has prevented my writing to you as I would wish, let alone my leaving here. Forgive me if I send you only these few bare lines when I would like to send so many . . . '

XII

Bembo continued to suffer from recurrent bouts of his fever. As soon as his son could travel, the Senator sent him to the Villa Bozza in the hope that the sweeter air of the country would hasten his cure.

The family as a whole never moved to the villa until the beginning of July, and Bembo welcomed the prospect of four weeks there alone. On the days when he felt strong enough, he settled down to finish the last pages of his book, working for an hour or two in the early morning and again in the late afternoon. He could work steadily and without interruption at the villa, and despite occasional days of fever, the writing went well. It had become a task pursued for Lucrezia alone, something which for both of them would bridge the months of waiting until they could meet at Codigoro. Nicola Bruno had accompanied Bembo to the villa. As soon as Bembo completed one of his scribbled and heavily scored sheets of manuscript, Bruno copied it in his precise hand for the printer. When a number of pages were ready, he travelled to Venice to deliver them to Aldo Manuzio.

One afternoon, towards the end of June, Bembo was lying on the marble bench under the trees, waiting for Bruno to return from one of his visits to Manuzio. He was thinking about his wool plans, as he often did when he rested during the heat of the day. They were maturing better than he could ever have hoped. The Senator was showing a growing interest in the speculation, and had even suggested that they should sell their cloth not only to the German merchants but in the markets of northern Italy as well. It had been agreed that Bembo should first explore markets in the Venetian cities of Brescia, Bergamo and Verona. Now in October, thought Bembo making his calculations for the hundredth time, Alfonso leaves for England. High summer, like the period of the winter fair, was a time of heavy trading in Venice, so he would not be able to leave for Brescia until the last of the summer fleets sailed in August. From Brescia he would move to Bergamo and

Verona. From Verona it was a mere step to Mantua where he could present his respects to Isabella, and from Mantua no farther to Ferrara. With careful timing, he should be arriving in Ferrara a few days after Alfonso had left.

He meant to spend as much time as he could with Lucrezia while she was free to remain at Codigoro. Ostensibly he would be staying at Ostellato for the hunting, and he would interrupt this as little as possible to deal with matters in Venice. In this respect, his illness had had its advantages. During the past few weeks, Bartolommeo had become accustomed to making his own decisions in the counting-house and had learned as much about his brother's wool scheme as Bembo had. Once it had begun operating, Bembo was convinced that it would function with little need of himself. Then he would be able to live for the greater part of the year outside Venice. After what Strozzi had said, he realised that it would be unwise to settle in Ferrara. The obvious choice for a home was Urbino. There he would be welcomed at court and encouraged to write; from Urbino he could travel swiftly and often to Ferrara, and there he would not be isolated from Lucrezia when war broke out.

He gazed with pleasure at the leaves above his head, and remembered the leaves round his window at Ostellato. October, he thought contentedly, October. He realised suddenly that it was growing late and Bruno had not returned. He walked down to the river and stood looking for the boat. After an hour, he went inside the house, feeling considerably uneasy.

It was after dark when Bruno eventually arrived. Bembo hurried down the bank to meet him. 'Cola, where have you been? I was worried – '

He stopped. In the light from the open doorway, he saw that Bruno was carrying some of the ledgers which from long practice were never removed from the counting-house.

'What are you doing with these?' he asked in amazement.

'Pietro,' said Bruno, breathing heavily with the weight of the ledgers in his arms, 'something has happened.' He carried the books into the study and laid them on the table. 'It's something serious that you have to know about.'

Bembo followed on his heels. 'Cola, what is it?'

Cola opened each of the ledgers at the last page of entry. 'I think it's best if you learn what it is from these.' He tapped them in turn. 'Merchandise account, shipping account, agents' account.'

'Just tell me,' said Bembo, growing angry.

Bruno shook his head. 'Read them, Pietro. I'll leave you alone.' He hesitated. 'I'm very sorry.'

Bembo, alarmed by his manner, sat down in front of the ledgers. Bruno closed the door behind himself and waited outside.

A few minutes later, the door was flung open. Bembo was carrying one of the ledgers and his eyes were blazing.

'Who wrote these figures?' he cried, striking the page.

Bruno swallowed. 'Bartolommeo. On the instructions of Messer Jacopo.'

Bembo stared at him. 'Do you know what he's done?' he shouted. He slammed the ledger in fury. 'My uncle has bought Cretan wine – Cretan wine! He's hired shipping for London. As debtors, we can't command credit, so he's sent gold ducats to cover both accounts to our agent in Rethimo.'

Bruno nodded without speaking. Bembo was shivering violently. 'Gold! He's used my wool money. Cola, my wool money. We shall lose it all.'

His fever broke out again, and he clung to the lintel of the door. Bruno and Lico helped him to bed and sat beside him, watching him anxiously. After a while the sweating abated and Bembo lay exhausted, thinking of the hours and hours of hard, uncongenial work that he had done to amass that sum of gold ducats. It was a very modest sum by Venetian standards, and when it was locked into the great iron-bound money chest in the counting-house it was almost lost. Bembo could remember that when he was a child the chest would be so full of gold Venetian and foreign coins that if the lid was lifted they would slither across the floor. It was a modest sum by those standards, yes, but it was enough to make a beginning in what he was sure would have been a sound and prudent venture. Now it was lost. From that little pile of gold, he could never have re-created the great Bembo fleets about which Carlo had dreamed, but he might have been able to settle some of the debts which weighed on his family.

'Bruno, why didn't my father stop him?' he cried.

Bruno bent over him. 'I don't think he knew, Pietro. Your uncle has as much power to act alone for the partnership as the Senator.'

Bembo groaned. 'Cola, you will take the ledgers back to Venice tomorrow and you will bring back Bartolommeo with you.'

But it was not Bartolommeo who returned with Bruno to the villa next day. It was the Senator.

He found his son dressed, but lying on his bed, haggard and heavy-eyed. The Senator spoke to him gently and with regret about what had happened, but he refused to listen to Bembo's outbursts against Jacopo. The launching of the wool venture had merely been delayed, he assured him, for another year.

'Another year!' Bembo closed his eyes, appalled at the prospect which this thought raised.

'What we have to discuss,' the Senator continued cheerfully, 'is how to raise the necessary capital.' He placed a sheet of paper in Bembo's hands. 'This is a list of our assets. As I see it, the only course open to us is to mortgage part of our property. The obvious choice is your mother's mill in Treviso and then, if necessary, this villa.'

'Not this villa,' protested Bembo. 'Must we risk the villa?'

'No, not necessarily,' said the Senator, pursing his lips in thought. 'There is, of course, another possible source of capital.' He smiled at his son. 'Marriage. A marriage with Madonna Veronica Gambara would bring us a substantial dowry.'

This abrupt re-introduction of the subject of marriage left Bembo too startled to speak. It was evident from the Senator's matter-of-fact reference to it that he had been considering the possibility for some time. 'I know,' he added, 'that when I first proposed this union you were not ready to contemplate it, but circumstances have changed for all of us since then.'

Bembo sought for the courage to give an answer. 'Marriage,' he said after a silence, 'would require my living in Venice.'

The Senator nodded. 'Of course.'

Bembo took a breath. 'Sir, that is something that I cannot do.'

He closed his eyes again to avoid the expression of disbelief and distress on his father's face. 'Is it fair, sir,' he asked miserably, 'to show such surprise? I have said before that I believe in the value of my work, and that I cannot work well in Venice.'

'You said that, Pietro, before you settled in Venice this winter and became interested in the work of the partnership.'

Bembo, with a mounting feeling of rebellion, tried to speak quietly. 'I have never settled in Venice, sir. I have stayed here during the past six months only because I was needed, not because I wished it. I have given the time and energy which should have gone to my writing to work which I disliked. I have given up much more than that,' he added bitterly, thinking of Lucrezia. 'Now I find the effort was fruitless. I have done everything that I could for the partnership of Bernardo and Jacopo Bembo, and to all intents you've rejected it – or rather my uncle has, and you have not tried to prevent him.'

'I have my work in the Senate.'

Bembo felt suddenly angry. 'I have my work, too. Yet you talk blandly of another year, of a marriage that would tie me to the counting-house for the rest of my life.'

'You're upset, of course,' said the Senator, looking round the room for a soothing drink. He fetched a pitcher of fruit juice and poured a little into a beaker.

As Bembo sipped the drink, shaken slightly by the way he had spoken to his father, he was conscious that, angry as he was, a change was taking place in his feelings. He was gradually aware of a sensation that he could only define with amazement as relief. As he examined it, he realised that it was not so much relief as a sense of release, of obligations absolved.

'Do I understand,' said the Senator, 'that you intend to abandon your wool project?'

'Bartolommeo can deal with it next year as well as I could,' said Bembo evasively. 'I'll go to the northern cities in the autumn as we arranged, but after that I would like to go back to Ostellato.'

'I see.' Bernardo stood by the window, looking out towards his trees. 'Are you telling me that you wish to dissociate yourself from the life and interests of your family?' Without waiting for Bembo to speak, he went on, 'When I am dead, you will be the head of this house. What, then, is to become of your mother, of your sister and her children, of Bartolommeo?'

Bembo sat crouched on the edge of his bed. He wished he could see the Senator's face. 'Sir, I swear to you that I would never neglect my responsibility to our family. All I ask is that I may be allowed to care for them in the manner I choose.'

'But, Pietro, how can you if you are not living in Venice, and not handling merchandise?'

'I don't know yet.' Bembo put a hand to his head. The Senator, turning to look at his son, saw that it was shaking and he was reminded of something that in the past few minutes he had forgotten – that Pietro had for many weeks been a sick man.

Bembo caught his glance, and realised wearily that all he had said was going to be excused as the expression of a feverish disorder. 'You must rest, Pietro,' the Senator was saying. 'We'll talk again later, yes?'

'Father, understand, please – ' Bembo broke off as Bruno came into the room. He looked uneasily at Bembo but addressed himself to the Senator. 'Senator, there is a stranger here, asking for Pietro.'

The Senator frowned. 'What does he want? Pietro needs sleep.'

'He refuses to say what he wants except to Pietro, or where he comes from. He's a foreigner. Spanish, I think.'

The Senator, who was not accustomed to receiving uninvited foreigners in his private villa, appeared displeased. Bembo said quickly, 'I'll come, Cola.'

He stood up and followed Bruno into the garden, where a man in travel-stained clothes was waiting. He stared narrowly at Bembo as he walked along the path towards him.

'You are Messer Pietro Bembo?'

'I am.'

'I asked to speak to you in a place where we should not be overheard,' the man said brusquely without any form of greeting. 'I am informed that you speak Spanish.'

Bembo replied in Spanish that this was so. The stranger nodded, and drew a letter from the pocket of his cloak. 'This is for you from the Duchess of Ferrara,' he said.

Bembo took the letter and broke the seal. The letter was in Spanish and unsigned, written in nervous haste. 'Complying with your good wish that has been made known to me, although I have legitimate cause for not writing to you, however having learned of your indisposition which has caused me great distress, I should believe myself lacking in courtesy if I did not in these brief lines inform you of this, which I do also to satisfy your request to have a letter from my hand because of the debts I have with you. It remains only to beg you to take as much care as possible of your health, and in the bearer of this message to have as much faith as I have myself.'

Bembo sat down on a garden bench, feeling himself enriched. The guarded and stiffly worded phrases told him of the anxiety it cost Lucrezia to get anything on paper, and her concern and devotion both humbled and exalted him. He sat holding the letter as though the paper which had come from her hands laid a blessing on his fingers. Then he looked up at the Spaniard and thanked him courteously for finding him. As he carefully folded the letter again, he asked if the man had been long in Lucrezia's service.

The man answered briefly that he had not. He had once, he explained, been a body-servant to Cesare Borgia. He had escaped with Cesare from Rome to Naples and, when Cesare had been betrayed by the Neapolitans to the Spanish king, had made his way to Ferrara, where he now served his master's sister. Bembo then tried to persuade him to talk of Lucrezia, but he refused to be drawn, saying only that the duchess hoped for a reply to her letter.

Bembo nodded with a smile and withdrew indoors. He wrote,

as she had done, in Spanish, assuring her that he was now well, and that he would be with her, whatever happened, in October. 'I will, if possible, come to you briefly before that, but I will not take risks that might deprive us of much more. In October, I will claim the debts that you owe me, and pay you mine, which are infinite.'

As he handed his reply to the Spaniard, he said diffidently, 'The Cardinal, I believe, has her highness closely watched.'

The man gave Bembo a tight smile of rebuke. 'You forget, excellency, that I was trained to serve Cesare Borgia.'

The Spaniard was lodged that night in the Villa Bozza. The Senator, though plainly disturbed by his unexplained presence in the house, made no comment until the following morning when the man had already departed. 'You must be aware,' he said gently to his son, 'that the Republic looks with distrust on private citizens who have dealings with foreign couriers, particularly if the manner of their arrival suggests a need for secrecy. Should you receive many other visits of this nature, you might find yourself submitting to questioning.'

Bembo sighed to himself. He was now, it seemed, to be suspected, among his other aberrations, of dabbling in political intrigue. Questioning by the Council of Ten, which protected the security of Venice, was not a pleasant experience either for the victim or his family. Yet Bembo could think of nothing to say which would dispel his father's alarm without betraying the truth. He merely answered, 'It is very unlikely that there will be further visits.'

The Senator, though not satisfied, made no further reference to the incident, but it added to his concern for the state of his son's mind.

XIII

At the beginning of July, the remaining members of the Senator's family arrived at the Villa Bozza. They brought with them Giovanni Matteo.

It was apparent to Bembo from their air of humouring an invalid that his mother and sister had been warned that he was still suffering from the effects of shock on a frame already debilitated by fever. Giovanni Matteo had been invited in an attempt to restore him to a more amiable mood.

Giovanni Matteo patted Bembo's arm heavily to express his great sympathy for someone who had been unable to enjoy the excitements of a summer in Venice. If only, he said, his face shining with delight at the mere thought of it, his uncle could see the city now. The galleys of Flanders, which had arrived in May after wintering in the Channel, were loaded, ready to leave again. The three eastern spice fleets – the galleys of Roumania, Beirut and Alexandria – which would be sailing early in August, were re-fitting in the Arsenal. The round-ships from Cyprus, Greece and Syria had also been docking throughout June. Sea-captains at midsummer were as common as dragonflies and could be seen walking the streets like mortal men, gold ear-rings, jewels and knives flashing in the sun.

Bembo enquired into the health of his cousin, Alvise. His father was very worried, Giovanni Matteo explained, because of his tin. It had come into Venice in one of the Flanders galleys, but it was still held in customs and he didn't know if it would be through in time for him to hire space in the Alexandria fleet.

Bembo realised that if Jacopo hadn't spent their capital he would probably have been haggling himself in Venice at that moment. 'Mm, I think I'd rather be here on a hot day,' he murmured gratefully.

'Do you like it here?' asked Giovanni Matteo.

'Yes, very much. I think I could be happy living here all the time,' said Bembo. 'Don't you like it here?'

Giovanni Matteo hesitated. 'Yes. But I wouldn't like it all the time.'

'Why not?'

Giovanni Matteo struggled for words to describe what he meant. 'It's so – so closed in.'

'Closed in?' Bembo laughed. He looked at the open fields

reaching to the horizon, laced by a network of streams glistening in the late afternoon light.

'Yes,' said Giovanni Matteo. 'There's too much land, and it's all round.'

Bembo stared at him in amazement. 'One day, Gian Matteo,' he said tartly, 'you will have an unpleasant shock. You will discover that you are a man, not a fish.'

'There was a Pope once,' retorted Giovanni Matteo, hoping to impress with his knowledge, 'who said that all Venetians were like fish.'

'Yes, but he didn't mean it as a compliment, if that's what you think. He said because fish lived in the water they had less intelligence than other creatures and the same applied to Venetians.'

'Oh!' said Giovanni Matteo, affronted. 'Why don't Popes like us?'

'Because we do what we want, and not what they tell us to do.'

'Well, that's right, isn't it?' said Giovanni Matteo. 'We understand what's best for us.'

They were sitting by a small stream, their backs against the wall that separated the private grounds of the villa from the rest of the estate. They spent part of each day there, away from the rest of the household, fishing, working at Giovanni Matteo's Latin, talking and dozing. Bembino lay on the bank beside them.

One afternoon, Bembino's barking disturbed them as they were bent over a book. Bembo glanced up and saw that Marcella, his eldest niece, had wandered out on to the bank and discovered their hiding-place. She stood watching them shyly, uncertain whether to come closer. It was not his displeasure that she feared, Bembo knew, but Giovanni Matteo's. She adored her cousin, who as yet was hardly aware of her existence.

Bembo smiled at her and beckoned. He was very fond of Marcella, a grave, even-tempered child of eight who lacked the waywardness of her mother and her two younger sisters. Giovanni Matteo, resenting her intrusion, gave her a long, unfriendly stare and then ignored her. Bembo patted the bank beside him. Marcella sat down and listened patiently until the lesson was over.

'Well, now,' said Bembo, closing his books with a snap, 'we'll all go on the river, shall we? Would you like that, Marcella?'

Marcella's grave little face lit up and she clapped her hands in a way that reminded Bembo of Lucrezia. Giovanni Matteo, however, turned his head away and muttered indistinctly.

'I can't hear you, Gian Matteo,' said Bembo. 'You don't want to come? Then we'll go alone, Marcella.'

He led her down the bank and lifted her into a small boat that drifted among the thick reeds and water-plants of the stream. Giovanni Matteo watched sulkily. With unhurried deliberation Bembo made his preparations to push off from the bank, and was within an instant of doing so when Giovanni Matteo changed his mind and scrambled in beside them.

With a brief nod at his nephew, Bembo settled behind the oars and rowed along the stream towards the Brenta. Marcella had a quick and curious mind, and once she had overcome her shyness was full of questions about the birds and animals along the banks. Bembo absorbed himself in his rowing and allowed Giovanni Matteo to answer. Giovanni Matteo always enjoyed displaying his knowledge and, like Bembo, derived even greater pleasure from sharing it with a responsive pupil. Marcella sat with her chin in her hand, listening to him talk; by the time Bembo turned the boat round to row back, Giovanni Matteo's manner to his girl cousin had mellowed and he was treating her with the same good-humoured condescension he bestowed on Bembino.

As he watched them together, Bembo found himself wishing idly that they were his own children. He thrust the thought aside, and then realising that this was foolish tried to examine it calmly. It was merely part of the choice which faced him: life in Urbino, where he could write and be near Lucrezia, or life in Venice as a merchant-patrician, married to Veronica Gambara. To the world he had to pretend that the decision lay between the work he wanted to do and the work he ought to be doing. In effect, being a man to whom personal relationships were more important than anything else, it was a simpler choice. Lucrezia or his own children by the little Gambara. He regretted the need for such a choice, but he had no doubt about what he was going to do. Whatever happened, as he had promised Lucrezia, he would be with her in October.

He glanced up towards the children. Marcella was almost asleep and Giovanni Matteo was trying to hold her up.

After this, whenever she could escape from her mother, Marcella sat on the bank, listening to Giovanni Matteo's lessons. She surprised Bembo by the amount she picked up in this way, and after a time he began teaching her properly so that she shouldn't misunderstand what she had heard. Giovanni Matteo decided to assist in the teaching and the chanting of Latin was then heard at odd hours all over the villa. Marcella loved it, even though, in Bembo's opinion, Giovanni Matteo tended to conduct himself like a galley-captain hectoring a crew.

They were coming back from the bank one afternoon when Antonia, Marcella's mother, came running towards them from the house. They stood still and Marcella slipped her hand in Bembo's. Antonia took one look at the books under her brother's arm and said accusingly, 'Pietro, you've been teaching Marcella Latin, without my permission. She doesn't need to learn Latin.' She snatched Marcella away from him.

Realising that life for a young widow was not easy, Bembo had always tried to make allowances for Antonia's uncertain temper, but there were times when she irritated him beyond bearing. 'Antonia,' he snapped, 'she has an alert, intelligent mind. Your idea of educating her is showing her how to bleach her hair and thump a clavichord. She deserves better than that.'

The moment he mentioned the clavichord, Bembo regretted it. Antonia dissolved into tears of self-pity. She devoted hours of her time to playing the clavichord under the disastrously mistaken impression that she was a gifted musician. The noise of her practising was a constant source of anguish to Bembo, particularly when he wanted to work.

Antonia hit back at him. 'I know why you're teaching Marcella Latin. You want to put her in a convent and save the dowry!'

Bembo seized his sister and marched her into the villa, away from the children. 'What do you mean by saying that?' he demanded furiously.

Antonia wailed loudly. 'What else do you expect me to think? What's going to happen to us all? You're going away, aren't you? Carlo worked for us all. You won't. You won't even marry.' She took a gasp of air and put a hand on Bembo's wrist. 'Pietro, do you know how rich Count Gambara is?'

'Antonia! Pietro!' The Senator, attracted by the sound of raised voices, emerged from his study. Bruno's face peered round the door after him. 'Antonia,' said the Senator again, looking severely at his daughter, 'I have forbidden you to discuss this matter with your brother. As it is, you will apologise to him for the discourteous remarks which I have just overheard.'

He turned to Bembo. 'You, Pietro, must understand that Antonia is naturally disturbed about the future of her children after my death.' He spoke quietly, but Bembo was aware of a rebuke.

He looked at Antonia and the bitterness passed as quickly as when they were children. Antonia kissed him on the cheek. 'Pietro, I'm sorry.'

Bembo returned the kiss. 'Antonia, if I choose to work outside Venice, it doesn't mean I shall forget my duty to you. I can't make money in Venice the way Carlo could. Our talents are different. But I'll use mine, I promise you, for all of us. As for Marcella's Latin, I was not trying to do something behind your back. It simply happened, Antonia. If you want me to stop, then I will.' He smiled at her. 'But I hope you won't, for Marcella's sake. Can't you see, she likes doing whatever Gian Matteo is doing?'

'Of course, Antonia's going to let the lessons go on,' said the Senator, putting an arm round Antonia. 'Now come along, my dear, and play to me for half an hour before supper.'

Bembo and Bruno were left looking at each other. Bembo followed Bruno into the study and from the window saw Giovanni Matteo and Marcella walking across the terrace, their heads close together. How nice it would be in ten years' time, he thought fondly, to make a match between them. Then he pulled himself up abruptly, remembering how much he resented his family's attempts at match-making on his own behalf.

He turned away from the window and watched Bruno for a moment as he sat copying a page of *The Asolani.* Bruno glanced up at him over his shoulder. 'Have you thought about it?'

'Thought about what?'

'How to find an income to support this family?'

Bembo frowned and shook his head. Bruno tapped the sheet of manuscript in front of him. 'You could make a start here. Sell your books to Aldo Manuzio instead of giving them to him.'

Bembo looked at Bruno in amazement. 'I could never accept payment for my writing,' he said. 'My father gives his time and his gifts to the work of the Senate. Does he accept payment? I see no difference in this respect between his work and mine.'

Bruno shrugged his shoulders. 'Then the only course open to you is the Church. Your Latin and your scholarship would find you a place in the Vatican.'

This was a thought that had been hovering unpleasantly in Bembo's mind and he rebelled hotly against it. 'How could I work in the Vatican? It's corrupt, it's full of the enemies of Venice.' He added childishly, 'I hate the smell of incense.' He hated the bigotry of the Inquisition, too, and the sly, cheating habits of mendicant friars.

'No,' he said firmly. 'Besides, Cola, if I took even minor orders, by Venetian law I should lose my rights as a patrician elector and a citizen. That would debar me from inheriting property in Venice.'

'When have you ever cared about your rights as an elector?' asked Bruno. 'And by the time you come to inherit your property in Venice, I suspect that you will find nothing but debts and mortgages.'

Bembo hit his thumb. 'Perhaps we should sell the Ca' Bembo now,' he said, half meaning it, 'and live here.'

Bruno looked as shocked as Bembo had done a few minutes before. 'You could never sell the Ca' Bembo,' he said in a hushed voice. 'How could a man of the Senator's birth and eminence live in a little summer villa?'

'Oh, I agree that it lacks the amenities of a real Venetian home,' said Bembo with sarcasm. 'No counting-house, no wharf, no warehouses – '

They stared at each other in silence. Then Bembo said lightly, 'Oh, well, who knows? Uncle Jacopo's wine might make a fortune, stocks might rise, the Portuguese spice ships may all sink – '

'Meanwhile,' said Bruno, 'you have your book to finish.'

'Yes.' Bembo closed his eyes to shut out the noise of Antonia's clavichord and Giovanni Matteo shouting outside.

He finished the book a few days later. On the first of August he drafted a dedication 'to Madonna Lucrezia d'Este Borgia, the most illustrious Duchess of Ferrara, from Pietro Bembo'.

He first explained to her that grief for the death of his brother, Carlo, had delayed the completion of this book which had long been promised to her, and apologised for the fact that he was still unable to leave Venice to present it to her himself. 'I hope,' he added, 'that these pages will speak in my place to your highness, to your dear Madonna Angela Borgia and perhaps to Messer Ercole Strozzi.'

He prayed that she might find pleasure in reading his work, for he knew that she was a lady who devoted as much time as she could to reading and writing, 'preferring to dress her soul with becoming virtues than to cover her body with fine clothes. Indeed, just as your beauty surpasses that of other ladies, so the delights of your mind eclipse those of your body. You love far more to experience an inward pleasure than outwardly to amuse others . . . I shall think it the most satisfying of rewards for this work of mine if I may believe that when you read my words you will feel yourself even more desirous of that wished-for experience. Kissing your highness's hand, I submit myself to your kindness and favour.'

He spent most of the day working on the dedication and it was late in the afternoon when he passed the draft to Bruno for copying.

Bruno cast a quick eye over the page. 'Isn't this rather odd for a formal dedication?'

Bembo was lying with his head against the back of his chair, his eyes closed. 'Why?'

'It reads rather like a private letter,' said Bruno. 'This reference to Carlo's death, for example – it has nothing to do with the subject of the book. Nor do the names of all these people. No one outside Ferrara will know who they are.'

Bembo opened his eyes. 'The last time I saw the duchess, we spoke of Carlo. It was his illness that caused my sudden departure from her court. That was several months ago, and I would like to remind her of this – ' he hesitated, ' – and of the conversation we shared on that occasion. As for the people I mention, I owe them much for their help and it seems a fitting way of expressing my thanks.'

Bruno was unimpressed by these arguments. 'I suppose we can always drop it from later editions,' he muttered. 'That isn't all, you know. The style is clumsy in places. Look, you've used the word "body" twice in as many lines. That's the sort of weakness of construction that you are usually so careful to avoid. Perhaps a few minutes spent in re-drafting – '

Unexpectedly, Bembo laughed. He thought of the sheets of paper he had destroyed in contriving the dedication as it now stood. 'Cola, I want it copied as you have it there.'

He closed his eyes again, too tired to feel as yet any sense of achievement in having at last finished his book. 'Tomorrow, Cola, tell Aldo that a rough proof-copy is to be sent to the duchess for her approval as soon as possible. Then in October – ' he smiled to himself, unaware that Bruno was watching him, ' – I'll present her with the proper bound version.'

XIV

Lucrezia was passing an afternoon in the garden of the Strozzi villa at Codigoro. The early October sun was warm and tender, the air spiked with the watery smells of the lagoon.

She was happy. Bembo was coming. He had left Venice for Brescia more than a week before, and from the plans that Tito Strozzi had explained to her she knew that he would now be riding towards Verona. Within a day or so he would leave Verona for Mantua, and then come to her at Codigoro. Nothing now could keep him away from her.

The villa at Codigoro was small, smaller even than Medelana, and Lucrezia had brought with her only a few of the most trusted members of her household. There was not a village, not even a peasant's hut, within miles and no one could cross the marshland without being seen against the horizon.

Lucrezia stretched out her hand to pick up the proofs of Bembo's book that lay on the grass beside her. In the two months since Aldo Manuzio had sent it to her, she had read some of her favourite passages so many times that the pages were ragged and torn loose from the binding thread. The book fell open at such a place and Lucrezia found that it was the part where a lover, separated from his lady, spoke of constantly seeing her in his mind's eye '... perhaps dancing, listening as she moves to the beat of the instrument, now advancing slowly to make a deep curtsey, now circling the floor with swift turns and swaying, hesitating steps; perhaps walking against the summer wind on the soft edge of the seashore, writing words on the smooth sand for one whom she knows is watching her ... '

Lucrezia closed her eyes. Bembo had described the dance she had performed in her white Venetian silk dress at the Strozzi ball, and had remembered the afternoon at Belvedere, when she had scratched a word in the damp sand with a stick and rubbed it out before he could read it.

The book slid off her lap as she lay half asleep in the pleasant warmth of the sun. Soon there would be no more need of memories. Bembo was coming. In a few days she would hear the sound of a horse, and it would be his. She would have the first glimpse of him that would send her heart spinning with relief to know that he was really there. It seemed to her that she could hear the horse now in her imagination, galloping steadily nearer.

Lucrezia roused herself. It was not imagination. The sound of hooves was real, and it was not the sound of one horse, but of many.

She sat up, frightened. The unexpected always alarmed her. Angela and Tebaldeo, who had been playing chess beside her, stared at each other, listening. Then Tebaldeo rose and went inside the villa.

When he re-appeared his face was solemn. He crossed the garden to Lucrezia. 'Highness, the members of the council of Twelve are here from Ferrara.'

Lucrezia gripped her fingers and began to tremble. She was always aware of the danger that threatened her through Bembo, and she assumed that they had come to arrest her.

'Their business is very urgent,' Tebaldeo urged her.

'Yes, I will come.' Lucrezia stood up and smoothed her dress. She was afraid of death, and the manner of being put to it, but she resolved not to betray Bembo, and not to behave in a way that would afterwards make him feel shame for her. With her head up, she walked firmly along the path and up the steps into the villa.

As she passed from the sunlight into the darkness across the threshold, she saw dimly a large company of men waiting for her. They turned towards her and each man knelt. Then Tito Strozzi rose, stepped forward and knelt again. 'Your illustrious highness,' he murmured and bowed his head.

Lucrezia realised suddenly that they had not come to accuse her; they were honouring her.

She offered her hand to Tito Strozzi to kiss. 'I beg your highness to forgive our precipitate arrival,' he said. 'I deeply regret to tell you, madonna, that we bear the gravest of news, and only for this reason would we have dared to disturb you in this manner.'

He paused, waiting for Lucrezia's permission to continue. When she nodded, he went on, 'Early this morning, our lord the duke was struck by a severe affliction. He was found in his bed without the power to move, or the power to speak.'

Lucrezia made a movement of distress.

'His physicians, madonna, are assured that he is dying. He may live for a few hours, or it could be a matter of days, even weeks, but death is inevitable. He is no longer in a state to govern Ferrara. Since the Duke Alfonso, your husband, is abroad, we come to lay the rule of Ferrara into the hands of your illustrious highness. We pledge to you our loyalty, and the loyalty of all Ferrara. We beg you to return to the city as soon as you may to govern as regent until Duke Alfonso returns.'

Lucrezia gave a gasping cry and buried her face in her hands.

Ercole Strozzi moved quickly to her side. 'We are all deeply touched by your highness's grief for the duke,' he said. 'But we entreat you to set it aside bravely so that you can serve the needs of Ferrara.'

Lucrezia raised her head to look at him. For a moment even Strozzi felt disconcerted by the misery in her face. 'Dear madonna,' he added quietly, 'nothing can be done about it. You must come back.'

Lucrezia left them then. An hour later, she sent Tebaldeo to announce that she was ready to ride back to Ferrara. When she appeared her eyes were dry, but her swollen face was pitiful to see. She entered the city and took her place in the ducal palace, too absorbed in her own pain to care whether or not the people in the streets or at court resented her authority over them as their regent, and this obvious indifference to power won her an initial grudging respect. Respect increased when she addressed herself uncomplainingly to the work that had to be done. She dictated letters to Alfonso at the court of King Henry in England, to Isabella in Mantua and Ippolito in Rome. Guided by Tito Strozzi, she signed documents and received visitors, accepted some petitions and rejected others.

She did everything with the same set, almost sullen, expression of despair. Only once did her face change. As Tito at one point bent close to her, she whispered urgently, 'Find Pietro. Tell him.'

One of the agents of Ferrara found Bembo in Verona. He spoke of the duke's approaching death and advised him, on Tito Strozzi's advice, to delay his visit to court. Messer Strozzi would of course be delighted, he added, if Messer Bembo still wished to stay at Ostellato for the hunting, but he would understand that neither Messer Strozzi nor his son would be able to join him as they had arranged.

Bembo's unresponsive silence puzzled the young agent. 'Was your business at court urgent?' he asked in concern.

Bembo made an effort. 'No, no, of course not.' He smiled briefly. 'My only reason for going was to present the duchess with a copy of my book. This is the least I can do since she has been good enough to accept the dedication. It would have been convenient for me now as I am travelling, and had planned to be in Mantua for a few days. It can easily wait for another time.'

'Mantua? Did you know that Madonna Isabella and her husband have already left Mantua to be with the duke? Messer Bembo, I'm very glad I reached you in time to save you so many wasted journeys.'

'Yes,' said Bembo. He fiddled with one or two of the things in the room. 'I was wondering if I ought to ask you to deliver a note for me to the duchess. She would realise, I'm sure, why I shall not be presenting myself at court, but I think it might be wise all the same to offer my excuses to her, and to assure her that I shall visit Ferrara at some later date.'

The young man agreed and put himself out to be helpful. 'Why not,' he suggested, 'arrange to go to Carnival?'

'Carnival?' Bembo repeated bleakly. 'That's a long time ahead. Five months.'

'Well, no one knows how long the duke's illness may last. Then there will be the coronation, and after that the period of mourning. You could plan several fruitless journeys during that time. By Carnival, however, matters are sure to be settled. Besides, the roads are good then and Carnival is an agreeable time at court. I really don't see in the circumstances that the duchess could find any discourtesy whatsoever in your delaying your visit until then.'

'It would certainly seem,' said Bembo wearily, 'to be a sensible suggestion.'

He wrote to her with the young agent almost leaning over his shoulder. It hardly mattered what he said. It was enough for the moment to tell her that he knew what had happened and to promise her that somehow, sometime he would come to her again. 'I had intended,' he wrote, 'to present my duty to your highness in the last few days before I returned home, having just arrived here from Bergamo and Brescia. I had planned to pass through Mantua, and from there to Ferrara. But when I arrived here, I learned that the lord duke, your father-in-law, had either passed from this life, or was not far from his passing, and that because of this news the Marquis and Marchioness of Mantua had already left for Ferrara. This made me change my mind, since it seems hardly a suitable time to make my reverence to your highness in that state of tranquillity that I would wish. And so, on the advice of the bearer of this letter, I have decided to delay my visit to Ferrara until Carnival. Naturally, every delay immeasurably displeases me – I fear your highness may think me a very weak and cold servant of hers if I can exist for so long without a sight of her . . . '

He added, 'the third of October, 1504, in Verona'.

XV

Bembo returned to the Villa Bozza.

'So you have decided not to go to Ostellato?' said the Senator pleasantly.

He had heard of the duke's illness, but chose not to believe that this had any bearing on Bembo's change of plan. He was now convinced that his son's earlier insistance on abandoning Venice was what he had always supposed it to be, one of the delusions caused by a prolonged state of fever. He congratulated himself on having encouraged Pietro to make his tour of the northern cities; the prospect of new markets had restored his interest in the wool venture and his sense of his proper place in life.

Bembo, deducing all this from the indulgent looks and remarks bestowed on him by his family, felt too dispirited to argue. He handed over to Bartolommeo all the notes he had taken during his journey and then refused to discuss anything further that concerned the counting-house. The Senator, accepting that his son might need time to heal his pride, was not dismayed.

Bembo waited restlessly for news from Ferrara. At the beginning of November, when the Villa Bozza was closed for the winter, the duke was still clinging to life. Back in Venice, Bembo spent most of his time with Aldo Manuzio, discussing plans for his book on the structure of the Tuscan dialect. They decided finally that part of it should be cast in the form of dialogues, like *The Asolani*, with Carlo and Ercole Strozzi voicing different opinions on the literary value and grammatical usage of Tuscan. Bembo threw himself into the work to escape thinking about the hated uncertainty of the next few months of his life. He still shied away from anything that touched the trading affairs of the Ca' Bembo, terrified of being committed again to something that would hamper his freedom to leave Venice when he pleased.

The Senator, however, had more subtle ways of embroiling his son in family responsibilities. He announced one evening at supper that he had decided to act as defence advocate in a law-suit. It was the first time for many years that he had pleaded in court, but he had been attracted to the case, he explained, because it involved obscure and contradictory points of property law. He suspected that it might require a search for precedents in the law records of the University of Padua.

Bembo, taken off guard, asked questions. The answers excited him, as his father had supposed they would. With the scholar's rapacious appetite for exploring abstruse problems, Bembo offered to conduct the research himself. It was only much later that he discovered to his fury that the defendant was Count

Gambara, but by that time he was working so closely with the Senator in preparing the case that it was impossible for him to withdraw.

The case, which promised to be a long one, was tried in Padua. The combination of Bembo's meticulous research and the Senator's oratorical skill produced a brilliant effect. Gratifying as this was, Bembo felt resentful and ill at ease in the presence of the count. His uneasiness turned to desperation when he received a letter from the count's daughter in which she begged him to think of her as his servant for life in gratitude for the help he was giving her father. She enclosed two sonnets which she had written for him, begged for one of his, and suggested that he visit her mother who was staying in Venice for the duration of the trial.

Bembo wrote urgently that same night to the Duchess of Urbino, reminding her of repeated promises to accommodate him at her court. All he sought from her, he pleaded, was two rooms in which to live and work, and the means to provide for himself and two servants. 'If I stay much longer in Venice, I shall find myself married . . . '

He replied later to Veronica Gambara's letter, regretting that he had been unable to visit her mother and expressing his courtesies in such a fulsome manner that she couldn't fail to see that they were insincere. After that, he attended the court only when it was necessary, returning to Venice whenever he was able.

He arrived one evening at the Ca' Bembo to find Ercole Strozzi talking to his mother.

'Ercole,' he cried delightedly, 'what are you doing here? I've been in Padua.'

'Yes, your mother has been explaining to me about Count Gambara's property.' From the lift of Strozzi's eyebrow, Bembo suspected that a hint had also been dropped about Count Gambara's daughter.

'Is the duke dead?' asked Bembo. 'Is that why you're here?'

'No, he's still alive, though still paralysed and without speech,' said Strozzi. 'No, I'm here on family matters.' He spoke with a hesitation that made Bembo look at him curiously.

They supped together that night not at the Ca' Bembo but, on Bembo's insistence, at Strozzi's elegant inn overlooking the Piazza San Marco.

'What's the matter with you?' Strozzi demanded. 'Why all this scurrying about?'

Bembo told him. Strozzi was amused. 'Oh, I thought from the way your mother was talking that you were weakening towards the little countess.'

'No,' said Bembo shortly. 'How could you think that, Ercole?'

'Still loyal,' asked Strozzi liltingly, 'despite my advice?'

Bembo said nothing. 'So is she,' murmured Strozzi. During Francesco Gonzaga's stay in Ferrara since the duke's collapse, Strozzi had tried to urge Lucrezia in Francesco's direction but with no success. 'You both amaze me,' he added.

'I don't see why,' said Bembo. 'Ercole, what are these family matters that bring you here?'

Strozzi smiled. 'In your present frame of mind I doubt if you will approve of what I am doing here – '

'Why?'

'Pietro, I am making arrangements for my marriage.'

Bembo almost overturned the wine-glass in his hand. 'Ercole – '

'You didn't know, perhaps, that Ercole Bentivoglio was dead? He was thrown by his horse and his foot caught in the stirrup.'

'So Madonna Barbara is free to marry you.' Bembo was genuinely overjoyed. Then he was struck by a thought. 'But why should you be arranging the marriage in Venice?'

'It will be a secret marriage.'

Bembo frowned. 'I don't understand.'

'Well, it is following in a somewhat irreligious haste after Bentivoglio's departure. However that's not the chief reason.' Strozzi sighed. 'I'm enchanted, of course, that he's dead, but I rather wish he could have contrived to fall off his horse a year later than he did.'

Bembo shook his head blankly. 'In another year,' Strozzi explained, 'Barbara's dowry would probably have been restored to her by the papal courts. Now it's passed to the Bentivoglio family, and as Barbara's husband her claim will become mine. Instead of a dispute between a husband and wife, it becomes a dispute between the Bentivoglio and the Strozzi. You know what we mainland Italians are like, Pietro. Appearance is everything, especially in matters of honour. The Bentivoglio will never countenance another house stripping them of what was once theirs. They're a violent family. If the marriage were made public, I don't think they would hesitate to kill either Barbara or myself to prevent this – '

'Oh, come, Ercole,' Bembo protested.

Strozzi laughed shortly. 'The Bentivoglio don't live on law and water like you Venetians. Besides, there is another factor here. The Bentivoglio are Ippolito's men. If they wanted my death, he would protect them; he might even incite them to act. How he would enjoy devising the method of my execution, eh, Pietro? No, it will be wiser, and legally simpler, for Barbara to pursue her claims as a widow.'

'Why pursue them at all?' asked Bembo. He was thinking of himself and Lucrezia in the same position. 'You have Barbara. Marry her openly and let the Bentivoglio keep the dowry. You're rich enough.'

'I am now, perhaps,' answered Strozzi impatiently. 'But Alfonso will soon be duke. You know what will happen to the Strozzi then. He'll take as much as he can from us. I need Barbara's money.' He rapped his fingers on the table between them. 'It's all very well for you to look at me with such disapproval, Pietro. You are an austere man at heart. You can live simply if you have to. I can't. If I can't live as extravagantly as I want, I shall destroy Barbara's happiness as well as my own. Can't you understand that?'

'No, I can't,' said Bembo, 'though I'm willing to accept that it may be true for you. In that case, why not delay the marriage until Barbara's dowry is restored to her. You've said you think it will be only another year.' He looked into his wine-glass. It was nearly a year since he had even seen Lucrezia.

'I daren't wait,' said Strozzi. 'Until now Barbara has been safe in Ferrara under the duke's protection. But I don't know what will happen when he dies. Ippolito, as we know, sides with the Bentivoglio in this and thinks Barbara should be sent back to them. Supposing Alfonso agrees with him, Barbara would be helpless. But as my wife, whatever becomes of me, she will be protected by the Strozzi in Ferrara and Florence.'

'Ercole, I can't help feeling uneasy – '

'Pietro, believe me, I've thought about this over and over again. I'm sure the only course open to us is to marry secretly now outside Ferrara.'

'Well, if you say so,' said Bembo, smiling at him. 'I'm sure it will make you happier than a Cardinal's hat would have done.'

Strozzi looked at Bembo thoughtfully. 'I wonder if you would ever have met Lucrezia if I hadn't been consumed by that ambition for a Cardinal's hat?'

Bembo's eyes glinted. 'You mean, would you have been consumed by ambition if Lucrezia and I hadn't been fated to meet?'

Strozzi snorted. 'You and your astrology.' He glanced out of the window towards the basilica. The gold mosaic glowed palely in the winter moonlight. 'Do you remember how we walked up and down here once – '

'Carlo was with us,' said Bembo.

'Yes. And at the time you were still appalled by my liking for the depraved Borgia.' Strozzi leaned across the table towards Bembo. 'Pietro, if you want to see her again, I think you ought to come back with me now to Ferrara.'

'The last time I wanted to do that,' said Bembo in surprise, 'you did everything you could to dissuade me.'

'Oh, make no mistake, I'd do the same if things were still as they were then. But they're changing. Even you must have accepted the fact that after the duke is dead you won't be able to visit her again.'

Bembo stared at Strozzi. 'Why do you say that?'

'Pietro, her life is going to be quite different. She'll be the reigning duchess. If you think she's watched now, what do you think it will be like then? The pattern of her days will be much more rigid, there'll be many demands on her time, she'll be swamped by protocol. Alfonso won't be travelling out of Ferrara as much as he used to, and I certainly won't be welcome at his wife's court. Besides, Pietro, you mustn't forget how much you and Lucrezia owed to the old duke's fondness for you. He wouldn't hear a word said against you. He won't be there to silence Ippolito any more.'

'Yes, I understand that,' said Bembo slowly. He sat crumbling a piece of bread. 'Whatever you say, I shall go back sometime. I promised her.'

'Yes. Exactly. So come back now. Take this last chance to say goodbye to her, if that's what you want. Alfonso isn't expected back from England yet, and both Isabella and Ippolito have had to leave Ferrara for a few days to deal with their own affairs. We'll find a chance for you to talk to her alone. It's a good moment, Pietro. There won't be any others.'

Bembo swept the bread angrily on the floor. 'Ercole, you know I can't come now,' he said savagely. 'I have to go back to Padua.' His resentment against Venice and his father's devices for keeping him there flooded over him.

'Do you have to be there? Supposing you were ill?'

'Of course I have to be there,' said Bembo, irritated further by Strozzi's irresponsibility. 'Anyway, Ercole, if I suddenly fail to appear in Padua and arrive at Lucrezia's side when everyone else is away, how will it look? For Lucrezia's sake, I have to have plausible reasons for going to Ferrara that won't point directly at her. If it weren't for this Gambara case, I could have said I was riding back to keep you company, but what advocate walks out of a trial for a reason like that?' He glared at Strozzi. 'Don't you think I want to come?'

Strozzi shrugged his shoulders. He called for a serving-man and asked for ink and paper. 'What's that for?' asked Bembo, frowning.

Strozzi smiled. 'For you. Surely you're not going to waste a good courier?'

Still upset and angry, Bembo poured out his bitterness to Lucrezia. 'I can do nothing, and I doubt if I shall ever do anything again if I don't break away from these ties here. I've had little time even to enjoy Ercole's company, having to spend the greater part of my time now in Padua. Every day I want to come to you . . .'

Before he returned to Padua, Bembo crossed to the island of Murano and in the glass foundry owned by Andrea Navagero considered designs for a nuptial cup. He chose one of violet-blue glass rimmed with gold, its shallow bowl decorated in vivid enamels with a sprightly wedding cavalcade. A week later Strozzi and his bride drank together from the cup, after their secret marriage in a small chapel on the Giudecca.

The Gambara case was concluded at last, with a judgement for the count. By this time Alfonso had arrived back in Ferrara. December came. The galleys from the Barbary coast and the Levant sailed into Venice for the winter fair.

Duke Ercole of Ferrara died in January. Towards the end he had recovered some of his faculties and he spent his last hours quietly beating time to the music of his lutanist.

SIX

Ferrara, 1505

I

Alfonso's coronation took place in the cathedral of Ferrara on a day of heavy snow. Tito Strozzi, as chief minister of the council of Twelve, placed the ducal crown on his head.

Wearing a white damask robe lined with squirrel fur, Alfonso walked from the cathedral between his brother, Ippolito, and the vice-domino of the Republic of Venice. On a path cleared in the snow, they moved in procession across the square to the palace.

Lucrezia watched from a balcony in the palace facing the great door of the cathedral. Under the heavy sky, the roofs and streets of the city were white. Alfonso's white damask gleamed between the scarlet of the Cardinal's robes and the crimson of the Venetian's. Behind them came Giulio dressed in tawny-brown velvet.

Lucrezia was also wearing white, with a band of diamonds in her hair and an ermine cloak across her shoulders. When Alfonso entered the courtyard of the palace in the swirling snow, Lucrezia appeared at the top of the covered marble staircase that he was about to climb. She ran down the wet steps and at the bottom knelt to kiss Alfonso's hand.

Alfonso was surprised and moved by the gesture. He lifted her and kissed her on both cheeks. They mounted the steps together, and then in the great hall of the palace stood together before a fire of blazing logs while the nobles and officials of Ferrara knelt in turn to pledge their loyalty.

When the ceremony was over, Lucrezia bowed to her husband and withdrew. Alfonso watched her thoughtfully. She had pleased him that day, just as she had pleased him by her sensible behaviour as regent when his father was dying. He was not attracted to fair, pale women of her type, but he began to feel a certain guilt at the way he had neglected her in the past year. The Duchess of Ferrara deserved better, and Ferrara needed an heir.

He beckoned for a servant and sent word that his Laura should not expect him.

Alfonso was no longer able to spend his days founding cannon or making majolica plates in his workshop. He sat instead in his father's room in the palace, laboriously striving to establish the state of harmony in which he intended to govern his duchy.

He had wanted to make a new pact of friendship with the Venetians, but he discovered that the old duke's embroilment in the Pope's secret moves to attack Venice was too close to allow him to withdraw without damaging Ferrara. Reluctantly, he turned, as his father had done, towards the French. Within his own state, however, he could act as he chose. He set himself to look first into the repressive measures sometimes imposed on his people. Many of them could be laid to Tito Strozzi, working through the council of Twelve. Twenty years earlier, after the devastation of Ferrara by Venice, when famine had followed defeat, Tito Strozzi's harsh laws had been necessary for survival. This was no longer the case, and Alfonso suspected that the two Strozzi now manipulated them for their own gain, although he doubted if he would ever be able to prove such a charge. Sooner or later, he had resolved to repress the power of the Strozzi, but he was prepared to wait for a time when it could be done without violence. In the meantime he set up a committee to hear the injustices done to private citizens. He considered very carefully whom he should choose to act as its chairman, and then invited his wife.

This arranged, he turned his mind to creating harmony between his brothers and himself. He had never felt any particular liking for either Ippolito or Giulio, but they were his father's sons and he wanted to end the bickering that had persisted throughout the old duke's life-time. One of his dearest wishes was to rule as the head of a united family. To this end he decided to give to each of his brothers what he believed they wanted most. To Ippolito he gave power, entrusting to him part of the administration of the duchy, including its treasury. On public occasions, Ippolito shared the dais of honour with Alfonso and Lucrezia, and sat beside Alfonso at the meetings of his council. To Giulio Alfonso gave independence; treating him as generously as he might have done another legitimate brother, Alfonso settled on him one of the Este palaces in Ferrara with an income to support a separate household.

Yet neither Ippolito nor Giulio were moved by gratitude or loyalty towards Alfonso. They considered that he had done no more than it was their right to expect. For the moment, however, they were not discontented, and Alfonso had the illusion of his united family.

His satisfaction was complete when he learned that his duchess was pregnant.

II

Tito and Ercole Strozzi waited on the duchess to offer her their congratulations on the expected heir.

Ercole now made only rare appearances at Lucrezia's court. Alfonso had not yet made any move against his father or himself, but he judged it prudent not to offend Alfonso's eye too much with his presence. The court, too, was still observing its period of mourning for the old duke's death, and Ercole disliked reminders of mortality.

Lucrezia was unwell and was lying on a day-bed. Tito and Ercole Strozzi each expressed their happiness for her, offering in turn a posy of winter roses. Lucrezia let the flowers fall in her lap, staring at them. Then her face slowly screwed itself up and tears trickled from her eyes.

'Your highness is displeased with the roses?' asked Tito in concern.

Lucrezia's tears fell more thickly. 'You gave me roses like this at your ball when Messer Pietro's play was performed,' she mumbled. She sat looking listlessly at her lap. Then with a sudden desperate movement she grasped Tito's arm. 'Why doesn't he come?'

Tito Strozzi glanced carefully round the room to see who might be within earshot. Assured of reasonable safety, he said, 'You know that it would not be proper for him to come to a court in mourning.'

Lucrezia sobbed. 'It is a year since he went away. I haven't been in mourning for a year.'

Ercole, who had had four sons by different mothers, was not unfamiliar with the irrational moods of early pregnancy. 'Why should you blame him if you haven't met? You promised to see him in Venice in April, and in June. You didn't go.'

Lucrezia stopped whimpering and sat up. 'But that wasn't my fault – '

'Nor is it Pietro's fault if he can't leave Venice. He, too, has obligations – '

'Many of which,' said Tito, more gently than his son, 'he has laid aside for your sake. Does your highness not realise that in the past year he has rejected the opportunity of a good marriage, and at great cost to himself has sacrificed the respect of his family because he refuses to go on living in Venice. He tells everyone that it is because he cannot write in Venice. You, madonna, surely know that this is far from the truth.'

Lucrezia covered her face with her hands. 'Yes, I do know.' She rocked herself backwards and forwards in distress. 'Why am I so unkind to him? I don't mean it.' She took her hands from her face. 'I wish he would write more.'

'Madonna,' said Strozzi impatiently, 'he doesn't write more because he cherishes your safety. He would write every day if he could find couriers he could trust.'

Lucrezia picked up one of the posies and smelt the flowers. Suddenly much calmer, she nodded at Strozzi. 'Yes, I know. It isn't important if he can't come or can't write, as long as he still needs to be with me. I can't live without his loving me. Messer Ercole, will you find some way of telling him that? You must tell him, too, that for me it is the same.' She looked up at Strozzi, pleading with him. 'Will it be the same for him? Will he hate me?'

Strozzi understood now the cause of Lucrezia's nervous state. She was afraid of Bembo's reaction to the child she was carrying. In Bembo's place he hardly knew what he would have felt and he hesitated, unable to answer her. But Tito said quickly, 'Madonna, it is not in his nature.'

As they withdrew from Lucrezia's apartments, father and son looked at each other. 'Will you try to let him know what she said?' asked Tito.

'Yes, of course. Why not?' said Ercole, surprised.

'Oh. I had an impression that Bembo was giving place to Gonzaga in your scheme of things.'

'My function,' said Ercole airily, 'is to serve her highness in whatever way pleases her best. Besides, Gonzaga won't be interested while she's pregnant.'

III

It seemed unlikely that Cesare Borgia would ever return from his Spanish prison to re-possess his two cities on the borders of Ferrara. While the Pope was preparing to claim them, they were quietly occupied by the army of the Venetian Republic. When Venice ignored the Pope's furious demands to relinquish the cities, she was commanded to send an ambassador to Rome.

Bembo, listening with only half an ear to his father's account of the quarrel, almost missed the information which followed. The Senate had chosen Bernardo Bembo to lead their embassy.

The Senator was elated at this honour, but his wife heard the news with misgiving. The Senator read her uneasy looks. 'My dear, there is no reason for you to worry. I shall be well enough. We shall be a large party and we shall travel slowly. And we shall wait until after Easter before we leave, when the weather is settled.'

Elena Bembo glanced at her son. A year before she would have asked him to travel with his father, but now she hesitated. Since the Gambara trial there had been a restraint between them. She and her husband now knew that he wished to live in Urbino and that the Duchess Elisabetta had agreed to accommodate him there. She was therefore surprised when he caught her glance and smiled back at her. 'Would you feel happier if I went to Rome as well?'

Elena embraced him gratefully. 'Pietro, yes of course I would.' She turned to Bernardo, who was nodding with pleasure, delighted by any happening that delayed his son's departure for Urbino.

Bembo's excitement at the prospect of the journey was as great as theirs, because it gave him a perfect excuse to travel unobtrusively to Ferrara. Since the recent arrival of a letter from Strozzi telling him of Lucrezia's fears, he had been searching urgently for a reason to take him to Ferrara. Nothing, he believed, would comfort Lucrezia more than the promise of a time when he would be with her. Even if Strozzi's warnings proved right and they were unable to speak privately, she would at least be reassured of his unchanged love by the sight of him at her court.

When he had first learned of her pregnancy, Bembo had suffered confused and turbulent emotions in which despair, jealousy, a hatred of Alfonso, a sense of rejection and helplessness had played their part. As his thoughts grew more rational, he had consoled himself with the knowledge that Alfonso neither loved nor wanted Lucrezia. Before long, every other sensation was forgotten in his abiding fear for Lucrezia's safety in childbirth. He had been disturbed by Strozzi's mention of her crying over the flowers. He knew how Lucrezia could abandon herself to passions of weeping when she was unhappy, and he was afraid of the effect of such states on her now.

He considered the plan of the visit to Rome. It had been settled that the party would travel through Ravenna. On the journey south, then, he could leave it at Padua, visit Ferrara on the excuse that he was obliged to present his book to the duchess, and be back in Ravenna in time to meet the embassy. On the return journey, he could make a similar detour, and to draw attention away from this second visit to Ferrara he would also stay briefly at the courts of the Duchess of Urbino and of Isabella in Mantua.

Delighted with this scheme, Bembo now sought for ways of getting a letter to Lucrezia. In her present state, there would be little comfort in sending her ambiguous courtesies or playing the fiction of FF. He had to find someone who could carry a letter safely, without being questioned, to Lucrezia herself. Neither Lico nor Bruno nor Alvise would be inconspicuous enough, and Strozzi's position at court was now too suspect to risk sending anything through him.

He stood up suddenly, left the Ca' Bembo and hurried through the dark streets to the printing-house in Sant'Agostino. The doors were barred for the night, and Aldo Manuzio was preparing to go to bed. He peered out of an upstairs window waving a candle about to try to see who was below.

'Pietro – ' he said, startled. He ran down the stairs and let Bembo into the printing-shop. 'Come upstairs, Pietro. Whatever's happened?'

'No, no, I won't come up. I'm sorry I've disturbed you like this, Aldo. I won't keep you very long.' Bembo paused to catch his breath. 'Aldo, will your father-in-law be taking any books to Carpi in the next few days?'

Manuzio held the candle to Bembo's face and stared at him. 'Is this all you want to know? My dear Pietro – '

'Aldo, please. Is he?'

'Well, someone is always taking books to Count Alberto in Carpi. In the next few days, though, I don't think – '

Bembo groaned faintly and leaned against the printing-press.

Manuzio pulled him up by the arm. 'What's all this about? Can you tell me?'

Bembo bit his lip nervously and then nodded. There was a most urgent letter, he explained, for the court in Ferrara and it had to be delivered secretly.

'Oh,' said Manuzio. 'So this is another of your letters to that Madonna Angela Borgia.'

'No, it isn't as simple as that. This time it's for – ' Bembo hesitated, 'it's for the Duchess Lucrezia.' He looked at Manuzio and Manuzio stared back at him. 'If the letter were lost,' Bembo went on desperately, 'or if anyone else knew about it, it could be – ' he took an uneven breath, ' – terrible for her.'

Manuzio was still silent. 'So, you see, Aldo, it must be taken not only by someone whom I would trust with my life, but also by someone whose presence in Ferrara would be taken for granted.'

'My father-in-law is a Venetian.'

'Yes, I know,' said Bembo wearily, 'but he takes books to Ferrara – '

'I, on the other hand,' interrupted Manuzio with a smile, 'am a Ferrarese by birth. When I was in the service of Count Alberto Pio and he was a ducal ambassador, I was often at court. And I still visit Cardinal Ippolito to discuss books on mathematics – '

'He is the dangerous one, Aldo,' said Bembo quickly. And then he laughed. 'Are you telling me you'll go to Ferrara for me?'

'If you can give me a little longer than a few days, why not? The winter fair is just over, and I always enjoy going home to Carpi.'

Bembo embraced Manuzio like a brother. 'And you will remember, Aldo, to give my letter only to the duchess. If there is the smallest risk, you must destroy it.'

'Destroy something written by Pietro Bembo? What a loss!'

Next day, in the February dusk, Bembo sat down to write the longest letter he ever wrote to Lucrezia.

'If I have been silent for such a long time, it is because of the wretched ill luck that thwarts everything I try to do,' he told her. 'You must know that from the first time I saw you, you set a mark on me that nothing can remove. I beg you not to be hurt or to make yourself unhappy in our love because life is perverse and contrary. Everyone knows how to love when all is going well.

But when one has to face a thousand hard and disagreeable things, a thousand absences, a thousand watchers, a thousand fences, a thousand walls, then *not* everyone knows how to love; or if they know, do not want to; or if they want to, cannot hold fast. And so it is rare. If, despite all our efforts, we should have to be separated, it will be good for us to remember that we were true and constant in our love, and in that memory alone we shall find happiness. You say you do not wish to go on living except in my love, and I tell you that I would not wish to go on living except in loving you, nor would I try . . .

'But I beg you to be careful that no one should know or discover these thoughts of yours, otherwise the ways that lead to our love will become fewer and more difficult than they already are. Do not trust anyone, whoever it is, until I come to you, which in any case will be just after Easter. The bearer of this letter, who is a good friend of mine, is going on to Carpi, and on his way back will return to know if you wish to command him in any way. By these means you will be able to send me a reply and give it to him secretly in complete safety. Please do this. Tell me about your life, your thoughts, tell me who you trust, what things upset you and what pleases you. But take care that you are not seen writing, because I know you are closely watched. I will come to Ferrara just after Easter, as I said, and then I shall be going on to Rome for a month or a little longer.

'Now I kiss one and now the other of those bright, dear eyes of yours that were the first, but not the only, cause of my love. Remember always that I can bear any stroke of misfortune as long as I know that I live in your thoughts and your love. I have no other blessing but you.'

Bembo laid down his pen for a moment. He had not mentioned the child. Instead he unfastened the agnus-dei that he wore round his neck. He had explained to Lucrezia once that Venetian women wore an agnus-dei to protect them in child-birth and that this one had been worn by his own mother in the months before he was born. He wrapped it into a small packet, and then took up his pen again.

'The enclosed agnus-dei that I have worn for a long time I would like you to wear sometimes at night, for love of me, if yo u are not able to do so during the day. Then your dear heart, that I would sell my life now to be able to kiss, will at least be touched by the token which has for such a long time touched mine. Keep well.''

Alfonso, having fulfilled his duty to his duchess and to Ferrara, had returned gratefully to his mistress. Lucrezia, alone in bed, wore Bembo's agnus-dei as he had asked. By day it lay hidden beneath the bibs of pleated white voile that covered her throat.

When Manuzio returned to his printing-house in Venice, he carried a letter for Bembo. Lucrezia had forgotten to answer all the questions he had asked her, but her words were none the less precious to him for that. 'Believe me,' Lucrezia had written, 'just as I realise more and more your continuing love for me, so my debt to you and my love for you grow and deepen.' She had been holding the agnus-dei as she wrote. 'How much I treasure this remedy against despair which you have given me,' she said.

IV

For the first time since they had known each other, Angela and Giulio were able to meet when they wished. A locked stair led to a private suite of rooms in Giulio's newly acquired palace, and Angela had a key to the stair. Lucrezia, absorbed in her work of hearing citizens' grievances, failed to notice the growing number of Angela's absences.

One morning when she was helping Lucrezia to dress, Angela fainted. Later, as she lay recovering on Lucrezia's bed, she announced defiantly that she, too, was pregnant.

Lucrezia was horrified. Her first thought was that she must keep the news from Alfonso. She decided that she would take Angela to one of the Este country villas, moving part of her household there on the excuse that she herself needed to avoid the harmful air of the city. Angela could stay in seclusion in the villa until after her child was born.

This Angela scornfully refused to do. She intended to stay in Ferrara and shame Alfonso into letting her marry Giulio.

'That you will never do,' said Lucrezia grimly. She tried to explain that, even if Alfonso was not planning a political marriage for Giulio, he would never accept into his family a woman who publicly declared herself unchaste.

'Unchaste?' Angela giggled. 'You think I should keep it a secret the way you did? Were you younger or older than me when you had a child by your father's courier? That *was* why Cesare stabbed him to death, wasn't it? They say he killed him on the steps of the papal throne and his blood spurted into the Pope's face. The Pope loved him, but he didn't try to save him from Cesare, so it must have been because of a child, mustn't it? A courier!'

Lucrezia, feeling faint herself, slapped Angela hard and gave her a choice. She must go to the villa of Belriguardo, which stood a few miles outside Ferrara, or she must go back to Rome.

A few days later, Lucrezia left for the villa with Angela sulking beside her. She allowed Giulio to escort them on the journey and agreed to let him visit Angela occasionally if he would promise to say nothing about the child. Giulio, who was delighted with his coming fatherhood, gazed at her with disappointment swimming in his lustrous, dark eyes, but nevertheless promised.

Giulio, however, didn't think the promise counted when it came to the boon companions who now flocked about him, helping him to squander his money. From them he had no secrets. Before long the story reached Ippolito.

The two brothers met one day in the courtyard of the ducal palace. Giulio was surrounded by his pack of young followers. Ippolito, apart from his secretary, was alone.

Ippolito hailed his brother pleasantly. 'Giulio,' he said, embracing him, 'I hear the most amazing rumours about you.'

Giulio blinked at him. 'Amazing?'

Ippolito looked into the beautiful vacant eyes. 'One might

almost say miraculous. Madonna Angela has always assured me that she worships you for your eyes alone. Did she realise what extraordinary powers of penetration they would possess?'

Giulio understood. His new wealth had taught him neither responsibility nor wisdom, as Alfonso had hoped, but only insolence. He laughed, snapped his fingers in Ippolito's face and pointed to his eyes. 'These have certainly seen things, brother, that you will never be asked to see.'

He turned his head to enjoy the sly smiles of his companions. Then, mounting his horse, he kissed his finger-tips rudely in the direction of Ippolito and the priest. At the gateway he swung his horse round to face his brother and pointed again, grinning, at his eyes.

Later that day, with only a single servant for company, Giulio rode to see Angela at Belriguardo. It was almost dark when he started back across the open fields to Ferrara. He put his horse to the gallop and quickly outdistanced his servant.

Waiting in the shadow under a clump of trees was Ippolito. He was accompanied by a hunting-party of a dozen men from his household, led by Alessandro Pio.

As Giulio came into sight, his hair flying loose, a cloak streaming from his shoulders, Alessandro Pio raised a hand. Three men, wearing the livery of the Cardinal's grooms, dismounted and crept up beside Ippolito. Ippolito nodded. 'The eyes,' he muttered.

The men slipped away and crouched by the side of the road. When Giulio was within yards of them, the first man leapt up with a shout and seized the bridle of the startled horse. The second dragged Giulio from the saddle, and the third drew his knife.

Ippolito heard Giulio's cry of surprise as he was taken, and then his shouts as he thrashed about in the grass, trying to free himself. Ippolito grew agitated. Giulio must not be struck unconscious. He must know and feel the work of the knife on his eyes. He plucked fretfully at Alessandro Pio's bridle. Alessandro Pio bent towards him and murmured reassurance.

Then Ippolito heard what he was waiting for. Giulio was screaming.

The members of Ippolito's household were accustomed to his brutality, but as these screams of horror and agony mounted the men remaining under the trees shifted uneasily. Ludovico Ariosto leaned from the saddle and vomited.

Ippolito's absorption was so intense that he failed to notice that not only was Giulio's servant in sight but that a party of horsemen was approaching from the direction of Ferrara. They had heard Giulio's screams and were using their spurs. Alessandro Pio shouted to his men. They leapt up, their work unfinished, and ran for their mounts. Ippolito started at the sound, as though emerging from a trance. For the first time he seemed to realise the enormity of what had been done. He felt no remorse, only terror at being discovered. He turned his horse and fled. He rode in panic through the darkness until he was over the border into Mantua, beyond the limits of Alfonso's justice.

V

The horsemen who had surprised the attackers were couriers travelling to Belriguardo. They found Giulio alive, but unconscious. His face was masked by the blood and water welling from his eyes, and they recognised him only by the ornaments on his dress.

Two of the party galloped on to Belriguardo for help, while the others remained to protect Giulio. Lucrezia, who could be brisk and composed at the onset of a crisis, despatched her physician with a litter to fetch Giulio. She sent at once to the University of Ferrara for surgeons, and demanded that Alfonso be found and brought to Belriguardo.

When the duke arrived during the course of the night, he found Lucrezia watching for him. Beside her was Giulio's servant. The men who had fled past him in the dusk had hidden their faces, but he had seen that their leader wore his hair in long strands over his shoulders. In the half-light it was the pallid colour of flax.

Alfonso listened to the man in silence and then went alone into the room where Giulio lay. When he came out, he sat for a long time with his head in his hands, trying not to accept Ippolito's guilt.

Lucrezia stood staring at him. She was exhausted by the hours passed at Giulio's side and she swayed to and fro on her feet without realising it. She was waiting for Alfonso to look at her and, when he did, she said harshly, 'Your highness will not let the Cardinal escape?'

Alfonso closed his eyes. He was haunted by a fear of that strain in the Este blood that made one member destroy another. His grandfather had killed his own son, Ugo. Now the strain was manifesting itself in Ippolito. He sensed that his longing to create harmony in his family sprang in part from this fear. His instinct was to punish Ippolito, as Lucrezia urged. But how could he be sure that this was the instinct of a just man, and not the Este strain moving in his own blood?

He clutched at a straw. 'Ippolito is a churchman. I cannot judge him by my secular law.'

Lucrezia's eyes narrowed and blazed. 'Then find him, and let the Pope condemn him.'

Since his arrival at Belriguardo, Alfonso had learned the reason for Giulio's visit. In his distress and confusion, he turned on his wife. 'Your cousin was in your charge, madonna! If you had watched her more carefully, this would not have happened.' He broke off, aware that this was hardly just, but in no mood to retract.

Lucrezia was trembling, frightened by the tone of his voice, but she went on. 'My negligence does not excuse the Cardinal.'

'He has not killed Giulio,' said Alfonso impatiently.

'Wouldn't Giulio have bled to death if my servants hadn't saved him?' cried Lucrezia. 'And if he hadn't, is what Ippolito was doing any better than killing?' She took a step towards him. 'My lord, I beg you. Stop him from doing this to other men.'

Alfonso noticed blood on Lucrezia's dress. He remembered his child, and said roughly, 'You need concern yourself no further in this. I shall consider what is the best thing to do.'

Lucrezia recognised that she was being dismissed, not only from his presence but from any further discussion of the matter. She bowed her head. As she was about to open the door, he added awkwardly, 'I am grateful to you for your care of my brother.'

As soon as it was possible, Alfonso moved Giulio to Ferrara, where he could visit him every day. The surgeons believed that they would be able to save the sight of one eye, but his face was terrible to see. Alfonso sat beside him in the darkness, for Giulio could bear no light in the room, and wondered what he should do. It seemed to him, finally, that the only wise proceeding was to forgive Ippolito and reconcile him with Giulio.

Ippolito was recalled from his exile across the border. For Giulio's sake, the court assembled at night, by torchlight, to witness the meeting between the duke's two brothers. Ippolito appeared wearing a large jewelled crucifix round his neck and behaved with an air of boredom, buffing his nails against a white leather gauntlet while he waited for Giulio to be fetched.

Giulio was carried into Alfonso's palace in a litter. He was helped to his feet, his hands groping in the air. One eye was a mass of swollen jelly. The other, in which some sight remained, was without the eyelid. Ippolito's glance flickered unmoved across the mutilated face. No one else in the room was able to look without distress. Alfonso's own eyes were wet with tears as he clasped Giulio in his arms.

He spoke gently, his voice shaking, to each of his brothers in turn, begging them to be reconciled for his sake and for the sake of their father.

Ippolito profferred a limp, white hand. 'I ask forgiveness, brother,' he said without expression.

Giulio allowed his hand to be held out towards Ippolito's, but as their fingers touched he suddenly cried out and snatched his hand away. Sobbing, he tried to find his way back to his litter.

Alfonso, tears still falling down his cheeks, grasped Giulio by the shoulders and pleaded with him. Three times Giulio had to be led to Ippolito before his hand rested in his brother's and the words of forgiveness were forced from his lips.

When Alfonso visited Giulio next day, he found him burning with fever. In his delirium he transferred his hatred of Ippolito to Alfonso, who had deserted him. The delirium passed, but Giulio's thoughts, as he brooded in his darkened room, remained wild and confused. Alfonso had allowed Ippolito to go unpunished. He must be pleased, then, with Ippolito. Perhaps Alfonso had encouraged Ippolito to try to kill him. Since the first attempt had failed, Alfonso would try again. I shall never be safe, Giulio declared to himself, until Alfonso is dead.

He decided that he must kill Alfonso to save himself, and he babbled about his fears to his companions. The malcontents of Ferrara began to gather round his bedside and among them they devised a plot to assassinate the duke.

Strozzi, staying at Ostellato, heard too late of the plot. He hurried back to Ferrara to reason with Giulio, but arrived only in time to see him led from his palace in chains, accused of treason.

Alfonso, unaware of Giulo's feverish terrors, was stunned by this new disaster. Swiftly, on his behalf, Ippolito arranged Giulio's trial. Bewildered and inarticulate, Giulio had no words to use in his defence, and the death sentence was passed and laid before Alfonso. Ippolito dipped the pen in the ink and Alfonso signed.

Isabella, who loved Giulio, was for once genuinely united with Lucrezia in pleading for Giulio's life. Isabella wrote passionately from Mantua, upbraiding Alfonso for his cruelty and stupidity. Lucrezia reminded him of his clemency to Ippolito. Isabella's letters Alfonso ignored. Lucrezia he warned not to interfere lest she be suspected of conspiring with Giulio.

The scaffold for Giulio's execution was erected in the courtyard of the castle, on the spot where Ugo and Paragina had died. When Alfonso and Ippolito had taken their places on the ceremonial dais, Giulio was brought up from the dungeons, shuffling sightlessly in his chains, whimpering with fear.

Ippolito watched with satisfaction, regretting only that Lucrezia and Angela Borgia had not been forced to attend. Giulio was pushed towards the block and on to his knees. Ippolito turned to his brother beside him, waiting for him to give his signal to the executioner. Alfonso was leaning back in his chair, his face unnaturally pale, his eyes closed. As Ippolito tapped him impatiently on the arm, Alfonso's eyes sprang open and he looked hard at Ippolito

'You will stop the execution,' he said.

VI

In Aldo Manuzio's private room above the printing-shop, Ludovico Ariosto sat with his head buried in his arms. Manuzio sat beside him. Bembo was staring out of the window. Ariosto had just told them what he had witnessed on the road from Belriguardo.

It was the beginning of April. Ariosto was passing through Venice on the way to Hungary, where Ippolito d'Este owned estates. He had gone, as he always did when he was in Venice, to the house of his compatriot, Manuzio, and had found him designing type-script with Bembo. Bembo had started up and come towards him, asking for news of Giulio. Ariosto had stared at him for a moment, and then broken down.

Ariosto lifted his head, brushed a hand across his wet eyes and said to Manuzio, 'Aldo, I am ashamed – '

Manuzio patted his shoulder. 'Why, my dear friend, why?'

'I haven't spoken of it to anyone since it happened,' said Ariosto. 'No one speaks of it in Ferrara.' He turned to Bembo. 'When I heard you say his name, Pietro, I suddenly remembered the day when we were all together on the duchess's terrace. He wanted to play a game – '

'Yes. Hide-and-seek. I remember,' said Bembo.

'We could hear him laughing. And now, dear God help me, all I can hear is his screaming.' Ariosto thrust his hands against his ears. 'I don't think I shall ever stop hearing his screams.'

'It will pass, in time,' said Manuzio gently. 'You know, Ludovico, the story you have told us is not the story we have heard in Venice.'

'No,' answered Ariosto. 'You will have heard that the Cardinal and his hunting-party were resting when a stranger galloped towards them. Fearing an attack on the Cardinal, his men drew their knives to protect him. In the struggle which followed, the stranger was cut in the face before it was realised who he was. The Cardinal's men could not be blamed. It was growing dark and no one would expect a prince to be riding alone.'

'So you have heard this story, too?'

Ariosto laughed bitterly. 'Oh, yes. I wrote it.'

Bembo looked at him in horror. 'You wrote it? Ludovico, knowing what you know, you gave your name to that?'

Manuzio observed the pain in Ariosto's face and said, 'Pietro, you've never had to live under patronage. You don't understand what it means.'

'You can't condemn me more than I condemn myself,' Ariosto muttered. 'But I have ten mouths to feed, as well as my own. If I refused to do what Ippolito wanted, I couldn't stay in Ferrara. I wouldn't dare to leave my sisters and my brothers and my son behind, and I can't afford to bring them all to Venice or Florence or anywhere else.'

'But there must be others who know the truth,' cried Bembo passionately.

'Who?' asked Ariosto sadly. 'Ippolito's servants? They won't speak. Who else will contradict me? I was there. In their hearts the duke knows and the duchess knows; so does anyone who really understands Ippolito. But they didn't actually see what happened.'

'So that monster escapes!' Bembo was beside himself. 'How is it possible?'

'I suspect, 'said Manuzio, 'that he is the kind of man who always will.'

'Yet, Giulio, who has done no harm to anyone, who has a good and simple heart, is savagely punished!'

'At least the duke mercifully spared his life.'

'Mercifully!' Bembo rounded on Manuzio. 'Is it merciful, after all he's suffered, to imprison him for nothing?'

'Not for nothing. He plotted treason,' said Manuzio mildly.

'If Giulio plotted treason, it was because of delusions caused by his pain. It must have been. Ludovico, you know him. He isn't brutal or ambitious.' Bembo paused. 'How long is he to be in prison?'

Ariosto shook his head in grief. 'For the rest of his life.'

'He's twenty-three,' cried Bembo. He thought of the dungeons in which Ugo and Paragina had been kept.

Ariosto read his mind. 'He is not to be put in one of the underground cells, but in a room at the top of one of the towers. He will have some light and air. His sight is returning in one eye, and he will be able to watch the street beneath.'

'Then he may be allowed visitors?' asked Manuzio.

Ariosto, with his eye on Bembo, hesitated. 'No,' he said slowly. 'The room has no door. There is a trap in the roof, through which his food will be lowered – '

'As though he were a dangerous beast? Is this Alfonso's mercy?' Bembo paced about the room in his distress. He was aware of an ambivalence in his attitude towards Alfonso. He felt an instinctive antagonism towards him, yet he was loath, for Lucrezia's sake, to believe him cruel. 'Was it mercy that let Giulio reach the block before pardoning him?'

'I think the duke was confused, not unmerciful,' said Ariosto. 'Though I fear these events inside his own family have changed him. He tried to be magnanimous and conciliatory. He believes now that this is only misunderstood as weakness.'

'And what,' asked Bembo, 'and what of the duchess in all this?'

'Oh,' said Ariosto vaguely, 'the duke is displeased that Madonna Angela was not watched more closely while living under his roof. He has appointed a mistress of her household to overlook matters, a woman who served his mother. He was not pleased, either, when she tried to help Giulio.'

More fences, more watchers, thought Bembo unhappily. 'But I mean her health – the child.'

'I understand she is well enough. I have not seen her recently. The duke advised her to remain at Belriguardo with Madonna

Angela. For that poor lady he is trying to arrange a marriage that will take her away from the duchess's court.'

Bembo had settled by the window again, his face pale, a trace of sweat on his forehead. 'Who would have thought Ippolito could have gained so much from gouging out his brother's eyes?' He spoke with a brutal flippancy that made Ariosto glance at him in surprise.

'Pietro – ?'

Bembo spread his fingers against the glass panes of the window. 'Ludovico,' he said in anguish, 'I pray God He protect – ' He stopped. ' – that He protect anyone whose life touches Ippolito's.'

VII

Lucrezia knocked on the door of her cousin's room at Belriguardo. There was no answer. She knocked again. When there was still no response, she opened the door and entered.

Angela was standing with her back towards her, half-dressed, her hair uncombed. 'Oh, it's you,' she said, over her shoulder. 'Well?'

Lucrezia seated herself before she spoke again. 'Cousin,' she said with dignity, 'you have my permission to sit.'

The formality of Lucrezia's manner startled Angela. Looking sideways at Lucrezia, she dragged out a stool and sat down in front of her.

'That's better.' Lucrezia smiled at Angela. She drew a breath. 'Angela, I have to talk to you at the duke's wish. What I am going to say the duke has asked me to say. The answer I give him will be yours. I shall not try to persuade you in any way – dear Angela, you know that I wouldn't.'

'I don't know yet what you're talking about, do I?' said Angela.

'No, no, you don't,' murmured Lucrezia. She paused for a moment, avoiding Angela's sharp eyes. 'Angela, the duke would like to arrange a marriage for you.'

'To Giulio?'

Lucrezia gasped in distress. 'No, not to Giulio.'

'Why not? Wouldn't that be a suitable punishment for me now?'

'Angela dear, there is no question of punishment, only what is wise for your future.'

Angela laughed scornfully. 'And who has been chosen for me?'

Lucrezia fumbled with her necklace. 'Messer Alessandro Pio.' She waited for Angela to cry out in protest as she had done when Alfonso had suggested the name. Alfonso had silenced her angrily, pointing out that their choice was not wide.

Yet Angela, surprisingly, said nothing. Faltering slightly, Lucrezia explained that Alessandro Pio had recently inherited the title of Prince of Sassuola. It was a very small principality, too poor even to support its lord, who had remained in the service of Ippolito d'Este. But if the marriage took place, Alfonso was prepared to allow the prince and his bride an income sufficient for them to live there independently.

Lucrezia was unhappy with the plan but, as she talked to Angela, she realised that Alfonso had in his own way not been ungenerous in his choice of a husband. It had always pleased Angela, during the life-time of Pope Alessandro, to be treated as the future Duchess of Urbino, and later she had counted on becoming Giulio's princess. Now Alfonso was offering her the title of Princess of Sassuola and the means to create her own tiny court.

'Alessandro Pio,' said Angela, sucking a strand of hair. 'Yes, I know him. His mother is one of the Bentivoglio of Bologna. They say he helped to arrange the attack on Giulio. Would you have told me that if I hadn't known?'

Lucrezia leaned forward and caught hold of her cousin's hands. 'Oh, Angela, there is no need for you to marry him. There is another way. You could go to live in a convent, perhaps with the nuns of the Casa Romei. Your baby could grow up there with you. I would look after you both. There you would be near Giulio.' For a moment, Lucrezia saw herself in Angela's position with Bembo as the prisoner in the castle. 'From the windows of the Casa Romei you would be able to see the window of his tower.'

Angela snatched her hands away and stared at Lucrezia in amazement. 'Do you really think I would live in a convent when I could be Princess of Sassuola?' She laughed. 'Giulio's window!'

Lucrezia shook her head in bewilderment. Angela said unkindly, 'The duke partly blames you for this, doesn't he? What would he say if he knew you weren't really trying to make this marriage?'

Lucrezia bit her lip. 'Angela, the duke has asked me to find out if you would consent to it, nothing more.'

'Do you expect me to believe that?' Angela stood up and looked down at Lucrezia. 'Oh, I'll marry Alessandro Pio. I owe you something. But there are conditions. I want you to give me a gold dress, like the one you had, for my wedding.'

Lucrezia nodded uneasily. 'Yes.'

'I want to be married in the cathedral in Ferrara, not in a private chapel somewhere.'

'Yes.'

'And will you let me wear your diamond crown?'

'Angela,' cried Lucrezia, 'the wedding ceremony is not the marriage. You must think – '

'I don't want to think any more.' Angela threw herself on her bed. 'If you were me you wouldn't have married Alessandro Pio, would you, because he helped in blinding Giulio? But he's like the rest of us who have no money of our own, he has to do what he's told.' As Lucrezia stumbled towards the door, she called out, 'I wonder which of us will hate Giulio's child most.'

On the stairs outside Angela's room, Lucrezia clung to a post, confused and sick at heart, grieving for Giulio and his unborn child. She felt for the agnus-dei at her neck. She wanted to close her eyes, let herself fall, and find Bembo's arms round her, supporting her.

She opened her eyes and saw Tebaldeo reaching out his hands towards her, and her ladies running to help her.

VIII

Bembo crossed the border into Ferrara, and rode through the flat fields of wheat and hemp towards the city. The sky was overcast, and the air unusually oppressive for April. It was like plague weather.

He rode across the moat and through the city gates into the sombre streets. At times, he was so possessed by the wonder and excitement of being close again to Lucrezia that he hardly knew how to stop himself from shouting aloud: at others, it seemed so natural to be near her that he might never have been away. He skirted the smaller moat that surrounded the castle, glancing up at the terrace where the orange trees grew, and at the balcony outside the room in which he had last seen Lucrezia sixteen months before. Above them rose the tower in which Giulio was imprisoned.

Bembo reached the cathedral square, dominated on his right hand by the ducal palace in which Alfonso and Lucrezia now resided. He turned his horse left across the square and continued his journey past the north wall of the cathedral towards the Casa Romei and the Strozzi palace.

Tito Strozzi received him lying in bed. The unnatural heat had tired him, he explained, and he considered himself old enough at eighty to indulge his weakness. 'But I rejoice to see you again, Pietro,' he said, embracing him.

Ercole was less cordial. 'You must be mad to come,' he said. 'You know I can't help you.'

'I hadn't come here to ask for your help,' Bembo answered patiently. 'You warned me, and I know that it is not your wish to give it.'

Strozzi relented a little. 'It isn't so much a question of what I wish, Pietro. As you know, I used to encourage Giulio to confide in me, and since that silly little plot of his was uncovered I am not entirely trusted myself. Ippolito, in his new glory, sees to that. I no longer have the opportunity to help you.'

'You have not perhaps chosen a very wise time to come,' added Tito. 'There is an embassy here at the moment from the King of France and the time of your Lucrezia is very much taken up with their entertainment.'

Bembo smiled. 'In a crowded court I may be less noticeable.'

'What! A Venetian at a meeting of two peoples pledging themselves to attack Venice?' exclaimed Strozzi.

'You'll have to pass yourself off as a Frenchman,' said Tito.

'Yes,' agreed Ercole. 'All you have to do is mince about, sweeping your bonnet off to everyone you meet, and stop washing for a fortnight.'

'Do I take it,' enquired Bembo, 'that you are less than enchanted by your new friends?'

'Oh, we can tolerate them as long as they keep their distance in hot weather,' said Strozzi. 'You Venetians are sweeter to live with, but this doesn't console us for your bland arrogance.'

Bembo raised an eyebrow slightly. 'I see,' he murmured good-humouredly.

'There's a perfect example of it,' cried Strozzi. 'You're immune even to insult – '

'We have the tolerance to realise that the fault lies not in ourselves, but in our attackers' lack of perception.'

Tito Strozzi reproved them, smiling, and Bembo hurried away to write a brief note to Tebaldeo, requesting an opportunity to present his book to the duchess. The servant who carried the note returned to say that the duchess would be pleased to receive him at court next morning.

From then on the hours that remained of the day seemed to Bembo to drag like lead weights. He had borne sixteen months of separation from Lucrezia with reasonable fortitude, but the last evening was unendurable. He had hardly expected to sleep that night, and was not surprised when he heard most of the hours struck by the clock in his courtyard.

Bembo descended from the Strozzi carriage at the foot of the covered marble staircase that led to the state rooms of the ducal palace. He carried a copy of *The Asolani* in covers of decorated leather, gilded with Lucrezia's name and titles. He was wearing the colours of his house, black and gold, a single gold ornament on a dress of black Venetian cut velvet. Lico followed him, carrying his cloak.

Bembo remembered how, returning from Medelana, he had felt stifled by the constraints of Lucrezia's court, but they had been slight compared with the formalities that now enclosed her. Bembo was escorted with ceremony to the ante-room of the audience chamber, and there left to wait. He was not alone; the apartment was filled with officials and petitioners, and with the attendants of the French emissaries w[illegible] were now, Bembo was informed, in conversation with her.

After nearly an hour, the doors of the audience chamber were opened and Bembo's name was announced. A steward beckoned him to the threshold with his wand. Facing him, at the other end of the room, in a chair placed on a low dais, was Lucrezia.

She was surrounded by people who were strangers to Bembo. He thought with pain of former times – Strozzi at her elbow, Angela smiling slyly, Giulio. She looked small and vulnerable in the chair of state, his timid goose under the spread wings of the Este eagle blazoned on the wall behind her. He recalled suddenly the night of the Torch Ball. 'Your highness does too much honour to a stranger,' he had said when she offered him the torch, and she had answered, 'You forget that I, too, am a stranger here.' He had taken her hand. 'Then let us form a league together – '

They were alone again in an alien company. Bembo felt as if the torch were burning again, casting into darkness everything except the path between them.

Stepping over the threshold, he bowed to Lucrezia in the manner of Venice, with his hand on his heart. When he was half-way across the chamber he bowed again without breaking the rhythm of his steps, as Venetians did in Venice. The unusual nature of the salutation was emphasized by Bembo's severe, dark dress in a court where men were aping the fashions of France in plumed bonnets and padded, slashed tunics of embroidered satin.

Lucrezia's eyes consumed him, delighting in his aloof bearing, the distinction of his dress, the graceful oriental movement of his hands. Since she had last seen him he had grown a beard, neat and clipped in the Venetian style. Her excitement and her joy in him made her body throb painfully, and its discomfort took her breath.

Bembo bowed for the third time at the foot of Lucrezia's dais, and then raised his head slowly to look at her.

She stared at him without speaking. He saw with concern that she was not well. Her pale face suddenly flushed.

Dear love, Bembo prayed silently, speak to me, for I must not speak first. He lowered his head again, afraid of the thought showing in his face. He was aware of the new mistress of her household standing beside her chair, watching him coldly.

Lucrezia gasped and murmured to the woman. A fan was passed into her hand. It was the fan with the black and white ostrich feathers and the spines of gold that he had seen her use often before. Perhaps the memory of this comforted her as it did him. The movement of its plumes seemed to restore her.

'Messer Bembo,' she said in a faint voice, 'I pray that you find the heat less exhausting than I do. I beg you to believe that there was no intention on my part of being so tardy in greeting you. You are truly welcome after so long an absence from our court.'

'Madonna,' said Bembo, 'I do indeed experience the heat of this room, but for me it is not disturbing. I rejoice in it since it is created by the flame of your highness's beauty. You have been more than gracious in giving your servant a moment to recover the composure that was quite taken away from him in entering your presence.'

Lucrezia inclined her head slightly in acknowledgement of the compliment. Bembo knelt on the lower step of the dais, proffering his book. 'May I beg your highness to accept, before it melts in my burning hands, this copy of my book, which in her illustrious condescension she has allowed me to humbly dedicate to her.'

Lucrezia leaned forward to take the book, but as her hands touched the leather cover which had just left his the strength which she had tried to sustain flowed out of her. Her face flushed again, and then faded to an unhealthy pallor. Bembo half rose as she thrust the book back at him, tried with a murmur of distress to stand and fell forward.

Bembo dropped the book and caught her. People surged towards them, but before anyone else could reach them Bembo had lifted her in his arms. The French ambassador, who had been standing by the dais, was the first at Bembo's side, offering to help him carry Lucrezia.

'I thank you, excellency,' said Bembo, speaking in the ambassador's tongue, 'but I fear it might be unwise to disturb her unduly. I can support her.'

He turned to meet the suspicious gaze of the mistress of Lucrezia's household. Bembo smiled at her. 'I beg you, madonna,' he murmured, 'to treat me as you would one of your own servants. If you would be so gracious as to walk before me – '

Startled by the unexpected sweetness of his manner, the lady smiled back and indicated the way to Lucrezia's private apartments. As she stepped ahead to guide him, the rest of Lucrecia's ladies crowded round. Bembo glanced at those who were pushing against him. 'I think you would be advised to keep back a little,' he whispered. 'I don't think for a moment that her highness has plague, but in this heat, you know – '

They fell back before he could finish. Lucrezia's eyes were now wide open. She had longed so often to find herself lying in Bembo's arms that for a moment she thought she was still dreaming. But then she felt the warmth of his body against hers, heard his breathing and the beating of his heart. He was looking down at her, and his name rose eagerly to her lips.

'Highness,' said Bembo sharply, 'do not speak. You will waste your strength.' Lucrezia remembered where she was and what had happened. She closed her eyes again, rejoicing that she was once more, if only for a few seconds, secure in Bembo's arms.

They were approaching the entrance to her apartment. Bembo gently pressed Lucrezia's arm and called out, as if to guide, 'Madonna, you must tell me where to go.' The lady nodded and beckoned him to follow her through the doors.

Bembo slackened his step as if tiring of his burden. 'If your highness were able to put an arm round my neck,' he said, 'I think you would find that I could support you with less discomfort.'

Lucrezia murmured and lifted her arm. Bembo lowered his head and briefly it touched hers. 'Tomorrow,' she whispered. 'The University.'

He carried her into her room, set her with the help of her physician on her bed, and withdrew with a series of his bows to the mistress of her household. Tebaldeo was waiting to escort him back to the audience chamber. As he entered, he found himself greeted by the sound of gloved fingers being politely tapped together. The King of France's gentlemen were applauding him.

The ambassador bowed to him. 'Monsieur, we entreat you to allow us to offer our felicitations on the exquisite dexterity of your wit. Your improvisation this morning, sir, commanded the admiration and envy of us all.'

Bembo bowed in return. 'Excellency, you owe no compliment to my words, only to the lady who inspired them.'

The Frenchman was delighted. 'Monsieur, you understand true gallantry. You are indeed a courtier.'

Tebaldeo bent down to retrieve Bembo's book from the dais. He looked at the Frenchman with distaste. 'I think Messer Bembo values the title of scholar more,' he said.

The ambassador gave a cry of protest. 'Ah, monsieur, what title is that for a gentleman? Why does the Italian consider that the complete gentleman must be trained in the arts of scholarship as well as arms and polite manners? What good is scholarship? In France we leave it to clerks and churchmen. If you were to come to the court of France tomorrow we should entertain you with the chase, with music and the dance, but certainly not with lectures in Latin.'

'Lectures in Latin?'

'Monsieur, have you not heard? Tomorrow afternoon the duchess escorts us to the University.' The ambassador shook his head ruefully.

Bembo smiled. 'Excellency,' he said, 'I wonder if you would be gracious enough to allow me to accompany your party – '

Bembo was about to step back into the Strozzi carriage when a soft voice called his name. He turned round to see Cardinal Ippolito's secretary gliding down the staircase towards him.

'Messer Bembo? His eminence has sent me to fetch you.'

Bembo hesitated, inclined to refuse an invitation framed so discourteously. Then he gave a curt nod and followed the priest back into the palace.

Ippolito was waiting for him in the room in which Bembo had often read Greek with the old duke. He extended a hand without rising from his chair so that Bembo was forced to kneel to kiss the episcopal ring.

'So, Messer Bembo,' he said, 'your meeting with the duchess was interrupted.'

It was a statement and Bembo saw no reason to answer it. Ippolito had changed since he had last seen him. He was still vain, with the long whitish-fair hair carefully arranged on his shoulders, but he no longer had an air of petulance. His manner had confidence and authority. As well it might have, thought Bembo bitterly. He had committed one of the most barbarous of crimes and emerged from it secure and powerful.

'How curious it is,' Ippolito went on, 'that your first visit here after so long an absence should occur when our good friends are here from France.'

Bembo acknowledged the coincidence.

'But is it a coincidence?' asked Ippolito. 'Messer Bembo, is it not a fact that your father is on his way to Rome to discuss certain points of dispute between Venice and the Papacy?'

Bembo said warily, 'Yes. I am on my way to join him at Ravenna.'

Ippolito nodded. 'The disputed cities lie on our borders. It is vital to your father to know how far the French are prepared to protect Ferrara against Venice if we attack those cities on the Pope's behalf. And he needs to know this before he reaches Rome.'

Bembo stared at Ippolito. 'Your eminence surely cannot pretend – '

'Pretend? Messer Bembo, my father once reproached me for accusing you of spying for Venice. At that time the thought had, frankly, never occurred to me. I presume we owe the misunderstanding, as we owe so much, to Ercole Strozzi. I must admit, however, that I now find myself grateful to him for putting the idea into my mind.'

'Eminence – !'

'Messer Bembo,' said Ippolito, 'you spoke to the French ambassador as soon as you left the duchess's apartment. You and your family no longer have any interests in Ferrara. What other possible reason could you have for returning here, if you are not spying for your father's embassy?'

Bembo stood silent, appalled at the neatness of Ippolito's trick. Then he drew himself up. He spoke with the contempt of the old Venetian families for the cunning of churchmen. 'I can assure your eminence that if the Republic sent an agent to Ferrara he would not allow his movements to be so easily observed as mine have been.'

'Ah, but you Venetians are devious. That is precisely what he might do, so that such an answer as you have just given me would serve to put us off our guard.'

'Your eminence,' said Bembo, 'is too subtle for me.'

'On the contrary,' murmured Ippolito, 'I rather suspect, Messer Bembo, that you have been too subtle for Ferrara and Duke Alfonso.'

IX

The schools of the University of Ferrara were housed in churches and halls scattered throughout the city. The church of San Domenico was the seat of the largest and most renowned of these schools, that of philosophy and medicine, and it was here that the French ambassador and his party were to be entertained by a learned disputation in logic.

Bembo had originally intended to travel to San Domenico in the company of the ambassador, thinking this would make excellent cover for his meeting with Lucrezia. But Ippolito had forestalled him. If he exchanged so much as a sentence with a Frenchman, Ippolito would make capital of it. He went, therefore, alone to the church, arriving unobtrusively on foot some time before Lucrezia's procession was expected. During his father's stay as vice-domino in Ferrara, he had often attended the lectures in philosophy of the celebrated Professor Leoniceni, and the rooms and passages of San Domenico were familiar to him. He wandered into the cloisters, mingling with the foreign students whom Leoniceni's work had attracted from as far afield as Poland and England. Among such outlandish groups, Bembo wryly hoped, the alien appearance of a Venetian might pass unremarked.

Hovering behind the Poles, Bembo witnessed the arrival of Lucrezia in her litter, surrounded by the jingling cavalcade of the French ambassador. The doctors and masters of the university were assembled to greet her, and she listened to addresses of welcome in Latin from the rector and from Leoniceni himself. Then she was lifted from her litter and, looking white and tired as she leaned on Tebaldeo's arm, she spoke a few words in the same tongue and then introduced the ambassador and his suite to their hosts.

Bembo was unable to hear what was said next. From her gestures, Lucrezia appeared to be regretfully declining the invitation to attend the disputation and Leoniceni, from his, to be indicating a room in which she might rest.

Bembo wondered how he could attract her attention. The rest of the company were beginning to move into the church to hear the disputation. Bembo hesitated, uncertain what to do next, as the crowd pushed past him and Lucrezia was led away in another direction.

He took refuge in the deserted cloister, conscious of how much Strozzi's help had meant in the past. A few yards separated him from Lucrezia, yet at that moment he might as well have been in Venice. He turned his head sharply as he heard steps in the cloisters. A young woman whom he had never seen before was coming towards him.

He was startled when she spoke to him by name. 'Messer Bembo? Messer Bembo, the duchess has sent me.'

Bembo's heart beat more quickly. 'How did you know who I was?'

'I saw you when you were received at court yesterday,' said the young woman. His surprise seemed to surprise her. 'Her highness knew that you would be here today and told me to find you.'

'And what was her reason for doing that?' asked Bembo gravely.

'She asks, sir, if you will spare a few minutes from the disputation so that she can apologise for the interruption to your audience yesterday.'

'I shall, of course,' murmured Bembo, 'be honoured to attend her highness.'

The young woman nodded and led him to the row of cell-like studies behind the cloisters used by the teachers of the university. Lucrezia had been accommodated in the largest of these, that belonging to Leoniceni. He was a man with an avid thirst for knowledge and the barely furnished room was overflowing with books, plant specimens, surgical tools, mathematical instruments, metals and acids. In a space cleared in the middle of this stood Lucrezia wearing a glimmering grey and silver dress. She was holding Bembo's book.

Bembo knelt down and kissed the hem of her dress. 'Your highness is gracious.'

'No, indeed, Messer Bembo, it is you who is being gracious in coming so promptly.' She smiled at her lady. 'If you wish, you may join the other ladies with the French ambassador. Messer Bembo will fetch you if you are needed.'

The girl took her leave gratefully and without curiosity. She was very young, and Bembo realised that to her he must appear, at thirty-four, as one who could be as safely left alone with the duchess as the seventy-year old Leoniceni. When he rose to his feet, he was already alone with Lucrezia.

They looked at each other. 'You are my grey goose today,' said Bembo, holding out his hands.

Lucrezia smiled as she took them. 'My ladies told me today that wearing grey has a special significance. Did you know that?'

Bembo shook his head, drawing her towards him.

'It is the colour of lovers, because it resembles the ashes of a heart that is always on fire.'

'I see,' said Bembo, kissing her fingers.

'You wore grey once.'

Bembo thought. 'Yes, the second time I saw you, at the Strozzi ball. So that is how you knew I loved you. I often wondered.'

Lucrezia laughed and they held each other closely. Lucrezia covered his face with kisses. 'It is just the same,' she said, 'just as if you went away only yesterday.'

'Sooner. An hour ago.' He kissed her mouth. 'Didn't you think it would be?'

Lucrezia sighed. 'Things have changed.'

Bembo fingered the gold chain round her neck. 'Is this my agnus-dei?'

Lucrezia nodded.

'I sent this to you so that you would know nothing had changed.'

Lucrezia rocked herself in his arms. 'Oh, I thought so. I hoped so.'

He felt her trembling, leaning heavily against him. 'Lucrezia,' he said in concern, 'you must sit down.' There was only one chair in the room and Bembo had to remove note-books and an astrolabe before lowering Lucrezia into it. He looked round with disfavour at the austere furnishings that boasted neither cushions nor a footstool, and then bundled up his cloak for her to lean against.

'Pietro, there is no need. I'm not ill,' Lucrezia protested gently.

'No? Yesterday you fainted. Just now, you had to be lifted from your litter. Do you know how pale you are?'

Bembo was kneeling beside the chair. Lucrezia bent forward and put her arms round his neck. 'Dear Pietro, truly it is nothing.

Only the excitement because you are here.' She felt for Bembo's hand. 'Please, Pietro, hold me safe now so that I can remember it when you are not here.'

Bembo put his arms round her, and held her head against his shoulder. She gave a sob of relief, and Bembo felt the old bitterness at being unable to comfort her when she had most need of him. Yet as they lay against each other, heads touching, he found that his distress, like hers, was gradually forgotten in the joy of at last holding and being held.

After a while, Lucrezia stirred. 'I love you.' She sighed with pleasure. Bembo was bending his head to kiss her when the sound of horses made them both start up.

'Ippolito!' cried Lucrezia, her hands flying to her face.

Bembo went to the window and leaned out. It was not Ippolito.

'Why did you think it was?' asked Bembo.

Lucrezia gave a helpless shake of her head. 'He seems to be everywhere, waiting for something.' She was desperately twisitng the chain of the agnus-dei round her fingers.

Bembo, watching her, made himself face the decision that he had been trying to avoid since his meeting with Ippolito. He went back to her side and gently unwound the chain. 'I should have put it on an iron cable,' he said, and he brushed his lips against the red weals on her fingers. 'There is nothing for you to be afraid of here. But, my love, listen to me. It is not wise for me to stay in Ferrara while the French are here.'

Lucrezia stared at him. 'Why not?'

Bembo explained to her what had passed between himself and Ippolito on the previous afternoon. 'This excuse gives him every reason to have me watched, and to persuade the duke to have me watched, too. And if they watch me, where will I lead them? To you.' Then holding her tightly, he said, 'I will have to leave Ferrara without seeing you again.'

Lucrezia's cry of misery broke Bembo's control. He shook her distractedly. 'Love, please, have some pity for me. I would stay with you always if it were possible. You must help me.'

'It's been more than a year,' sobbed Lucrezia.

Bembo rocked her in his arms. 'Listen, listen a moment. I will come back. Not in a year, but in six weeks, on my way back from Rome. If I go now, Ippolito's story loses its point, and there will be nothing to stop my returning in June. If I stay, even without seeing you, it is possible that I could be banished from Ferrara.'

Lucrezia lay without moving in his arms. 'Yes,' she said. 'Yes, I suppose so.'

'In June,' said Bembo, comforting her, 'you will be able to go to Medelana again, and I will come to Ostellato. We shall be safer there. Here in the city I can't tell who is watching me, but when I ride across the fields to Medelana no one can follow without my knowing. And at Medelana you can choose which people you have about you. We shall see our garden again, and our balcony.'

He was thinking also as he spoke of the little room that overlooked the kitchen court. He wondered if he would ever make love to her again. He laid his head in her lap to hide the tears that came unexpectedly to his eyes.

Lucrezia's fingers rested in his hair. 'And after Medelana?' she whispered. Bembo was not sure whether she was speaking to him or to herself. He shook his head in her lap, unable to answer.

X

While he was in Rome, Bembo went every day to the Vatican to look at Pinturicchio's fresco of Saint Catherine in one of the empty Borgia apartments. It was said by some to be a portrait of Lucrezia. Bright hair streamed over the little saint's shoulders, a strand above each ear fastened at the back of her head. Her thin fingers were twisted together. Her pale face was gentle and apprehensive. The first time Bembo had seen it, he had smiled to himself. There was no doubt: it was his white goose when she was barely out of childhood.

He wandered through the other deserted rooms and through the streets of Rome, seeing with new eyes the places which Lucrezia had known and for which she was often homesick. Wherever he went, he found himself haunted by a sadness in the gaze of the Lucrezia on the Vatican wall that disturbed him. Yet he was unwilling to explore the reason for his uneasiness and instead he fixed his thoughts resolutely on the days to come at Medelana.

For much of the rest of his time he moved in the enlightened circles of Roman society. His book had been read with acclaim and his company was widely sought among the elegant summer villas near Tivoli. He was honoured by a summons from Cardinal Giovanni de Medici, regarded by many as the next most likely candidate for the papal throne. The Cardinal was one of the sons of Lorenzo de Medici, and Bembo had known him when they were boys together in Florence. His plump, impassive face masked, Bembo remembered, a brilliant, ambitious and scholarly mind. The Cardinal questioned Bembo on a number of literary matters, and then enquired how he would remedy the debased and corrupt Latin in which Vatican documents were produced.

'The only way to eliminate barbarisms,' said Bembo promptly, 'is to force all clerks to use only the syntax and vocabulary found in Cicero.'

The Cardinal blinked at Bembo, and Bembo was not sure whether he accepted the answer or was even interested in it.

The Senator's stay in Rome was less pleasant than his son's. No negotiations as such were possible with Pope Giulio. His attitude to the Venetians was one of implacable hostility, and his demands for the two disputed cities were larded with threats and abuse. Bernardo Bembo's reply to the indignity of his treatment was to combine a meticulously correct regard for protocol with a calculated insolence of manner. The Pope was goaded to fury.

'Show me,' he roared on one occasion, 'any document which gives you a claim to those cities.'

Bernardo Bembo barely hesitated. 'Your holiness will find our claim written on the back of the deed which granted Rome and the Papal States to the fisherman of Galilee.'

The Senator left the papal court with the Pope shouting after him that whatever else happened he would destroy Venice.

Bernardo Bembo had no doubt that he would do everything in his considerable power to achieve it.

He spoke that night to his son. 'You have not yet said when you intend to leave Venice for Urbino,' he began carefully. 'I have no wish, Pietro, to enquire into your affairs, but if you were not committed to leave in the next few weeks I should be grateful for your help at the Villa Bozza.'

'For what kind of help?' asked Bembo, equally careful.

'I would like you,' the Senator explained, 'to help me make an inventory of everything we have of value in the Villa Bozza and decide how we may accommodate the articles at the Ca' Bembo.'

'You're selling the villa?' cried Bembo. 'You've never spoken of this before. A mortgage, yes, but – '

The Senator held up a hand. 'Pietro, let me finish. I am not discussing our debts. I am only concerned now with the coming invasion of Venetian territory. The Pope's resolve to attack us is now in the open. It may come next year, it may come in five years' time, but it is inevitable.'

'Yes, but what has this to do with our villa?'

'There are times, Pietro,' said the Senator tartly, 'when you surprise me by talking like a typical Venetian. Our mainland borders, you know, are not inviolate as so many of our countrymen appear to imagine. When this war comes, we shall be fighting against every Italian and foreign prince who has an eye on a piece of our territory. The Pope will be virtually offering Venice for sale. We shan't be able to hold our borders.' He drew lines on the table in front of him with his finger. 'As I see it, the papal forces and the French, using Ferrara, will attack from the south. The Germans will move eastwards from Verona towards the lagoon.'

Bembo felt the prickings of concern. 'Surely if they get as far as the Villa Bozza, Venice itself will be taken.'

'That might just be remotely possible if a Spanish or a Genoese army were to march on the lagoon, but this will be a German one. Have you ever seen a German fall into a canal? They're terrified of water. Even if they occupy all the land between Padua and the shore, the lagoon will save Venice. And then we shall wait,' added the Senator thoughtfully. 'We shall wait until this unlikely company of allies falls out. Then the Pope will remember that he is an Italian, and he will beg for Italian help against the foreigners.'

'I see,' said Bembo, who was not certain that he did. 'Of course, I'll help with the inventory.'

The Senator nodded gratefully at his son. He was not unaware of the success Pietro had enjoyed in Rome. While the rest of the Venetian party had, by choice, remained aloof and apart in Roman society, Pietro had behaved like an Italian among Italians. He had a chameleon quality that could be of incomparable value to Venice in the difficult future ahead. The Senator allowed his mind to dwell on a time when Pietro's obstinate insistence on living in Urbino would have burnt itself out, like his earlier predilection for Ferrara. Then all they would need to do would be to persuade the electors that Pietro's lack of provincialism was a diplomatic asset to be exploited.

Had the Senator been told at this point that before another ten years had passed the Papacy would be suing for a Venetian alliance, he would hardly have been surprised. Nor would he have been surprised to learn that his son would be the chief figure in these negotiations, conducting them with skill and elegance.

What he would not have believed was that Pietro Bembo would be an ambassador of the Papacy and not of the Republic of Venice.

XI

Bembo had reached Urbino, the last stop on his journey back to Ferrara.

Entering the city, he was conscious of the sort of pleasure which he always experienced when he arrived in Asolo. Urbino, perched on its hillsides, like Asolo under its snow-peaked mountains, gave him a welcome sense of protection and seclusion. Unlike Giovanni Matteo, he felt no hunger for the vast horizon and exposed waters of the lagoon. In Venice, men pushed and hurried along their flat quays; in Urbino, they moved with leisure up and down the sharply inclined streets.

Inside the ducal palace of Urbino, Bembo was taken, although it was still afternoon, to the apartment known as the evening room. It had acquired this name because it was here, in the evenings, that the duchess liked to gather about her all those men of wit and learning who gave her court its fame as a centre of polished conversation. It was a gracious room, paved with tawny-coloured burnished bricks, its hooded marble fireplace carved with climbing honeysuckle. On one side, its windows faced the city, and on the other looked across a hanging garden towards the wooded hills of the Apennines.

As he was admitted into the room, Bembo saw the reason for its use at this unusual hour. Against a background of this distant landscape the Duchess Elisabetta was sitting for her portrait. A very young man with long black hair was working at the easel, and another man of Bembo's age, wearing a yellow tunic, was watching over his shoulder and at the same time reading aloud from a sheet of manuscript.

The duchess moved and held out her hands to Bembo. He had last seen her in Venice, before the duke's exile had been brought to an end by the capture of Cesare Borgia. He congratulated her on their restoration.

Elisabetta had none of the spirit and exuberance of her brother, Francesco Gonzaga. She was noted, by contrast, for her quiet and controlled refinement of manner. Bembo could understand, but not entirely forgive, her contempt for Lucrezia's simpler and unschooled behaviour.

'To think,' Elisabetta was saying, 'of that creature, Cesare, living inside these walls!' With a delicate shudder, she looked at her silk tapestries and silver-mounted pictures and mirrors as though contact with Cesare Borgia might have coarsened them.

Bembo expressed his sympathy, and he thought of Cesare Borgia sitting for three days and nights by Lucrezia's sick-bed.

'You are here for only a day or so,' said the duchess regretfully as Bembo bent over her hand. 'When are you coming here to live? It is several months since you wrote to ask me if I might find rooms for yourself and your servants. They are ready, Messer Pietro.'

'You must forgive my delaying,' Bembo stammered, 'but my affairs are – are unsettled. I shall probably join you in the early autumn.' He was not sure why such a date came to his lips. He was nursing a foolish secret hope, perhaps, that by some miracle he might be able to spend all the summer near Lucrezia; certainly, he felt too much on edge to commit himself to anything until after the birth of Lucrezia's child.

'In the autumn? Good, good.' The man in the yellow tunic came forward. Bembo peered at him, then gave a cry of recognition. 'Bernardo Bibbiena!'

Bibbiena had the bland, smiling face of the adroit man of intrigue. It crinkled suddenly into laughter. 'So you remember me? I wondered if you would. How long is it? Twenty-five years?'

Bembo was laughing back. 'I saw Cardinal Giovanni in Rome. And now you.'

'At one time, madonna,' Bibbiena explained to the duchess, 'we all took our lessons together in Florence – Giovanni, his brothers, myself and our little Venetian here. We taught him to speak good Florentine Tuscan and you'll notice, madonna, that he still does.'

They grinned at each other with the amusement of men who have known each other as boys and can never quite accept each other as adults.

Bibbiena laughed again. 'Welcome, Pietro, to the ante-room of the Vatican.'

'What was that? What did you call it?'

'Messer Bernardo has the impertinence,' said the duchess indulgently, 'to refer to my palace as the ante-room of the Vatican.'

'Well, isn't that what it has become since the Medici were banished from Florence, madonna?' asked Bibbiena.

Duke Guidobaldo and Elisabetta, familiar through experience of the plight of exiles, had offered refuge in their palace to the exiled house of Medici. Bibbiena, who from childhood had identified himself with the ambitions of Giovanni de Medici, had accompanied him into exile. They divided their time between the Cardinal's house in Rome and the palace of Urbino.

'You surely heard talk in Rome,' said Bibbiena to Bembo, 'of Cardinal Giovanni as the next Pope?'

'Yes, I did hear some people speak of it,' answered Bembo.

'Well, when that happens, we shall desert our ante-room here,' Bibbiena's eyes glinted, 'and we shall occupy the opulent chambers of the Papacy.'

'You may,' observed Bembo, 'have to cool your heels a long time. Pope Giulio appears to be in robust health.'

'Indeed, yes,' Bibbiena waved a hand in the air. 'So, meanwhile, we take our indolent delight in Urbino.'

'Doing what?' asked Bembo.

'How can I describe it to you? We walk out into the air, we laugh, we invent games, we sup together. A few of us study a little. Some of us make love, and all of us talk about it. Sometimes we compose verses and read them to each other. We write plays and act them.' He tapped the paper in his hand. 'If her highness approves this small effort of my own, we shall perform it for her on Sunday. We are always in a hurry with so much to do. Why, there are times in summer when from these windows we see the dawn rising above the hills before our conversation flags.'

Bembo smiled, thinking of life in the counting-house in Venice. Then he said, 'But I am not coming here to be indolent. I want to work.'

Bibbiena shook a finger at him. 'Then,' he said severely, 'you must be decently discreet about it.' He glanced towards the young painter. 'Not like Messer Raffaello here, who fidgets himself to desperation if he has to spend a minute without his brush on a canvas.'

The young man blushed and laughed. 'I'm sorry, madonna,' he said, appealing to the duchess, 'but the light is beginning to change – '

Elisabetta, with a kindly smile, resumed her pose. Raffaello darted forward to position her fingers on the cushion that represented the pet dog which would appear in the finished portrait. 'Messer Bembo,' she said, 'this is Raffaello Sanzio. He belongs by birth to our city of Urbino, but his heart, like Messer Bernardo's, already yearns for Rome.'

Raffaello smiled at Bembo. 'You have just come from Rome,' he said, as though this bestowed a special grace on Bembo. 'Did you see the murals in Nero's villa? And the Apollo – ?'

His eyes shone, and Bembo found his enthusiasm infectious. 'I like the bronzes.'

Raffaello nodded eagerly. 'Yes. Think how many more there may be just beneath the earth. I started to make a plan once of a system for excavating the city in sections – ' He snatched up a brush and began to sketch lines on an empty portion of his canvas.

'Raffaello, the light,' murmured the duchess. Raffaello gave her a rueful enchanted smile and selected another brush.

Despite his impatience to see Lucrezia, Bembo remained for five days in Urbino. Much of the time he spent with Bibbiena, watching Raffaello at work.

He felt at first that he had little in common with Raffaello. Urbino, which Bembo loved, was regarded by Raffaello as confining and provincial. He had left the city as a child of eight to be apprenticed to the painter, Perugino, and in later years he rarely returned except to fulfil commissions for the duchess. He was now only twenty-two, but he already enjoyed a considerable fame. Yet he had a startling lack of self-consciousness that reminded Bembo of Lucrezia. He was not surprised then to learn that Raffaello had once refused a number of valuable commissions in Perugia and left unfinished an altar-piece in Siena to go alone to Florence to study the work of Leonardo and Michelangelo. There he had sat in front of frescoes and sculptures, drawing for hour after hour, learning new techniques to transmute those he had already mastered.

In the house which Raffaello owned in Urbino, Bembo looked at his Florentine note-books. His imitative skill was extraordinary. Even as a boy in Perugino's studio, his execution had been so like his master's that it was said to be impossible to distinguish them.

'Copies,' said Bibbiena, glancing over his shoulder. 'Brilliant, but only copies.'

Bembo shook his head. He recognised that the sketches were not the copies of an artist who lacks his own originality of style, but of one who is greedy to learn every technical secret of his craft. 'When I was a young man, I did the same sort of thing. I made myself imitate the verse of Catullus and Petrarch and the Provençal troubadours until I was satisfied that I understood how every effect of rhythm and sound was achieved.' He smiled at Raffaello, realising that he had met someone who shared his scholar's temperament.

'Are you going back to Venice?' asked Raffaello. Without waiting for an answer, he hurried on, 'I must go to Venice, too. They say that in Venice paintings have such a richness of colour that one can taste the painted fruit, and smell the flowers, and your madonnas have warm, glowing flesh – ' He laughed. 'How is it done, Messer Bembo?'

'I don't know – '

'They paint like that because they never look beyond the flesh,' interrupted Bibbiena. 'They have no understanding of the spirit.' He glanced sideways at Bembo. 'But when you come with us to Rome, Pietro, we will lead you beyond such limitations.'

'To Rome?' Bembo shook his head. 'I fear I shall have to stay here with my sensuous limitations. I could never afford to live in Rome.'

'I don't think you understand me,' said Bibbiena quietly. 'I mean as a member of the papal court.'

Bembo stared at him. 'My dear Bernardo – '

'Cardinal Giovanni has written to me,' said Bibbiena. 'He was impressed by the methods you suggested for reforming Vatican Latin.'

'But, Bernardo,' protested Bembo, 'we spoke of it only in passing.'

Bibbiena waved this aside. 'Giovanni de Medici is not a soldier like Pope Giulio, who sees the Papacy as a means of destroying

Venice. Giovanni is a scholar. What he would like to do as Pope is to revive in Rome something of the Rome of the Caesars.' He smiled broadly, so that Bembo was not sure whether he was speaking seriously or not. 'He has Raffaello to restore its treasures. He would like to have you to restore its language.'

'And how do you suppose I could do that?' enquired Bembo.

Bibbiena shrugged his shoulders. 'Well, perhaps if you were one of the papal secretaries, it could be arranged that every document leaving the Vatican passed through your hands.'

'That would mean taking orders,' said Bembo sharply, remembering an earlier conversation with Bruno.

'Only minor ones. Isn't it worth it for the sake of the benefices that will flutter into your lap like plump birds? No more mortgages, Pietro, no more debts.'

'No,' said Bembo. 'No, it isn't possible.'

'I thought you were running away from Venice to avoid marriage,' said Bibbiena. 'There's no better protection than minor orders.'

'No,' said Bembo again. 'You don't understand, Bernardo. I'm a Venetian.' He glanced at Bibbiena. 'One of your unspiritual Venetians. Hardly fitted for the Vatican.' He couldn't explain that Rome was too far from Lucrezia in Ferrara. Instead he added lamely, 'I prefer to stay in Urbino.'

Bibbiena observed his growing agitation and allowed the matter to drop. 'Well, when are you going back to your carnal city, Pietro – tomorrow?'

'I'm not going back to Venice, but to Ferrara,' said Bembo. He felt obliged to add something more. 'I shall be staying with Ercole Strozzi.'

Bibbiena glanced at Raffaelo. 'Pietro,' he asked gently, 'have you received any news of the Strozzi recently?'

Bembo felt a prickling of alarm. 'Not since I arrived in Rome. Why do you ask?'

Bibbiena hesitated. 'Messer Tito Strozzi died two weeks ago.'

Shock and grief overwhelmed Bembo for a moment. 'He was very good to me,' he muttered. He saw Raffaello nod in sympathy, his face filled with distress. 'Do you know how he died?' he asked Bibbiena.

'It is believed that it was plague, but you must understand that the information has come to me at second hand, through the house of Strozzi in Florence.' He paused. 'They also sent news concerning Ercole Strozzi.'

Bembo looked at Bibbiena nervously. 'Yes?'

'You will know that he shared the leadership of Ferrara's council of Twelve with his father. Alfonso has dismissed him. Alfonso has also reclaimed a number of the estates which the old duke bestowed on Tito Strozzi.'

Bembo took a quick breath. 'Do you know which ones?'

Bibbiena shook his head.

XII

'Oh, yes, he's taken Ostellato,' said Strozzi bitterly.

As he had ridden towards Ferrara, Bembo had tried to prepare himself for such a blow. The effect of it was still shattering. Bembo felt as though he himself had been robbed of Ostellato. It hurt him to realise that never again would he be able to sit in the turret room which he regarded as his own, and see the leaves brushing the window or look out at the garden beneath. Ostellato was alive with his earliest memories of Lucrezia and it had been torn from him. Yet that was nothing compared with the knowledge that without Ostellato there could be no more visits to Medelana, and without Medelana there was no safe place left for them in Ferrara.

'He's taken a lot else,' Strozzi was saying, 'besides Ostellato. Now perhaps you can understand why I must have Barbara's money.'

Bembo, ashamed of his preoccupation with his own grief, enquired after Barbara Strozzi's health.

'She is well,' said Strozzi. 'We will sup with her this evening, and she will take pleasure in thanking you for our wedding cup.

I've taken a house for her on the outskirts of the city. It's sheltered and secluded, and we shall go by a devious route.'

Bembo found this secrecy unwholesome. Even in Strozzi's present position, he found it impossible to see any wisdom or need for hiding the marriage.

'Surely some one will eventually see you,' he protested. 'Why go on like this?'

'Human nature is fortunately uncharitable. If I were seen, who would assume in these circumstances that I was married to the widow Bentivoglio?'

'But it could be years before the courts make a decision. We never know how little time we may have – ' He broke off, aware of Strozzi's indifference to what he was saying. He was unable to be silent any longer about Lucrezia. 'Ercole,' he murmured, 'have you any news for me? Am I to see Lucrezia?'

Strozzi said unkindly, 'I was wondering how long it would be before you had to ask. Yes, she's waiting for you at Belvedere.'

'Belvedere? But that's so close to Ferrara.'

'You will have to lodge now in Ferrara, so isn't that what you want?' snapped Strozzi. 'It's the best that can be done. It's on an island in the river, so you can see if you are being followed.' He stared morosely at Bembo. 'My father, like Ercole Bentivoglio, died too soon. He should have waited until after this visit of yours.'

'Ercole – '

'At least while my father lived, Alfonso allowed us some semblance of authority. Even six weeks ago when you were here, my father's position protected you. But now you are nothing more than the friend of a man who has been disgraced and whom the duke regards as an enemy; as such you are not a fitting person to consort with the duchess. Do you understand, Pietro?'

Bembo nodded and stared at the ground. 'Yes,' he muttered. 'You are only putting into words what I know, and pretend not to know.'

Strozzi's harsh manner relented slightly. 'There is some consolation for you,' he said. 'My father is said to have died of plague.'

'Yes, so I heard in Urbino.'

Strozzi shook his head. 'I don't think so. He had an attack of plague, but it was only slight. I think he began to die slowly from the night when he saw what Ippolito had done to Giulio's eyes. Ippolito killed my father.'

Bembo said nothing. After a moment, Strozzi sniffed and laughed coarsely. 'But Ippolito thinks it was plague and he rushed away to Modena. So my father's death isn't altogether untimely, is it? He's given you a few days' grace before Ippolito can discover that you are here and return to Ferrara. You would be wise to go before he does get back.' Strozzi paused. 'In fact, you would be very unwise not to go before then.'

'Yes, yes I know that,' said Bembo.

Strozzi leaned towards Bembo. 'Of course, it would be even wiser to go now.'

'Without seeing Lucrezia?' Bembo smiled. 'No, Ercole.'

Strozzi shrugged his shoulders. 'I have two men who will ride with you to Belvedere when you go.'

'I don't want two of your men. Why should I draw attention to myself like that?'

'It is her wish, not mine,' said Strozzi. 'You are not to go anywhere alone in Ferrara.' He put out a hand and touched Bembo with something of his old friendliness. 'Be advised, Pietro. Giulio thought he could ride alone.'

XIII

Bembo stepped on to the green island of Belvedere. He was met by the majordomo, who was expecting him, and informed that the duchess was resting and would not appear in public until later in the day. Surprised, Bembo thanked him and announced that he would pass the time enjoying the gardens until her highness pleased to send for him.

Uncertain what was expected of him, Bembo strolled past the ornamental fountain, through the formal gardens and into the parkland beyond. Ahead of him were the little loggias built into the wall overlooking the river. He had sat in one of them once, watching Lucrezia on the shore. He wandered about idly, trying to decide which it had been. Then, where the screen of trees was thickest, a flicker of movement caught his eye.

He hurried across the grass and through the trees. In the loggia facing him, he could see the silk of a woman's skirt. He pushed aside the hanging vine tendrils. Lucrezia was sitting on the marble bench. For a moment his joy was complete; nothing else mattered to him except the sight of her.

Lucrezia sighed with pleasure. 'You guessed where I was.'

Bembo smiled ruefully. 'No. I walked this way by chance.'

Lucrezia shook her head. 'Not by chance. In your book someone says that people in love are joined by an invisible chain. I watched your boat arrive and then I wound in our chain.'

'So that was it?' Bembo laughed. He took both her hands and kissed the inside of her wrists and her palms. 'Love, are you well?'

'Yes, well.' She seemed stronger, less exhausted by her pregnancy than when he had seen her in April.

'Are you alone here?'

'Oh, yes. Since I have come to Belvedere it is understood that I rest alone here in the afternoon. No one is allowed to disturb me. You, Messer Bembo, have broken my rules.'

'Is that my fault when you have just admitted that you dragged me here yourself?'

Lucrezia laughed and held out her arms. 'Let me kiss you.'

'Lucrezia – ' Bembo glanced round anxiously.

'The trees hide us from the garden, and there is no one near on the water.'

She drew him on the bench beside her, and kissed his hair and his eyes, and then his mouth. 'You allow me no freedom of my own, do you?' murmured Bembo, grasping her fiercely.

Later, when they sat side by side, fingers linked together, heads touching, Lucrezia said, 'Tell me about your journey.'

'In Rome,' said Bembo, 'I saw your portrait. I went to look at it every day. And in Urbino I met a young painter whom I wish could paint you now for me. He would understand you, because he has the same unawareness of himself that you have. Raffaello.' He touched her hair. 'And you, my love, what has happened to you in these last few weeks?'

Lucrezia sat up. 'Angela has been married. She has gone to Sassuola. I don't know when I shall see her again.'

Bembo sensed Lucrezia's distress and gripped her fingers more tightly. 'We are quite alone now,' he said in a soft voice.

Lucrezia looked round at the river and the park. 'Yes – '

'I didn't mean that.' Bembo hesitated.

'Tell me,' said Lucrezia gently.

Bembo sighed. 'In one sense we have always been alone, as we were in our circle of torchlight. Yet close to us, helping us and watching for us, we had people like Angela and the Strozzi and the old duke. Now Tito Strozzi and the duke are dead, Angela has gone, and Ercole either can't or doesn't want to help us. No one any longer stands between Ippolito and us.

'That's what I meant when I said we were quite alone now. You and I, love, we are still together in our circle, but what surrounds us now, like the water round this island, is fear.'

'Pietro – '

Bembo turned towards her and touched her face. 'Your Saint Paul promises us that perfect love casts out fear. For ourselves perhaps it does, but it doesn't cast out the fear we feel for those who are dear to us.'

He had tried to ignore the uneasiness weighing on him in Rome, but Tito Strozzi's death had made it impossible for him to run any longer from the truth. With a groan, Bembo took Lucrezia again in his arms, hiding his face from her. Then he said with difficulty, 'Lucrezia, there is something I must say to you – but, oh love, how? I don't know how – '

Lucrezia lay very still in his arms. 'I think I know what it is.'

Bembo raised his head to look at her. 'I am afraid, too,' she said to him, 'afraid of what may happen to you, Pietro, if you ever come back to Ferrara.'

Bembo had expected Lucrezia would be the one to falter and

protest. But it was Bembo who laid his head in his hands with a sob. 'Lucrezia, do we have to stay apart from each other?'

Lucrezia cradled him as he had so often done to comfort her. 'There are times when I think I can't bear it. I know that I would risk any harm to myself rather than give up trying to see you.' She raised a hand to brush away a tear from his cheek. 'But then I make myself remember Giulio with his eyes destroyed. Then I know there is no choice.'

She gazed across the strip of brilliant water that protected them from the city. 'Ippolito,' she said, 'there is no curbing him now, not after the story Ludovico Ariosto told.' She sighed. 'He was your friend, Pietro.'

'He still is,' said Bembo. 'Lucrezia, Ariosto did what he did because he, too, was frightened for those he loved. Try not to condemn him.'

Lucrezia suddenly cried out, 'Ippolito always wins.'

'But does he?' Bembo asked her. 'Whatever he suspects about us, does he really know what happened at Medelana, or in my house in Ferrara? I don't believe so. Does he understand what conformity means? Think about that when you see him.'

Lucrezia smiled shakily. 'Yes. But thinking about it won't bring you back. Oh, Pietro, don't go now, not today.'

Bembo smiled. 'My goose, I couldn't leave you today if Ippolito was already on his way across the river. And we know he's not. He's not even in Ferrara. I think we can risk another four days together before he can interfere.'

'Four days!' Lucrezia's eyes shone. 'Perhaps longer? It's possible no one will tell him you're here – '

Bembo put a finger to her lips. 'We mustn't demand too much of our luck. Remember I'm on my way back to Venice from Rome. I broke my journey for five days at the court of the Duchess of Urbino. I am now spending four or five days waiting on the Duchess of Ferrara, and then I shall pause for a few days at Isabella's castle in Mantua. Three visits of courtesy, Lucrezia, not one of which should appear any more remarkable than the others. It may not deceive Ippolito, but it will pass as a reasonable travelling plan to everyone else. Five days, after all, may be nothing to some – ' he kissed her tenderly on the mouth, ' – but to us, after the last eighteen months, it will be a life-time.'

'Yes, it will,' whispered Lucrezia. 'For the next four days, when you leave me in the evening, I shall be able to say, "Tomorrow he is coming again". That has never happened to us before, not for four days, one after the other.'

She was smiling, but Bembo saw tears suddenly spring into her eyes. He reproached himself angrily, 'I shouldn't have spoken yet. I should have waited till the last day.'

'Oh no,' said Lucrezia quickly. 'This is better. You would have dreaded it more and more, and it would have spoilt these last few days we have together. And, after all, I knew what you were going to say. Now we have time to grow used to it together. We shall not be alone when we have most need of each other's comfort.'

Before he could answer, she stood up. 'Pietro, you must go now. They will be coming to fetch me. Walk in the garden. I will send for you and then we will sit sedately discussing your book until supper.'

She held out a hand to him. He rose and stood beside her, looking down on to the beach. Lucrezia pointed. 'Do you remember when I wrote something in the sand over there for you?'

'Of course. Didn't I write about it in our book? But you rubbed out the words before I could read them. What were they?'

'I told you before that I wanted you to guess. It was only one word, Pietro, and I'll help you: it has more than one letter and less than ten.'

'So have most words,' said Bembo. 'I can't guess. Tell me.' He hazarded the obvious. 'Crystal?'

Lucrezia shook her head impatiently. 'No. It's a word that's very special to me, yet very easy for you to guess. You must think about it.'

'I'll think about it.' Bembo looked at her. 'Do you remember that it was there, too, that your hair blew loose and I wanted to touch it.'

'Yes,' said Lucrezia, laying her head on his shoulder. 'The next day I cut off a piece and sent it to you.'

Much of the time they passed together during those few days was spent in this way, recalling the earlier days of their love. Each afternoon they contrived to meet alone in one of the loggias. Bembo ate in the evening at Lucrezia's table and after supper, when the rest of her household danced or played cards, sat apart with her, pretending to read aloud. By Lucrezia's wish, he was back in the Strozzi palace before the summer darkness covered the city.

To their surprise, they were happy. In the rare pleasure of being together parting seemed to belong to a time that would never really come. They were once more within a circle of torchlight so brilliant that nothing beyond its light had any form or substance.

Yet the last afternoon came. They sat behind a screen of vine-leaves, stricken and for a long time speechless. Lucrezia spoke first, in a flat, quiet voice, almost as though she were talking to herself. 'I don't know what I shall do. You will be gone, and Cesare – '

'Cesare?'

'I mean that I don't think I shall ever see Cesare again, or my baby, Rodrigo – '

Lucrezia's hand lay between Bembo's palms and he chafed it gently. 'Soon you will have your new child. When you are the mother of the heir, you will have great influence here in Ferrara. In time you could make it stronger than Ippolito's, and you could try to undo some of the harm that he has done.'

At the mention of the child, Lucrezia's hand had strayed to the chain of the agnus-dei at her neck. 'Yes,' she said absently, and drew out the jewel to look at it.

The action touched the fear that Bembo always felt for her in her pregnancy. She was not strong and death in childbirth was common. He took the agnus-dei from her hand and pressed his lips to it. Then, gripping her tightly, he said, 'You must promise me that you will do everything that is sensible and careful. Tomorrow, when I have gone, you must not make yourself ill with crying – ' He broke off helplessly. 'Lucrezia, you are crying now. My love, don't – '

Lucrezia's face was screwed up with crying, and trying not to cry. She thrust a handkerchief in her mouth and bit the corner hard. Then between the tears that were flooding down her cheeks and choking her, she said, 'Shall we never see each other again?'

'My pet,' said Bembo, shaking her in his distress, 'no one can talk about "never". If things have changed so much for us in the last two years, why shouldn't they change as much again in the next two, or three, or five? We must always hope for that.'

Lucrezia opened her eyes wide and looked hard at him. 'But you do not really think they will change.'

Bembo hesitated, and then answered her. 'It is not impossible. But I think it unlikely.'

Lucrezia stood up and clung to the rim of the balcony. She gasped and cried out, 'I shan't know where you are, or what you are doing – '

'But of course you will know what I am doing,' said Bembo. 'You will have my letters.'

Lucrezia turned round. 'Letters?' She spoke the word again, not believing it. 'Letters?' Her face was transformed. 'You will write to me?'

'As you will write to me, surely.' Bembo laughed at her tenderly. 'Sweetheart, how could I leave you now if I were not sure that, from time to time, I should see something and touch something that had come to me from your hands? Our letters may never be anything more than polite greetings, but we both know how to read what is not written.'

Lucrezia was clinging to him, sobbing now with relief. 'Pietro, you will let us write. We shall not be completely lost to each other.'

Bembo spoke to her almost in surprise, yet with great gentleness. 'Whether we write or not, we shall not be lost to each other.' He stroked her hair. 'Most lovers part because one of them is fickle or bored or disillusioned. I think the worst misery in loving is not having to part, but loving someone who no longer cares. Do you realise how blessed we are because we share the same grief in parting? Remember that we are being separated for no cause that is in one or both of us, so how can either of us be lost to the other?'

He sat down with her on their bench, still holding her. 'I told you once that the cruellest thing that could happen to me would be knowing that you no longer loved me. Nothing in life could hurt me as much as that.'

'I do love you,' said Lucrezia.

'Yes, and because I know that, other misfortunes are less difficult to bear – even leaving you. My dear love, let it be the same for you.'

He felt her head move against him. 'To think of these things may not help us much in the next few days. But later, I think they will.'

He pulled loose a strand of her hair and laid it across her cheek. ' "Hair, like clear amber, as by a miracle blown across fresh drifts of snow",' he murmured.

'That is in your book,' said Lucrezia, pleased.

Bembo smiled. 'Yes, that, too. Do you remember? Do you remember the afternoon in my house in Ferrara? We have loved each other well, haven't we? Yet we've both learned that when we can't share each other's bodies, when we can't even see each other, love doesn't have to change. Perhaps we are lucky that we've been able to discover this truth.' He smoothed the loose hair back into place. 'Most people think it's an illusion.'

He knelt down in front of her. 'But we will never stop hoping.'

Lucrezia looked back at him. 'No, never.'

'Remember, that as long as Ercole Strozzi is alive, there is a way between us. If you need me, he will always know how to find me, wherever I am.'

Lucrezia sighed. 'Yes. Messer Ercole. Will you be going soon to Urbino?'

'Yes, soon. But first I want to go home to the Villa Bozza.' He smiled at her sadly. 'I want to be there alone for a while.' He paused, and then added, 'Then I have some work to do there for my father that may take a month or two. I think when your baby is born in September I should still like to be in Venice. If it won't make you angry, I should like to have his horoscope cast for you.'

Lucrezia bent forward to kiss him. 'No, it won't make me angry,' she said, tears again in her eyes. She brushed them away. 'And then you will go to Urbino?'

Bembo nodded and stood up. 'Life is curious. I have turned mine upside-down so that I could leave Venice to be closer to you, and now that everything is arranged I dare not see you any more.'

'Then wouldn't you rather stay in Venice?'

'No. I shall go to Urbino. Because of you I've made myself escape from a way of living that would eventually have stifled what talent I possess. Without my need for you, I wouldn't have found the energy or the courage. In that sense, whatever I write from now on belongs to you – ' He broke off abruptly. 'Oh, my love, the afternoon is nearly over. When I leave this evening I shan't be able to say goodbye to you as I would want. Let us say goodbye now.'

Lucrezia caught his hand. 'Pietro, does it have to be the last time today? Let me go back to Ferrara in the morning. Come to me in the palace as you leave.'

'But, Lucrezia, it would have to be such a brief meeting. I could say nothing to you there.'

'I know, but at least I would see you again. I shall have one more night of knowing that I shall see you again. We've had so little time. I can't bear to lose even a few minutes that I might share being in the same room with you.'

'But won't it disturb you less if I leave you here – '

Lucrezia held his hand to her lips. 'Pietro, please.'

'Oh, my love, anything you want. But you will have to find some reason for going back so suddenly.'

'Pregnant women have whims,' said Lucrezia. 'Then, when you have gone tomorrow, I will go to the nuns in the Casa Romei.

You will be at the Villa Bozza, and we will both be alone and know we are thinking of each other.'

Bembo nodded. 'Yes,' he said quietly. Then he asked, 'And what excuse shall I have for coming to the palace tomorrow?'

'You are going to Mantua, and I have a letter for my sister, Isabella.'

Bembo smiled. 'Very well.' They looked at each other without speaking. Bembo took a step towards Lucrezia. 'But this is still the last time that we shall be alone together.'

He held out his arms to her.

XIV

Lucrezia received Bembo next day in the balconied room which overlooked the cathedral square.

He wore riding dress and apologised loudly for his appearance of haste.

'No, Messer Bembo,' said Lucrezia, 'it is I who must apologise for delaying your journey.' She beckoned Tebaldeo and took from his hand a sealed letter. 'This,' she added, rising from her chair and moving towards the window, 'contains certain private matters for my sister – '

At the reference to private matters, Tebaldeo and Lucrezia's ladies discreetly withdrew a few paces.

'Keep well, my love,' whispered Bembo. He took the letter and bowed his head as though reading the superscription. 'I shall not turn round when I go. Promise me that you will not watch me.'

'Yes.' Lucrezia took a breath. 'Write to me.'

'Very soon.'

They took one brief, helpless look at each other. 'You must send me away now,' murmured Bembo.

Lucrezia closed her eyes tightly, but she turned back towards the room and held out her hand in a gesture of dismissal. 'I am most grateful, Messer Bembo.'

Bembo brushed her hand with his lips. 'Your highness's servant always.'

Lucrezia resumed her seat, and listened to his steps crossing the floor and passing into the rooms beyond. Her head was bent as though she was attending to what Tebaldeo was reading to her, but her mind was following Bembo along the corridors of the palace, down the covered marble staircase to the courtyard, out through the gate into the cathedral square.

She stood up abruptly. 'I'm too hot,' she gasped and moved clumsily towards the window. Tebaldeo ran ahead of her and unfastened the catch. She leaned against the side of the window, staring across the balcony. Bembo was crossing the square. He stopped, turned and looked up at the window.

They stood gazing at each other until Bembo saw Lucrezia move her head as though answering someone behind her. He became aware then of people watching him, glancing round to see why he was staring at the palace.

He began to walk slowly backwards. At the corner of the square, where the road led to the Strozzi house, he stopped again. He placed his hand on his heart and bowed his head slightly. For an instant, Lucrezia leaned out of the window, her fingers clinging to the chain at her neck.

Bembo's arm fell. Then he made himself turn and walk away.

EPILOGUE

Villa Bozza, 1542

After a month of quiet leisure at the Villa Bozza, Cardinal Pietro Bembo was arraying himself in the scarlet silks of a prince of the Church. The summer was over, and the Cardinal was preparing for a brief stay in Venice before travelling to his bishopric of Gubbio, where he would pass the winter. His admission to the sacred college was sufficiently recent for him to feel satisfaction at the brilliant image reflected in his glass. He had never been an ambitious man, and had not become so in old age, but it pleased him to have thwarted the enemies who had opposed his election. Their objections had not lacked weight, and it had taken three years of protracted argument before Pope Paolo was able to bestow on Pietro Bembo the office of Cardinal Deacon of Saint Ciriaco in Thermis, and later that of Bishop of Gubbio.

Now, after only a brief period as a member of the sacred college, it was being whispered that Bembo's dignity, his intellect, his experience of Vatican diplomacy, his literary reputation abroad rendered him 'papabile' – one fitted to be considered as a future Pope. Bembo himself was not unamused by this. Faith had never been a thing that troubled him greatly, and theology interested him less. He was not disposed to lobby for the Papacy, but if it offered itself, he would not resist.

He took one final look in the glass and held out a hand to Lico for his gloves. They were of white leather, the cuffs fringed with gold. On one corner of each cuff the Bembo device had been stitched in black silk and gold thread. The Cardinal liked to affect a certain richness of detail in his ecclesiastical dress. On his hands were huge cabuchon stones selected from his own collection and mounted to his own design by a goldsmith on the Rialto. He was, as always, determinedly Venetian when he moved outside the Republic. His lace was fragile Venetian rose-point, and his silks were woven in the Mercerie.

He drew on one of his gloves, almost ready to leave. His barge was waiting, and his household had been assembled. In the adjoining room, which was his study, Nicola Bruno was packing the last of the books, pictures and antiques which Bembo wished to take with him to Gubbio.

The Cardinal's vast collection of antique and beautiful objects was acknowledged to be one of the finest in Italy. It was committed to the care of Bruno, who supervised the disposition, cataloguing and cleaning of every piece, from the ancient Egyptian table of bronze and silver to the hundreds of coins, medals, gems and cameos. The frequent movement of such treasures between the villa and the Cardinal's palaces in Venice, Padua, Gubbio and Rome was a constant source of worry to Bruno. He dreaded particularly the departure from the Villa Bozza at the end of the summer. Bembo expected the packing and sorting to be completed as quickly as in the days when there were no more than a couple of cases to be cleared. When, this year, Bruno had begged for more time to arrange the work, Bembo had refused but had offered Bruno instead the assistance of his son, Torquato.

Bruno had accepted this compromise with mixed feelings. Torquato was seventeen, the last of Bembo's three children. Lucillo had died as a boy and Elena, his sister, was married to a Venetian patrician. Torquato was lonely and bored in his father's house, and he resented the fuss made about the collection. He packed with an ill grace and a carelessness that tortured Bruno's nerves.

'Torquato, don't do that,' he screamed, as Torquato tipped a tray of intaglios into a linen bag. 'Each one wrapped separately, please.'

Torquato grunted and emptied the bag. 'Cola,' he said, 'why can't we go straight to Gubbio? I don't want to go to Venice.'

'Of course you do,' said Bruno. 'You'll enjoy a few days there.'

'I would, if we weren't going to stay with bloody Cousin Gian Matteo.'

'Torquato!'

Bembo's uncritical affection for Gian Matteo was another source of resentment to Torquato. 'I hate him,' he mumbled.

'No, you don't. He's always very kind to you. Get the ladder and fetch down your father's portrait.'

Torquato groaned rudely and set the ladder against the wall. As he put a foot on the first rung it rocked slightly, but he was too lazy to climb off and set it square. He mounted higher, made a lunge for the portrait and slipped. The ladder fell, striking a smaller picture from its place. Torquato yelled as he hit the floor.

Horrified, Bruno snatched up the picture. 'Are you hurt, Torquato?'

Torquato shook his head. Bruno stood clutching the picture, almost afraid to examine it for damage. He listened. 'Perhaps your father didn't hear,' he whispered.

But the Cardinal was always alert to any sound that might spell harm to an item of his collection. The communicating doors were flung open. Bembo stood on the threshold, his gaze taking in the fallen ladder, the picture in Bruno's hands and Torquato sitting on the floor, rubbing an elbow.

'What has happened?' he enquired deliberately.

Since his election as Cardinal, Bembo tended when annoyed to make simple questions sound like the rhetorical utterances of an Old Testament patriarch. Titian had painted him in such a mood: upright, austere, the dark eyes fierce under frowning brows

Bruno, holding the picture close to his side, tried to sound unconcerned. 'We had a small accident with the ladder, Pietro. I apologise if the noise disturbed you. It is nothing that need take up your time – '

'Accident?'

Bruno cleared his throat. 'A small tear in a canvas, Pietro. It can easily be repaired.'

'I will see the canvas,' said Cardinal Bembo.

Bruno carried the picture over to him. Bembo drew in his breath angrily and glanced, hawk-like, at Torquato. 'This, no doubt, is the result of your carelessness. Get up off the floor and come here.'

Torquato joined his father and Bruno. He peered at the damaged picture. The tear was in one corner, not more than half an inch long. 'Is that all it is?' Torquato smiled at his father. 'It doesn't matter, does it? It's an ugly, old-fashioned picture that you never look at. Who was Ercole Strozzi?'

In the silence that followed, Bembo's displeasure gathered strength. He advanced into the room with a commanding rustle of stiff red silk, and then turned to address his son. 'I hardly know whether to attribute your opinions to insolence or deficiency of feeling.' He paused. 'I have given you, Torquato, at no small cost to myself, an education as fine as that enjoyed by any prince in Europe. I hoped that you might have learned from your tutors that a son has an obligation to respect what his father values.'

Torquato fixed his eyes on a point beyond Bembo's left shoulder. 'Yes, Father,' he said meekly.

The meekness was overdone. Bembo made an obvious attempt to control his anger. 'I appreciate,' he went on, 'that the portrait is a poor one compared with many others in this house, but if it hangs on my walls, Torquato, it should be evident to you that I prize it. It happens to be the only likeness I possess of a man who was once a very dear friend of mine, and whose violent death I have never ceased to lament.'

Torquato said nothing.

'Oh, go away,' said Bembo irritably. 'Get the dust off your clothes. I refuse to have you enter Gian Matteo's house in that state.'

A flicker of temper crossed Torquato's face, but behind Bembo's back Bruno hastily shook his head and pointed to the door.

When Torquato had gone, Bembo sat down with a sigh at his

desk. On its immaculate surface lay a crumpled list that Torquato had made for Bruno. Bembo idly smoothed out the paper, read it, and then struck the desk with his fist. 'Cola, have you seen this? The boy's illiterate. He can't even spell his own language! And I worry about his Latin.' He sniffed. 'Illiterate,' he said again. '*My* son. Would anyone believe it?'

Bruno looked at him. 'Fathers are often disappointed because their sons are not like them.' He paused. 'Your own father was.'

Bembo glared at him. 'What do you mean by that?'

'Your father wanted you to stay in Venice and become an ambassador of the Republic, like himself.'

'Yes, well that might have been difficult since no one showed any inclination to elect me to office,' snapped Bembo.

'And why was that?'

Bembo frowned, waving a finger at Bruno across the desk. 'Might I remind you, Cola, that my father was present when I addressed the whole of the Greater Council, in the presence of the Doge and Senate, as ambassador – '

'Yes, as papal ambassador, Oh, he couldn't fail to take pride in your oratory, or to enjoy the banquets given in your honour.'

'Well?'

'He was also shamed to witness his own son acting for Rome. He never again took public office in Venice after that.'

'Is that surprising?' shouted Bembo. 'He was over eighty then. Don't forget, Cola, that my work in the Vatican during those years saved this villa and fed you all.'

'Yes,' said Bruno, 'that's true. I agree that there is something to be said on your side. Perhaps there is on Torquato's. You didn't want to be a Venetian merchant and ambassador of the Republic. He doesn't want to be a scholar.'

'Scholar!' Bembo screwed up Torquato's list again. 'You always take the boy's part,' he grumbled. 'Leave me, Cola.'

Bruno ignored him and went on with his work. Bembo said nothing more. They had known each other for nearly fifty years and they wore each other's moods like old clothes. After a time, Bruno picked up the Strozzi picture and studied it carefully.

'How bad is it?' asked Bembo.

Bruno laid it on the desk without answering Bembo's question. 'Torquato might have hurt himself when he fell.'

Bembo smiled. 'But he didn't. I knew he wasn't hurt when I saw you weren't clucking over him.'

Bruno smiled back. 'Pietro, try not to keep talking to him about Gian Matteo.'

Bembo appeared surprised. 'Do I?'

He turned his attention to the picture. He propped it up so that Ercole Strozzi's sharp eyes looked back at him. There was some truth, he had to admit, in what Torquato had said. There had been long stretches of time when he had barely glanced at the picture, just as he had given only a fleeting thought to Strozzi himself. But Torquato was wrong if he believed that this was still the case. In recent months Strozzi had been much in his mind, as had others, many years dead, who had once been close to him. He was aware that he had reached that period in an old man's life when he recalls the past with ease. He sometimes forgot conversations that had taken place in the previous week, but what Carlo or Raffaello had said forty years ago he remembered without effort. And among the memories of his boyhood in Florence, of the two years he had spent as a young man in Sicily, of Urbino and the early years in Rome, those that came most clearly and most often belonged to the time when he had known Strozzi, to the time when he and Lucrezia Borgia had been lovers. It needed only a small incident, like the tearing of the picture, to people his thoughts again with Angela and Giulio, with Tito and Ippolito, with Lucrezia herself.

Lucrezia.

Lucrezia had been dead now for nearly a quarter of a century. During those years he had never ceased, when reminded of her, to think of her with tenderness and a grateful heart. He had continued to believe that he worshipped her because it had become a habit to do so, but as his life moved on the image in his mind grew fixed and pale, like a rose pressed in a book. Now, suddenly in old age, the rose was springing fresh and alive again into his hand.

Bembo rejoiced in this. He saw again the snowflakes of Asolo and a dancing Lucrezia; Lucrezia running through the garden at Medelana among the white birds; Lucrezia leaning against the doorway of his house in Ferrara. And as these memories illuminated his mind, growing ever more and more vivid, he had the sensation that he was no longer an old man thinking of the past, but an old man who had found a way of stepping into some pocket of time where he was able to live again the most treasured experience of his life. Perhaps he had stumbled on the road back into that secret circle of torchlight that had once encompassed them –

How extraordinary, thought the Cardinal, that I can remember that evening so clearly, even the heat of the flame in my hand and the bite of the snow-laden air on the terrace. I can remember what I said: 'No waters can quench love'. So many waters had flowed since then. Bembo found a tear standing in his eye, and realised that he was passing again through the hour of his parting from Lucrezia.

He fumbled for the key to his private drawer and unlocked it. Inside lay the box of Lucrezia's letters.

He remembered coming home to the Villa Bozza, after those last days with her in Ferrara, to nurse his grief. He had sat at this same desk writing to her, trying to suggest a courage and a hope which he did not feel. Her answers had come back to him, brief and guarded, but precious enough. One of his letters had been sent to her as soon as he had heard the news of her son's birth; one of hers had reached him when she was well again.

He had had the child's horoscope cast by the most distinguished astrologer in Venice. When he read it, he had thrust it to the back of a drawer. Only when the baby died two months later did he retrieve it and send it to Lucrezia, hoping that 'your highness will take comfort from seeing that by our stars we are in a great part governed'.

She had given birth to other sons who had happily survived.

The eldest was now Duke of Ferrara, and another sat with Bembo in the sacred college. They had both been born during Bembo's stay of six years in Urbino. Urbino. Bembo recalled fleetingly, with pleasure, his growing friendship with Bibbiena there, their pride in Raffaello's soaring fame. Strozzi had been a frequent visitor. He had talked little of his own affairs during those visits. Yet there had been one occasion, when he had limped with Bembo on to the city walls to enjoy the view of the hills around them. The month was May. It was almost three years since Bembo had parted from Lucrezia. Strozzi, with a smile, had mentioned that Barbara, his wife, was awaiting their first child, and he felt that the time had now come when he must make a public declaration of their still secret marriage.

Bembo never saw him again. Within a month his dead body had been found in the alleyway that ran beside the Casa Romei.

With the loss of Strozzi, a change had come over Bembo's life. He began to realise that he couldn't live idly in Urbino for ever, hoping – hoping for what? Alfonso's death? He hardly knew. Reluctantly, he made himself attend to Bibbiena's talk about Rome. He acknowledged, at last, that only in the Church was there likely to be any future for such as him.

This was not the only capitulation that followed Strozzi's death. He allowed himself to become the lover of one of Elisabetta's ladies. The affair lasted only briefly, and it was followed by others. After each of them he felt a sense of shame at having pretended to the words and acts of love when his heart was not touched. Some time later, in Rome, he had met Morosina. It had been in the year after his appointment as papal secretary to Giovanni de Medici, then Pope Leo X. With Morosina he had not pretended. He offered her tenderness and affection; he took from her comfort and companionship. She had been twenty-five years younger than him, in some ways more like a daughter than a wife. He hoped that he had made her happy. He had cherished her with growing fondness during the years they lived together until her death, and in the end he had been able to obtain for her the thing which he believed she desired most in the world – the legitimisation by papal brief of their three children. She had never known about Lucrezia, nor of the letters that passed between them.

The Cardinal became conscious of one hand resting on the box of those letters. He lifted it from the drawer and raised the lid. The letters were arranged in two bundles. In the first were those that Lucrezia had written to him when they were lovers, and in the other those that belonged to the years between their parting and Lucrezia's death. While they were both alive, they had never stopped writing. Bembo slipped his hand beneath the two bundles. At the bottom of the box lay the crystal case with Lucrezia's strand of hair, the colour of yellow amber.

Only one person, the Cardinal recalled, had ever seen what lay in his private drawer. He had shown Bernardo Bibbiena the letters and the hair when he had been unnerved by the shock of hearing that Lucrezia was dying. He remembered that day with great clarity. Ariosto had come. Before that, Bibbiena and Raffaello had sat on the edge of his little wood, tasting the early strawberries.

The Cardinal mused sadly. He had foolishly supposed then that for many years to come, his two dear friends would ride north to share the pleasures of his villa when the heat in Rome became unendurable. Yet, before the next crop of strawberries had ripened, they had both been dead.

A noisy sigh broke into his thoughts. Bembo raised his head, and the present surged back. The sigh had been Torquato's.

'What is it?' said Bembo testily.

Torquato approached the desk. 'Everyone is waiting.' He added with a certain satisfaction, 'you're late, Father.'

Bembo stood up with the velvet box in his hand. 'I am ready, Torquato, but before we leave there is something I wish to say to you.'

Torquato's face became sullen as he anticipated a lecture on one of the many shortcomings which his father found in him.

'I am aware,' Bembo was saying, 'that you have little interest in the things which I have devoted my life to collecting, and that on my death you will probably dispose of them without compunction.'

Torquato was noisily sucking in his breath when his father's words took a turn that surprised him. 'You will do what you wish, of course, with most of my things.' He raised the velvet box. 'But I forbid you to part with this box or its contents. It is to remain within our family. When you die it is to pass to your children, or if you have none to your sister's. Do you understand me, Torquato?'

Torquato, startled into a courteous reply, nodded, 'Yes, sir.'

'You promise me that you will not allow it to be lost, or its contents scattered?'

Torquato looked at his father gravely. 'I promise.' He took a step forward. 'May I see what is in it?'

Bembo lifted the box out of his son's reach, and gave him one of his rare, brilliant smiles. 'You must allow old men their secrets, Torquato.'

He walked in to the hall of the villa to greet the officers of his household. Then, preceded by his steward and walking between his chaplain and Torquato, the Cardinal emerged from his door on to the river-bank.

He raised a hand to bless the people gathered to watch him. Then he entered his barge, moving across the swaying deck in his heavy robes with as much dignity and unconcern as if he were on solid ground. It was an impressive sight, and the Venetian in Bembo was not unaware of its effect. He seated himself under a silk canopy on silk cushions as his suite scrambled into the boat behind him. The gilded oars of his boatmen flickered through the water and they moved away from the shore, followed by a fleet of smaller boats carrying his servants and his baggage. Bembo usually travelled quietly and simply. He was too active to give much time to display. But occasionally he chose to travel in state, and then his style was magnificent. This was such an occasion. He was making a visit to Giovanni Matteo Bembo, High Admiral of the Most Serene Republic of Venice, and Gian Matteo was worthy of any honour that might be paid to him.

On both sides of the river, people ran to the water's edge to see him pass. Some of the children ran along the path, keeping pace with the barge. As they rounded a bend in the stream, a boy writing in the mud with a stick glanced up and joined the other children. Something stirred in Bembo's memory, and then eluded him.

He was still trying to recapture it as they crossed the open lagoon. The day was mild, sea and sky were the colour of egg-shell blue. Ahead were the coral-red walls and spiked bell-towers of Venice. In recent years, Bembo had been invited by the Senate to write the history of Venice and also to act as custodian of its great libraries; his feeling towards the city of his birth had therefore mellowed to one of condescending approbation. Riding along the grand canal, he glimpsed the tall chimneys and attic windows of the Ca' Bembo, high in the sky beyond the Rialto bridge. He had not visited the house for many years. On his father's death, it had passed to another branch of the family, since as a churchman he was forbidden by Venetian law to inherit property within the city. The Senate had bestowed on him as a gift a palace in another quarter of Venice, but he rarely used it. He wondered what would have happened if Jacopo had not spent the wool money. Would he have been living now in the Ca' Bembo? His instinct about wool had been sound; in the last thirty years, trade in the weaving and dying of wool had risen from two hundred pieces a year to several thousand.

The barge turned into the network of smaller canals that led to the Campo Santa Maria Nuova where Giovanni Matteo lived. The closer they came to the campo, the thicker grew the crowds clustered on bridges, leaning from windows and gondolas to salute him. This was not entirely, Bembo appreciated, on his own account. His Venetian birth, and his fierce defence of Venetian rights in Vatican councils won him applause whenever he visited the city, but the warmth of his welcome on this occasion was due more, he suspected, to the fact that he was the kinsman of Giovanni Matteo Bembo, and Gian Matteo, conqueror of the Turkish fleet, was the darling of Venice.

The barge approached the water-steps of the Campo Santa Maria Nuova. Gian Matteo's was one of the few patrician houses in Venice that had no water entrance, and the packed earth of the campo had been spread with carpets from the canal to the door of his house. Other carpets and streamers hung from the balconies of neighbouring houses, flowers wreathed the well-heads, bells began to peal from the tower of the church. And there was Gian Matteo himself, walking with his four sons to the edge of the water as the barge came to rest.

Giovanni Matteo Bembo was dressed in the full panoply of a High Admiral of the Republic: a polished breastplate, a sash fringed with gold, a ceremonial Turkish sword, and a scarlet cloak caught on the right shoulder with six knots of gold cord, insignia of supreme naval rank. In contrast, his thick grey hair was cut short, and his hands were bare except for a plain wedding ring.

They progressed along the carpeted way. From the roof of Gian Matteo's house hung the enormous triangular pennant of his flagship, red silk embroidered with the winged gold lion of Venice, and the black and gold shield of the house of Bembo. Below it, on the wall of the house, was the plaque which Gian Matteo had placed there to commemorate the most notable of his naval victories.

'You seamen were always over-fond of display,' murmured Bembo.

Gian Matteo glanced at the rings on his uncle's hands. 'Seamen?'

Their eyes met and twinkled. Neither of them had ever overcome his amusement at the other's dignity.

They turned together to acknowledge the crowd again before entering the house. Marcella, Bembo's niece and Gian Matteo's wife, was waiting for them. Bembo took her in his arms. The happiness of their marriage was an abiding joy to him.

They led him to their own room. Bembo protested that a smaller one would do as well, but when he saw the trouble they had taken to prepare it for him he ceased to argue. Gian Matteo shared Bembo's love of antiquities and arranged about the room were the treasured pieces which he himself had excavated in Cyprus when stationed there as a young man with the fleet. An alcove contained Gian Matteo's carefully assembled library of his uncle's books: his sonnets, his history of Venice, his grammar of the Italian language, *The Asolani*, a collection of the passages of Latin prose that he had composed during his years as papal secretary, the innumerable editions of the Greek, Latin and Tuscan texts that he had prepared for printing, even his very early work on the flowers and trees of Sicily, composed in Latin verse for his father.

On the table beside a silver bowl and ewer, Gian Matteo placed an hour-glass and promised to fetch his uncle when supper was ready.

'Asparagus and kid,' whispered Marcella. It was his favourite dish.

Lico appeared, carrying his warm furred robe and a plain cap. He helped Bembo to remove the scarlet robes and folded them away in a chest. Left alone, Bembo poured water into the bowl, and bathed his face and hands.

He glanced at the hour-glass. Sand and water, he thought idly. He recalled the boy he had seen earlier in the day, writing by the river's edge with a stick. And suddenly he knew what he had been trying to remember as he sat in his barge. He saw Lucrezia on the beach at Belvedere, writing in the sand and then erasing what she had written before he could read it. She had never told him what the word was. In their last hours together it had been driven from their minds. What was it she had said to him? More than one letter, less than ten?

The bells of Santa Maria dei Miracoli were beginning to strike the hour of six when Gian Matteo came to fetch his uncle for supper. He found him sitting with the hour-glass in his hand, smiling to himself.

'We have kept you waiting?' asked Gian Matteo in concern.

'No, of course not,' said Bembo. 'I was merely trying to solve a problem.' He set the hour-glass on the table. 'It had to do with sand.'

The bells of Venice were ringing now all over the city.

'As a matter of fact,' said Bembo, 'it is a problem of nearly forty years' standing.'

'And have you solved it?'

'I have time,' said Pietro Bembo.

LOCATIONS

The Piazza San Marco, with its basilica and the doge's palace, has changed little since Bembo's day. He would also recognise the Arsenal, and the many surviving Veneto-byzantine and Gothic palaces and warehouses on the grand canal. The fish and vegetable markets, and a row of goldsmiths' shops still occupy the old exchange quarter round the Piazza San Giacomo, and the Mercerie is still a street of luxury shops.

The wooden Rialto bridge was replaced during Bembo's lifetime by the present bridge, but it can be seen in the painting in the Accademia in Venice of 'The Miracle of the Relic of the Holy Cross', which was executed in about 1500 by Bembo's contemporary, Vittore Carpaccio.

The CA' BEMBO still commands the Riva del Carbon (the coal wharf) close by the Rialto Bridge. It was extensively restored in the seventeenth century when its original Gothic balconies were removed, but much of it is still as Bembo would have known it. It is now divided into offices, shops and apartments, and the state rooms of the 'piano nobile' house a permanent commercial exhibition of the crafts of the Veneto. (The term CA' is an old Venetian abbreviation of the word 'casa' – house. It was given to great patrician houses before the later term 'palazzo' became common.)

GIOVANNI MATTEO BEMBO'S HOUSE still stands in the Campo Santa Maria Nuova.

On Murano, the boat-station 'Navagero' indicates the place

where ANDREA NAVAGERO'S VILLA and orchard once stood. The remains of the house are now part of a glass factory.

The Villa Valier, once referred to as the Villa Valier-Bembo, at Mira on the river Brenta, could well stand on the site of, or even be part of, the old VILLA BOZZA. The immediate surroundings show a number of startling similarities to the descriptions of the villa found in Bembo's letters.

The CASTLE AT ASOLO of the Queen of Cyprus remains, and part of the gardens which Bembo used as the setting for his book *Gli Asolani* (*The Asolani* – the inhabitants of Asolo). A narrow street leading from the piazza at Asolo is called Via Pietro Bembo.

The EVENING ROOM in the PALACE OF URBINO is the room in which Castiglione placed the conversations recorded in his *Cortegiano* (*The Courtier*). The book refers to the period when Bembo was living in Urbino and he appears as one of its characters, together with the Duchess Elisabetta. Both the palace and RAFFAELLO SANZIO'S BIRTHPLACE are museums.

The ESTE CASTLE IN FERRARA, like the ducal palace, is now used for local administrative offices, but the state rooms, the terrace-garden and the dungeons can be visited. The CASA ROMEI, with Lucrezia Borgia's apartments, is also open to the public, as is LUDOVICO ARIOSTO'S HOUSE, on which the description of Bembo's house in Ferrara is based. The STROZZI PALACE, next to the house in which Savonarola was born, and facing the Casa Romei, is now a medical institution. A plaque on the wall of the Casa Romei commemorates the place where Ercole Strozzi's body was found on the morning of June 8th, 1508.

In the small country town of Ostellato there appears to be no known record of the Strozzi villa. It probably stood just outside the town near the river where today one sees a few ancient, isolated farm dwellings.

It had not been possible to trace any district, village or site called Medelana.

75 10 9 8 7 6 5 4 3 2 1